C000172086
Historical Fic...

LOOK AWAY NO MORE

Carol Owens Campbell

LOOK AWAY NO MORE

Copyright © 2023 Carol Owens Campbell
Reynolds Street Press
Cover Art: Creative Commons 0 (creativecommons.org)
Cover Design by Griffin Owens Campbell (rendered with Stable Diffusion, CC0 license)

All rights reserved. This is a work of fiction and a product of the author's imagination. Character names and locales are used fictitiously. Views expressed herein are the sole responsibility of the author. No part of this book may be reproduced in any form or by any electronic or mechanical means, including information storage and retrieval systems, without written permission from the author, except for the use of brief quotations in a book review. (Please contact Carol at: www.carolowenscampbell.com. Thank you.)

Songs: (Appreciation to these artists for the inspiration of their songs)

"Can't Help Falling in Love," songwriters Hugo Peretti, Luigi Creatore, George David Weiss; sung by Elvis Presley, Album: *Blue Hawaii,* 1961
"Dixie," lyrics and music by Daniel Decatur Emmett, 1859
"Get Ready," songwriter Smokey Robinson, sung by The Temptations, *Gordy*, 1966
"Moon River," lyrics by Johnny Mercer, composed by Henry Mancini, 1960; sung by Andy Williams, 1962, Academy Award for Best Original Song, 1962.
"Ohio," lyrics by Neil Young, sung by Crosby, Stills, Nash and Young, Atlantic, June 1970
"The Night They Drove Old Dixie Down," lyrics and music by Robbie Robertson; sung by The Band, 1969

Book Excerpts:

A History of Knowledge: Past, Present, and Future, Charles Van Doren, Ballantine Books, New York, copyright 1991
A Moveable Feast, Ernest Hemingway, Scribner, The Restored Edition, 2009, original copyright 1964, by Ernest Hemingway, Ltd.

Published by: BookBaby Publishing Company, Pennsauken, New Jersey 08110, 877-961-6878 (Published in USA)

ISBN 979-8-35091-201-2

This novel is dedicated with love and appreciation to:

John, my sweetheart, my husband, who held my hand through every step of this journey and kept me laughing through all the detours. Thank you, John, for sparkling my life with your optimism, brilliance and love, and for believing in me and my dearest dream to be a writer.

Griffin, our son, who is my kindred spirit in celebrating the power of art and the integrity of writing. Thank you, honey, for brightening my life with your humor, creativity, joy, and love, and for your generous encouragement of my dream to be a storyteller.

In Remembrance

Sandy Scheuer, William Schroeder, Allison Krause, Jeffrey Miller

Look Away No More

One

A thin, dark cloud slunk past the moon, a funeral ribbon across a white wreath. Mesmerized, Tally stood atop a sand dune, one hand over her heart. With the other, she pulled strands of hair from her eyelashes in time to see the wisp of cloud disappear into the indigo sky.

She marveled at the déjà vu-feeling of seeing this same wonder in the heavens not long ago. Last summer she and her brother had been sitting on one of the sandbars that famously polka-dotted the water off the coast of Hamper, Georgia when they observed the identical twin to this take-your-breath-away moment.

The marshmallow-white moon hovering just above the horizon. The charcoal-slinking mist. The crisp-ice stars. The ink-velvet sky. The soothing feel of warm ocean breezes.

Her brother, a philosophy grad student, had said the image was a haunting one because it reminded him of what grief looks like, the way grieving moves from being observed by others to slowly disappear into the quiet of one's soul.

Tally was in awe. How could her big brother, four years older, have such deep thoughts? She had complimented him and encouraged him to write a poem before sheepishly saying how cheerful the image was to her.

She had said the moon reminded her of the giant spotlight at the football stadium, tilted to focus on the field. The skinny cloud had reminded her of the water boys in their gray uniforms who streaked across the circle of light to deliver water to the players before disappearing into the dark.

"You know, the boys who don't get chosen to play football but still deserve their time in the spotlight?"

She remembered jumping up and tossing her baton higher than the fronds of a Royal Palm. Catching it behind her back, her "signature move" as former Head Majorette for the Hamper High School squad, she had bowed.

Her brother had shaken his head and clapped.

"Only you, Squirt. Only you would think that way."

She smiled now as tears blurred her eyes. Private Shaw Philippe McCall, nicknamed "Shawl McCall" by his tennis buddies at the Hamper Country Club, had last written from Da Nang on March 15th, 1970.

Now it was Saturday, May 2nd, seven weeks later, and Tally wanted to believe that wispy cloud was Shawl's reminder to her about grieving or his way of applauding her from afar.

As the moon loomed higher, it reminded her of the globe of an ancient lamplight shimmering a path across the ocean.

"To guide a sailor home." Tally blew a kiss to the intoxicating light.

Surely, her brother would write soon, her boyfriend would write soon, and everything would be alright soon. She dabbed her fingers on the moisture streaking her cheeks. Bubbles of hope, as effervescent as champagne fizz, began to tickle her spirits.

Tally scooped her baton from the seagrass where she had dropped it in her dash from the mansion to the beach.

Breezes puffed blue spangles on her majorette costume. Peach blossoms, ripped from nearby trees and fragrant as the fruit, hopped on the air.

It was that time of night in early May when winds kicked up on the Georgia coast. If only she could bottle those breezes. If only she could spritz their exuberance over her body. If only her concern about Shawl and worry about her sweetheart Rye could disappear into the ether like that cloud.

A horn blared. Silhouetted in sparkle, a shrimp boat trudged along the Georgia shore past the sorority houses with their private beaches. Outrigger booms, cantilevered from both sides of the boat, cast an exaggerated smile on the water as if celebrating the grin on Tally's face as she ran barefoot toward the ocean. She waved. A herald light on the boat flicked twice.

Sounds of "Joy to the World," Three Dog Night's newest hit, blared from a radio on a distant beach. A bonfire smoked the air. Car horns honked near Hamper Park.

Amidst the noise, a bell bonged from the clock tower at Hamper University, Georgia's oldest coastal college. Each boom warned students to enjoy their final carefree hours that Saturday night before the school year ended, before the weekend curfew, before Hamper Police issued tickets outside dorms, fraternity and sorority houses, and before Finals Week began on Monday, May 4th, 1970.

"Tally! Stop! You forgot!" A Southern accent floated on the breeze.

Tally turned to see Becca, wearing yellow polka dot pajamas, rushing towards her.

"Your whistle, silly." Becca placed the filigree chain sporting a miniature gold whistle around Tally's neck. "Someone has to look out for you."

"Becca, you're an angel, plain and simple." Tally hugged her sorority sister, best friend and Shawl's fiancée. "Too much on my mind. The announcement, Finals Week, the Gala--"

"One breath at a time, Tally, one breath at a time."

Echoes from the bonging stopped.

"Gotta scoot! Cake in the oven." Becca squeezed Tally's hand. "You know you shouldn't be doing this."

Tally grinned, nodded and blew the whistle softly.

Warm water splashed her ankle bracelet as she hopped over scallops of foam. A stream gurgled down troughs in the sand that separated the beach from the sandbar. In the moonlight, the ring her parents gave her for her nineteenth birthday twinkled like a constellation of diamond stars around a pearl moon.

Seagulls swooped past her head. She flinched at their screeches. Were they welcoming her to their private island or warning her of dangers inherent there?

Undaunted, she stepped onto the mound of white sand that looked like a giant vanilla cookie floating in the ocean.

She closed her eyes. Inhaled tangy air. Clutching her baton in front of her with both hands, she twirled in circles, gathering speed. The sand burned hot under her toes. Practicing swirls, counting spins, calculating how high her baton could soar, imagining the trajectory of its peak before its rapid plunge toward her outstretched hand was second-nature to her senses. She heard bands playing, trumpets blasting "Sweet Georgia Brown" in her memories. Spinning in circles during a show-stopping routine was the only time she could look away from her somersaulting baton once it was launched to the heavens.

She stopped. Tried to get her bearings. Squinted. The world zipped by. Moonlight, navy sky, bright stars, mansion lights, shrimp boats in the distance, revolving lighthouse beam. If only she could find a visual anchor to stop the dizziness from swirling out of control.

The beam from the lighthouse swanned over the bronze historical marker on the cliff. The perfect anchor.

Of all the historical markers, this was her favorite. The one that revealed the hidden history of Georgia and the one fact that no one except historians and history majors, like herself, seemed to know.

It was the marker that stated how the Royal Colony of Georgia in 1732, in its written charter from King George II, banned slavery, outlawed slavery, prohibited slaves in Georgia in its legal decree, the *only* colony of the Original Thirteen Colonies to do so.

Forever furious at the thought of Georgians' noble intent changing to immoral actions years later, Tally threw her baton toward the sky as hard as she could. It spiraled in a moonbeam toward the stars. As it reached its pinnacle, the baton soared with Tally's highest hopes to be named the nominee on Monday for the History Honor so she could--

"Tally Gigi McCall! You better not drown. Coconut cake's ready."

Gulls frenzied their wings. Squeals pierced the quiet. In a flutter of white, the birds soared to the grove of mimosa trees on the cliff.

The baton plopped to the sand with a thud.

Becca Bambi Brown, ever the cheerleader, waved a megaphone in her hand. She was illuminated by moonlight and a crystal chandelier on the second-floor sleeping porch at the rear of the Chaucer Sorority mansion.

Tally pressed an index finger to her lips and waved back.

"Sorry!" Becca boomed into the megaphone.

Tally pointed to Becca and saluted.

"And no hiccups about tomorrow, Tally."

The roar of Becca's voice softened even through the horn.

"You'll be the best Chaucer Day Hostess ever. Hurry home."

Biting her bottom lip to keep emotions in check, Tally hoped Becca was right. Factually, Tally would be the *first* Chaucer Day Hostess of the "Third of May-Chaucer Day" event after she encouraged her sorority to begin an annual tribute to Geoffrey Chaucer. She had reminded her sisters that Chaucer celebrated the English language spoken by commoners in his writing instead of the French language preferred by nobility and aristocrats after the Norman invasion. Cheering, they reminded her that Chaucer is still revered as "The Father of English Poetry" before she even had a chance to finish.

Yet the words "hurry home" gave her pause. They were the last words she had said to Shawl before he left for Vietnam.

She pressed her palms together as if praying. No sense shouting with breezes hungry to swallow her words. The girls blew each other a kiss.

Becca dimmed the chandelier to night-light softness. Rows of iron bunk beds, decorated with yellow comforters and pink pillows, disappeared in the darkness.

"Coo. Coo-coo." Tally sat akimbo on the warm sand, crooning to the gulls returning to the sandbar and beginning to nest. Their chitters harmonized with the chirps of grasshoppers, croaks of frogs, thumps of a party boat against the rubber bumper along the pier, and lullaby of waves lapping the private beach. She stretched her legs on the warm sand crystals. She closed her eyes. As if in prayer, she whispered lines from her second-favorite poem about a sandbar.

> *"Twilight and evening bell....*
> *The flood may bear me far,*
> *I hope to see my Pilot face to face*
> *When I have crossed the bar."*

She loved sandbars. The sand was different on a bar than the sand on a beach. Harder, thicker, firmer, less fly-away sand to get in your eyes when spinning. The fun of tossing her baton as high as she could, free from palms, mimosa trees or shadows, was the release of energy she needed. Being on a sand island all by herself was the privacy she craved.

If only Tennyson had chosen another metaphor. If only his poem, *Crossing the Bar,* had referenced a sea wall or a pier instead of a sandbar as the place that is crossed when life sails toward the ocean of death.

Tally stood as seagulls inched closer. Whitecaps lapped the edges of the bar. She must hurry. Tonight was "Chaucer Eve" and tomorrow would be the brightest day.

Water thick as sludge swirled at Tally's knees. The force almost knocked her down.

The bar, oh, my gosh, just a sliver. Waves. Devouring. The beach a mile away.

Don't panic. Hurry. Move with the undertow 'til you find your path forward. Focus. Paddle. Lift feet. Eyes on the mansion.

Teetering, keeping her balance by holding her baton above her head, she hopped on crunchy shells, a sign she was nearer to the beach than ever. *Hurry. Hurry. Keep going.*

A wave spanked her thighs, pushing her closer to sandcastles on the beach. Her feet sank in oozy sand. She could not imagine anything sucking her toes that would feel more glorious.

Breathing as if she had just marched for miles in a Christmas parade to a band playing "Silver Bells," her favorite holiday song, she sucked in salt air that had the feeling of Christmas.

The next day, Tally stood at the front door of the historic mansion, home of *The Hamper Herald,* Georgia's oldest coastal newspaper. She dangled kitten heels and her pocketbook in one hand as she struggled to twist the brass doorknob with the other. Rocking chairs along the veranda banged against the wall of white-painted bricks. A porch swing zig-zagged sideways scraping flecks of paint from black iron shutters. An old rope hammock twisted, pretzel-like, as ocean breezes swelled.

She pulled strands of frosted hair from her strawberry lip gloss. Her white silk miniskirt swooped to her chest, exposing a vision of lavender lace. Good grief.

She tucked her shoes and bag under her arm while tying her flouncy skirt in a knot so high on her thigh, she might as well have been wearing hotpants.

An envelope of thick cotton-rag floated from her open handbag. It landed on a gardenia bush at the bottom of the stairs.

"Got yourself a scented envelope now, Tally."

A young Black man, his hair a halo of shimmer in the bright sun, grabbed the envelope before it blew away. His painter's pants, white as gardenias with creases ironed down the front, and his blue t-shirt sporting "Caught by Crockett" next to an image of a shrimp boat, rippled as he ran up the stairs.

Tally grinned and lifted the cotton square to her nose.

"Franklin, I could swoon. It's fragrant as can be. Thank you so much."

Tally tucked the envelope deep in her pocketbook. She felt grateful for Franklin's kindness and for an opportunity to look away from his eyes if, heaven forbid, he had seen her bikini panties. Of course, he was such a gentleman, she would never know.

"Least I could do. You working on Sunday?"

"Turning in an assignment. See you at the event later?"

"Try my best. Got another drag with Papa." He held up white shrimp boots.

"Oh, Franklin, I don't want the afternoon party to interfere with your trawling or studying for finals."

"You know when gulls call, no time for--."

A snap, loud as the crack of a whip, interrupted.

Tally dropped her shoes.

A copper bowl, lush with ferns, smacked against the porch column again.

"Dadgum breezes!"

Good grief. Her nerves were a mess. The sorority event in a few hours. The Candlelight Ceremony at the sorority house tonight. Finals Week ahead. The big History Award announcement tomorrow. The Gala. Why can't things slow down?

Franklin shook his head as he knelt. "Hold still, Cinderella."

Tally squeezed her knees together. Her pocketbook dragged the brick floor. She laughed as Franklin slipped her lavender kitten heels snug on her ticklish feet.

"Franklin Roosevelt Crockett to the rescue."

Tally saw a group of young men, wearing "Hemingway Fraternity" jerseys and carrying surfboards, stroll past the grove of Mimosa trees. Franklin was still kneeling. Shoot. Hurry. Think.

"Of course, Franklin." She said loudly as Franklin stood and turned. "Here are newspapers you can use to line the boat."

Tally lifted a red brick that weighed down a stack of free newspapers by the front door, scooped up several papers, slipped them into a courtesy cellophane bag meant to protect hands from getting black newsprint on them, and gave the bag to Franklin.

The frat boys yelled.

"You okay, Tally?"

Franklin's hands squeezed hers.

"Just chatting with my good friend, fellas. Good luck on finals."

She waved to the Hemingway boys, smiled at Franklin as he gave her a salute, and placed her newsprint-smeared hand on white silk just above her heart.

Franklin ran in the direction of the dock as church bells boomed. Good grief. Noon already. In her rush, she had left her watch at the sorority house. At least the breezes had died down.

Tally dipped her hands in the ice water-depths of a pewter trough positioned by the stack of newspapers. As the best antidote to newsprint on one's skin, the ice-water tingled Tally's fingers until they were almost numb. She marveled that the pewter did not show how black the water could get. Neither did the black paper towels weighted down with a single white brick on a table nearby. The water felt so cold on her skin, it gave her the shivers. So did the headline of that day's Sunday, May 3rd, 1970 edition of *The Hamper Herald*:

Couple Last Seen on Sandbar Feared Dead

Tally squeezed the brick, sucked her breath, skimmed the article. The couple. A young man, a senior at Hamper University. His girlfriend, a freshman. A picnic on a sandbar near South Hamper Beach and a planned proposal at sunset, according to his fraternity brothers. Fears the couple drowned. Hamper citizens in a flotilla of boats, searching the shoreline.

Oh, please be safe, please be safe.

What had she just read in her elective class on the "History of the New Testament?" That Hebrews 6:19 reminds us: *Hope is the anchor of the soul?* What if the couple was rescued by a shrimp boat? What if they swam to a cove further down by the beach, cuddled beneath a sand dune and fell asleep?

Oh, heaven forbid! What if someone found out she was on a sandbar last night too?

She dashed through beveled doors into the foyer. Wetting a washcloth in the ladies' room, she dotted the handprint on her blouse. Thank goodness the shape dissolved in cold water. She washed her hands, untied her skirt, shook her hips as if doing the Twist and looked in the mirror.

Her hair was so windblown, it looked as big as Franklin's Afro. She closed her eyes and inhaled a deep breath. Surely, the day could only get better.

Searching for the wrought-iron, see-through-cage elevator centered in the swirl of the grand staircase, she spotted it hovering at the third-floor.

She hesitated. She could run faster up the stairs than wait for the slow-as-molasses elevator. She could not be late for her Chaucer Sorority's "Third of May-Chaucer Day" celebration that afternoon. There was also work to do on her final project for Georgia History Class, and she had to hurry and type her newspaper submission by today's 12:30 p.m. deadline.

She raced up the stairs. The elevator began moving downward at turtle-speed.

"Fancy a ride, Tally?" Mr. Bentley, the most beloved and longest-serving employee at the newspaper, tipped his straw hat behind crisscross iron gates as she reached the second floor.

Her mother's guiding principle echoed in Tally's ear.

The greatest gift you can give someone, cherie, is to honor one's relevance.

Waving at Mr. Bentley, Tally smiled.

"Merci beaucoup, Mr. Bentley." Tally's soft Georgia drawl grew louder as the accordion door clanged shut.

"Don't fret now, Tally. I'll get you to the third floor quick as can be."

Mr. Bentley's frail hand squeezed the lever, pushing it to the left. The antique cage lifted at a snail's pace past urns of peonies adorning the staircase. Mr. Bentley sat on a stool and stuck a wrinkled thumb under one of his red suspenders.

"Mr. Boudreaux thanks you too." Tally sucked her bottom lip.

Her boss, Jax Boudreaux, the Managing Editor of the paper, had warned her twice in the past month about her tendency to be late for work citing a new "three strikes, you're out of a guaranteed internship your senior year-rule" if she was late again.

"You just tell Boudreaux I needed to talk to you about the Kentucky Derby." Mr. Bentley coughed. "Reckon you watched it yesterday, being a history major yourself."

"Oh, yes sir. Wasn't it thrilling?"

The sight of Mr. Bentley's blue veins and gossamer white skin next to his red suspender seemed oddly patriotic triggering her memory of the moment last week when he confided in her his lifelong regret.

After asking about her brother, Mr. Bentley had told Tally that he himself was born in 1900, too young to serve his country during World War I and too old to serve during World War II.

Mr. Bentley said he truly sympathized with her worries about her brother serving in Vietnam and encouraged her to think how each day Private Shaw Philippe McCall was closer to coming home.

Mr. Bentley even had tears in his eyes when he said he wished he could switch places with "such a fine young man" for he longed for "that rite of honor and duty" denied him by his birthdate.

If only Mr. Bentley knew.

Her brother was in Vietnam because his birthdate, September fourteenth, was the first date chosen in the military draft lottery.

"Never thought I'd live to see the day," Mr. Bentley pulled the lever gently to the right, "when a girl, how old was she?"

"About my age, sir. Nineteen."

If only the elevator had the speed of a Derby colt.

"When a young *woman* finally got to be a jockey in the Derby."

"Yes, sir, she sure is a pioneer. May 2nd, 1970 will go down in history thanks to Diane Crump from Florida riding *Fathom*."

She did not want to mention the fact that Diane, called "The Darling of the Derby," also had a brother serving in Vietnam.

She pulled the envelope, with the words, "Reminder: Military Gala, Monday Night, May 4, 1970," written in navy ink, from her purse.

"Mighty fine job she did. Showing folks how a Southern girl can make history."

If he only knew.

Tomorrow, she, Tally Gigi McCall of Hamper, Georgia, might make history too.

Reaching the third floor, Tally thanked Mr. Bentley, gave him the envelope, grinned as she saw him sniff the cotton, and twirled through the revolving door into the newsroom. The clock near the Palladian windows registered 12:21 p.m.

"McCall! Copy editor needs that text. Nine minutes."

"Yes, sir, Mr. Boudreaux. Just need to type a bit more, sir."

"Well, hurry. And McCall," Jax Boudreaux lit one of his H. Upmann cigars. "How many times have I told you to address staff by their last names? I'm tempted to stop the reminders and actually give you an 'F' if you keep calling me *sir*."

He had threatened to give her an F for months. For not using last names. For being late. For wearing perfume that intoxicated the male reporters. For bringing a sterling silver bucket to the newsroom, filling it with ice water and placing black washcloths on a silver tray next to the bucket so reporters could soak their hands to get rid of newsprint ink. Too ostentatious for the newsroom, Mr. Boudreaux had berated her.

Good grief! Nothing she ever did seemed right.

"Newsroom boundaries apply even in the South, McCall. And, lest you forget, as Managing Editor, I make the rules. You follow. Last names, McCall."

Tally still wondered what the big deal was.

Mr. Boudreaux shouted to the only reporter still in the newsroom.

"Sandbar couple. Press conference at one. Chief Parish's son, Mike, at the mike."

Mike Parish. Tally had not heard from him since they broke up in March. She still felt awful about dislocating his finger. Yet when he kissed her ear, whispered in his drunken state that he could not wait any longer and moved his hand under her miniskirt while they were in his car, she had no choice but to push his hand away, with unintended, trip-to-the-emergency-room results.

"Mr. Boudreaux, I read the headline and, sir, as dire as it seems, I'm not giving up hope."

"McCall. Anyone delusional enough to be on a sandbar, with no concern for safety, deserves the consequences. And anyone who works in this newsroom knows how many sandbar fatalities we've covered."

The more he rubbed his bald head, the pinker his skin became.

"Yes, sir, however, I don't find sandbars to be any riskier than--"

"Begs the question. Just what have you learned about the newsroom, McCall?" He blew a circle of smoke above her head and tamped his cigar against the green glass ashtray on her desk.

"Sorry, sir, Mr. Boudreaux. I'm trying to meet today's deadline per your instructions. I have to hurry."

"You have six minutes."

"And, sir, the truth is, as I've tried to explain to you a bunch of times before, I just can't call older people by their first or last names. It's disrespectful not to say, *sir* or *ma'am*."

"McCall. Just like protocol in the military," he tugged on his *Semper Fi* tie pin, "journalists have rules."

"Yes, sir, as an officer in my sorority, I appreciate how rules-"

"McCall, you're a history major. Here's a revolutionary thought. Newsrooms are the great equalizers. Within these walls, there's no North versus South. No old versus young. No male versus female. No Black versus White. No fame versus--" He pointed to the clock and stomped out his cigar. "Hell. Time to go."

Tally's teeth made baby bites on her bottom lip.

She wanted to remind him.

When there is no choice, there can be no equality.

"Boudreaux."

He turned around, a grin on his face.

"Thank you for your courtesies to me, sir. I'll try my best tomorrow."

Tomorrow, Monday, May 4th, 1970 would be her final day at the newspaper, the first day of Finals Week, the day of the big announcement about the Award to study at Oxford which she so wanted to win, and the Military Gala tomorrow night. She would just have to impress him tomorrow with hopes to win another internship during her Senior Year at Hamper University.

"See that you do. And get that *Meet the Staff* copy to Johnson, pronto."

Tally positioned carbons between sheets of thin typing paper. Only one more thing to add to her biography for Tuesday's annual feature, *Meet the Staff*. She scanned the highlights of the form, required in column style, that would be placed under a photo of the staff:

Name: Tally Gigi McCall

Birthdate: June 15, 1950

Interesting personal fact: Dual citizen of France and USA

Family: Mother ~ Babette Maree Bouviette McCall, (Co-Owner with Vera Velmarie Sanders of Babette's Bridal Boutique)

Father ~ Delphi Aviary McCall, (Named after his Papa's love of doves; a Georgia Federal Court Judge)

Brother ~ Shaw Philippe ("Shawl") McCall, Private First Class, U.S. Army, Vietnam. (Nicknamed "Shawl McCall" by his tennis buddies at the Hamper Country Club)

Accomplishments:

"Georgia Girl Award," 1963 (with "Bama Boy Award-winner," Larchmont Leroy Lee)

Miss Georgia Peach Majorette (1968)

Chaucer Sorority Historian (1968-present)

Fort Hamper Military Gala Queen (1970)

She added:

"Honored to be an Intern at *The Hamper Herald* under the leadership of Managing Editor Jax Boudreaux"

Tally zipped the page from the typewriter, ran to the Copy Editor's desk and dinged the oval deadline bell with its thick center protrusion that reporters called "the nipple." For months, she had blushed whenever reporters signed the daily deadline log on her desk, winked at her, and told her they had just "rubbed or patted or tapped or tickled the nipple." Tally would keep typing, thank them for signing the log, and wonder if her lace push-up bras needed a boost of padding to hide hers, especially since her breasts recently had a growth spurt.

One day, already frustrated that too much gauze for Initiation ceremonies had been delivered to the sorority house, she placed a caller on hold after a reporter made his usual comment.

Standing, she faced the grinning reporter and said, in her quietest voice, "Ben, could you please help me?"

"Sure, Tally." Ben leaned closer and whispered back. "What's up?"

"Well," Tally's voice strengthened, "I'm just wondering where the sign that says 'Male Locker Room' is hanging. Is it above my desk?"

She heard Mr. Boudreaux laugh. Ben looked sheepish. He apologized as if he had just remembered his Southern manners.

Within moments, Mr. Boudreaux typed a memo and tacked it on the bulletin board reminding the newsroom staff that: "A lack of decorum is a lack of professionalism and a lack of professionalism leads to the lack of a job."

Now Tally had hit the bell for the first time and could add her name to the log.

"Right on time, McCall. Appreciate the courtesy."

"You're so welcome. And, may I say, I have loved working with you."

"Likewise, McCall. You make a bright addition to *The Herald*. Your godmother must be plenty proud."

Tally grinned.

Charlie Johnson was the only employee who knew that Tess Hamper, the Publisher and Executive Editor of the newspaper, and his high school sweetheart, was also Tally's godmother.

With time to spare before putting on her costume to host her sorority's "Chaucer Day" event, Tally plopped into the swivel chair at her desk. Exhaling, she looked around the newsroom. The Sunday skeleton crew of reporters was out on assignment. The newsroom was quiet. She wanted to lay her head down on her desk and nap like she used to do in kindergarten.

Tally's smile at her favorite memory of kindergarten was interrupted by a yawn. She covered her mouth and remembered the first day of school when asked by her kindergarten teacher what she wanted to be when she grew up.

She had famously said she wanted to be a breeze.

"Did you say a *breeze*, honey?" Mrs. Castellow pinged C-sharp on her piano. Giggles from children, seated on the floor, froze in mid-air.

"Yes, ma'am."

Tally felt so proud to wear the dress her mother had designed for her. The lilac organdy dress, with mint green crinolines underneath, featured appliques of baby sea turtles that looked like they were crawling along the scalloped hem, and a taffeta sash her daddy said was an absolute miracle match for her green eyes.

"And a majorette too."

"Gracious! How versatile."

Mrs. Castellow led the children and also the parents in the back of the room, men dressed in seersucker suits, ladies dressed in a rainbow of polished-cotton pleats and pearl earbobs, in applause again, just as they had clapped for each of the other children's ambitions.

Mike Parish, who had said he wanted to be a pirate, swung his toy sword in the air.

Becca Brown, who said she wanted to make cupcakes and sell them at a lemonade stand, jumped up and cheered.

Jimbo Carson, who said he wanted to be a baseball pitcher, licked all his fingers, put two in his mouth and whistled.

Khaki Carson, Jimbo's twin, who said she wanted to make babies because her mama told her friend on the phone that making babies was the best feeling she had ever had, put her hands over her ears.

"Thank you, children. Thank you, parents. Now why do you want to be a majorette, Tally?"

"To touch the moon."

"With your baton?"

Tally had nodded and waved to her parents.

"Well, honey, the way you are twirling your baton through your fingers right now makes me think you'll be a fine majorette one day. And why do you want to be a breeze? Speak louder, dear."

Tally shouted, "CAUSE I WANT TO MAKE THINGS MOVE!"

Tally sank her toes into the plush crimson rug. Maybe she could just take a little, little nap. She yawned, nestled her head on her arm as whiffs of Ma Griffe perfume lingering on her skin lulled her eyes to close. The full moon. Slow-dancing with Rye. The deck. The ship. The band. The Spring Break cruise. Rye's arms, so strong. Beneath the stars, before they—

A familiar voice swooped her off the deck.

"Hey, girl, wake up."

"Winston?" Tally placed her hand over her mouth as she yawned. "What are you doing here?"

"Sorry to wake you, girl. Got to type that form for Boudreaux before the deadline. Forgot about it, then remembered it, then ran like the dickens from the shrimp stand to get here."

"The *dickens?*"

Winston grinned. "That's what happens when you're up all night trying to get your brother to understand the ending of *A Tale of Two*

Cities for his English Lit final. He keeps getting Sydney Carton and Charles Darnay confused."

"Everyone does, right? I hate to say it but it helps me to remember that the guillotine had a *cart* beneath it." Tally winced and pointed to the clock. "And, Win, I hate to say it but it seems you missed the deadline."

"Nope. Got 'til 1:30."

"What? Mr. Boudreaux told me the deadline was 12:30."

Winston shook his head, sheen twinkling on his Afro under the chandelier, and raised an eyebrow.

"Looks like somebody's got your number, girl."

Tally tossed his pack of Newport Menthols at him.

Winston laughed, sat down at Mr. Boudreaux's desk and pounded keys.

Tally marveled at Winston's confidence. Not only was Winston the first Black student to intern at the paper, he was also the only Black employee at *The Hamper Herald* other than the janitor. And no one ever sat in that burgundy leather chair but Mr. Boudreaux.

The click of typewriter keys was the first sound Tally heard when she met Winston Crockett, a double major in drama and history, and his twin brother Franklin, a liberal arts student. Winston had been typing the script for his play in their "Intro to Acting" class, freshman year.

The play was a tribute to Winston's passions. Besotted with airplanes and history, he drew diagrams of bi-wings in his notebook. He sailed paper airplanes in the classroom whenever their Acting professor stepped into the hallway. Winston wanted to be a pilot.

Winston's play was one he wrote and directed about the Wright Brothers.

His premise? What if the brothers had been Black?

Titled *The Wrong Brothers,* Winston portrayed Orville Wrong, the pilot of the first manned flight, while Franklin was cast as Wilbur. Tally played Amelia Earhart who, she insisted for dramatic effect and historical accuracy, exited the stage and never returned, not even for the curtain call.

She flipped her hair over her shoulder. No surprise that Winston, with his writing skills, his brilliance, his devotion to history, and his joie de vivre, was the front-runner for the Oglethorpe-Oxford History Honor and the chance to study at Oxford.

Abruptly the ticker of the *Associated Press* wire service pounded. Tally ripped paper from the machine.

"Hey, Win, no byline. One of those private citizen-reporter stories, you know, one of those color stories the *AP* picks up."

"Girl, did you say *colored* story?"

Tally strolled to Winston's side, raised an eyebrow and pinched his arm.

"Ouch." Winston laughed. "Read it to me. Got to keep typing."

AP, Sunday, May 3, 1970. Kent, Ohio

CANDLELIGHT RAGE by Anonymous

In amber light, a young man with long hair paces by a first-floor window, punches a pillow, and flings it against a wall. On the second floor of the dorm, a hand shoves a windowpane sideways. A young woman leans over a row of jittery flames, sticks her middle finger in the air and shouts, 'Screw you!' at the helicopter hovering above.

Through an open window on the third floor, Fogerty's voice growls a swamp-rock plea to "Run Through the Jungle" as two girls sway, their hands snaking above their heads as if they are about to be frisked.

Smoke, from nicotine and weed, bitters the air, still chilly for the first Saturday in May. The constant thwacking of copter blades over the dormitory, the barking through bullhorns of curfew updates, the clapping and chanting from a crowd of students marching past the buildings, and the honking of car horns make studying for Finals Week impossible.

In the parking lot at the foot of Blanket Hill, a white VW Beetle wedges between an orange Torino and a lamppost. The Beetle sports a giant iridescent decal of a peace sign on its roof, the image Nixon recently dismissed as 'the footprint of a chicken.'

The full moon, as opaque as a ghost, lingers over the campus like an omen. A military jeep jerks to a stop at the entrance to the parking lot. Two National Guardsmen jump out, slam doors and patrol an adjacent football practice field. Rifle straps hang on their shoulders. Barrels are clutched tight in their hands.

The copter's spotlight focuses on the dorm. Students cover window panes from the glare. Bed sheets, posters and art paper, painted blue and yellow, the school colors of Kent State University, proclaim one cry in unison:

"O-hi-*O-HELL NO*! We Won't Go!"

Winston lit a cigarette.

Tally stared at Winston.

Ceiling fans whirred.

Two

Hours after the "Third of May-Chaucer Day Celebration," Tally and Becca sat on beach towels, licking coconut flakes from their fingers. It was their tradition as the end of each school year. The cake. The laughter. The beach. The reminiscing.

"So, Becca, who's having a Candlelight tonight?" Tally poured sweet tea into a cup.

"Can't figure it out. I've gone through every sister's name. The hint for this one is 'Military.' I think it's Rayleigh and Travis." Becca accepted the tea. "He just got back from 'Nam and they are crazy in love."

"Who do you think, Tal?"

"Becca! Tally! Sorry, girls. Time to get ready for the ceremony, Becca." Virginia, the sorority sister in charge of preparing the living room for the Candlelight, yelled from the first-floor sleeping porch.

"Be right there, Gin." Becca scooped up paper plates, forks, cups and a thermos of tea. "Love you, Tally."

"Always, Becks." Tally blew Becca a kiss and waved at Virginia.

Becca juggled the items, laughed as the thermos dropped, and puckered a kiss in the air.

Tally pulled her compact of Pot O' Gloss from the pocket of her aqua chiffon peignoir. Mesmerized by the sight of the full moon, she slowly stroked shimmer across her lips. Why no letter or phone call from Rye? If only she could break the rules, flaunt decorum, pick up the phone, and call Rye without worrying that he might think her too forward or too interested in him or too ready to go all the—She blushed. She could not wait to share that intimate experience for the first time with a sweetheart she adored. If only she could hear Rye's voice.

She plopped her compact on the towel, rubbed her sticky fingers on the sand, hurried to the water's edge and dipped her hands in the warm saltwater.

A few feet away, a sandbar beckoned.

Tempted as she was to wade out to it, she rushed back to the beach blankets. She dried her hands, shook the towels, rolled them like logs and placed them on the rope hammock. Her honey-brown hair, streaked with blonde, waterfalled from a ponytail down her back as she removed her peignoir, placing it on the towels. She shivered in the breeze.

She imagined her French negligee, in the bright moon glow, hid nothing. Her bra was in her suite. She could only wonder if her silk panties were transparent too.

"Who cares? No one will see us, right?" She chatted to a heron marching in the sand, its beak poking at the foam.

Gliding her feet through the sand, she clutched her baton, and gazed at the sandbar again. She wanted to sit there, think about the day's events and tomorrow's too, toss her baton again and again. Yet the couple last seen on a sandbar gave her pause.

She sailed her baton toward the moon.

"Whisper the Creed, Tally. Whisper the Creed, girls." She could hear the voice of her high school majorette coach, Miss Grace Melody, instructing her as Head Majorette along with the entire award-winning Hamper High Majorette Squad. *"It helps you focus as you watch the revolution."*

The majorettes had laughed.

Miss Grace Melody had meant "revolutions" of the baton, not the French Revolution they were studying in class.

Tally locked her sights on the spinning object high in the air, whispering the Majorette's Creed, rapid-fire.

"Whether a baton is cartwheeling through your fingers, circling above your head, or tumbling about your neck, a Majorette will not be distracted from her singular talent and acquired ability to focus solely on keeping the baton from crashing to the ground."

She stretched her arm to the sky, twirled and scooped the baton behind her back in her trophy-winning move.

If only the Georgia Historian's Creed, *"The true purpose of History is to illuminate how life can change in an instant,"* were not so heartbreaking.

Pressing her baton close to her heart, Tally glided in the dance steps the Hamper High Majorette Squad had performed during the funeral for their beloved majorette coach, twenty-two-year-old Miss Grace Melody Parker.

The majorettes, wearing their pastel bridesmaids' dresses, had twirled their batons to the plinks of a harpist playing "Amazing Grace" in a farewell tribute to their mentor, a heartbroken bride-to-be who, after her fiancé called off their wedding just hours before the event, had returned each wedding gift with a handwritten apology note before slipping into her satin wedding gown and the blue water of her parents' pool.

Two years had passed since that awful day yet Tally had never forgotten the dance steps she and Khaki Carson choreographed for the funeral or the lyrical voice of Miss Grace Melody or the history of tragedies happening to brides in Hamper, Georgia.

Rolling the baton in Figure Eights through her fingers energized her. Tally rushed back to the hammock, the satin ribbons around her ponytail dancing on her shoulders, and scooped a beach towel under her arm. Instead of risking her safety on the sandbar, maybe she would skinny-dip again.

She laid the beach towel under the canopy of a weeping willow tree at the edge of the beach. Drooping fronds formed an umbrella about her. She exhaled. No one could see her from the sleeping porches of the mansion. Not even the moon could find her. She could finally be alone with her thoughts.

She imagined her sorority sisters studying for finals or on dates with their boyfriends before curfew or gathered in the den in their pajamas guessing which sister would blow out the candle at the "Candlelight," their sorority's most anticipated ceremony.

If only her own anticipated ceremony tomorrow night at the Military Gala could bring honor and hope to her parents while taking their minds off Shawl. She grinned. Shawl McCall seemed the perfect name for a person as funny, as one-of-a-kind, and as comfort-personified as her big brother.

Unfortunately, Shawl was not giving her much comfort now. Her grin melted. Why hadn't he written? Was he on a secret mission? Was he in a hospital somewhere? Wouldn't the Army notify her parents?

A flash of gold streaked through willow fronds above her. Caught in the circling beam from the lighthouse, the Georgia Historical Marker on the cliff sparked a burnt-orange glow that reminded her of a sunset in the moonlight.

Oh, my gosh! That's it!

The image to anchor her essay and oral presentation for Oxford if named the nominee. She could compare Georgia Historical Markers to lighthouses.

She could remind those lost at sea and those lost at seeing the power of the past that the present has all the questions and the past has all the answers.

She could illuminate, using a Historical Marker as a guiding image, the intentions of the Founding Fathers of Georgia, members of British nobility, who conceived the thirteenth colony named Georgia as the first utopian experiment in the New Land.

She could show a Marker splashing verbal sunshine on Georgia's history as the only colony of the original thirteen to ban slavery and outlaw the slave trade in Georgia in its Trustees' charter, her favorite surprise historical fact.

And she could imagine a Marker shining a light of awareness on the truth that folks in Georgia who feel dismissed and defeated throughout history will rebel.

If only she knew if she would be nominated or not. She exhaled, closed her eyes, arched her back, pressed her palms behind her on the towel and inhaled citrus air. Her breathing slowed. Her pulse stopped pounding her forehead. Her nipples perked as they always did when she felt she wanted to toss her clothes, wade into the sea, and swirl in the warmth completely naked.

She had done it once, just after she returned from the Spring Break Cruise in April. Without a thought to the undertow or the fact that no one knew where she was, she had shed her nightgown and bikini panties, having earlier shed her bra, and immersed herself in the waves. The chill of the water had shocked her as much as her sudden rebel energy.

Yet her body had flushed hot at the risk of entering the tide in the dark and at the rush of knowing she was closer than ever to the moment her body had been anxiously, tenderly anticipating.

That night she had stroked her arms, fluttered her feet, and rubbed the tightening flesh around her navel. Shivers coursed through her body, tumbling, effervescent tingles like the ones she always felt at the top of a Ferris Wheel before plunging over the peak, helpless to stop, free-falling into the most intense bliss deep inside, warm waves of restlessness and force gushing into the most exhilarating rush she had ever felt.

At that moment, she had imagined Rye Somerset, the handsome, *Sundance Kid*-lookalike with sandy hair and blue eyes, the Syracuse senior she met on the cruise three weeks ago, now standing on the beach, untying the strings of his swimsuit, before swimming out to hold her and kiss her until—the thought of what could happen next, of allowing a sweetheart to touch her where no else ever had, and finally making love for the first time—made her cheeks blush hot.

Scandalous as it was, she had decided she would not wait until marriage to have such an intimate experience with a sweetheart for she had no intention to marry. She just wanted to be in love with a sweetheart for the rest of her life.

Her mother, the co-owner of Babette's Bridal Boutique, the South's most elegant destination for wedding dresses, would be apoplectic when she found out.

Tally stood and lifted the hem of her gown to her shoulders.

A beam of light flashed through fronds.

Her hands froze. She squealed, shimmying her gown down to her hips, as she heard a familiar voice.

"Tally? Tally-ho? Hot damn. What the hell are you doing out here all alone?"

Oh, dear lord! What did he see?

"Mike? Mike Parish? You scared me to death. What are *you* doing here all alone?" Tally wished her peignoir were closer. "Mike, please turn that flashlight off. The moon is already bright as can be."

"No can-do. Not on my new beat, Tally-ho. Police rules. Page 17. Line 4."

She had never been so irritated by numbers in her life.

The beam focused on the party boat pulling on its rope from the pier as if trying to escape.

She heard Mike swear about the damn moon being a pain in the ass after just buying batteries for his flashlight before his beam meandered back to Tally.

With a gasp, Tally grabbed the ribbons atop her head and surfed them down the full length of her ponytail before dropping them to the sand. Thick waves cascaded over her shoulders. Scooping her hair over her breasts, she hoped she was fully covered.

"What rules, Mike?"

"Now you didn't have to cover up those beautiful breasts."

"Mike Parish! You're incorrigible."

"Just teasing. Feels good to tease you again, Tally-ho, like old times. Besides, you know I like your hair down." Mike rested his hand on his holster and pointed to his chest. "Look. So, you won't get upset. I'll put the light on me. See anything new?"

Tally saw nothing new, only the face of her childhood friend and former boyfriend.

"Just a handsome man in a uniform."

"Shoot-fire. You sure know how to make a fellow feel good, Tally-ho." Mike grinned. "See this new badge? Just got named the youngest Lieutenant on the Hamper Police Force."

"Wow. Wonderful. Congratulations, Mike."

With the light splashed on his face, she could see his face redden.

"Thanks. Got a new assignment. Sorority Row. Well, officially, Poet's Row. You'll be seeing me around the cul-de-sac checking on the sorority houses, day and night. Also, I'll be checking on sandbars from high on the cliff. Especially after that couple disappeared."

"Mike, isn't that the saddest thing?"

"Can't believe anyone could be that stupid. Who would risk their life just for the fun of a sandbar?"

It did seem absurd. Sometimes it was hard to understand why others did what they did. Never mind. Keep the focus on Mike.

"Mike, your dad must be proud as can be."

"You know better than that, Tally." He plowed his fingers through ginger hair as he moved closer to her. "Just 'cause dad's the Chief of Police doesn't mean I get any favors."

"Mike—" Tally moved backwards. The woodsy scent of his Brut cologne intoxicated her. She had not been this close to Mike since the night they drove to the emergency room to get a splint on his finger.

"Need to get my peignoir."

"Your what?"

"My robe. I'm feeling a bit chilly and—oh, my goodness." Tally glanced at Mike's watch gleaming in the moonlight. "It's almost time for our Candlelight."

"Your what?"

"Our Chaucer Sorority Candlelight Ceremony. You know, when a sorority sister blows out a candle to announce if she's lavaliered, pinned or engaged."

Scooping up her baton, she whooshed her beach towel from the sand, closing her eyes as sand scattered.

"Damn, Tally." Mike dropped the flashlight. "Just got sand in my eyes."

"Mike, I thought you saw me when I bent over to—You okay?" She leaned toward him.

Without warning, he wrapped his arms around her. He kicked the flashlight, its beam rolling on the sand at her feet.

"Tally-ho, you know how I told you the 'ho' is short for honey?" His voice was a whisper. "Look, baby. I'm the one who's sorry. C'mon. Let's give it another try." His hands stroked her back. His lips nuzzled her ear, her second-most ticklish spot.

In a flash, she kissed his cheek, lifted his hand, and twirled underneath its arc as if dancing the Jitterbug they learned in ballroom dance class with their teacher, Miss Jenna.

"Mike Parish, cheers to the most gallant boy who first wore a police uniform that Halloween in, what was it, third grade?"

Moonlight streaked through the willows. Tally saw him shake his head.

"Still got the moves, Tally-ho. Yep, third grade." Mike rubbed his eyes as if coming out of a trance. "The year Miss Jenna let us wear our Halloween costumes to the dance recital. You were Pocahontas. Jimbo Carson grabbed your Baby Ruth candy bar out of your papoose that Halloween—"

"And you told Jimbo you were arresting him, handcuffed him with those toy handcuffs—"

"And my dad had to use garden shears to get him loose." Mike laughed. "But I got that dadgum Baby Ruth candy bar back for you!"

Tally laughed, juggled her baton and towel under one arm, picked up the flashlight, and dusted sand from its handle.

"Leading with Thank You" was Rule One in a Southern girl's pocketbook of persuasion. "Getting Folks to Laugh to Ease a Sticky Situation" was Rule Two. "Distraction" was Rule Three.

"Mike, I've been in your debt ever since!"

She handed him the flashlight.

Rushing to the hammock, she slipped on her peignoir.

"Good Lord. You sure know how to pay someone back. It wouldn't be Halloween without that box of Baby Ruth bars you send to the house every year. Mama loves you."

"Well, that's the least I can do for my protector and his sweet Mama."

Mike looked at his watch. "Hot damn. 9:00 o'clock. Gotta go, Tally-ho. Wait. Shoot-fire. Meant to ask earlier. Heard from Shawl?"

She wanted to hug Mike just for asking.

"Hey, didn't mean to upset you." Mike took a handkerchief from his back pocket and patted Tally's cheeks. "Look. That big brother of yours is probably teaching a philosophy class in Da Nang by now. I bet he's telling all his buddies in 'Nam about, you know, that cave story he likes so much."

Sniffling, Tally nodded. "You remembered? Oh, Mike. His favorite story."

Tally smiled at the thought of her brother regaling his Army buddies with Plato's *Allegory of the Cave*, the story of the prisoner who broke his chains, left the cave, saw the sun for the first time, and encouraged other prisoners to follow him and see the light.

She squeezed Mike's hand.

He winced.

"Oh, Mike. It still hurts? I didn't mean to—"

"Yeah. Acts up sometimes."

Tally lifted his hand, kissed his finger and stared into his brown eyes.

"Mike, thank you for caring about me and thinking about Shawl."

Mike put his hand in his pocket as he cleared his throat. "Great guy. Bet you a Baby Ruth, he'll be home soon."

She put her hand through the triangle of his arm like she did when they walked into her debutante ball together. They strolled under the willow canopy into the moonlight. She waved as he zigzagged his flashlight beam past the fence. She grabbed towels from the hammock.

Slipping into the shadow of the Chaucer House, behind a curtain of ivy cascading from the first-floor sleeping porch, she pushed a hidden door. The historic tunnel beneath the sorority house smelled of musk and patchouli, fragrances emanating from earthen walls and flickering candles.

She bolted the door from the inside, blew out the candles, inhaled the sensual smoky-scent, and paused at the final candle by the stairs to the secret Initiation Room.

Soon it would be time to join her sisters for the final Candlelight Ceremony of the school year.

Three

Girls in off-the-shoulder white peasant blouses, green tea-length skirts, yellow sashes, and daisy wreaths on their heads gathered by a window near the front door. One girl pointed to a sign. Bordered by yellow, white and green ribbons, the colors of Chaucer's favorite flower, the English Daisy, the stenciled words read:

CANDLELIGHT TONIGHT!!!
May 3, 1970   10:00 p.m.
Who is lavaliered, pinned or engaged?
HINT: "MILITARY"

Voices whispered, chattered and laughed. One girl clapped. Several girls embraced in a group hug. One girl, walking into the room, squealed.

"A Candlelight?" She hugged the suit of armor standing guard by the door. "Could there be a more perfect way to end the year?"

To the girls of the Chaucer Sorority, a Candlelight Ceremony heralded the most thrilling tradition of all their school events. Nicknamed the "Candlelight," it was more reverent than Initiation; more surprising than Big Sister-Little Sister Reveal Day; more fun than the annual Mother-Daughter picnic each April with the other sororities on Poet's Row; more sentimental than the Father-Daughter Dance in the ballroom of the mansion at Christmas-time; more memorable than the "Third of May-Chaucer Day" tribute to Chaucer, the greatest of English poets; and more exciting than car washes with fraternities, charity barbecues with sororities, and rehearsals for skits during RUSH.

Sentimental pictures from "Candlelights" through the years adorned tapestried walls in the Canterbury Room. Amidst these keepsake photos were images of girls hugging and showing off diamond rings next to photos of girls surrounding the statue of a black stallion, its front hoofs raised as if ready to jump over the wrought iron fence. Around its neck lay a wreath of berries with a sterling tray dangling from it, as if a Tiffany necklace and bar locket, engraved with the words, "Our beloved mascot, Canter Berry."

"Why is a Candlelight so special?" Chaucer Sorority pledges often asked before their first time. A sister would gently inform them that a Candlelight was the moment between not knowing a secret and knowing one, you know, like not knowing what it is like to fall in love and what it feels like once you have or, in hushed voices, what it feels like before you make love and what it must surely feel like after.

The thrill of a Candlelight was the moment a sorority sister could announce her happy relationship news and finally be able to wear her boyfriend's lavaliere fraternity necklace around her neck or position his fraternity pin one half inch above the nipple of her left breast or wear her sweetheart's two carat, or more, diamond engagement ring.

Girls would gather in a circle in the darkened living room, light a tall tapered candle, and gently hand the candle from one sister to the next, making sure the candle flame still flickered.

If a sorority sister was announcing her new status of being lavaliered, the happy girl would blow out the candle when it reached her during the first go-around.

If a sister was announcing her news about being pinned, she would blow out the candle during the second circle.

If the announcement was of an engagement, the ecstatic girl would blow out the candle during the third and final passing of the candle as squeals, cheers, hugs and tears commenced.

One sorority sister with hair as black as a turtle shell amidst a beach of sandy blondes further distinguished herself from her sisters still dressed in "Third of May-Chaucer Day" costumes. She was the Chaucerette in charge of ringing the Waterford crystal bell. At the sound of the chiming, voices hushed to whispers.

"Chaucerettes! Our last Candlelight of the school year!" Nora Faye reminded the girls that no Candlelights could be held during Finals Week. "Time to guess who is going to blow out the flame."

The chandelier above them cast a soft glow on the girls raising their hands as if bridesmaids hoping to catch a bride's bouquet.

"Did anyone see who put up the sign?"

"I saw Tally in the Arts & Crafts room in the turret where the stencils are!"

"No. She was working on her poster for that big history award she wants to win."

"Everybody, let's say a prayer for Tally tonight! The big announcement's tomorrow."

"Great idea, Nora Faye. Now shouldn't we focus on the hint? MILITARY!"

"Okay, that settles it. Has to be Tally McCall. Her brother's in Vietnam."

Southern accents leapfrogged over each other.

"No. It can't be. She broke up with Mike Parish months ago, remember?"

"But how 'bout that fellow she met on the Spring Break Cruise?"

"Remember how they snuck off to the island?"

"And rode bikes down that private 'No Trespassing' road?"

"She blushes every time we say his name."

"Are y'all crazy? Tally would never accept a fraternity lavaliere from a Yankee!"

"Who cares? He looks just like Robert Redford in *Butch Cassidy and the--*"

"Oh, lord. What if she and the *Sundance Kid* went all the--"

"Wait. It could be Virginia Dodge."

"You're right. Her Mama's President of the Hamper Chapter of the United Daughters of the Confederacy and Virginia's got a crush on--"

"Hold the fort! I have an idea." A voice with a British accent chimed in.

A collective gasp galloped through the group.

"LeeLee Gigi Clark!" A sister put her arm around the girl from Britain. "Honey, remember? No one ever says that phrase in Georgia."

The pledge, a Hamper U freshman hailing from Brighton, England who was a Chaucer Sorority legacy through her grandmother, Mrs.

Penny Grace Hamper Clark, a former President of the Hamper Chapter, placed her hands together as if in prayer, shook her head and looked as if she might cry. "I keep forgetting that 'hold the fort' is taboo."

Girls groaned. "Don't say it again!"

Phoebe, the President of the sorority, and LeeLee's Chaucerette "Big Sister," shushed the group. She tugged a tiny sachet filled with tangerine petals from the top of her yellow satin push-up bra and gave it to LeeLee.

"Take a deep breath, Lee. I made this fresh before the ceremony."

"How come?" Nora Faye asked.

"Well, Nora Faye, I knew I'd be reciting quotes from Chaucer at the ceremony right after Tally's welcome to our distinguished guests and Becca's beautiful Sorority Prayer so--"

Phoebe twirled a tendril of LeeLee's buttercup-blonde hair. "I tucked this sachet inside the bridge of my bra to whiff when my head was bent over before the Amen. You know, to calm my nerves."

LeeLee closed her eyes, held the tangerine sachet to her nose and inhaled.

Phoebe smiled. "I'm sure your sweet grandmother, Miss Penny Grace, told you, LeeLee, that girls in Hamper--"

A chorus interrupted her in singsong voices, "--are taught to be resourceful like the women of Hamper, Georgia who helped our town become the only one spared by Sherman on his March to the Sea."

Laughter rippled through the group as girls pretended to wave invisible fans near their cheeks.

Phoebe rolled her eyes. "And, LeeLee, because William Tecumseh Sherman was the person who originated the phrase, 'H the F,' we never use that phrase in Georgia."

"And, Lee, in Georgia, we never, *ever*, name baby boys 'Sherman' either!"

Nora Faye clanged the bell loudly as everyone whooped and hollered.

Phoebe took the bell, slipped off her ballet flats, and stood on a brocade ottoman. "Shhh! Girls! Do we want Miss Perry to come out here and cancel the Candlelight?"

Giggles ceased.

Phoebe reminded the group that it was Finals Week and everyone must study and get enough sleep to earn the best grades they could.

"Do we want the other sororities to win the 'Honor Roll Award'?" She held her finger to her lips. No one spoke.

"Just remember what Chaucer said: *'Time and tide wait for no man,'* so let's hustle, bunnies, to make A's on our finals, and get ready for the Candlelight."

Phoebe held up her hand as if in afterthought. "However, before we go, bunnies, let's remember our manners and ask LeeLee, what was it you were wanting to say, sweet pea?"

LeeLee exhaled as she opened her eyes and nodded to the group.

"Could our Candlelight Sister be Rayleigh? She sure loves Travis Brinkley and he just got back from Vietnam and isn't her father a General at Fort Hamper?"

Tally heard none of this as she paused at the final lantern illuminating the plaque by the door to the Initiation Room.

She read the words on the plaque for the hundredth time. The voice of Lily Lois Scarborough, her fourth-grade teacher who inspired Tally to love history, echoed in her thoughts.

"Children, if Leonardo da Vinci was standing right here in this classroom, he would say that historians must read about history with *sapere vedere* which means '*to know how to see.*' But he's not and I am. So, if you can't remember Latin, just remember what I always say, 'History rhymes with mystery.' There's a whole lot of our history still to be discovered. And a whole lot to try to understand."

Tally's fingers traced the words as if they were Braille:

CHAUCER SORORITY HOUSE

At this site on May 3rd, 1850, the Chaucer Sorority established the first Sorority House in the state of Georgia at Hamper University, Georgia's oldest Coastal college. Under the mansion, a secret tunnel once connected the Sorority and Fraternity houses before barriers were placed underground between the houses to create bomb shelters for residents.

During the War Between the States, the tunnel protected slaves navigating the Underground Railroad to the safety of ships waiting for them in the harbor beyond the private Chaucer Sorority Beach.

During Prohibition, the tunnel protected Caribbean rumrunners storing barrels of rum in the tunnel for delivery to private Gentlemen's Clubs in Georgia.

The State of Georgia, hereby, honors the Chaucer Sorority for its history and its Creed of "hospitality to all Canterbury pilgrims, whether sinners or saints" while retaining exclusivity of membership for the South's finest young women.

The Honorable Carl E. Sanders
Governor of Georgia, May 3, 1965

Tally scooped the key from the hook next to the Initiation Room, swung open the door, turned on a lamp inside, and extinguished the candle inside the lantern, leaving the tunnel pitch black. Sweeping past panels of sheer white gauze used in Initiation ceremonies, she tossed her baton and beach towels on a sofa and snuggled into the overstuffed navy velvet chair in the corner.

Calculating the hours ahead, her hand shook as she wrote on a notepad:

10:00 p.m. Candlelight Ceremony

11:00 p.m. Final practice (History Class presentation)

12:00 a.m. Prayers for Shawl

6:00 a.m. Wake up to a history-making day (Fingers crossed!!!)

She looked at the digital clock on the desk. 9:14 p.m. She shivered. Why does it always happen? All her life, without fail, whenever she looked at a watch or a clock, even Big Ben in London, the time would inevitably correspond to a date with special historical reference or personal meaning to her. She had never understood why.

9:14 p.m. September fourteenth. The date she both cherished and despised.

She smoothed the navy velvet on the arm of the chair with her palm, back and forth, again and again, until her hand burned hot. With each swipe, the nap of the fabric changed hues. Darker, lighter, darker, lighter. She sniffled, lifting a handkerchief from the stack of cotton squares on the silver tray beside her.

The bright joy of celebrating her brother's birthday on September 14th was now shaded by the dark sadness that his birthdate was the first date chosen in the Military Draft Lottery for immediate deployment to Vietnam on that night of December 1st, 1969.

Shaw Philippe McCall was in graduate school at Hamper U earning his Ph.D. in Philosophy only months ago. Although he had college deferments and a father with political connections, Shawl's personal philosophy would not allow him to ask for another deferment when his "birth mates" had no choice. He strolled into the Army Recruiting Office on December 3, 1969, completed basic training at Fort Hamper in late January, and was deployed on February 15th, 1970 to Da Nang.

Tally, her parents Babette and Delphi, and Shawl's girlfriend Becca Brown were in shock. President Nixon had only signed confirmation on November 26th, 1969 directing the first draft lottery since World War II to be held.

Five days later, *Mayberry RFD* was interrupted on TV for the live on-air lottery event. Blue "Birthdate" capsules were dumped into a big Bingo bin before being tossed around in the spinner and drawn out one at a time. No young man from the ages of 19 to 26 wanted to hear his birthdate being called, especially early in the lottery. Even if that happened and his buddies were cheering, consoling, and buying him beer, the young man knew his life would soon be changed forever.

The happiest news before Shawl left for 'Nam was when he asked Becca, his girlfriend of a year, to marry him. Becca squealed, "yes," before he showed her the three-carat emerald-cut diamond with fluted baguettes that had belonged to his paternal grandmother, long deceased.

The Brown family hurriedly hosted a Valentine's engagement dinner-dance at the Hamper Country Club, and Becca, her mother Dee Julee, and Babette McCall began planning the wedding of the year.

They just did not know which year.

Tally smiled. She could hear Shawl's voice in her memory.

"Squirt," Shawl had held the umbrella as they left V.V. Vaughn jewelry store in February, where he picked up a slender box wrapped in vanilla and white polka dot paper, that morning he left for 'Nam. "Remember the novel *The Member of the Wedding*?"

"You mean Georgia-born Carson McCullers' novel made into a movie and Broadway play?" She had laughed and hopped over a puddle.

Ever since she was a little girl, her brother had challenged her to play the game he created called "More, More, More." Whenever either of them would ask each other a question, the other would answer with more information and they would keep adding more until the winner was the one who finally offered the most.

"Yes. The one with the protagonist Frankie Addams." Shawl had detoured from their route to the car, ushering her to the back of their favorite diner and into their favorite cherry red booth where they ordered vanilla fountain Cokes and fries.

"Of course. The twelve-year old girl who wanted to go with her brother and his new wife on their honeymoon because--" Her voice had trailed off.

"Because," Shawl had said in that slow, deliberate way he spoke when he explained the merits of his favorite philosopher Heraclitus or any philosophical view to her, "Frankie did not want her brother to leave."

The sound of pouring rain, the quiet of the diner, the smell of fresh-brewed coffee and the two of them together, like old times, before Shawl would change into a soldier and, eventually, a married man, had overwhelmed her. She grabbed a napkin and placed it over her face.

Without saying a word, Shawl had moved beside her on the bench, put his arm around her shoulders. She leaned against him.

The waitress appeared with a fresh bottle of ketchup and Tally heard Shawl say, "Thank you, Connie May. Yes. We're doing fine. Now don't you start crying too."

Connie May had told him there was no charge for the Cokes and fries, just her gift to him before he left for 'Nam. Shawl had thanked Connie May, asked about her new puppy and her twin, Nora Faye. Tally reached for another napkin as Shawl slipped a twenty-dollar bill behind the saltshaker.

Tally cried with Shawl's arm around her until her eyes were puffy. By the time Shawl moved back to his bench across from her, she had heard Johnny Mathis sing "The Twelfth of Never," Connie May's favorite song, two times on the jukebox.

Shawl had said, "Squirt, I thought it would be the twelfth of never before I could give you this." He slid the vanilla and white polka dot box across the table. "You okay now?"

She shivered again just as she did that day. She had babbled something like, "For me, Shawl? I thought it was for Becca."

It was the gold Baume Mercier bracelet watch she wanted for her twentieth birthday. Shawl had laughed when she squealed. He showed her the special blue moonlight feature so she could see what time it was, night or day. She had jumped up, hugged him, dropped a quarter in the jukebox and played Shawl's favorite dance song, the one Connie May put in the rotation cycle just for him. Shawl had clapped at the first guitar twangs of "Run Through the Jungle" by Creedence Clearwater Revival and laughed.

When she slipped back into the booth, Shawl sounded serious.

"Listen, Tally, I need your help." He never called her Tally. "While I'm deployed, I want Becca and Mother preoccupied so they don't fret about me all the time. I need you to keep them upbeat and focused on the wedding. Good to go?"

She had nodded. "Good to go, Shawl."

Tally wrote him last week. "Your plan to keep Mother and Becca busy is brilliant, however, if you don't write one of us soon, and I mean *soon*, Shawl, your plan will fray."

Shawl had kept his promise to write to Becca, Tally and his parents every week. For a month, he did. Now no one had heard from him since the Ides of March.

Tally's nerves were fraying in the absence of Shawl and his letters. She struggled to keep her own spirits up. How could she keep Becca's and her parents' hopes up too?

"And how do I do that after Nixon just up and decides to invade Cambodia?"

She balled the handkerchief, threw it across the room, stranding it in a cloud of gauze while shouting, "Dammit!" Surely her Daddy could call Commander Hemming at Fort Hamper to remind him that Shawl only agreed to go to Vietnam, not Cambodia, and to ask, once again, if Shawl was okay.

The surprise announcement to invade Cambodia had just happened days ago, on Thursday, April 30th. Not only was Nixon's decision confusing and upsetting to Tally, it also begged the question: *Don't people ever look at dates?*

Tess Hamper did.

Tally sucked her bottom lip as she remembered Tess's scathing editorial as Publisher in today's paper with its Editorial Page headline:

APRIL 30th: THE DATE HITLER COMMITTED SUICIDE AND NIXON DID TOO

Tally's recurring, albeit delusional, dream? That Shawl would make his dutiful military visit to "the South Pacific," be assigned an office job there, write every week as promised, and be home for a week of R&R on June 15th, 1970 to celebrate her twentieth birthday. Maybe he would surprise her. She hated most surprises with a passion yet seeing Shawl was her only birthday wish. He had to be home. She had never celebrated a birthday without him. Besides, his actions on the day she was born saved her life.

She wanted Shawl to come home just like he left. He could not come home like Travis Brinkley who lost his leg when a mine exploded or Clay Dobson who used to know everybody's name and now could not remember anyone's or Billy Callaway whose gravesite was adopted by the Chaucer Sorority as their "Hamper Hometown Hero" where they visited each month, pulled weeds and placed tiny flags by his tombstone.

Tally wondered why she heard horses galloping. Was that actually her heart beating so loud she could hear it?

She jumped at a knock on the door.

"Tally. You in there, baby?" Lula, the longtime sorority house cook, sounded worried.

Tally scrambled to the door and opened it to see Lula frowning.

"Hey, Lula. Everything okay? Need help?"

Tally heard horses galloping again.

Lula shook her head. "No, baby. Appreciate your offer but I already got platters of quiche sitting on warming plates on the kitchen counters, for after that Candlelight ceremony. And my ambrosia with all the fresh oranges and shaved coconut is in the icebox. You girls need to eat if you're going to be up late studying."

"Ambrosia? Oh, Lula. The food of the gods." Tally closed the door, tucked deep beneath the Grand Staircase, and locked it. Her baton would be safe inside until tomorrow.

She gave Lula a quick hug.

"Lula, you darling, you. Thank you so--Good grief. Does it sound like horses running down the Knight's Hallway or am I going crazy?"

"You're not crazy, baby girl. Miss Perry changed the doorbell from chimes to some tape she made of horses galloping. You know how she loves her horses."

Tally rolled her eyes. "But how come?"

"She says it sounds just like the horses those pilgrims were riding in *The Canterbury Tales*." Lula arched her eyebrow. "Lordy. Even I know those folks weren't galloping their horses to that church. No sirreee. They were going mighty slow so as to tell their stories to each other. Now, baby girl, you got a caller at the front door. Phoebe says to tell you."

Tally gave Lula a kiss on her forehead, thanked her for the quiche and ambrosia, and rushed down the Knight's Hallway.

Amber light from candles, flickering in elegant lanterns, brightened yellow brocade walls, oil paintings, alcoves, and suits of armor as she wondered who could possibly be waiting on the other side of the door.

Four

Tally waved at sorority sisters gathered in the living room where the Candlelight would be held. She dimmed the light of the chandelier and peeked through the beveled glass of the front door.

"Franklin? What's he doing--?" She knocked on the glass and held up her index finger to Franklin. He nodded. She grabbed Phoebe's arm as she walked past.

"Phoebe! Did you order shrimp salad to be delivered? Lula made quiche, remember?"

"Maybe Khaki did or Becca." Phoebe shrugged her shoulders. "Hey, Tally, have you seen the dripless candle for the Candlelight? Mercy. With so much happening today, I'm losing my mind."

Tally stood on tiptoes, the way she used to march on tiptoes in her white majorette boots during half-time at football games, and massaged Phoebe's shoulders.

"Phebes, we need our Hamper U Poet Laureate to relax."

"Just give it up, Tally. I mean it. Quit your quest to win that History Award. Enough with going to Oxford. Just give your fabulous massages instead. I beg you." Phoebe moaned as her hands went limp. "Oh, my lord, that feels so good."

"Phebes, you need to go to the sleeping porch, sit in a rocking chair and look at the moon. It's gorgeous."

Phoebe turned and smiled. "Can I go *now*?"

"No, you nut. You have to preside over the Candlelight. The dripless candles are in the chiffarobe. Do you have your key to the Initiation Room?"

"I do." Phoebe gave her a hug. "Oh, my word, Tally McCall! You smell like Brut. Are you seeing Mike Parish again?"

"No, Phoebe Gigi Pope! You must be in one of your romantic hazes again. Now scoot. I have to see Franklin."

Phoebe shouted from the entrance to the Knight's Hallway. "*Methinks ye doth protest too much*! Hustle, bunny. Thank Franklin for me. From Becca and Khaki too. Oh, shoot! Khaki! She said for me to tell you she put a letter from that Syracuse fellow under your pillow. She said she meant to give it to you when it arrived a week or so ago and forgot. Typical Khaki."

Tally felt exhilaration and rage all at once. She wanted to strangle Khaki. Most of all, she wanted to read Rye's letter. She would talk to Franklin, rush upstairs, read the letter from Rye, slip into the circle of the Candlelight in the darkness a little bit late, get a good night's sleep, and practice her presentation tomorrow morning, bright and early, before the big announcement.

Her fingers squeezed the doorknob. In the swirl of delight that a letter from Rye waited upstairs for her, she almost forgot.

Thank goodness an internal warning stopped her. She pulled her hand away from the door as if it were a hot potato. She tossed her hair over her shoulders and took a quick glance at her peignoir in the mirror, only to have her fear confirmed. Through the silk, she could see too much. And her French bra? Upstairs, of course. On the window seat where she had tossed it.

Her nipples puckered the fabric. They were the size of the pearls adorning the collar of the yellow taffeta duster she grabbed from the coat closet to cover herself.

Quickly, she opened the front door.

"So sorry for your wait, Franklin. Come on in."

"Naw. Just be chilling here." Bowing his head, Franklin handed a sack to her.

"Well, you know you're welcome to come into the foyer, Mister Crockett. It's not curfew yet. Oh, my gracious. That shrimp salad smells so good."

Franklin stuck his hands in his pockets. He was rattling coins. As Tally looked up, his Afro threatened to block the moon. Something's wrong. Did he have a fight with his girlfriend?

"Franklin. I'm not sure who placed the order."

"Oh, nobody. Mama just figured y'all needed some shrimp tonight and sent me over."

"Franklin! Your Mama's the sweetest person I know. Please thank her for us."

"She says y'all order so much shrimp salad through the year, it was the least she could do as a surprise."

"Well, she's a sweetheart."

Franklin nodded. "I'll tell her you said that. Well, 'bye Tally."

"Wait. Sorry, Franklin. I've been so overwhelmed today, as you know, with the 'Third of May-Chaucer Day' activities and working on my history final and, well, you know, tomorrow's big announcement, I haven't asked how you're doing with finals and all." Feeling anxious always made her babble. "I didn't want to interrupt you talking to that Army Sergeant today. Still, I wanted to thank you and Winston after you saved my life at the Chaucer Day event. And for your help during the whirlwind breezes this morning too. So, thank you, Franklin. And I sure wish Winston all the best for the award tomorrow."

Franklin shrugged. "Mama keeps telling Winston it's good to have your name start with *Win*."

Tally chewed her bottom lip.

Shoot! Even if she were named the finalist, should she demure, for history's sake, for justice's sake, for friendship's sake, and forfeit so the finalist could be Winston instead? Would that be the proper thing to do? Offer a deserving young Black man a chance to represent Georgia? But wouldn't justice be served if a girl won too?

The tower bell on campus chimed one time, the final curfew warning.

"And I guess your mama knew you'd always be 'frank.'" Tally teased although it was one of the qualities she admired most about Franklin.

Franklin glanced at the moon. "Good night for shrimping."

"Hey, Franklin, I hope delivering shrimp salad this late didn't interfere with your studies."

"Naw. Can't remember those dates anyway. Hey, got a question. How come is the third of May called 'Chaucer Day'?"

"Oh, May third is the only date Chaucer ever mentioned in *The Canterbury Tales* or any of his other works."

"How come?"

"No one really knows. That's one reason why I want to study at Oxford to find out. Well, that is, if I were to be named the finalist from Hamper U and write the winning essay." Tally shook her head, her hair dancing down her back.

"Or I could visit Winston there and follow him to the library to do research. Who knows what will happen?" She tried to sound nonchalant. "What I *do* know, Franklin? Easy ways to remember dates. I've always loved them. Always believed in their patterns. Hey, come over sometime. I'll show you."

"Come here? To Sorority Row? In the daylight?"

"Franklin, you'll be my guest – or maybe we could meet at a picnic table in Hamper Park." She touched Franklin's arm. "Would you wait a second? I'll be right back."

She dashed to the nearest suit of armor nicknamed Geoffrey. Becca, a Home Economics major and Design Engineer minor, had crafted a secret shelf inside Geoffrey's chest plate where she and Tally kept envelopes of cash in case a delivery was made and there were no gift bags of freshly-baked sugar cookies ready to give the delivery professional as a 'thank you.'

Within moments, Tally returned holding an envelope.

"Franklin, here's extra tip money for you and your mama. From Phoebe, Khaki, Becca, Virginia, Rayleigh and me. We so appreciate you understanding we need shrimp salad or we'll never make it through Finals Week."

He took the envelope and nodded.

"Franklin?"

"Did I forget the dressing? Thought I put it inside."

"No, no. I just wondered. Is everything okay with your family? Winston? Your Mama? Your Daddy?"

He shrugged. "Shrimp boats are full." It was his standard answer for 'all is well.'

"It's just that you seem a little bit down." Tally's voice softened. "If there is any way I can help you, you'll tell me, right, Frankie?"

The nickname she had called him since they met slipped out. He had asked her to call him Franklin at the beginning of their junior year so he could get used to hearing it before his name was called at graduation a year from now.

"Sure, Sunshine." He whispered her nickname too. "Got to go. Can't worry Mama more than she already is." Franklin saluted as if he were a soldier saying goodbye. "Tell the girls 'Thanks.' Wait, are the crackers in the--oh, yeah--wrapped in tin foil."

"Frankie, wait." Tally put the sack on the cobblestone floor. "Can I ask you something?"

He jiggled his keys.

"Can I please give you a hug?"

Without waiting for an answer, she reached for the switch near the door. She flicked off the portico light. Her arms circled his torso. His arms floundered before finding a place to land. Tall and thin, he seemed as if he had lost weight. She felt him squeeze her, like old times, and nuzzle his nose in her hair. He always did like her lemon shampoo, how soft and smooth her hair felt, how different he used to say. His arms felt strong. His shirt smelled of shrimp. The feel of his strength reminded her of the many times they hugged when they were on stage in the play Winston wrote, the one that made the audience gasp when she and Franklin first touched, until the more they witnessed, just like Winston predicted, the more they clapped and whistled at the final hug.

Franklin abruptly let go. In the moonlight, she could see his eyes. He looked as if he were searching past the gate, into the park where willows swayed in the breeze.

"Thought I heard something."

"No one can see us, Frankie. It was just an innocent hug. You're like a brother. Besides we could always say we were practicing for one of Winston's plays."

Franklin laughed. "Remember how many times we hugged in that play based on the Wright Brothers? Every time we said goodbye. Every time we said hello."

Tally shook her head and grinned. It was more fun chatting when they were not in the spotlight of a stage or under a spotlight on the portico.

"Who knew Amelia Earhart had a thing for Wilbur?" Tally punched his shoulder. "And Orville too."

Franklin grinned. "You know what Mr. Drama King would say right now?"

"Oh, he'd be scolding me for not being upstairs practicing my presentation."

"But first he'd be saying, '*You'll catch your death of cold, girl. Barefoot in the cool night air is fine for Frankie's black skin but that white skin of yours can't handle it, girl.*'"

Tally laughed. Winston might as well have been standing in front of her.

Franklin kept mimicking Winston. "*Better be glad it's dark, girly-girl. Or some redneck fool's fixing to shoot Frankie for that hug and asking questions later.*"

"Franklin Roosevelt Crockett. You sound just like him."

"That's what Papa says. Figure it's from listening to the seagulls real intense-like, their chitter, their screeches, their squawks, their coos. Just reckon I got a good ear for sounds. It's what I do on the shrimp boat. Wait for the trawling to start. Listen to the gulls. Think about Win, the way he talks, and just start talking like him. Papa says he feels like both of us are on the boat with him."

"Hey, what the fuck? What's going on here?"

A male voice barked from the walkway.

Tally heard Franklin swear under his breath. She recognized Louie's voice and Khaki's squeal. They sounded loud. Shoot. Hurry. Think.

Tally grabbed Franklin's hand and raised it.

She flipped on the portico light.

"Franklin Crockett! You're an angel. Thank you so much for fixing that light that burned out."

Franklin looked stunned. He dropped his keys. Bending, he picked them up, his hair brushing against Khaki's bronze satin sleeve as she stepped into the circle of light.

"Hey, boy. Watch it."

Even a foot away, Louie reeked of rum.

"Khaki. Welcome back. Made it in time for curfew. And shrimp salad." Tally lifted the sack to show her.

"No talk of food around me." Louie burped and spit into the boxwood hedge. "Hey, Khaki. Come give me a kiss, sugar."

"See you around, Tally." Franklin saluted. "Sorry 'bout bumping you, Khaki."

"Oh, hey, Winston, I mean, Franklin." Khaki seemed giddy. She squeezed Franklin's arm. "Good to see you."

"Khaki, take your hand off that boy's arm right this--"

"Franklin," Tally interrupted, loudly, "thank you for the shrimp with chunks of avocado, hot pasta and creamy dressing."

Tally raised her eyebrow at Louie who glared at her.

"And good luck with finals, Frankie. I'm cheering for you!"

Tally waved at the outline of Franklin's body blending into the darkness.

Five

The formal living room was dark except for the lighted candle that looked as if it were floating up and down around a giant lifesaver ring in the ocean at night. Tally hoped someone was lavaliered so the ceremony would be over quicker. It was taking forever for the candle to be passed around the circle and all she wanted to do was read Rye's letter. After Franklin left, she ate a scoop of shrimp salad to hush her growling stomach with no time to rush upstairs.

Instead of her wish coming true, she passed the candle to Khaki who, as the Chaucerette at the end of the circle, passed the candle to Phoebe, the Chaucerette who began the circle. Muted squeals punctured the quiet. After a suspenseful second time around with no one blowing out the candle, it was the beginning of the third time the candle would be passed from one Chaucerette sister to another.

Becca, the last Chaucerette to have an 'engagement Candlelight," whispered, "Someone's engaged."

Tally turned to her left and smiled at Rayleigh, her Chaucerette Little Sister, whose curlers, framed by the glow from the portico light, made giant O's. They looked like an abbreviation for The Oglethorpe-Oxford History Honor. The O-O-Honor. Her hands felt icy. In a few hours she would know.

Her worry that Rye was unaware she had not seen his letter churned her stomach. She felt hot, queasy, tired. The shrimp salad she had just devoured rested heavy. She needed to move, drink water, get cool. During the second pass of the candle, her hand had felt so jittery the candle shook.

The sisters huddled closer to each other. The air could have jump-started a curling iron. Electricity coursed through the room as the candle slowed and each girl's face was seen in its tiny spot of light.

Tally counted the girls ahead of her. Pamela, no, she's lavaliered, you can't go from wearing a boy's fraternity necklace to being engaged. Robin, no, unless she and Red got back together. Jane, no, she and David have been engaged since high school. Mary Pat, no, she and Buford just got pinned. Barbara, no, she's so proud of her four-carat diamond from Steve. Laura, can't be, she just got pinned to Brandon. Belita, no, she and Price got pinned in April. Shannon, no, she's already engaged to Shep. Sheila, no, she and Jeff set a wedding date. Nancy, heavens no, she and Sonny are so in love, they might as well be married already. Virginia, no, she just started dating Jimbo. Rayleigh, no, she'd tell me. Oh, my god! It's not me. It's—Khaki!

A group of girls giggled. Others whispered, "Shhh." Tally started to panic. Her nose itched. She just wanted to give the candle to Khaki, get the celebrating over with and go upstairs to read the letter from Rye. But now she heard her name whispered.

"Tally. Must be Tally." Some said, "Khaki. Bet it's Khaki." Virginia was holding the candle as if to build suspense. Hurry up, Virginia. Nose. So itchy. No time to think of distractions. Rayleigh pushed the candle into Tally's hands.

Tally knew if she whisked it to Khaki, the yellow flame, already squatting instead of stretching, would flicker out. If she sneezed, the flame would, oh no. She couldn't stop. She said "Sorry," sneezed, and the flame disappeared.

In the commotion that followed, during the squeals and the shouts that Tally must have accepted a ring from that Syracuse student, the one she met on the Caribbean cruise during Spring Break, what's-his-name, Rye Something, her only consolation was that her mortified, guilty, embarrassed face was in the dark.

Tally tried to apologize. She tried to calm the room. She asked everyone to be quiet, assuring her sorority sisters she wasn't engaged. She turned on a lamp. She apologized to Khaki who accused her of doing it on purpose to ruin her night.

Tally took the lighter Becca offered. Her hand shook as she lit the candle. She turned off the lamp, and handed the candle to Khaki who was shouting, a little too loudly, no doubt the result of too much gin during her stroll with Louie in the park, "Not fair. I made the signs. I made the flyers. I chose the hint. Did anyone even guess that khaki is the color of army military uniforms? Dammit, Tally. It was MY Candlelight!"

Tally nodded and encouraged Khaki to take the candle. Khaki refused. Tally had ruined Khaki's night, her special moment. She felt terrible.

"Khaki, please forgive me. We all want to celebrate you and Louie."

Rayleigh began to hum "Edelweiss." It was the song she always sang in the talent portion of beauty pageants. Within moments, the girls were singing the lyrics. Tally moved out of the circle. Her palm was cupped around the flame. She gave the candle to Phoebe who started the Candlelight Ceremony all over again, as if no one knew that after three full circles Khaki would finally announce her engagement.

Tally tiptoed up the backstairs to the sleeping porch on the top floor. She drank water, washed her face, patted moisturizer under her eyes, dotted white fade cream on the tiny tan freckles sprinkled across her nose and cheeks, brushed her teeth, and streamed her fingers through her hair. Thick strands tumbled over her shoulders. She tugged through tangles with bristles of the engraved silver brush Tess Hamper had given her years ago. As each hair pulled her scalp, sharp pricks of pain triggered hot tears to spill, but not from tangles.

She flung open a drawer, grabbed a pair of scissors and chopped at her hair. Baby-fine hairs cascaded to the white shag rug. She shook her head. The ends of her hair bounced atop her shoulders. She sucked her bottom lip. Twisting her head from one side to another she glanced at her reflection in the mirror. If he could see her now, Shawl would tease her for another of her rash decisions or make some wacky comment about her hair.

Like the time he winked at Cyndy Jean behind the counter at the Goo-Goo Bakery after she congratulated Tally on turning thirteen and raved about the soft glow of her first-ever frosted highlights. Shawl asked if Cyndy Jean would agree that his sister's hair was now the color of a donut drizzled with butter pecan icing. Cyndy Jean laughed, gave Tally a surprise box of her favorite almond bar cookies, and offered

Shawl a gift of donut holes with her phone number and a red heart drawn on the top of the box.

A gas pain struck. Don't think of food. She burped, the taste of shrimp rising in her mouth. It tasted like the first time she swallowed seawater with its warm brine taste.

The time a sudden wave had whooshed her downward into a spiral of gray that long-ago afternoon, moments before a tug of her hair pulled her up, bouncing her like a puppet in the water. Shawl had scooped her against his chest, turned her like a football under his arm, side-stroked to shore, and slapped her back as she coughed out seawater.

"Squirt, didn't I tell you not to go out that far? Didn't I tell you about the undertow? Damn it. I knew I'd better keep an eye on you." His voice still barked through a tunnel of time. "Listen up. You're not drowning on my watch. Not on my watch."

His favorite phrase? *Not on my watch.* She shook her head. Does every know-it-all big brother say that?

"No." He would yell at her when he was on babysitting duty in the back yard. "You and Becca are not jumping off the balcony onto those sofa cushions and breaking your necks. Not on my watch."

At Hamper Park, he used to embarrass her when he would shout, "Tally! Becca! You two are not wandering down the boardwalk by yourselves. Not on my watch."

She wondered if he was still wearing the stainless-steel Swiss Army watch she gave him as a surprise going-away present.

She opened the shuttered doors of the white French armoire next to her bunk bed on the sleeping porch. She rubbed the braided bracelet of her watch between her fingers and pressed the blue nightglow button. Now she could check the time throughout the night. She could not, would not, be late for class tomorrow, on what could be her big day.

She positioned a box of engraved stationery in front of a picture of her family in Paris when they last visited her mother's childhood home. The stationery would remind her of her promise to write Shawl after the Military Gala tomorrow night to tell him about the festivities, the Gala's celebrity guest, and whether she was nominated for the O-O History Honor. Surely, wherever he was, he had too much to think about to be kept in suspense. Besides, once he got back from whatever secret mission he must be doing, the Army would need to give him a month off just to read his mail.

Smiling at the thought, she heard cheers. Finally. Khaki could show off her ring and announce a wedding date. If only Tally had just observed. If only she had not participated in the Candlelight. That is what historians do. Observe. Not participate. Remember that.

Tally crawled onto her top bunk bed on the screened-in porch that faced the beach. A breeze was blowing wind chimes. The trilling soothed her. She smelled brine in the air and a whiff of cigarette smoke. Somebody must be smoking on the porch below. Tally yawned. Tomorrow she would go with Becca to check her mailbox for letters and—*oh, my lord! Oh, my gosh! Rye's letter.*

She lifted the pillow, tore open the envelope and unfolded the typewritten page dated April 23rd, 1970.

Dear Tally,

You Southern girls sure know how to make a Yankee feel welcome "south" of the Mason-Dixon. And, no, I'm not implying, in case Khaki Carson finds this letter and reads it, that anything "untoward" happened during our excursions off the ship to the island. That's between the two of us, right?

I'm up late. Getting law school applications sent to Columbia, Kentucky and a little school with an excellent reputation named Hamper University in Hamper, Georgia. Guess I'm fond of schools and ladies with sterling reputations. Speaking of ladies whom I admire, I happened to see my little sisters at the airport when I got home from the cruise. Those two are growing like kudzu.

How's that for a Southern reference? See. Slowly but surely, this Yankee from Niagara Falls is being won over by all things Southern. Of course, I'm most charmed by a certain green-eyed girl I look forward to knowing better.

Tally, in that hope, I'll be visiting the Hamper U campus on Monday, May 4th. There's a tour of the law school scheduled that day and a barbecue. Would love to see you and treat you to some barbecue and a bottle of Pepsi.

Now don't get all riled up, Georgia. I can see those cute little freckles scrunching up on your nose right now. Settle down. I'm just joshing. I remember what you said. "Coca-Cola is the only thing, besides sweet tea, that we drink in Georgia. After all, it was discovered here."

And, just to be accurate--since that's what lawyers and purported historians, ahem, are supposed to be--Coca-Cola wasn't "discovered" in Georgia. However, I admit its formula was crafted and patented in your lovely state.

Tally, I'll call your sorority house on Monday, May 4th, when I arrive in Hamper. If you'll still see me after reading this letter, I vow to be on my best behavior.

I would hate to miss the chance to kiss the sweetest lips in Georgia once again.

Rye

Tally felt a tingle from her lips to her toes. Tomorrow could be the best day ever.

She tucked the letter into its envelope, slipped it under her pillow, jumped off the top bunk, and ran to the powder room to wash that freckle fade cream from her face.

Six

Tally blew bits of gold glitter from the stenciled letters on her poster. After reading the title, "The Trail of Tears," and subtitle, "The Descendant Honor Bestowed by Georgians to the Cherokee Nation," out loud one last time, she tied gold ribbons around the white poster paper as Becca tenderly held it in a giant roll on the dining room table.

Exhaling, Tally smoothed her white suede mini-dress, the one she had purchased at Candy's Couture especially for this day. What could be more appropriate than a white dress to represent the innocence of the Cherokees forced at gunpoint from the only homes they knew, forced to walk in moccasins through mountains in snow and freezing blizzards, and forced to watch their loved ones die senseless deaths?

With her guitar upstairs, she positioned her guitar case, holding a surprise item inside for her presentation, by the front door. Strolling with Becca to the kitchen, she cheered as Lula lifted peach-cinnamon rolls onto a serving platter lined with napkins.

"Lula, do I look okay?" Tally poured water into a goblet.

"Gorgeous as always, baby girl. Cute new hair-do too." Lula offered the girls a roll.

"Thank you, Lula. But no thank you. I mean 'thank you' for liking my haircut. But 'no, thank you, Lula,' for the rolls. Goodness. I'm a mess. I mean I'm too nervous to eat, Lula."

Tally kissed Lula on the cheek.

"Too nervous or too guilty?" Khaki sauntered into the kitchen. She poured a steaming mug of hot cocoa. No matter the season, hot cocoa and peach-cinnamon rolls were staples of a Chaucer Sorority House breakfast.

"Morning, Khaki." Tally raised her goblet. "Soon to be Mrs. Louie Larson."

"Hey, Khaki." Becca chimed in, munching one of the two rolls she had placed on her Lenox plate. "You'll go from Khaki Carson to Khaki Larson. How about that?"

"Yes. Khaki Carson Larson has quite a nice ring to it." Khaki nodded before tilting her head as if to ponder the engraving on her future thank-you notes.

"Oh, Khaki. Your ring." Tally oohed and ahhed over the three-carat marquis-cut diamond, tilted on crisscrossing gold prongs. "It's, well, it's stunning."

"That's because Louie designed it himself."

"Who knew Louie had such artistic vision?" Tally pressed the glow button on her watch to illuminate the time. 7:30 a.m. July 30th, 1730. The day James Oglethorpe petitioned King George II to establish the colony south of the Carolinas that would become Georgia, the last of the thirteen colonies. Hustle, bunny, as Phoebe always said. Or be the last student to class. She placed her goblet on the marble counter.

"He *is* a drummer, Tally. Drummers are musicians. Which makes them artists. Look at Ringo." Khaki rolled her eyes and tucked a curl of copper hair behind her ear.

"Touché." Tally winked at Becca, and hugged Lula, the woman who often told her that she wished Tally could be her granddaughter after having four boys and eleven grandsons. "Wish me luck, Lula Lou. Today's the day."

"Good luck, baby." Lula wrapped an egg salad sandwich in waxed paper, a teacake inside a square of tin foil, and placed them in a paper sack. "Hope this helps."

"Lula, you angel, you. Thank you so much." Tally hugged Lula again. Her nose brushed Lula's tight black curls that smelled like oranges as she whispered, "Shhh! Rye's calling today. Ask him to meet me here at 4:30. Please?"

"Tally, you know I love you too." Lula squeezed Tally's hand.

"Fingers crossed, Tally. Soon you'll be the nominee from Hamper U." Becca stopped licking her fingers and blew a kiss.

"Yeah. Good luck. Oh, let me see your new haircut." Swiftly, Khaki reached, tousling the ends of Tally's hair, as her other hand holding her mug bumped Tally's elbow with force.

Hot cocoa splashed Tally's dress, seeping brown splotches into the white suede.

Tally felt liquid drip down her legs. Her new pistachio green Pappagallo flats were dotted with tan spots.

"Khaki Carson! How dare you!" Tally's eyes blurred with tears. The grandfather clock, set by Miss Perry to chime at frenetic intervals before classes each day to hurry the girls along, boomed. Tally panicked. Only fifteen minutes to get to class and set up her project.

How would she have time to murder Khaki, change clothes and still arrive before Professor Dodge locked the door?

"McCall, you moved away then--Wow. That is one ugly--Sorry. Give me a napkin, Lula, and I'll wipe it off."

"No. Khaki, you'll smear it." Tally blotted her legs with a dishtowel. "And I don't have time to change."

"Now that's not the end of the world, baby." Lula took a pink marker and put a check by Khaki's name on the Demerits list Miss Perry asked her to keep in the kitchen. "Those melted polka dots look like a little Indian baby smeared mud on your dress."

Becca grabbed Khaki's arm. "Uncalled for, Khaki. She didn't mean to sneeze last night and blow out your candle."

Khaki wriggled from Becca's grip, scooped a roll onto a napkin, and sashayed past Tally.

"Touché yourself."

Tally rushed to class, taking a shortcut past students strumming guitars and singing "Where Have All the Flowers Gone?" near the spot where Frisbee throwers had trampled gardenias in the quad.

Knocking on the classroom door as a bell at the nearby church rang eight times, she thanked Ivy who opened the door for her. Tally thumbtacked corners of her poster to a corkboard, all the while apologizing for being late. Professor Dodge shook his head and pointed to the clock. Tally wiggled into her desk-chair holding her hem down until she could cross her legs.

Professor Dodge explained that each student in today's final group of the Georgia History Pedagogy class would have ten minutes for his or her presentation and question-answer follow-up. Tally would give the first presentation, Winston the last, with a restroom intermission, during the two-hour class.

He complimented the class on their attire as future History Teachers dressed according to the Georgia History topic or prominent Georgian he or she had researched. The novelty of their costumes would earn them extra points toward their final grade as could cordial participation during a classmate's presentation.

"Just a reminder, class. Your costumes are an example of how to create a visual impression for your future junior-high and high-school students. History is often considered a dull subject filled with dates and facts, difficult to remember. Today you will show how vibrant history truly is." Professor Dodge applauded the students. "Your colleagues will pretend to be your students asking you questions or posing dilemmas to enhance your teaching ability."

Professor Dodge also announced he would take pictures of each student with his new Leica 35 mm camera and flash attachment.

Winston, dressed as Otis Redding, raised his hand.

"Professor D., I'll be changing from Otis to Dr. King. Singer to Saint. You'll be needing two pictures of me for your scrapbook, right?"

Tally grinned. Winston. There was no one like him in the world. Brash. Brilliant. Butters up everybody to get his way. And everyone knows. And no one cares.

"Good point, Winston." Professor Dodge lifted his camera in the air to show to the class. "Yes. If anyone is changing costumes, like Winston, and, I suppose, Tally who may be changing from her, whatever, then yes. I'll take two pictures. Thanks, Winston."

Winston made a motion toward the professor as if his index finger were a gun. Point. Jerk. Pow. Professor Dodge smiled.

Oh, my gosh. There is no doubt. Winston is going to be nominated. Tally looked at Winston then the Professor. What a fool she was. Of course, Professor Dodge would choose Winston as a finalist. He would want to make history himself by giving a deserving Black student a chance to win the inaugural Oglethorpe-Oxford History Honor.

She wanted to sit in the private tunnel under the sorority house where she could be alone in the quiet and figure out what to do next. What would she tell Rye? Her parents? Shawl? Becca? Her sorority sisters? She wanted to see Rye, snuggle in his arms again and feel safe.

Winston leaned toward her. He put his arm around her shoulders as Professor Dodge excused himself to go into the storage closet to load his camera with film.

"Girl." His voice was a low drawl. "What's the problem here? Other than that awful costume."

"Winston. I, I feel dizzy."

"Suck it up, girl. Stop acting the ingénue. You're getting nominated. If you don't feel brilliant, *act* brilliant." His massive hand covered her fist. He cushioned her hand in his until she relaxed her fingers. "Now listen. No tears on 'The Trail of Tears' except for the Cherokees. You're their voice today. *Their* voice. Got it?"

Tally sucked her bottom lip, looked into Winston's eyes, and saw him wink.

"And, girl, after this shindig is over and you're nominated," he put his hand back on his knee, "rightfully so--"

"Winston, I'm sorry to interrupt you and I thank you so much for your...look, here's the thing. I just want you to know how much I think you deserve the finalist spot. If either of us gets nominated, I'll be tickled." Tally's fingers zigzagged through layers of hair behind her right ear, flipping the ends up in her coquettish way. "However, Mister Observant Historian, you haven't even noticed I cut my hair."

"I noticed, girl. I noticed. Once a fox, always a fox."

Tally blushed. "You and your sweet compliments, Winston Churchill Crockett. You know what I say? Once a friend, always a friend. So, Winston, is everything all right, you know, with your family?" Franklin's demeanor last night still troubled her.

Professor Dodge banged the door to the closet, emerged with the camera on a strap around his neck and a grade book tucked under his arm.

"Got a favor to ask, girl. Just between us. Later, gator."

Moments later it was her turn. Tally stood next to her poster. In a clear voice, she thanked her "students" for their attention and participation. She thanked Professor Dodge for his indulgence of her topic. She stated that, unlike everyone else today, she would indict Georgians, not praise them. She stated that she was taking a risk. However, someone had to be true to the original Georgians: The Creek, the Cherokee, the Chickasaw.

She stated that hot cocoa was spilled on her dress that morning allowing her no time to change. She emphasized the word *change*. She told the class, in a voice brimming with tribute, that instead of the white of her dress representing the innocence of the beleaguered Cherokees, her dress now would represent something else. Something they would be able to guess soon. Winston leaned forward in his chair.

She reminded her students of the Supreme Court case, *Worcester v. Georgia*. She reminded them that the Supreme Court had declared the Cherokee Nation a sovereign nation and a *"distinct community with self-government in which the laws of Georgia can have no force."*

Yet when an illegal treaty, signed by only a handful of Cherokees without full tribal authority on December 29, 1835, was announced, it effectively dismissed the Court's ruling. The unauthorized signatures of the suspect Cherokees granted Georgia the Cherokee land. It was this unlawful treaty that was voted on by Congress and ratified on May 23, 1836, forcing a nation of people to lose the right to stay on the land they loved, the only land where they and their ancestors had ever lived.

"How many votes in Congress ratified the *Treaty of New Echota* to supersede the original Supreme Court ruling?" Her voice hushed.

"One vote by one Senator," a smattering of voices answered.

One vote, she emphasized in a now monotone voice, to change the course of history, to mandate the removal of an entire nation of Cherokees; one vote that ultimately ended the lives of four thousand Cherokees forced to journey through a brutal winter without proper supplies.

Connie May blurted, "And that doesn't even count how many spirits were crushed. Or all the hearts that were broken."

"Thank you, Connie May. You're so right. And that toll is not included in any statistics. The psychological terror of uprooting people from their ancestral land, from the place where they buried their loved ones, from the place where all their memories were made, was devastating, according to personal testimonies found in books on the subject."

"In fact," Tally quieted her voice, "there is the legend of a Cherokee woman who arrived home from working in the fields all day. Her newborn baby was crying in a papoose on her back and her toddler was clutching her leg. Confronted by soldiers pointing guns at her babies, she was ordered by the soldiers to gather her belongings immediately and start walking. She pleaded for time. Her pleas were dismissed. Her tears dropped to the red Georgia clay where she finally collapsed across the foot of a soldier, her hand still squeezing her toddler's hand, and died."

There was a hush in the classroom.

Connie May dabbed tears from her eyes.

Tally pointed to a quote by John Donne from *Devotions upon Emergent Occasions* that she had copied with a Magic Marker felt pen on her poster. She passed out purple mimeographed papers with the typed quote on each one as a take-home surprise for the class.

She asked the class to read it.

Their voices sounded like horses' hoof beats, clomping at different speeds, before joining in unison.

"No man is an island, entire of itself; every man is a piece of the continent, a part of the main. If a clod be washed away by the sea, Europe is the less, as well as if a promontory were, as well as if a manor of thy friend's or of thine own were; any man's death diminishes me, because I am involved in mankind, and therefore never send to know for whom the bell tolls; it tolls for thee."

She asked for a moment of silence.

Without warning, she rang a bell, a sterling silver Tiffany bell engraved with her initials and given to her parents by the First Lady, Bess Truman, when she was a baby.

Classmates, acting as her students, looked startled. She passed around a tomahawk she had carried in her guitar case. She asked the class to appreciate the power within each of them during their lifetimes not to allow dismissed and defeated people to suffer further, including Georgians of all skin colors, all races, who feel dismissed and defeated and want to rage and rebel.

She asked her students to own their own power. She challenged them not to let a travesty of man's inhumanity to man happen to any group of people again.

"The source of your truth?" She pointed to her poster. "Descendant honor."

She acknowledged that no Georgian alive today could comfort the Cherokees who lived through "The Trail of Tears." No Georgian alive today could apologize to those Cherokees who actually endured the mass exodus. No Georgian alive today could beg for forgiveness from those who actually suffered, who lost loved ones, or who died.

The transformative power of "Descendant Honor," a title she told the class she had originated for this project, is that each Georgian alive today could instead have the decency and the honor to vow that this injustice will never happen again -- not in his lifetime, not in her lifetime, not in his actions, not in hers.

She asked the class to take a good look at her dress, to see it with fresh vision. She asked them to see not only the white representing the innocence of the Cherokee nation. She asked them to imagine these Native people who had always lived on Georgia soil, who began adopting the ways of Europeans in dress and speech, who modeled a governance to be more like Georgians, who developed a written language, and who interacted with Georgia colonists with sophistication, education and generosity.

She asked her students what truly led to the Cherokees' grave misfortune.

Buford shouted, "Living on land where gold was discovered."

She thanked Buford and reminded the class that the Gold Rush in Georgia, where gold was found in a North Georgia creek on Cherokee land in 1829, started a stampede of prospectors two decades before the Gold Rush in California. She emphasized the lack of empathy by President Andrew Jackson who wrote the Cherokee people and told them in no uncertain terms, *"You cannot remain where you are now."*

She asked the class to see the brown splotches staining the white on her dress in a metaphorical way and share what they saw before she would offer her conclusion.

"The brown man is a stain on the white man?"

"Jack, we're talking redskins." Laura countered.

Tad raised his hand. "Okay. The brown stain reckons to be Georgia soil, except Georgia dirt is mostly good ol' red clay. Hey, maybe I don't get metaphors."

Gene, an English Lit major, said, "Easy to remember, Tadpole. Best metaphor? *Fog comes on little cat feet.* Carl Sandburg."

"Got it. Okay, the white could be the snow the Cherokees had to suffer through and the, uh, brown? Guess it could be the color of blankets that covered the dead bodies."

Patricia's tentative voice joined in. "Tad, that's so sad! I think the brown represents the Cherokees who died and the white represents heaven."

"Tally, I mean, 'Miss McCall,' I have an idea." Heads turned toward the girl who had to be coaxed to say anything in class. If Gloria had something to share, Tally had done her job.

"What if the brown represents dirt covering chunks of gold that rightfully belonged to the Cherokees?" Gloria asked. "And what if the white represents the white men who claimed it as theirs?"

"Wow. Great job, everybody. Thank you, Gloria. What a fresh idea. Connie May, Laura, Tad, Patricia, Gene, Buford, Jack. You all have such interesting guesses and views. I would never have thought of those." Tally saw other hands raised.

"Hey, brilliant girl, I mean, 'Miss McCall,' what do you say?" Winston challenged.

"Why thank you, Winston, for your compliment and your question." Tally's voice strengthened. "I think of my white dress now splotched with brown as my homage to the paint ponies who were forced to carry the devastated Cherokees on their backs and whose hoof prints made history along 'The Trail of Tears.' The metaphor abides in the image of both the ponies and the Cherokees being forced to risk their lives without being shown mercy or freedom from others."

At the moment she said the word, "forced," Tally remembered Charlie Johnson's favorite quote. One slow day at the newspaper when Mr. Boudreaux was gone, Charlie told her about Leonardo da Vinci's belief that *"restlessness and force were the supreme principles of the cosmos, not statis and rest."* Charlie quoted da Vinci as eloquently as if he had been on a stage that day.

"Anything could be understood if a person knew what forces had been and were being brought to bear upon it--the forms of animal and human bodies, the shapes of trees, and of women's faces, the structures of buildings and mountains, the courses of rivers and the contours of the seacoasts."

Charlie gave Tally a copy of the essay his cousin, Charles van Doren, wrote on *The History of Knowledge*. Charlie encouraged her to read it on her summer vacation. She had underlined the passage he quoted and memorized it already.

Tally wrote, "Restlessness, force, mountains, women's faces," on the chalkboard. She added *"sapere vedere,"* explained da Vinci's *"to know how to see"* personal Creed and his view of restlessness and force, and handed Gloria a tissue.

A majorette knows a big finish, with flourishes, lifts spirits.

"In conclusion, thank you so much to each of you for your ideas. You proved what Professor Dodge once said about each of us seeing history differently."

"Like the *Titanic*?"

"Yes. Great memory, Ivy. Professor Dodge, as I'm sure you remember, made this observation on the first day of class: 'From the view of passengers on the *Titanic*, the rockets shooting into the night sky must have meant hope of a rescue. From the view of the ship's crew, the rockets flaring must have meant horror for it proved the ship was sinking. Yet from the view of the *Californian*, a ship only fifteen miles away, the fireworks must have seemed like a party to celebrate the ship's maiden voyage across the sea.' Right, Professor?"

"Correct, Tally, I mean, 'Miss McCall.' It all comes down to how each person sees, like da Vinci's Creed. One's understanding of history is fueled by the energy one puts into research, contemplation and analysis." Professor Dodge pointed to their textbook. "And by how much one studies. Only then is one able to determine when truth rings."

After Tally's presentation, for which she received applause, there was anticipation for the big announcement and the other presentations by future History teachers dressed in a variety of attire for their assigned topics:

Connie May wore a shirtwaist dress, hat, gloves and pearls with a pencil behind her ear to honor Georgia author Margaret Mitchell;

Gene, as "The Misfit" in a garish shirt with parrots painted on it, would be honoring Georgia writer Flannery O'Connor and her short story, *A Good Man is Hard to Find*;

Buford was dressed in a white doctor's coat to honor Georgia's very own Dr. Crawford W. Long who performed the world's first painless surgery using ether as an anesthetic;

Tad, in dungarees as a gold miner, represented Georgia's "Twenty-niners;"

Gloria, in a custom-made Brownie uniform and serving a platter of Thin Mint cookies, would honor Juliette Gordon Lowe who started the Girl Scouts in Savannah;

and Winston wore bell bottoms and a silver polyester shirt to honor Otis Redding before he would change into a red Kool-Aid-stained white shirt with black tie and black trousers while holding a family Bible to honor Dr. Martin Luther King, Jr.

Professor Dodge called Winston's name and took his photo as Winston sat on the edge of the Professor's desk, his long legs dangling in a wide stance. Winston pulled a harmonica from his pocket, cupped his palm around it, and blew a plaintive tune through the instrument. The notes, reminiscent of the whistling at the end of "Sittin' on the Dock of the Bay," got the class humming as Winston played the intro notes on his harmonica and pointed to classmates. In unison everyone sang lyrics with emphasis on the beginning of verse two when the singer leaves his Georgia home.

"Thank you, Otis, my man, for your words, your truth. Thank you for telling it like it is. Folks without hope, nothing to dream about. Can you dig that feeling of hopelessness, students? That feeling of no way out? That feeling of no purpose, no power, no path to follow? That feeling, I remind you, fellow students of history, is the connection for people with black skin throughout their history in Georgia."

Winston's voice sounded riled up.

"Yessiree. That is the connection. Lack of hope through the years is what connects Negro slaves to the words of Black soul singers. Yet, there was a glimmer of hope in the glory of our modern-day prophet, a man whose life was cut short only two years and one month ago today. Dr. Martin Luther King, Jr., who will appear just as soon as I change outfits, will encourage you to think of hope in a whole new way. These two Black men, Otis and Martin, died within four months of each other. Otis in a plane crash. Martin assassinated. Their personal hopes died with them. Their words, however, did not. Now y'all keep singing, whistling, humming. Back soon."

While Winston changed, Professor Dodge took pictures of the students. Without Winston, the group reflected the image of the first colonists of Georgia, all Caucasian settlers, where no Black residents lived.

Winston walked back into class as Dr. King. He addressed the class in hushed, dramatic tones. He reminded his students that Georgia was originally chartered by a group of men in England, led by James Edward Oglethorpe, a social reformer and philanthropist, who wanted to found a colony in the new land; a colony not only named for, but also given a royal charter by, the King of England, George II; a colony envisioned as a utopia in the New World.

Fifty acres of land would be granted to each colonist; small agrarian farms that would not require outside labor, only family members to toil the land, would be offered; Trustees would oversee the colony; and the Trustees' "Charter of Rules" would be the governing law.

Winston held his Bible in the air.

"As Georgians, as descendants of the original Georgians," he nodded at Tally, "you must never forget. Those rules not only included the planting of mulberry trees so silkworms could flourish in the warm, sunny weather and the silk trade could provide a way to make money for the colonists--" Winston paused, bent his head, and after a moment, looked up. "Those rules also included the words *'No Slavery'* in the Georgia-land. That's right. Georgia was the only colony among the original thirteen that legally outlawed slavery in its charter."

"Therefore, my fellow Georgians and my students, our hopes as Negroes and as Caucasians are intertwined. Our mutual hope is simple. We want the original intent of the law in Georgia to be acknowledged by all Americans as pure intent, utopian intent. What led to that change of intent by Georgians will, we also hope, be studied for a long time."

"We, as Georgia History students, know what happened. A group of wealthy settlers, mostly from Scotland, did not need help from the Trustees financially when they arrived in Georgia. These settlers grew tired of the hard labor it took to farm the land in Georgia's heat and humidity. These colonists, called 'The Malcontents,' stirred up trouble in Georgia when they saw the leisure-life of plantation owners who had slaves in South Carolina and wanted that lifestyle too. We know the Malcontents wrote letters to Parliament in England, wrote letters to the King, and published pamphlets to demand slavery and rum in Georgia."

Tad raised his hand. "I would have petitioned for rum too."

"I hear you, Tad. Only problem?" Winston grinned. "The Malcontents didn't have Coke to make those rum and Coke drinks you like. Now, let's get back to you being my *teenage* student."

"Reckon I'd be content just to have rum," Tad whispered to Gene, "right about now."

"Well, you would have been frustrated back then, Tad. Oglethorpe refused the Malcontents' pleas. So did Parliament. Years later, in 1751, circumstances and relentless persuasion forced Parliament to allow, with restrictions, the presence of African slaves in Georgia."

"Oglethorpe acknowledged that Georgia's original ban on slavery was a 'lost cause.' Yet today, the words, 'lost cause,' reference the supposed chivalry and honor and pride of the South that was lost after The War Between the States. Curious, right? Folks who loved the antebellum days of slaves and plantations still pine for the glory of that time and rally for that 'lost cause' just as folks who take pride in Georgia as a colony without slavery pine for their 'lost cause' too."

"You know, I bet Dr. King would ask us, as historians, for all citizens are historians in one way or another, to lead the way to a 'new cause.' Digging deep into what caused this change of intent from the original Trustees' rules, to try to understand, as Miss McCall said," Winston pointed to the words Tally wrote on the chalkboard, "the force and the restlessness of settlers who reckoned that slavery was morally acceptable. That is, my fellow historians, where we will discover the true gold and the answer to why our Georgia History is so fraught with hatred, horror, honor and hope."

Winston held up the Bible. "Dr. King would surely want us to be modern-day Malcontents. People who will not be content with the status quo. Citizens who are not content with the way some Whites treat Blacks in Georgia. Citizens who are not content with the way some Blacks treat Whites in Georgia. Citizens who will never be content with injustice to another human being. I'll leave you with a quote from Dr. King. *Injustice anywhere is a threat to justice everywhere.*"

Winston concluded with a prayer for peace among people in Georgia and in the world as he said Dr. King would do.

The class, after bowing their heads, stood and applauded.

Professor Dodge congratulated Winston. He took a picture of the class with Winston in the center.

In a quick-thinking gesture, Winston opened the door, disappeared momentarily and returned with the janitor who leaned his mop against the bulletin board long enough to learn how to hold the camera and snap a picture of the class that included Professor Dodge.

Moments before class ended, students gathered around the professor for the important announcement.

"Students of Georgia history, today is a historic moment. Today, Monday, May 4th, 1970, is a day of tribute to Georgians, past and present, who are often ignored for their intelligence, their curiosity, their awareness, their original intent. People," he pointed to Tally, "often dismissed and defeated, as Tally mentioned in her presentation."

He cleared his throat.

"Students, early this morning, in a telephone call with Lord Hughes in London, I was granted special permission from Oxford University in Oxford, England to nominate both Winston Churchill Crockett and Tally Gigi McCall as finalists from Hamper University for the inaugural Oglethorpe-Oxford History Honor. Congratulations to our two deserving Georgia History students."

Tally could not believe what Professor Dodge had just said. Her dream had come true. She was nominated. A girl. In Georgia. To study at Oxford. A way to make her parents happy. A way to take their worries off Shawl. And Winston nominated too? Hallelujah. All is right with the world.

Amidst the cheering, Tally grinned, hugged Professor Dodge, and patted Winston on the back. Winston shook Professor Dodge's hand while Tad and Gene started singing "Dixie." Professor Dodge posed Tally and Winston, still dressed in their costumes, by his colonial map of Georgia.

Between clicks of the camera, Winston whispered in Tally's ear. "Time to be rebels, girl. Let's both win this thing."

Tally stood on tiptoes and whispered in Winston's ear, "Winston, let's do it. Oh, and promise? Let's never forget this day."

Seven

Still giddy at the news of her nomination, Tally arrived at her Speech class not caring one whit about the Final Exam. She already had an "A" in the course. The written test would be a breeze. She had other things to think about.

Waving at Virginia Dodge across the room, she saw her sorority sister clap her hands in the air without making any noise. Oh, my gosh. Virginia knows. Her daddy, Professor Dodge, must have told her to keep the secret. Either that or Virginia, who had always dreamed of being a hairdresser, really liked Tally's new haircut.

Tally smiled and blew Virginia a kiss.

Their Speech Professor called the class to order. He announced he had changed his mind about a written test. Instead, he would assign each student a topic from an article in *The Hamper Herald*, *The Fort Hamper Gazette* or, for fun, *Photoplay Magazine* with the student giving a extemporaneous, off-the-cuff, persuasive or expository speech about the topic. Students would have five minutes to read the article before addressing the class.

What? *WHAT?*

Students were aghast, groaning, raising their hands to remind the professor they had studied for a written test and changing the rules at the last minute was not fair.

Tally was given a front page from the Monday, May 4th, 1970 edition of *The Hamper Herald.* An article was circled. Unfortunately, it was not about the sweethearts on the sandbar for she would have had much to say. Instead, the article was about that school up north, Kent State University. She speed-read "Trouble Brewing in Ohio" and took notes.

Trouble Brewing in Ohio
by Tom Barker
AP Staff Writer, Louisville, Kentucky

Over the weekend, the 96th Kentucky Derby drew a crowd of happy, mint julep-drinking gentlemen and fancy hat-wearing ladies at Churchill Downs in Louisville. Diane Crump, a female jockey, made history competing in the race on a horse named *Fathom.* Hometown writer, Hunter S. Thompson, attended the event with an illustrator friend. Thompson stated to this reporter that he plans to write an article on the Derby for a sports magazine. The working title is *The Kentucky Derby is Decadent and Depraved.*

A few hours away, in Kent, Ohio, a long-haired, jean-and-tee-shirt-wearing crowd of students, fueled, it seems, by frustration about the war and end-of-school-year rowdiness, proceeded to trash cars, break downtown store windows and, ultimately, burn the abandoned ROTC Building, the building already designated for demolition at the edge of The Commons, on Saturday, May 2, 1970.

National Guard troops, originally sent to Akron, Ohio earlier in the week to quell a truckers' strike, were reassigned by Governor

James Rhodes to the Kent State University campus to guard against further riots.

With National Guard troops on patrol, a rally for peace and U.S. withdrawal from the Vietnam conflict will be held by students on Monday, May 4th, on "The Commons" field by the Victory Bell at noon.

The grassy field known as "The Commons," where the Victory Bell signifies a place of honor and tradition, is also the place on the KSU campus known for touch football games, picnics, concerts, Frisbee throwing, and student gatherings.

It will now be known as the place where a group of history students named "World Historians Opposed to Racism and Exploitation," (with an acronym in the original *AP* article that our readers might find offensive, therefore, editors at *The Hamper Herald* have found it unnecessary to print) buried the U.S. Constitution under the Victory Bell, the bell which was originally meant to clang for KSU football victories.

The group asserted on purple mimeographed flyers handed out to fellow students or nailed to oak trees on campus as well as in a speech at the Victory Bell site on Friday, May 1st, 1970 that "President Nixon had murdered the Constitution when he announced on Thursday, April 30th, 1970, his plans for the U.S. to invade Cambodia."

Therefore, in reaction to the President's decision, the KSU history students buried the document in the ground.

Tally stood at the podium, observed her classmates, saw Virginia and Jimbo flirting, heard one boy humming as he circled phrases in his article, saw another with a transistor radio to his ear, saw a girl putting on lipstick, heard a group of girls talking about the sandbar couple.

The only connection between Hamper University and Kent State, like the South and the North one hundred years before, was how individuals with freedom, did what made sense to them in each climate, in each culture, in each moment of urgency or lack of it.

Eight

Tally raced past the historical marker in Hamper Park celebrating Hamper, Georgia as the only town Sherman spared from destruction in his March to the Sea before he spared Savannah because of its breathtaking beauty. She rushed past the bandstand decorated with striped bunting left over from May Day celebrations, past the marble statue nicknamed *The Two Men*, past the deserted Red Cross station sporting red and white balloons punching each other in the breeze. The clock on the theater marquee read 11:30 a.m.

Tally's plan to arrive early for her final day at *The Hamper Herald* was right on track.

Bounding up the spiral staircase inside the mansion, guitar case in hand, she stopped at the sound of creaks from the elevator in slow descent. Through iron gates, she glimpsed the janitor, with his bucket and mop beside him, manning the lever. Oh, my gosh. Is Mr. Bentley okay?

"Morning, Miss Tally."

"Gus, good morning." Tally entered the elevator. "Is Mr. Bentley alright?"

"He is fine. Excited about something and needed a new suit. Mr. Boudreaux asked me to take over during Mr. Bentley's lunch hour."

"Oh, thank goodness, Gus. Wow. It smells so good in here. Love that pine scent."

"Recipe I made up. Pure pine flavoring with a tinge of eucalyptus keeps it fresh. Like being in a forest."

"Smells like heaven to me."

"Here you are, Miss Tally. Third floor."

"Thank you, Gus. And I was so hoping to see you this morning. Please forgive how late this is. It's been the craziest, busiest time."

She handed him an envelope with "You are Cordially Invited" engraved on the front with an asterisk beside her handwritten words, "Please wear your medals."

Reporters nodded to her as they cradled phones on their shoulders and typed. One reporter pointed to the clock on the wall, wrapped a black curly phone cord around his neck, pulled it tight and stuck his tongue out. Another pointed to her mini-dress, covered his phone, and spit gum in his coffee cup. Another blew her an air kiss.

She dropped the guitar case on the floor beside her desk and did not even stoop to close it when it popped open. She sat down in her chair and focused on envelopes sporting the words, "Farewell, Tally," "Good Luck, Tally" and the inevitable "Tally Ho!" in a trail of pastel squares across her mahogany desktop.

One note propped against a scented candle proclaimed, "No one holds a candle to you when it comes to sweet-talking callers."

Blinking rapidly, she grabbed the last tissue from the box on her desk, touching it to her eyelashes. Tiny amethyst elevens arched across the soft white paper.

She could not believe the events of this day. She had been nominated for the highest honor she could imagine. All she wanted to do was call her mother. But her mother was in Paris buying wedding gowns for her shop.

She wanted to call her daddy. But he would be driving to his weekly Monday lunch that took place behind closed doors at the Country Club with other judges in Hamper, Georgia.

She wanted to call her brother but how could she when it was almost midnight in Da Nang?

She wanted to tell her sweetheart, Rye Somerset, the happy news but what if he was upset with her? Good grief. Rye had written that he would be at Hamper University touring the law school as a prospective student today and would call her before he left to go back to Syracuse. But without hearing from her, would he still call?

She wanted to phone Lula at the Chaucer Sorority House to tell her the good news and ask if Rye had called. But Lula would be busy fixing lunch for the Chaucerette sorority sisters and it would not be fair to disturb her.

Her emotions were a jumble. Yet the more she thought about her name being considered by Oxford University officials in England for the opportunity to earn her graduate degree in History there, the more she wanted to win the award. If only she and Winston could figure out a way to win as a team.

"McCall! Daydream-time is over."

"Mr. Boudreaux. Sir. I mean, Boudreaux." She stood, nearly knocking over a vase of daisies. She grabbed an envelope with a crest engraved in the corner. "Thought you were at lunch."

"Saw your grand entrance. Early on your final day as an intern? Impressive."

"Yes, sir. After my final in Speech class, I ran as fast as I could through the park." She pointed to the guitar case sprawled open, stuffed with a rolled-up poster and tomahawk. "Oh, sir, you'll be so proud. I presented 'The Trail of Tears' from the Cherokee Indians' point of view for my Georgia History final today." She fanned herself with the envelope.

"Impossible." He lit a cigar, dropping the match in the flower vase. "Can't be done. Can't report the Cherokees' point of view unless--"

"Unless?"

"You interviewed a Cherokee who was there." He blew a ring of vanilla smoke in Tally's direction.

She grimaced at the smell and twirled a lock of hair. "Well, I tried to imagine."

"And what in God's name do you have on? Earth to McCall. Moretti's shooting the group photo today, the one for tomorrow's *Meet the Staff* edition."

"I didn't forget, sir. I asked Mr. Moretti yesterday what I should wear."

"And he said to dress like a giraffe?"

Tally blushed. "No, sir. Mr. Moretti told me in his darling Italian accent, 'Miss Tally, with your hair the color of caramel, your baby freckles the spice of cinnamon, your eyes as green as--'"

"Spinach?"

"No! 'Green as mint and lips the color of peaches, there is one color to wear.'"

"Good God. Pray tell."

"White. He said the contrast would be stunning. Don't you love how Italians have such a glorious way as word-artists to describe colors?"

"McCall, white isn't a color. And except for Dante, Italians are known for art. Not the written word. And, Miss Forever Gullible, Moretti's from Rome. Rome, Georgia."

"Really? But his accent? Oh, my gosh. Isn't that the oddest thing?" She wanted to challenge him. The written word is art.

"Anyway, I told him I was already planning to wear white. You see, sir, I saved this white suede dress to wear today to represent the innocence of the Cherokees being forced from their homes. But then hot cocoa was splattered on my dress this morning and I didn't have time to change."

Boudreaux closed his eyes, tilting his head from one shoulder to the other.

"So, I looked in the mirror, saw splotches soaking the suede, and, quick-quick, made a decision. I announced to the class that my dress was my personal tribute to the brave paint ponies that were forced to carry the Cherokees from their homes."

He rubbed his temples. "Only you, McCall. Only you would see things that way."

He tossed a business card, featuring a grinning pig, at her black typewriter cover.

"McCall. Chief Parish is meeting me at Blue's Bar-B-Q, the one on Fort Hamper Highway. If Tess Hamper calls, tell her I'm researching my editorial on students out of control, campus shenanigans, toilet paper in the mimosas, loud music, curfews. All that."

"Yes, sir. And Boudreaux?"

He raised his eyebrow and sported a cocky smile.

Stop acting the ingénue. Winston had said those words to her just before her history presentation.

"Boudreaux, sir, I need your signature on this form, please."

"I'll sign it later. It's nearly noon."

"But what if you get busy and forget? I have to submit it tomorrow."

"I'll sign it when I get back from lunch. Wait. What am I signing?"

"I need you to write something positive about my work ethic."

"For whom?"

"For Oxford University in England." Her voice sounded reverent.

The moment she said the words out loud, she knew, once again, that she wanted the award more than ever. Oxford. England. The home of her beloved Chaucer. She felt happy to be nominated for this honor, but, most of all, hungry to be hugged.

Through sniffles she said, "You, Boudreaux, sir, you're the first person I'm sharing the news with."

"What news? And what's with the tears?"

"I just learned that Professor Dodge is nominating me as a finalist for the very first Oglethorpe-Oxford History Honor."

"Wait. You're nominated for something? You didn't win anything? You're just nominated and you're crying because you're nominated?"

Boudreaux pulled a handkerchief from his back pocket and handed it to her. "Time to toughen up, McCall."

"That's what Winston said." She blew her nose on his handkerchief.

"By the way, where is Winston? I didn't see him working on obits in the library."

"Sir, Winston and I left class at different times. And we had different classes to attend after that. I'm sure he's here."

Soon he would be asking for Boudreaux's signature too.

"What's with this nomination you're so happy about that it makes you cry?"

Tally laughed at the absurdity. "The Oglethorpe-Oxford History Honor."

"Didn't we run a sidebar on that months ago?" Boudreaux waved to Miss Jane, the Book Editor, spreading books from her slush pile across a table for employees to take home. "Something about a history major from the state of Georgia studying at Oxford."

"Yes sir. Oglethorpe, the founder of Georgia. Oxford, his alma mater. The person who wins goes to Oxford, all expenses paid, to study for his *or her* graduate degree in History. And guess what?"

She couldn't stop for his answer.

"The winner represents the state of Georgia, along with dignitaries, in planning America's Bicentennial events for 1976. And history will be made if I should win because not even an Oxford Rhodes Scholar can be a female."

"Curious. So why did Dodge choose you? What made you stand out?"

Boudreaux sounded like the beat reporter he used to be.

"Professor Dodge told me that he liked my essay comparing the military draft in The War Between the States to the military draft today and how I connected the military draft to Georgia history."

"The draft, you say? And your conclusion?"

"My conclusion is a military draft is modern-day slavery. And Georgia is the only colony of the original thirteen to outlaw slavery in its royal charter with King George."

"And you're being crowned Military Gala Queen at Fort Hamper tonight?"

He shook his head, signed his name, wrote something on the work ethic line, started toward the revolving door, abruptly turned, and said, "Keep the handkerchief."

At the sound of campus bells clanging the noon hour, seagulls screeched. The shrieks continued, as they did every day, until echoes of the bells died down prompting the gulls to settle on window ledges outside the newsroom.

Inside the mansion, reporters clicked off electric typewriters, slammed dictionaries shut in such rapid-fire succession they sounded like gunshots, and shouted to each other about where to meet for lunch. They saluted to Tally at the reception desk, and whistle-cheered when she saluted back.

Finally. All gone. Quiet as a morgue.

Strolling from her desk to a row of windows overlooking the shore, she watched four kites in the distance. One sailed high above the waves, one glided over a volleyball net where students jumped and cheered, one dipped near a snow-cone stand, while one plunged dangerously close to the grove of mimosas by the boardwalk.

The newsroom echoed the hush that comes over Southern towns, even those with college campuses, in the middle of the day. In Hamper, Georgia, students slept in, studied on the beach or gathered at sorority or fraternity houses for lunches served on white linen tablecloths. Folks closed offices and stores, meandered home for a nap, or strolled to the local diner for a lunch special of chicken 'n dumplings, fried okra, turnip greens, sweet tea, rolls, and egg custard pie.

Tally plopped down in her swivel chair. She slid Lula's teacake in her mouth, dusted flour from her fingers, closed her eyes and sucked on the mound of soft cookie. Ummm. Fresh lemon. She listened to ceiling fans purr, tickertape machines hum, phones sleep. According to Mr. Boudreaux, shoot, *Boudreaux*, on the first day they met, nothing newsworthy ever happens in the middle of the day.

"McCall," she could still hear his voice as he made his concluding comment, "just sit here and babysit the phones. Nothing newsworthy happens in the middle of the day."

"What about President Kennedy being shot in Texas at 12:30 p.m. Eastern Standard Time, Mr. Boudreaux?" Tally remembered asking her new boss this question after her introduction to internship duties at the newspaper. What else was she supposed to say after his pronouncement that burglaries, rapes, and murders don't happen at noon, only at night, and that her job was to babysit the phones, take messages, look pretty, and follow orders. Did he expect her to ignore the facts?

"Listen to you, McCall." His sarcasm reverberated in her ears. "Aren't you the clever one?" The metal rim of his pencil had struck the black telephone on her desk with annoying pings.

"Thank you, sir. I'm majoring in history at Hamper University." She had curtsied, pulling the sides of her scarlet velvet mini-skirt into a crooked smile. Struggling to keep her skirt from flouncing up her thighs, she had knelt down, knees together and scooped his pencil off the Oriental rug where he dropped it. "Sir, I have a theory that if we look at history with a fresh point of view, from the eyes of the dismissed or defeated, especially Southerners of all races who are doomed to eternal inferiority, we'll know how to solve problems and see life in a revolutionary way."

By the time she looked up, however, Mr. Boudreaux was swaggering between desks, barking an order to Winston, the other new intern, to meet him, *pronto*.

Mr. Boudreaux was probably driving down Fort Hamper Highway at that moment, pulling into the gravel parking lot at Blue's Bar-B-Q for his meeting with Hamper's Chief of Police to discuss vandalism at Hamper University. Police Chief Parish and Boudreaux would probably continue their long-standing feud about the duty of a college town's newspaper.

Everyone in the newsroom knew Chief Parish's stance. His letters to Jax Boudreaux were on the bulletin board. He proclaimed that a newspaper's job was to work with law enforcement to warn rebel-rousers of consequences. Boudreaux disagreed. He had no problem with any consequences. He just insisted that a newspaper must be independent. Not beholden.

Yet over the May Day weekend, complaints of rowdy parties at fraternity houses, toilet paper streaming from mimosa trees and loud music on Sorority Row had already prompted curfews and the cry that something had to be done. Hamper, Georgia was, after all, the "Mimosa Tree Capital of the World" and there would be lots of tourists arriving in the month of May, "Mimosa May," according to the Chamber of Commerce.

Shutting her eyes, she took a deep breath. Pine oil, as sharp-sprite as the smell of fresh-cut Christmas trees, was used to polish the desks on Monday mornings. Gus's homemade scent soothed her. She opened her shoulder bag, pulled Rye's letter out, and read his words again. He said he would call today when he was on campus. He said he wanted to kiss "the sweetest lips in Georgia 'Hello' again." The thought of his kiss triggered tingles to tumble down her body. If only they could be back on the island, at the bonfire, where he kissed her so tenderly, his arms cradling her, his tongue--

Her face flushed. In her Botany notebook, she drew an iris, its tongue longer than its petals. She slammed the notebook shut, tucked the letter back in her bag. Focus.

She lifted her fountain pen, writing on a fresh page in her notebook, a quote by Adlai E. Stevenson, Tess Hamper's dear friend.

"All progress has resulted from people who take unpopular positions."

Writing the date, Monday, May 4, 1970, she printed in capital letters:

"TODAY MY LIFE CHANGES."

A paper airplane sailed past her nose, skimmed her desk and crashed into the *AP* wire ticker. She grabbed her fountain pen as her closest weapon and jumped up.

"Winston! Scare me to death!"

"Scare you? Me? Six foot two? Black guy with an Afro? In the South? Now that's a shock!" Winston jiggled coins in his pocket and shook his head. "You're just jumpy after the announcement today. Nerves all affray."

Winston was right, as usual.

"Win, did you get Mr. Boudreaux to sign your certificate for the award?"

"Haven't seen him. Mine's back in the library. Don't let me forget."

Winston seemed more scattered than she did.

Winston's assignment at the newspaper was to read microfiche of news stories about prominent Georgians then type notes for confidential files in anticipation of their deaths. That was the job Tally had wanted, but no. Winston couldn't be seen at the reception desk. He was "colored," according to one of the reporters who explained the assignments to her. Besides, she met the most important criteria for the job. She was a girl.

"Winston. Can you believe we're both finalists? Now that's the shock."

"Tell me about it. Mama will freak out. Frankie will be grinning from ear to ear but not surprised. You know, he predicted it. He said we would both be nominated."

Winston shook his head and frowned.

"Reminds me. Need to talk to you. Got a favor to ask."

"Is it about the award, Winston? Have you figured out how we can both win?"

Winston did not smile. She had never seen him so serious. She tossed Winston her egg salad sandwich still wrapped in waxed paper. He bent his head in a theater bow, his hair a giant Brillo pad. Winston bit into the sandwich. Tally grabbed a straw from the jar where she kept the reporters' spitball weapons, took a sip from Winston's can of Tab, energized by the sweet soda fizz tickling her throat as she swallowed.

Winston glanced at the clock. He looked like he had just witnessed a plane crash.

"Bad news." Winston crushed the wax paper from the long-gone sandwich into a ball and arched it into Mr. Boudreaux's trashcan. "It's Frankie. If he screws around, sorry 'bout the language, girl, if he messes up finals and can't get college deferment for his senior year, his birth date could be his death date. Or, at least, be the cause of it."

"What? What are you talking about? Franklin's your twin, for heaven's sake. Are you saying you worry about him being drafted? But y'all have the same draft numbers so you both just have to go to grad school or get married, have kids, wait this thing out and--"

"Wait. Don't you remember?"

"Winston. Are you telling me you have a disability? Franklin doesn't?"

"No. I'm telling you life's a damn crapshoot. Sorry 'bout the language. Thought I told you ages ago. Freshman year. Even though Frankie and I celebrate our birthday together, Frankie was born on April 24th, one minute before midnight. Me? I jetted out like a bullet on April 25th. My draft number? 351. Frankie's? 2."

Tally's fingers squeezed the handkerchief. Goosebumps puckered her skin. All Franklin ever wanted to do was be a shrimper and keep the family business going. Listen to gulls squawk from sunrise to sunset. He started college just to get a military deferment like a lot of young men did. Now she knew what was bothering Franklin last night. Clearing her throat, she put an index finger in the air.

The phone rang.

"Winston, I'm so sorry."

"It's killing me. Mama cries every night. Frankie's flunking history again. Draft board sent another letter about call-up times. His only hope is to stay in school. So, girl, can you tutor him for summer school? He'll listen to you. Not me."

The phone rang again.

"In a heartbeat, Win. Daddy always quotes George Herbert, you know John Donne's godson, by reminding folks, '*Where there's a will, there's a way.*'"

"Well, I say, 'Power to the people.' You're fixing to change Frankie's life, girl."

The phone rang for the third time.

"Bet it's the Prayer Lady." Winston hummed The Temptations' tune, "Get Ready," flashed the peace sign, and sauntered to the tickers where his paper airplane had nosedived into one of the gray machines sitting silent atop a pedestal.

"*The Hamper Herald,* Georgia's oldest coastal newspaper. May I help you?"

"Tarnation! You know I call each day at 12:25 to celebrate when Jesus was born."

Tally blew feathery bangs from her eyelashes and shook her head. She wanted to say that Jesus' birthdate was arbitrarily chosen long after his death and that he was not born on 12/25 yet it would not matter. Logic was not the foundation of belief systems.

"Ma'am, I do apologize. I just finished my lunch, yes ma'am, a teacake."

The teletype machines began to ping like woodpeckers on speed.

"Lordy, girl. Don't you know angels are serving teacakes in heaven right now to folks just arriving to the glory? Child, what is that commotion?"

"Ma'am, I'm so sorry. The wire service printers are just typing up a storm."

"Sounds like machine guns, Tommy-guns, it does."

"Ma'am, I'm going to have to check on the news coming from-- I'm sorry, my other line is ringing. May I put you on hold? Be right back."

"But I need to ask a question."

Tally knew the question. Every day the elderly woman called to ask the same question. Today she would just have to wait.

"Yes, ma'am. One moment please." Tally punched a button putting the woman on hold, the white light blinking. She observed Winston's face as he glared at the paper beginning to waterfall from the ticker. What's wrong now? She welcomed the new caller.

"*The Hamper Herald*, Georgia's--"

"Tally. It's Tess. Damnation. The wires sound like the SOS from the *Titanic*. Is it the Pulitzer announcement?"

"I haven't checked yet. Both tickers just started going crazy at the same time."

"Boudreaux there?"

"No, ma'am." The white light on her phone blinked again and again. The caller who called herself "The Prayer Lady" still waited with her daily question and Boudreaux was still gone. "He's having lunch with Chief Parish."

"Tally-love, I need you to pull that copy from the tickers. Then read it to me. Something's happening somewhere."

"Yes, ma'am." Tally covered the phone before a laugh escaped.

She needed to laugh. Tessie's favorite saying, the motto on the masthead of the paper, stated: *Something's happening somewhere*. Come on. Get a grip. Act like a professional.

"Miss Hamper, may I please put you on hold again while I go get it?"

"If you must. And, Tally, if nobody's around, good Lord, just call me Tessie. You know I hate being called 'Miss Hamper' by you, honey."

"Yes, ma'am. Winston's here. Oh, my gosh! I forgot to tell you. Winston and I were just nominated for the History Honor. Can you believe it?"

"Congratulations, Sugar. And yes, I can believe it. You two are mighty smart. But I hope Winston wins. I don't want my goddaughter going all the way to England for two years."

Tally cupped her fingers around the phone receiver and whispered, "Tessie. I know. I'd miss you so much. Back in a second." Tally placed her on hold then pressed the blinking button of the original caller.

"Ma'am, Miss Prayer Lady, there's news happening right now that I have to attend to. Will you kindly call back later?" Please. Call back later. When my shift is over. When I'm gone.

"No. I need to ask something. I'll wait."

Tally rolled her eyes. For a split second, she considered hanging up. Instead, she pressed the hold button again. Winston stood by her desk, a look of shock on his face.

Tally grabbed the paper from Winston, saying, "Sorry, Win. It's Miss Hamper on the phone and I have to read this—Winston--Win. You look awful. Are you okay?"

He turned to the window and shook his head.

Tally began reading the text to Tess Hamper:

AP (Ohio) Monday, May 4, 1970. FLASH.

At approximately 12:24 p.m. Eastern Standard Time a confrontation escalated between Kent State University students protesting the recent U.S. invasion of Cambodia at a rally and

National Guard troops sent to keep the peace by Ohio Governor James A. Rhodes.

It is reported that the troops fired a barrage of bullets into a crowd of students, presumed to be unarmed. Four bodies in prone positions are lying lifeless, according to eyewitnesses, in an adjacent parking lot. Other students appear to be injured.

Ambulances arriving. Updates forthcoming.

Nine

As students were collapsing on gravel and grass at Kent State University in Ohio, students were collapsing on beach towels and hammocks at Hamper University in Georgia. Unaware their peers had just been shot, Hamper U students listened to the Doobie Brothers, the Allman Brothers, and Creedence singing in a constant loop on their radios without news or commercial interruption.

Today marked the beginning of "F Week" at Hamper University. It was the Monday each year when the manager of the local FM radio station pre-taped music, commercials and his familiar patter without news reports so he could take the week off and students could listen to energizing music while they studied for final exams.

Signs for "F Week" dotted the Hamper University campus, Hamper Park and the sand dunes above the beach. Letters of turquoise and lime, the Hamper University school colors, spelled out the battle between students and administrators. Student-painted signs on campus celebrated the "Fun" of "F Week" while the Administration's professionally-painted signs reminded students of the importance of "F Week" to their "Futures."

Hamper University Administrators hung signs reminding students that most final classes, tests and field trips had been scheduled for the morning hours that week, with a few exceptions. According to the signs at the cafeteria, this scheduling would allow Hamper students to be up at dawn after curfew the night before, eat a hearty breakfast, and be mentally ready for the day, much the way their teachers would.

Signs at the library reminded students that their afternoons were free of tests and classes, excluding unavoidable "F Week" science class field trips, to allow students to spend their free time studying.

Hamper U students, however, had their own meanings for the "F" in "F Week." For some, the "F" stood for "Forever Week," a reminder that administrators were forever clueless about the real needs of the student body. The mere mention of "Forever Week" on a sign was also a written wink to classmates that Finals Week only *feels* like "forever."

Signs attached to antique lamplights on Poet's Row, the cul-de-sac where the Chaucer, Kipling, Shakespeare and Browning Sorority Houses were located, touted "Fun Week." Drawings of volleyball games, kite-flying contests, Frisbee-throwing tournaments, and sun tanning on Hamper Beach were featured.

Likewise, on Prose Street where the Twain, Poe, Hawthorne and Hemingway Fraternity Houses were located, banners hung from balconies with giant letters proclaiming, "Fraternity Week," as blanket invitations to year-end keggers.

There were also signs anonymously poked into the soft, moist earth of flower gardens near the quad. These hand-painted signs, most likely the work of fraternity pledges, asserted that the "F" in "F Week" meant "Flirting, Flattering and *Favors*," a euphemistic reference to the other "f word" rarely used in public.

To ROTC students at Hamper U and their dates, "F" had an additional meaning: "Fort Hamper Military Gala." This festive event, held each year on the first Monday in May at Fort Hamper, feted World War I, II and Korea veterans, honored fellow soldiers serving in Vietnam, and introduced the VIP Military Personnel to Senior ROTC cadets of Hamper High School and the ROTC Student Commanders at Hamper University.

At each Military Gala, a Gala Queen was presented. She would be featured in a picture on the front pages of *The Hamper Herald* and *The Fort Hamper Army Gazette.* According to Fort Hamper's tradition of fifty years, a celebrity guest, preferably from the state of Georgia, was asked to present the Gala Queen with the Fort Hamper Honorary Service Medal for her to wear when representing Fort Hamper at nursing homes, the Veterans Administration Hospital, food pantries, and parades.

The Queen also received a scepter.

Tonight, the new Gala Queen would be Tally Gigi McCall who was chosen because, as the proclamation stated, "her brother, Private First-Class Shaw Philippe McCall, had enlisted in the Army, trained at Fort Hamper, and was presently serving in Vietnam."

The celebrity guest, however, was still a surprise.

Hours before she would meet and be photographed with the celebrity at the Fort Hamper Military Gala, Tally was still in the newsroom of *The Hamper Herald* hearing the words "God damn" echo in her ear.

"God damn Nixon." Tess Hamper's voice sounded hoarse. "After that weekend mess up there, I expected violence. But not this. Good Lord, not this. Shooting students. Tally, dear, I apologize."

"Please, no need to." Tally observed Winston snatch another stream of paper from the ticker. "Your language just expresses your upset, Miss Hamper."

"Tally-dear, I'm not talking about my language. Hell. If words are meant to be precise, then, by God, these are the exact words to express my precise feelings. I despise euphemisms. I'm talking about how sorry I am as a woman who has seen too much hate in her lifetime that the killing of innocent students now impacts your life too."

Tess's voice sounded older than Tally had ever heard it.

"Dumpling, if this stirring's too loud, I apologize. I'm making a hot toddy to settle my nerves. Are you alright?"

"Yes, ma'am. I'm trying to grasp it all. I can't imagine what that campus must be like right now." A white light continued to flash on her telephone. "Miss Hamper. I'm sorry. May I please speak to the caller I put on hold?"

"What'd you say? Sure, sure. Take your time. I'm watching Cronkite. He's trying to explain this mess on TV."

"Thank you, ma'am."

Winston stood in front of her desk reading the updated *AP* release. He put it down gingerly, as if it were a ransom note, and stared out the window. He struck a match. Touching the flame to the candle on her desk, a rush of cinnamon infused the air. With the same flame, he torched the tip of a cigarette and took a long drag. Smoke streamed over Tally's head.

"Winston, what is happening? What's going on in the world?"

"You mean, 'What's going on in the world--except here?'"

"Thank goodness. Can you imagine students being shot here? At Hamper U?"

"They'd have to protest first."

"That would be surreal." Tally cupped her hands around the glass jar holding the candle.

Touching her temples, she felt the warmth from her fingertips and palms soothe her skin.

"Winston, we may be the only two students at Hamper U who know about this."

"Except for sorority girls watching soap operas. Bet Cronkite's interrupted the shows with the news and ruined their day."

"Hey, Mr. Crockett. I'm a sorority girl. Harper Lee was a Chi Omega at the University of Alabama. Pearl Buck and Georgia O'Keeffe were Kappa Deltas."

"I stand corrected, Miss McCall."

"Thank you, Mr. Crockett. Besides, Hamper U students can't be faulted with not knowing."

"I agree. The fault lies with what they do once they *do* know. Remember, girl. Once a person becomes aware, he or she can't claim unawareness. Shoot. It's Acting 101. Isn't that why you refused to show your face on stage after you uttered your final words as Amelia Earhart? You knew Amelia would never be seen again. You also knew the audience knew. If you had returned for the curtain call, you would have been, what's that word?"

"Disingenuous?"

"Man, you get it. *To be or not to be* true to the power of awareness."

Tally nodded. The more Winston talked, the more she knew. He should win the O-O Honor. She rubbed her palms together rapidly.

"Win. Feel my fingers. They're icicles."

Winston dangled the cigarette from his mouth and covered Tally's hands in his, squeezing them again and again with his rough skin, rubbed raw from ropes on the boat.

"Girl, we won't forget where we were on this day. Shock of our nominations to shock from these killings. And, can you believe it? Ohio is my favorite Yankee state. The Wright Brothers were born there. Now? It's going to be remembered as the place where the revolution started." Winston's eyes narrowed as he released her hands. "Unlike Orangeburg."

"Orangeburg?" Odd. Why did that name sound familiar?

"South Carolina. Remember? February '68. Tet Offensive sucked up all the news. Three Black students shot and killed at a college that night. One just in high school sitting on a step waiting for his mama to get off work. Innocent. All of them. National Guard and local police were there. And why? 'Cause those Black students knew all about the Civil Rights Act of '64 and were protesting for their right to bowl in the town's only bowling alley--"

"Which was Whites-only. Oh, my gosh, Win. I do remember reading about that. February 8, 1968. The day Laddy Carmichael was riding his bike near Hamper Park and a drunk driver—"

"Yep. Hit and run. There was a big article in *The Herald*."

"And right below it, in the February 9th, 1968 newspaper, was a small article about the Orangeburg Massacre, the protests and the murders." Tally had that very article in her scrapbook at home.

"Damn, girl. How the hell, forgive my swearing, do you remember all that?"

"Oh, I, well, somehow, just do."

Tally did not want to explain that her photo as the winner of the Miss Georgia Peach Majorette of 1968 Award was on the front page of the paper that day, February 9, 1968, above the wire story of the Orangeburg Massacre.

She also did not want to explain why the story, heartbreaking as it was, had faded from her memory. Was it because she couldn't understand why the students were shot? Or because she didn't understand why protesting about bowling was so important and worth risking one's life? Or because she wondered why someone in the Black community didn't just open up a bowling alley for Blacks-only and solve the problem to everyone's satisfaction? Or because she was too happy at the time about her majorette routine and she didn't think about Orangeburg again? Oh, my gosh. Two years ago. She felt like a different person now. Or was she?

"God help me. If Oxford chooses the winner based on dates, I'm history." Winston tapped his cigarette on the ashtray, pulled a Newport Menthol cigarette halfway out of the pack and pointed it toward her. "Want one? It'll calm your nerves."

"Winston, I wish I could--"

A phone rang in the library.

"Girl, I told you, 'Stop being the ingénue.' No one's here but us. It won't ruin your reputation to have a cigarette."

"Winston! I was about to say I wish I could *throw* something. That would calm my nerves."

"Alrighty now. That's the spunk I like to see, girl. Spoken like my favorite Yankee from Rye, New York, Miss Amelia Earhart." Winston picked up his paper airplane, grinned, and placed a cigarette and a matchbook on her desk.

"Got to answer my phone. Stay strong." He shouted back at her before closing the library door.

Rye, New York. Is Rye Somerset in Hamper? Has he called the sorority house? Dammit. She really did want to throw something.

Most of all, she wanted to see Rye today. She wanted to show him her favorite spot deep inside the mimosa grove by the boardwalk, the place she had discovered long ago, the clearing tucked away from the breezes, hidden by thick mimosa ferns drooping down, laden with cucumber-scented pink blossoms. She wanted him to put his arms around her, hold her, kiss her, talk with her, help her make sense of it all.

One minute she was overjoyed about her nomination for the O-O Honor. The next minute she felt overwhelmed that students were shot on a college campus and apoplectic they were killed by an armed government force, something that had never happened in the history of America before. Well, never before….at least….in the daylight.

Tally knew Tess would still be watching Cronkite on television. The Prayer Lady had been waiting and would continue to wait no matter how long it took. The tickers pounded. If Tally could listen to her heart through a stethoscope, the beats would be racing. The constant noise was giving her a headache. She imagined reports of more students dying. She felt helpless.

She looked at the clock. 12:33 p.m. Twelve. Thirty-three. The two ages of Christ mentioned in the Bible. At least Jesus lived to be thirty-three.

She squeezed her fingers against the candle to warm them as she wondered about the parents of students at Kent State. They may not even know their children were shot. Or dying. Or dead. How could they? A mother might be shopping at the grocery store unaware her son would never be home for supper anymore. She might be reading a magazine at the beauty parlor with her hair in curlers under the hair dryer. What if she heard about it on television? Would she scream at Walter Cronkite, "Why did someone shoot my child?"

The phone rang. All three buttons now flashed. She picked up the phone, stumbled over words of greeting.

The caller said someone at the filling station thought shots had been fired at kids on Kent Street. Is that true?

She said, "No, sir. Kent State."

The caller said, "Never heard of it."

An abrupt dial tone buzzed in her ear.

She pressed each white blinking button. She told the ladies she would be back with them as soon as she could and thanked them for waiting.

With no one in the newsroom, she pushed her swivel chair away from the desk and began to twirl. Faster and faster. Desks, ferns, windows, silence blurred around her. She felt dizzy. She kicked her shoes past a row of vacant desks.

Sunbeams bounced off beveled glass. Tiny rainbows scattered across the polished hardwood floor. She grabbed the stick Gus used to open the plantation shutters, squeezed it with both hands, calculated weight and span, and tossed the slender hickory high into the air. The second it reached its apex, spinning like a propeller, she shut her eyes, counted revolutions, whispered the Creed, twirled twice, and caught it behind her back.

She still had it. Her signature twirling move, the one Khaki could never copy. The twirling maneuver that had infuriated Khaki when Tally and Becca skipped second grade, moved up a year, and Tally became Khaki's majorette competitor.

"*To know how to see.*" Tally announced to the Boston ferns as she propped the stick against the wall, slipped on her shoes, and rushed to her desk, energy surging through her.

Tally pressed the first blinking button. It was time to focus on the Prayer Lady.

"Ma'am, I sure am sorry." She could feel her pulse in her temples. "Thank you for waiting. I appreciate your patience."

"Been told I got the patience of Job. You familiar with Job in the holy book?" Sounds of throat-clearing turned into sounds of a coughing fit.

"Yes, ma'am. Are you okay? I'm sure you must be needing to go. Thank you for calling. Sorry it's been a whirlwind around here today."

"Is there a whirlwind? Haven't been outside in a week." Her coughing started again. "My neighbor Judy, you know the sister of Suzanne who's married to Peter who--"

"Yes, ma'am. They're the dearest." Tally placed the phone down, still hearing the woman's voice as she continued to babble, before bringing it to her ear again.

"Well, she checks on me. Brings *The Herald* but I can't see to read no more. Just look at the pictures. That's how come I need your sight so I can see, child. Now tell me. Who needs my prayers today?"

"Kent State." Tally's voice hushed.

"Baby boy of the State Family on 14th? The one that went in to have his adenoids removed?"

"No ma'am. That was little Clark Kent State. He's fine now."

"Thank the Lord. Now is there a name I could add to the prayer list at church? That's all I was wanting. Didn't mean to take too much of your time, child."

"Thank you, ma'am. I appreciate you asking. But instead of reading a bunch of names from the paper today like I normally do, could you just pray for Franklin Crockett and Kent State and college students everywhere?"

"I'll pray steady 'til tomorrow this time. But how come these children?"

"Cause they're all in dire straits, ma'am. And, somehow, it feels like we could all be in danger."

Tally said goodbye after reassuring the Prayer Lady she would return to intern at the newspaper when her senior year started in September.

She punched the flashing button.

"Tessie, thank you for waiting. It was the Prayer Lady on the other line."

"I already figured, sweet pea. Our oldest subscriber, the Prayer Lady. Bless her. She's nearly blind, yet, she has a unique way of seeing things, wouldn't you say?" Tally heard admiration in her voice. "Now, who did you advise her to pray for today?"

"College students."

"Tally Gigi McCall. That's it, darling. That's the lead for the human-interest story I'm assigning you to write, as a college student yourself. When's your next class?"

"Botany at three-thirty. But I have to change clothes at the Georgia Glen Cabin, get my picture taken there at three, the Gala's tonight and I planned—"

"Yes, I agree. Time's a-wasting. Call the restaurant where Boudreaux's dining, read him the latest ticker. Then call sorority and fraternity houses, talk to anyone who answers the phone. Ask for reactions to the shootings at Kent State. Be very specific when you write down their quotes. Be sure to get their names, ages, hometowns. Type up the comments for tomorrow's paper. And earn your first by-line, dearest."

Moments after Tess Hamper hung up, Tally pulled the latest news from the ticker.

Four students confirmed dead at Kent State. Nine students injured. One possibly paralyzed.

Following that update was the announcement of the 1970 Pulitzer Prizes. A reporter named Seymour Hersh won for exposing the My Lai massacre in his article in *The New York Times*. Author Erik Erickson won for his book, *Gandhi's Truth*.

She crumpled the paper, stared at the ferns on their pedestals, all four of them, alive and thriving. Squeezing the paper in her hand, she bowed her head and prayed for people she would never know.

Opening her eyes, she smoothed the wrinkled paper, pressed it inside her Botany book to later add to her History Scrapbook, and picked up the phone to alert Mr. Boudreaux.

Tally dialed every sorority and fraternity.

"McCall! That sidebar ready?"

"Not yet, sir. By the way, have you seen Charlie, I mean, *Johnson*?"

"His department took him to a long lunch for his farewell. Write the sidebar."

She may have spent too much time calling the Chaucer House. The phone had been busy each time she tried. Who could possibly be on the phone for so long? There was a five-minute limit for each phone call. If she didn't get through soon, how could she ask Lula if Rye had called? And this was taking so long, now she wouldn't have time to run to the sorority house, drop off her guitar case, and tell Lula about her nomination in person before dashing to the Georgia Glen Cabin for the photo shoot as planned.

After gathering comments from sorority members at the Kipling, Shakespeare, and Browning Houses on Poet's Row, she still needed to locate someone at a fraternity house on Prose Drive to interview. Not even pledges were answering the phones.

She glanced at the clock. 2:01 p.m. Okay. February 1st. Texas secedes from the Union, 1861. First meeting of U.S. Supreme Court, 1790. Clark Gable's birthday, 1901. Mary Shelley's death, 1851. Lisa Marie Presley's birthday, 1968. Calm down. Almost done.

But how could she type the rest of the assignment, run to the Georgia Glen Cabin, get her picture taken, and end up at the boardwalk for Botany class on time?

Frustrated, she dialed the Chaucer House again.

It rang four times.

"Chaucer Sorority House. Thank you for calling. May I help you?"

"Lula, it's Tally. Thank goodness you answered. I've been trying for over an hour to get through."

"Hey, baby girl. That Miss Priss Khaki has been on the phone talking to her boyfriend, that Louie."

"All this time? Isn't Miss Perry there to stop her?" The Chaucer sorority housemother had stopped Tally from talking too long on the phone when she was dating Mike Parish. "Good grief. I had to polish silver pitchers after I talked for ten minutes to Mike. Remember?"

"Wrapped those pitchers in velvet, took one out the other day and it still shines like a mirror, thanks to you, honey." Lula's voice sounded like she was smiling. "But Miss Perry's at a luncheon and fashion show at the Hamper Country Club today."

"The 'Parasols in Paris' Fashion Show. Lula, oh, my gosh. So much has happened today. I don't have time to tell you everything. But you know that nomination I wanted? The one to study in England?"

"The one I've been saying prayers about all day?"

"Lula Louise Burton. I could hug your neck. Guess what? I got nominated!"

Tally held the phone to her chest to muffle Lula's 'Hallelujah' while pivoting to search for Mr. Boudreaux. He was offering a cigarette to the Book Editor, rumored to be his new girlfriend.

"Tally, honey, your mama, your daddy and Shawl, they're going to be so tickled."

"I can't wait to tell them. Lula, I forgot to thank you. Lunch was delicious."

"Making Sweet Potato Pot Roast tonight. Going to tuck some away for you in the icebox. You can heat it up in the oven at 375 degrees. Reckon you'll be too nervous to eat much at that Gala."

"Lula, you are an angel. Wish I didn't have to hurry. Gosh. Almost forgot. Did Rye call?"

"Honey, I bet you he tried. But that Khaki's been hogging the phone all lunch time. Nobody could get through."

Tally picked up the cigarette. If only she could light it without reporters teasing her.

"Good grief, Lula. Please tell her to stay off the phone. Please tell her you're expecting an urgent call from Miss Perry. And as you say it, please show her that other drawer of tarnished silver trays that need cleaning. Most of all, Lula, please tell Rye, if he calls, I sure do hope to see him today."

"Twain Fraternity House."

Finally. An answer. Hurry.

"Hello. May I please take a moment to ask you a question?"

"Shoot."

"What?"

"Shoot. Ask. Then it's my turn to ask a question."

"Sure, okay, fair enough. I need a comment from someone in your fraternity about an event that happened today in Ohio for an article in tomorrow's *Herald*."

Sentences tumbled out so fast she felt energy seep from her body with each word.

"And you are?"

"I'm sorry. Tally. Tally McCall. Tally Gigi McCall."

"And the event in Ohio would be? Miss Tally *Gigi* McCall?"

"Yes. The news. First things first though. Do I have your permission to quote you for the article? Oops, sorry, I don't know your name."

"Ted. Ted Beckett. Ted Alton Beckett granting permission, Gigi."

Touche'. At least he couldn't see her blush.

"Thanks, Mr. Ted *Alton* Beckett. Please forgive the rush, however, I'm on deadline so I need to be quick. I'm composing an article about reactions by students at Hamper University to a story being reported by the *AP*, the, uh, *Associated Press*, and *UPI, United Press International*. Here's the report, and may I say I'm sorry to have to tell you tragic news. An hour and a half ago at Kent State University in Ohio, four students believed to be unarmed while participating in a rally to protest the Vietnam War were shot and killed by National Guard troops."

Each time she said the words out loud, her voice softened.

Boudreaux, standing in front of her, frowned and wrote in capital letters on her paper: EMOTION TAINTS RESPONSE.

She monotoned, "How do you respond to this news?"

No answer.

"Ted?" She could hear thumping, in an echo, a beat, like hands hitting pants.

No answer.

"Ted? Are you there?"

"You can't print my response."

"Well, Ted, you gave permission."

"It's unprintable."

"But, I--"

"Instant Karma." His voice sounded certain.

"Instant? I'm sorry I don't know what you mean."

"K-a-r-m-a. John Lennon's song. 'Instant Karma.'"

Great. A goof-ball answers the phone. How can I use this in the paper?

"Ted, could you talk a little slower?"

"That's what I'm talking about. You want me to speak slower, right? This better?"

"Much. I'm in a huge rush to get this to the editor."

Boudreaux nodded then strolled to the newsroom library.

"Instant Karma, the concept not the song, is *The Golden Rule* on speed."

"Wait. I'm trying to get this down. Did you just refer to drugs?"

"No. I don't do drugs, well, secondhand smoke at gigs. All drummers do. Look. Karma is based on *The Golden Rule*, 'Do unto others as you would have them do unto you.' If you treat others the way you want to be treated, your life on earth is better for it. I'm talking philosophy. Not religion."

"I'm a member of Hamper Beach Church." Get a grip. Interview *him*.

"And I don't go to church."

She did not know anyone who did not go to church.

"Look, Gigi. What happened is tragic, despicable. Karma in an instant. Think about it. Would those four students kill National Guard troops? No. Honorable people who *don't* want war *don't* kill. They want the killing to stop."

"True." So hard to think, answer, write at the same time. How do reporters do it?

"Hey, Gigi, you've got a deadline. Sorry."

"Ted, it's fascinating. Oh. My editor's waving at me. May I put you on hold? Please?"

"Can do."

Tally pushed the hold button. Good grief. The *Meet the Staff* photo. She rushed to a place beside Winston in the back row of gathered reporters under the clock. Boudreaux whispered something to Moretti.

"Miss Tally? Bella? Would you please come to the front? You are too petite, Bella, to stand beside Mr. Winston."

"But I'm just an intern and I thought I should be next to the other intern."

"McCall." Boudreaux's words sliced like a guillotine. "Follow orders."

Winston whispered in her ear, "Can't have a White girl next to a Black man in a picture, Missy Tally. Better go, girl."

His Afro tickled her neck. She elbowed his stomach.

Tally moved to the center next to Boudreaux. Moretti shook his head. Scooping his black drape, the one used by photographers when they need darkness to change film and prevent light exposure, he tossed it to Tally and pointed to the splotches on her dress.

Blushing, she wrapped the drape around one shoulder and tied it in a bow at her hip. Moretti kissed his fingertips, shouted, "Bellissima," and clicked shot after shot.

When everyone moved away, Boudreaux asked Tally, "Are you done yet?"

"No, Mr., I mean, Boudreaux. I'm still interviewing someone at the Twain Fraternity House. I'll be finished by the deadline, sir," her voice sounded irritated, "if I can just get back to the phone and not be interrupted again."

Boudreaux nodded. "Feisty looks good on you, McCall. Speed it up. Got to put this paper to bed."

Tally raced to her desk. "Ted, I'm so sorry."

"No sweat. Gave me time to think. So, you want a quote? Look. Paraphrase this however you want. I trust you. Ready? I'll go slow."

"Ready."

"The instant those bullets killed innocent students," he paused as if waiting for her to catch up, "karma started killing the guys who pulled the triggers. Something inside them died. Yet those students. Their legacies. They'll keep shining. You know, Lennon wrote and recorded that song in one day. Last February. Bet he wasn't thinking about it being a tribute to people being shot -- but it is."

She heard someone call Ted's name. Tally wrote as fast as she could, abbreviating words, scribbling in symbols, trying to get his quote accurate.

"Got to go, Gigi. Got a phone call on our private phone, urgent. Bet my mom heard the news. Better call the folks, Gigi. If parents aren't fretting about the damn draft, now they got this to scare them to death. Bet they're fit to be tied, needing Alka Seltzers or a bottle of wine tonight. Look, Gigi, next time? I expect you to call with better news."

Tally laughed. What a charmer.

Boudreaux pointed his finger at her and then the clock.

"Wait, Ted, I need to know what year you are, your major and your hometown. Sorry if that's too personal."

"Nope. Hold on." He must have put the phone to his chest. She could hear faint thumping. His voice was an echo. "Hold your horses." Louder, he said, "You first."

"Wait. Me first about what?"

"Your major and hometown."

"Gosh, thanks for asking." Boudreaux would skewer her. "I'm majoring in History, Georgia History specifically. Hamper's my hometown. And I'm in the Chaucer Sorority."

"Great sorority. Fine reputation. And Hamper? Cool. Nice place. Glad to be leaving for summer though. That is, if I don't have to return for Summer School. Done with junior year if I pass these finals. Me? Double major. Philosophy and Music. Hometown? Key West."

His voice sounded muffled. "I'm coming! Sorry, Gigi, got to go. I'll ask my question another time. Good luck with that article. Wait. Hold the fort. Why didn't I think of that? Just thought of a great quote, one of my favorites. Don't write it. Just hear the cadence. Here goes: *It is the chirping of grasshoppers beside the immortal question whether justice shall be done. However feeble the sufferer and however great the oppressor, it is in the nature of things that the blow should recoil upon the aggressor.*"

"Ted. That's what you were talking about. How beautiful." Thank goodness she had ignored him and scribbled it anyway. "Who said that? Rod McKuen?"

"Not said. Written. By Ralph Waldo Emerson in a letter to President Martin van Buren. Emerson wrote to protest what the government was doing in his name and in the name of American citizens that ended in 'The Trail of Tears.' Emerson called it '*the terrible injury which threatens the Cherokee tribe.*' Hey, Gigi. Take care today."

The phone clicked. The flicker of the candle on her desk blurred as tears filled her eyes. What he said about "The Trail of Tears" was profound. She wanted to talk with him again. He knew things she wanted to know. For a moment she heard the echo of his voice, rugged, funny, pulsing, energetic, fading into silence, abrupt and deep. The sensation felt as soothing as if he had cupped his hands over her ears with the warmth of velvet earmuffs.

Boudreaux barked orders so loud she wished she had earmuffs. Thank goodness for her typing class in high school.

"McCall, you're not writing an essay. Just a sidebar." Boudreaux hovered.

"What?"

"An ancillary column to the main, wait, you don't think you're earning a by-line, do you? McCall, a sidebar's like the dessert table at Thanksgiving. Over to the side."

Good grief. Where's the White-Out jar? Just typed 'supper' instead of 'shooter.'

"Don't look so disappointed. You're doing what Winston's doing. He's writing a sidebar on the irony of a book on Gandhi's non-violence winning the Pulitzer on a day that's going to be known for violence, unprecedented violence at that."

Winston. The first Black person to write for the paper. What a coup.

"Whew. Done. Have to rush to class."

Boudreaux scanned the page.

"Curious quotes you got here, McCall. From 'Yankees stirring the pot," to "It wouldn't happen in the South," to "Instant Karma." Wait 'til Johnson at the copy desk gets hold of this. He'll cut it down to size. And, McCall. Good work. I'll even consider a by-line."

"Thanks, Mr. Boudreaux." She just couldn't call him anything else.

"See you back here in the fall, McCall." He gave her a salute. "And see you at the Gala tonight." He sauntered off, his moccasins as quiet as his bark was booming.

She blew out the candle on her desk, sparking a déjà vu flash of the candle fiasco hours ago. She waved to Winston, blew kisses to reporters with phones to their ears, and hurried through the revolving door on her way to the Georgia Glen Cabin where another innocent youth had been killed before her life was barely lived.

Ten

His spectator shoes caught her eye. Tally tiptoed over to the man dozing in a hammock on the porch of the mansion. The patter of her ballet flats on the teak slats sounded as loud as tap shoes to her. If she could slip by unnoticed, she could rush down the stairs, take a shortcut through the park and still make the photo session at the Georgia Glen Cabin on time. She opened her guitar case, lifted the surprise gift she had made Charlie Johnson for his retirement, placed it on the wicker table, and turned to leave.

"Heard you typed a piece on that college shooting up north, McCall."

Dammit. She had not wanted to wake him. She needed to hurry. She also did not want to trigger more upset and sadness talking with Charlie about his retirement.

"Oh, hey, Charlie. So sorry to wake you. I wanted to give you a token of my appreciation for all your help this year! And that piece I typed? Just a sidebar."

She had no time to talk. She had no time to wonder if addressing colleagues by their last names in the newsroom was still in effect once you shut the front door. It would not matter to Charlie. He had always told her to call him by his first name.

The hammock creaked. His brown and white spectators landed on the porch.

"Mighty kind of you, McCall." He stood and opened the card. He wiped his eyes with a handkerchief. "Did not expect any—well, I'll be. My favorite quote right here on a plaque."

He rubbed the raised letters of newspaper clippings on the wooden typewriter shape with a shiny coat of decoupage-glimmer covering them. He had a look of awe on his face, as if he could stroke his beloved quote for the first time without getting newsprint on his fingers.

He read:

"Restlessness and force are the supreme principles of the cosmos."
Leonardo da Vinci

Tally frowned. Charlie's baritone voice boomed strong at the beginning of the sentence. By the end of the quote, his voice faded to a whisper as if under a weight of emotion.

"Charlie, you should have seen how black my hands were as I cut all those words from a stack of newspapers. My sorority sisters teased I was composing a ransom note."

He smiled. The round-rimmed bifocals resting on the middle of his nose inched upward. His hand lifted the plaque the way a preacher lifts the Bible during a sermon.

"Well, I sure appreciate your time, McCall. And all the ice-cold water you had to endure to get your hands from black to white again."

He chuckled. "It seems restlessness and retirement are mirror images. Guess I'll just *force* myself to go fishing as often as I can." He coughed his emphysema cough. "Keeping this on the wall of my screened-in porch."

Charlie stuffed his handkerchief in the front pocket of his tweed pants.

"And if your 'bar makes final edition, you'll be seeing it around sunrise, McCall. Heard you did a good job meeting the deadline. By the way, did you know the word 'deadline' originated in Georgia at Andersonville Prison and was documented as such?"

"Is that right?" Tally's voice climbed an octave. She knew all about the historic 'deadline' at Andersonville. She had studied the court case against Colonel Wirz, the despicable commander of the camp who was the only person convicted of war crimes during The War Between the States and who was hanged for his crimes. In his testimony, Wirz admitted that if a prisoner, in an attempt to escape over the stockade walls, crossed the line that Wirz created around the perimeter of the walls, the prisoner would be shot dead.

Still, Tally knew it was not polite to tell someone older, especially someone you respect, that you already know what they most want to tell you.

"Yep. You should look it up sometime. Sure does have importance to the newspaper business. Don't know what we'd do without deadlines." He cleared his throat. "Well, have yourself a good summer, now. Been a pleasure working with you, McCall, and I'll see you around town."

"Thank you, sir. I'll be back next fall. Senior year." She waved. "But the newsroom won't be the same without you there."

"Keep that sweet smile of yours." He waved back. "Break time's over. Time to put this paper to bed."

Tally's "Thank you so much, Charlie" was swallowed by campus bells bonging three o'clock. Good grief. How would she ever get to the cabin in time for the photo?

She ran down steps bordered by two curved swirls of pink Georgia marble. They reminded her of a lady's arms outstretched to welcome folks to the mansion. If there was anything she needed right now, it would be arms outstretched for a hug.

A sudden wish for her mother not to be in Paris buying bridal gowns and accessories for her boutique but instead to be here in Hamper so she could tell her all about what had happened today made her feel as if she was about to cry.

Mon Dieu. A twenty-year-old young woman doesn't need a hug from her mother. Well, almost twenty. Only six more weeks to her brand-new decade.

Guitar case in hand, her fringed shoulder bag bouncing against her hip, she dashed down the path under the live oaks, past the historical marker honoring the Confederates who died at the Massacre of Hamper Park, only to stumble near *The Two Men* statue. She could not go any further. Her feet were killing her.

She plopped down on the ledge of the statue, her shift dress sliding up past the lace of her powder pink bikini undies. She did not care. The smooth marble cooled her thighs.

Easing off her flats, she grimaced at the skin rubbed raw on the back of her ankles. If she did not dab Mimosa Miracle Oil on them soon, she would be forced to wear gold satin bedroom slippers to the Military Gala tonight or, better still, go barefoot.

She propped her ankles against the marble to chill her tender skin. She wanted to yell, "If you intend to be on time but get there late, do your intentions count?"

In a courtroom, intentions counted. Her daddy taught her that.

As Frisbees sailed in the distance and shrieks of laughter surfed on the breeze, she was struck by the idea of intent. What was the intent of Kent State students this morning? What was the intent of National Guard troops firing at them, especially when the latest *AP* and *UPI* reports she read confirmed the students were unarmed?

She tossed her shoes in the guitar case next to the tomahawk and the smushed poster from her history presentation. She wondered if anyone would remember this day years from now. She closed her eyes silently promising the students who died and those students who were wounded that she would never forget them.

Neither would she forget what her daddy's friend, Dr. John W. Gardner, cautioned her when she was ten years old. After he shuffled through her autograph book, he found the only gray page among all the pastels. It was the color he said he liked because it was the place between black and white where people could 'pause and ponder, not panic' as he wrote:

"History never looks like history when you are living through it."

The air smelled of shrimp. Tally could not wait to see the sign in front of the historic log cabin named for Hamper's most famous citizen, Georgia Glen. The cabin was once the home of the Gable Glen family whose only child, sixteen-year-old Georgia, was shot and killed on her wedding day. Georgia Glen is noted in history books as the only civilian killed during the Massacre of Hamper Park on April 17, 1865, eight days after Lee surrendered to Grant.

Not knowing The War Between the States had ended, not knowing Lincoln was dead, not knowing the Confederate soldiers carried rifles with no ammunition, Yankees crept from their ship at night onto the beach near Hamper Park and hid beneath the dunes.

At dawn the next morning, the Yankees startled the ragtag Confederates asleep under the oaks and weeping willows. The Confederate soldiers, once hailed as rebels with a cause, had been too weary, too sick, too defeated to walk the final mile to Fort Hamper the day before. They never stood a chance when the battle began because they never had a chance to stand before being slaughtered.

According to a letter Georgia Glen's grieving mother penned to relatives, her beautiful daughter, Georgia, already dressed in her wedding gown that fateful morning, heard seagulls chitter in the dewy darkness before dawn, moments before the massacre began. She ran to the porch with hopes her sweetheart, Private Josiah John Flournoy, was approaching. She saw the sun rise, turned to her mother and exclaimed, "Come see the most beautiful morning, Mama," her last words before being shot in the back. She died instantly. Her bereaved and distraught sweetheart vowed never to marry.

The morning of their wedding day became his day of mourning, a day that stretched out in his memory until the day he died.

Even though citizens voted him Mayor of Hamper for his pledge to keep alive Hamper's reputation as "the town where quick-thinking triumphed over Sherman," his true mission, he acknowledged on his deathbed, was to keep his sweetheart Georgia Glen's memory alive too.

One hundred and five years later, the results of his devoted efforts to honor his beloved could now be seen on a plaque near the cabin's front door citing the Georgia Glen Cabin as a National Historic Landmark on the Register of National Historic Places. It was dedicated on Friday, April 17, 1970, the day Apollo 13 returned to earth bringing home loved ones safely from the heavens.

Near the cabin stood the sign, secured inside protective glass and planted in cement, shaped like a wedding bouquet:

Welcome to the Georgia Glen Cabin

The Place Where a Love Story Will Never Die

The sign was painted white and etched in pure gold leaf. The gold came from a mine in Dahlonega, Georgia, where the metal was discovered on Cherokee land in 1829 igniting the gold rush of "Twenty-niners" years before folks rushed to California.

It is legend that a woman hailing from Georgia, Mrs. Jennie Wimmer, was the first person to confirm that the gold found at Sutter's Mill in California was the coveted treasure. Mrs. Wimmer, who cooked and did laundry for the hired help at Sutter's Mill, did not need to test it. She knew it was gold the minute she saw it. Still, for the sake of doubters, she confirmed it by throwing the nugget into a pot of boiling lye. The next morning when the lye had cooled to make soap flakes, she scooped the nugget out and it was shiny as ever.

Mrs. Jennie Wimmer's kinfolk in Hamper, the ones who always referred to her as a "fine Southern woman from Georgia," knew what she knew too. To hear them tell it, Cousin Jennie had seen so much gold in Georgia that the tiny little nugget out west was "just a bitsy little smidgeon" compared to what the state of Georgia had to offer. However, Cousin Jennie did not brag. That is not what a Southern woman does.

Tragically, Georgia Glen never grew to be a woman. She did not live to experience the glory of her wedding day or the wonder of her wedding night. Therefore, to honor Georgia Glen, whose life ended before her life truly began, brides came from all over the South through the years to be photographed on the porch of the Georgia Glen Cabin in their wedding dresses. Georgia Glen was their "Juliet of the South," their icon of romantic love.

According to her mother's letter, Georgia Glen's wedding dress, a white polished cotton heirloom, puddled like a halo around her strawberry blonde hair when she fell. It turned scarlet from blood seeping out the center of the bow in the back.

As if to prevent the tragedy, as if to freeze this beautiful young girl in a state of hope, the Georgia Glen Collectible Doll in her pristine white gown, her face wearing a smile, her eyes looking upward to the sun, was constantly in demand. The legend of Georgia Glen was also credited with why so many baby girls in Georgia were named *Gigi*, for Georgia Glen's initials *G.G.*, as a way to honor this Hamper, Georgia sweetheart.

Tally sprinted by the Tess Hamper Performing Arts Theater, the park's replica of Loew's Grand Theatre in Atlanta where *Gone with the Wind* premiered. The giant hand on the antique clock over the entrance moved. 3:09 p.m. A comet of historical events streaked through her mind. Students streamed past her from the matinee. She zigzagged through the crowd while saying "Hey" to folks she knew.

3:09. March ninth. Easy. Napoleon and Josephine marry. A seagull screeched so loudly Tally felt she was in that Hitchcock movie, *The Birds*. She imagined that would be the sound her mother would make when Tally told her mother of her recent decision to never get married.

Tally rounded the white and pink azalea garden and saw another sign, closer to the picnic tables. It looked as if its letters were announcing the Law School Barbecue. The breeze was curling it upward.

The barbecue. What if she did not see Rye at all? He probably had expected a letter from her. If they missed each other, she would never speak to Khaki again. Khaki. Miss Bride-to-be. Who never gave her Rye's letter.

Tally smiled for the first time as she fingered the weeping willow fronds that swayed near her like dangling harp strings. Just remember, Khaki. You *will* need a wedding dress and my mother has the most exclusive wedding dresses in Georgia.

Tally frowned at the irony that she herself never would. Here she was the only daughter of a Parisian-born beauty who married at twenty, moved to Georgia, designed a revolutionary bridal brassiere with sensual support, comfort and allure, a brassiere hand-sewn with the finest cotton from Sea Island, Georgia. She opened Babette's Bridal Brassieres Boutique with Vera Sanders, the best seamstress in Georgia. She later changed the name to Babette's Bridal Boutique, and now buys couture bridal gowns in Paris, yet her only daughter would never wear one.

Tally dreaded the day when she would be forced to explain to her mother why she did not want a wedding or a marriage and why she only wanted a sweetheart. She could not discuss anything upsetting with her mother now. Her mother was too frantic about Shawl.

Tally scampered over soft zoysia grass and patches of sand by the putt-putt golf course next to the carousel. She heard her name shouted by her sorority sisters from the porch of the log cabin. After tucking the fattest part of her guitar case under her arm, she pulled her white mini dress to the top of her thighs and jumped over the stream instead of taking time to cross the bridge. Only after she made it to the other side did she realize Mr. Moretti was leaning against a porch beam with a smile on his face.

"I'm so sorry for being late. Mr. Moretti, may I change quick-quick into my uniform? I left my ROTC uniform in the cabin yesterday so I wouldn't have to carry it all day or wear it on campus."

Mr. Moretti's grimace looked like his feet were hurting him too.

"Miss Tally, I regret not to grant your wish, Bella. No pictures can develop by tomorrow's edition if we don't start now. We need to take photos. Every minute more the light is fading."

"Tally, what the hell? Why are you still wearing that dress?"

Khaki grabbed the guitar case.

"And where are your shoes, Tal?" Becca tugged Tally's fringed suede bag off her shoulder as Tally pulled her shoes from the guitar case. "Did everything go as you hoped it would today?"

Tally nodded, hugged Becca and whispered, "Oh, Becks. SO much to tell you."

"Tally, Shawl will be beside himself!" Becca whispered back.

"Wait. I have an idea. We're all wearing our white uniforms since it's after Easter." Virginia scooped a hairbrush from Tally's bag and began brushing her hair. "So, Tally could just stand in between us and we could cover up her dress and folks won't know she's not wearing her Honorary Lt. Colonel's uniform."

"Virginia Dodge. You brilliant girl." Tally hugged Virginia who whispered in her ear how much she liked her new haircut.

"Mr. Moretti? Could I stand in the back and let the girls cover the front of my dress?" She quickly switched shoes with Becca whose platform sandals would give her height. She eased the straps of Becca's sandals over her heels. Pain squinted her eyes. The skin on her heels felt so tender, she gritted her teeth.

"Brava, Miss Virginia. That works. No splotches now, Miss Tally."

The girls grouped together surrounding Tally. Becca, Virginia and Khaki wore their ROTC Honorary Captain uniforms, denoting their junior status with fewer ribbons than Tally's senior Lt. Colonel uniform would have shown. Each uniform consisted of a white A-line skirt, a starched white cotton, long-sleeved blouse, a row of military ribbons above the left breast near one's heart, and thick gold braids waterfalling from each shoulder.

"Not fair." Khaki pinched Tally's arm. "Mr. Moretti, we were here on time. We wore our uniforms. But now you want us to gather around Tally like she's the bride and we're the bridesmaids? When we know that's not true."

Khaki smoothed her hair with her left hand adorned with her engagement ring.

"Rank has its privilege." Becca elbowed Khaki. "Right, *Lt. Colonel* McCall?"

"*Preferer noblesse oblige.*" Tally stared at Khaki. Good grief. There would be no splotches without Khaki. "I could call rank, *Captain* Carson."

Khaki threw her hands in the air. "Why is it that the captain of a ship is the highest rank a fellow can have? He's the person who makes all the rules, the man who goes down with the ship because he's so dadgum honorable and thoughtful. And he's the officer who can marry a couple on a ship. So how come is Captain not the highest rank in the military? Not fair."

By the time Mr. Moretti repositioned his tripod to take the first shot, Khaki complained that the breezes were swirling her hair. Soon they were all picking at tendrils getting stuck on lip-gloss and mascara.

"Ladies, grazie. The breezes, they are excited today. With most regret, we must do this another time." Mr. Moretti bowed and unscrewed the bulb from the camera flash.

"Mr. Moretti?"

"Yes, Miss Tally?"

"Can we go inside? Light the kerosene lamps on the mantle and pose by the fireplace? I know Mr. Boudreaux wants this picture on the front page of the paper tomorrow. At least he did before, well, you know, the news from Ohio."

"Yes. The sad news. The Editor's always right. Right, Miss Tally?"

"Right. And Mr. Moretti, you don't have to call me 'Miss.' Why don't we pretend we're still in the newsroom? Would that be okay, Mr., I mean, Moretti?" She reached her hand to shake his.

He bent and kissed the back of her hand.

Tally blushed.

"Italian men. Gotta love 'em." Khaki whispered in Tally's ear.

"He's from Rome. Rome, Georgia." Tally grinned at Khaki's perplexed look.

"Wait. What sad news?" Becca and Virginia chorused.

"Tell you later." If Becca started crying, they would never get the picture taken. And they would all look a mess.

"Got to hustle. Botany Field Trip-Final Exam starts in ten minutes." Tally took a key from her coin purse and pushed open the heavy log door. A stream of daylight brightened the room.

"You have a key?" Moretti patted his hand on the wall as if to find a light switch.

"Tally works here as a tour guide on weekends." Virginia dutifully signed the guest book.

"You won't believe all she knows about Georgia Glen. What she ate that tragic morning. Her last letter to her sweetheart. How she died before the Massacre of Hamper Park began. On her wedding day." Becca put her arm around Tally and gave her a squeeze. Tally leaned her head on her best friend's shoulder.

"Bellissima. I promise to tour someday but now, Bellas, we must hurry."

Eleven

Tally lifted the glass chimney of a kerosene lamp. She struck a match, twisted the key on the base, and observed kerosene soak into the thick cotton wick just as it caught fire.

A spark of memory flashed an image of the last time she had lit this lamp during Saturday's tour before her sorority sister's nautical wedding.

Whenever she demonstrated to tourists how a kerosene lamp worked, for invariably there were visitors who had never seen one, she reminded them of a fact, as she did last Saturday, that was flagrantly missing from any debate about The War Between the States.

"Why do you keep calling it The War Between the States when everybody knows it's The Civil War?" A man with a Northern accent had asked that Saturday afternoon.

"Thank you for asking your question, sir. It comes from how I grew up. My daddy always says that Southerners tend to take their time explaining things. He says Yankees know how to hurry 'cause when it's cold, you have to move fast. And Southerners like to go slow 'cause when it's hot, you sure need to take your time. He says lots of folks in other parts of the country call it 'The Civil War' because it's faster than saying 'The War Between the States.' However, my daddy says 'The Civil War' is an oxymoron just like 'jumbo shrimp' or 'postal service' because there is nothing 'civil' about war.'"

A few in the crowd had chuckled when she mentioned the post office offering service.

"Besides," Tally continued, "saying 'The War Between the States' gives the heft of words, specificity and a measure of reverence, Daddy says, to a conflagration so horrific that we are all still affected by it as a country today, even 105 years later. Does that answer your question, sir?"

"I'm still thinking about it."

"Take your time. Now as I was saying about the kerosene lamps--"

Tally kept to the script explaining that Northerners were portrayed as railing against slavery, as being America's utterly innocent spectators calling out the horrors of the despicable slave trade, demanding that Southerners be punished, or killed, even before hostilities escalated and The War Between the States began.

Yet it was curious to note, she would tell the tourists as she opened the hourglass chimney of the lamp for them to peek inside, that citizens in Northern states had no qualms whatsoever, not in their speeches and not in their actions, about advocating for cotton to be plentiful or about buying cotton for their clothes, their feminine toilettes, their hats, their curtains, their quilts, their sheets, their handkerchiefs, their wedding dresses.

Every Northern citizen who used paraffin wax lamps, whale oil lamps or kerosene lamps to light their homes, their carriages and their trips to the outhouse, used wicks made of one product. Cotton.

Cotton, she would note, that could only grow in hot weather, and, therefore, could only be planted, grown and harvested in the Southern States.

King Cotton was coveted, needed, demanded by consumers in the North, East and West and in Europe, yet folks who acted as if they played no part whatsoever in slavery and the horror of one man owning another man, continued to purchase the cotton harvested by slave labor seemingly without guilt.

"Therefore," she would quote the script, "it is important to pause before we continue the tour to acknowledge that each man or woman in the country who used a kerosene lamp to provide light and a measure of warmth on a cold night was a participant and also a beneficiary in the history of America that shredded our collective souls."

Invariably, just as happened Saturday, a voice, usually male, would tell her she was wrong, tell her she was an apologist for slavery as most Georgia Crackers and other Southerners were, and that the South was treasonous for seceding from the Union.

The accusations were legitimate. One hundred and five years ago those White children who lived through The War Between the States—those who saw dead bodies, both White and Black, in their backyards, those who witnessed Negroes being lynched, those who observed their chickens and silver stolen by Yankees, those who felt staggered at the loss of their fathers killed in war, who watched their mothers succumb to fear or rage or grief or poverty, who listened to words of hate, revenge and the new battle cry, 'The South Shall Rise

Again,' those who were forced to accept the invasion of people from the North who spoke and acted so differently, who treated them as if they were poor White trash, even if they were not, while the invaders supported the freed slaves instead—grew up to be the revengeful adults who parented another generation of dismissed and defeated White Southerners yearning to rebel.

The question Tally struggled with was not "How could generations of Southerners grow up to be so racist, so vengeful, so cruel?" but instead "How could generations of Southerners grow up not to be?"

What had always enraged Tally was the absurd notion among Southerners themselves that The War Between the States had shocked Southern genteel sensibilities and impugned Southern honor when, in fact, the actions of slave owners were inherently dishonorable, completely indefensible, outrageously barbaric in an otherwise civil society. The War just put an end to the enslavement, not the delusion that the South was innocent.

Still, as a student of history and a Southerner, Tally knew that pulling historical times apart, like cotton candy, could get sticky sometimes when all the facts were not present to understand and discern how individuals living within the rules and norms of their culture acted the way they did.

The cabin walls had surely absorbed the words she had stated in her rebuttal a dozen times already that year.

"Yes sir, well you see, I appreciate your views about the state of Georgia and the South. With your kind indulgence and that of the other folks on the tour, is it okay if I take a moment to respond to this gentleman's comments?"

Folks nodded their heads. Tally looked at her watch, knew she had to get ready to slip on her navy pleated mini-dress with green piping and sheer billowing sleeves for her sorority sister's nautical-themed wedding, and knew she couldn't address every accusation the man made.

"So, what have you got to say for yourself and all the treasonous racists down here?"

The woman next to him punched her elbow into his rib and shushed him.

"Well, first, I would ask y'all to please enjoy more sweet tea from the pitcher over there if you want some. And I'd also ask if you would follow me outside to the garden where we will conclude the tour, quick-quick."

The group exited the cabin and oohed and ahhed over the stunning array of pink Gerber daisies, ferns, and violet forget-me-nots.

Time is not only elusive, Tally knew. Time also allows one to breathe, to think, to plan, to be introspective, to ponder. Time is the quest of every historian to document its passage precisely and the element most needed in a historian's research. Tally just needed time to pull apart her frustration at the constant accusations that Southerners were of one mind.

Tally heard a few tourists saying how it was still snowing up north and how in the South spring had truly sprung. She grinned. She had once written an essay in fourth grade on "New Ideas to Win a War" suggesting that dropping snow on troops fighting in Georgia during The War Between the States would have made everyone pause and maybe have snowball fights instead. Miss Scarborough had given her an A for creativity yet wrote "See me after class. I'm calling your mother and father!" on the paper.

Fortunately, her daddy was traveling on the Federal Court circuit in Savannah with Judge Scarlett and her mother was in Paris with Vera

Sanders for a fashion show. The next day Tally had brought Tess Hamper, with whom she was staying, to see Miss Scarborough instead.

Miss Scarborough told Tess Hamper that Tally's other creative idea, to "dump saltpeter on the troops," was scandalous because she did not want a student of hers advocating for the least creative idea to dump the very essence of dynamite or gunpowder on fellow human beings, for goodness' sake. Tally had raised her hand.

She explained to Miss Scarborough that her big brother Shawl had told her about "*testerone*" or something like that and he had told her that dumping saltpeter on soldiers would make them act more like ladies and surely make the fighting stop.

Tess Hamper had burst out laughing.

Even Miss Scarborough had smiled.

"Thank you, ladies and gentlemen." Tally put her hand to her heart.

"Could you please gather round so I don't have to shout my response to the gentleman from—Where are you from, sir?"

"New York City--Brooklyn."

"Yo! No kidding? I live in Flatbush. Name's Sal. Your wife drag you here too? Small world."

The men shook hands.

"I appreciate your time, ladies and gentlemen. And I'll try to talk as fast as I can so I hope you can understand me. My response to your comment, sir, begins and ends with the word *incandescent*. When a cotton wick soaked in kerosene is heated with flame, the result is incandescence, literally white-hot cotton glowing amber from kerosene.

"Incandescent bulbs, which replaced kerosene lamps, as you all know, burn white-hot through wire filaments heated by electricity inside white bulbs. My white-hot stance is that I want White Americans, especially Southerners, to get white-hot about issues we must face as descendants of a horrific legacy and about issues we can solve.

"However, my white-hot attitude about Southerners is similar to my white-hot stance on Northerners. If all Southerners are regarded as racists, with no factual justification for that broad assumption, then it would only be fair to say that all Northerners are part of the Mafia which is patently absurd. Some Southerners are racists. Some are not. Some Northerners are racists. Some are not.

"Were Southern states the first to propose secession, a supposedly treasonous act, in the United States? No. The state of Maine seceded from Massachusetts in 1820. Furthermore, in 1844, one of the earliest advocates for the secession of the Southern slave-holding states was not a Southerner. William Lloyd Garrison called for secession of the Southern slave-holding states and he hailed from Massachusetts."

She was speed-talking and fired-up.

"Garrison, an abolitionist, publicly burned a copy of the Constitution, condemning it as a *'covenant with death, an agreement with Hell.'* He was referring to the compromise that had written slavery into the Constitution. Secession was not unilaterally ruled a violation of the Constitution until *Texas vs. White* in 1869, four years after The War Between the States, and eight years after the Southern states had determined secession was their chosen, albeit risky yet legal, recourse.

"Please remember, sir, that Jefferson had slaves. Washington had slaves. Ulysses S. Grant had slaves. There were slave auctions near the site of Wall Street in New York City, across from Brooklyn, sir. What I ask each of you is to understand the notion of *descendant honor.*

"Those of us who are White Georgians, those of us who are White Southerners, those of us who have grown up as descendants of a legacy we despise, can do nothing about the legacy of slavery a century later. We cannot change the fact that many of our ancestors allowed it to happen and participated in brutal, criminal acts.

"We are still immersed in a physical, emotional environment and culture where long-ago battles were fought on our soil, where widows of Confederate soldiers--whether their husbands were slave owners or not--still live among us, and where those of us who hate the legacy of Southern ancestors owning slaves wish we could confront those ancestors who did.

"Yet Southerners cannot do anything today to change the past or our horrific history. However, there are enlightened, educated, enraged Southerners who are white-hot with incandescent grief, guilt and gut-wrenching helplessness about the past. As descendants, we can only distinguish ourselves during the history in which we are all living and breathing each day. We can only honor those who were the innocent victims of criminal, racist behaviors based on hate, unawareness, fear or what White Southern settlers perceived as "honor" of their own race and heritage. Sir, I'm sorry to be so flustered. It's just that I've lived in Georgia all my life. It is my home, my heart, my hallowed ground. No matter where I travel, I take Georgia with me in my memories, in my manners--"

"And in your sweet accent too. Just beautiful, honey." Several tourists mumbled their agreement with the woman in a seersucker dress who gave Tally a floral paper fan from her pocketbook.

Tally smiled, thanking the woman as she fanned herself.

"Please know I wish I could change the history of Georgia that disgusts me, mortifies me and breaks my heart yet I cannot do anything about the past. I can only learn from it. I wish I could stop the despicable actions of Jim Crow racists in Georgia today yet I can't. All I can do is search Georgia's history for answers to questions about how Georgia became what it is now. All I can do is ask for equal awareness on the part of Northerners who are racists and Americans who are racists and who have also victimized the Original Native Americans and all individuals with hopes and dreams who are just like us but for the color of their skin.

"Thank you for listening to my rant, sir. Thanks so much to all of you who honor the innocent victims, the slaves, the Cherokees, the children, and Georgia Glen, the only civilian casualty at the Massacre of Hamper Park. Now here are brochures about the Hamper Park Massacre, the tragedy of Georgia Glen on her wedding day, and the history of the colony of Georgia. Before we go, I'll be happy to entertain discussion. Any more questions?"

That Saturday there were none.

After lighting the second lamp on the mantle, the cabin glowed. Helping Becca move the red velvet rope and brass posts from their semi-circle around the hearth, Tally gently rolled the worn sisal rug to safety by the fireplace as an idea dawned on her.

She asked the girls to take off their shoes so as not to block the watercolor painting of Georgia Glen in her wedding gown. They agreed. Hallelujah. After the freedom of going barefoot, she could not stand to wear Becca's sandals a minute longer.

Smiling, the girls posed for one photo after another. Moretti raved about how the soft light haloed their faces, how beautiful the girls were, how the gold braids on their uniforms seemed to sparkle, what lovely manners Southern women have.

He asked them to pause while he moved the American flag beside them. He requested that the girls look at the camera and salute. Finally, he clapped and bowed.

"Grazie, Bellas. I go to the darkroom to develop. Grazie. Ciao."

The girls waved and offered their thanks. Tally turned the key on the lamp, lowered the wick and cupped her hands over the chimney to blow out the flame.

Becca and Virginia repositioned the velvet ropes. Khaki moved the flag. Tally and Becca rolled the rug back in place. When everyone was ready, they bolted out the door, all barefoot, in a race to the boardwalk for their final Botany class of junior year.

Twelve

Hot pink pom-pom blossoms, scattered on branches of mimosa trees by the boardwalk, looked like giant cupcakes from a distance. Tally was starving. Lunch was a distant memory of a lemon teacake. Winston had devoured her egg salad sandwich. Now her stomach squeezed tight as a fist. Looking at cupcakes bouncing in the wind, she felt dizzy. There was no way to concentrate on Botany experiments if she didn't get some food.

She waved at Becca and shouted, "Be there soon. Cover for me? Merci beaucoup!"

She ordered a cup of sweet tea and a shrimp-cocktail from Mrs. Crockett at the Caught by Crockett shrimp stand. Easy to prepare, easy to gulp down, she could chat quick-quick with Mrs. Crockett, Winston's and Franklin's mother, while she ate.

"Mrs. Crockett, the shrimp smells divine. How much do I owe you?"

"Tally McCall. Don't you dare even ask that, child. Winston just told me you said you'd tutor Frankie in history for Summer School. Oh, bless you, child, for answering my prayer. I asked the Lord how can one twin be so smart and the other so--"

She shook her head and waved a paper fan from Stork's Funeral Home as she talked.

"Now my baby won't flunk out of school. Now he won't be fixing to go get drafted. You're saving his life and the only thing I can give you in return is shrimp for a lifetime."

She wiped her eyes with an orange bandanna before tying it around her Afro.

"Lord Bless you, Tally. Lord Bless you."

Tally saw her arms outstretched and her eyes filling with tears. She walked around to the side of the booth and hugged Mrs. Crockett who started crying on Tally's shoulder.

"Mrs. Crockett, ma'am. Everything will be just fine. Winston told me all about it. We're not going to let anything happen to Frankie. Promise."

She did not want to tell her how worried Winston was about her. Tally also did not want to mention Winston's O-O Honor nomination. What if Winston was waiting to tell her in some special way?

"Tally, if I'd just been able to hold Frankie inside of me a minute longer," she dabbed her eyes with a paper napkin, "Oh, if I could go back and keep him safe until after that midnight time. I swear it's all my fault."

"Hey. Need to order a fried shrimp sandwich and some gumbo." A man in a Hawaiian shirt and brown Bermuda shorts that fit snug on his plump pale thighs snapped his fingers. The other hand flicked a cigarette lighter again and again in what seemed a nervous tic.

"Yes sir." Mrs. Crockett kissed Tally's cheek then returned to the counter. "Sweet tea and hushpuppies with that?"

"Is the Pope Catholic? And put a move to it. I'm in a hurry." He turned his head and spit tobacco juice on the sand.

"Won't take but a minute."

Tally gathered her things, apologized to Mrs. Crockett for rushing, scooped the last shrimp in homemade pineapple-cucumber sauce, plopped it in her mouth, gulped a swig of sweet tea, and began jogging to the boardwalk.

Within moments she returned.

"Good grief, Mrs. C. I forgot to tell you that I just saw Police Chief Parish's son, Mike, remember him, big tall linebacker for Hamper High, anyway, he's the new park security cop now and he just told me he and his partner are on their way over for some shrimp gumbo. He wanted me to be sure and tell you to please get some ready."

Tally stood by the counter talking to Mrs. Crockett in a loud voice while glancing at the man.

"In fact, I'll help."

"But you'll be late to class, Tally."

"Hey." The man pointed at Mrs. Crockett. "Could you stop jawing and start frying?"

"Yes sir. It's just about ready."

Tally stashed her guitar case and bag behind the counter.

"I can see my class from here. They're just sitting on the boardwalk. So, I'll be happy to help."

"How much longer?" The man clutched the beam where red, white and blue bunting flapped. A tattoo of Jesus on the cross waving a Confederate flag was visible on his upper arm.

Tally poured sweet tea in a cup for the man. Steam rose from the platter Mrs. Crockett slid onto the counter. The man tossed two dollars and two quarters on the counter.

"Took way too long. No tip for you." He demanded another napkin and walked to a distant picnic table.

"Child, I've got this. I can get the gumbo for Mister Mike Parish ready by myself. You go on to class now 'cause Winston tells me how you hate to be late." She laughed. "If only I could get my boys to be on time."

"Mrs. Crockett. I'm sorry to disappoint you about the gumbo and all."

"You feeling okay, child? You look a little flushed. Here, have some mint pillows to soothe your tummy."

"Thank you, ma'am." Tally sucked on the cool, mint candies as they melted on her tongue. "It's just that I lied about seeing Mike Parish. I made that whole story up because I was worried about you being here all alone with that man."

Mrs. Crockett got a big grin on her face.

"Tally, child, come here." She pulled something from the pocket of her flouncy skirt in its African print of blue, brown and yellow. "See this? Now don't you worry about me. 'Cause I know how to use it."

In her palm sat a giant orange whistle.

Thirteen

The longer Tally sat on the boardwalk with classmates, waiting for their Botany professor, Dr. Logan, to arrive, the more she wanted to slip between mimosa trees and find her favorite place in the clearing.

The more she thought about what could be happening at Kent State that very moment, the more she wanted to curl up on the sofa at the sorority house and listen to news reports on TV. The more she wanted to hear Paul Harvey share news on the radio, the more frustrated she felt by Dr. Logan's refusal to allow transistors on field trips for fear of causing vibrational harm to the plants or trees when music played too loudly.

With Khaki, Becca and Virginia volunteering to go to the end of the boardwalk to look for Dr. Logan, and the boys staying behind to smoke cigarettes, she nestled on cool sand under a mimosa. Her dress was ruined anyway. Might as well get sandy.

She looked at her watch. 3:42 p.m. March of '42. Hmmm. March of 1842. Dr. Crawford W. Long performed the first surgery using ether as an anesthetic in Jefferson, Georgia. Dr. Long had attended "ether parties" and observed how the men whiffing ether would fall down, bruise their legs, arms or head yet not feel a thing. He decided to try this organic chemical compound on his patients.

Of course, folks in Boston would beg to differ about Dr. Long being the first to perform surgery using ether. They would argue a Yankee doctor was the first. They would be wrong, of course. Dr. Long did perform the first surgery. He just didn't announce it in scientific journals right away. Seems he was not looking for glory as his Yankee counterpart, William T. G. Morton, appeared to be in 1846.

Dr. Long, as legend has it, was looking for his patients to be comfortable and wanting to verify the procedure with several surgeries before announcing it to the world, for that was more important to him than accolades.

"Wonder what Dr. Crawford W. Long would think about the statue of *The Two Men* in the park?" Tally mused aloud as she muffled a yawn. The tribute to Dr. Long in pink Georgia marble depicted him leaning over Mr. James M. Venable, the first patient on whom he conducted surgery while administering a towel of ether over the patient's face. The sculptor was careful to elongate the towel to cover the tumor, protruding ominously, on Mr. Venable's neck in appreciation for the gentility expected in a public place. The plaque near the statue told the story of how vital Dr. Long's discovery was to the doctors performing surgeries and to soldiers enduring amputations during The War Between the States.

After the brouhaha from Yankees that Dr. Long was not the first to use ether during surgery, another plaque was added stating that Dr.

Long's discovery was so profound as the first surgeon to use ether to benefit both the South and the North on battlefields and in hospitals, Dr. Long was chosen to be one of two individuals representing the state of Georgia in Statuary Hall in Washington, D.C.

Later, another plaque was added to the statue stating:

"Dr. Crawford Williamson Long was also a cousin of dentist Dr. John Henry Holliday, famously known as Doc Holliday, of Griffin, Georgia, who is a Georgia legend in his own right. Dr. Long operated on John Henry's cleft lip, presumably using ether as an anesthetic, before John Henry grew a mustache, moved to Texas and joined in the Gunfight at the O.K. Corral."

She dug in her pocketbook for a mirror, inspected her white, straight teeth that her dentist, Dr. Jordan, had pronounced close-enough to perfect once he removed her braces in eighth grade, and proceeded to smooth strawberry gloss over her lips.

What she would not give for a wisp of ether to put her into deep sleep right now. The dry, warm breezes made her yawn. She licked her finger, tasting strawberries before rubbing her finger on the sand. She leaned her head against her guitar case, the perfume of cucumber-fresh mimosa blossoms lulling her to nap.

She closed her eyes. Rye's face drifted before her. Wind gulping their words that night they met on the cruise ship. Spring Break. Alone on the deck. The full moon. Their toasts to the Apollo 13 astronauts home safe that day. Toasts to Rye's birthday that night too. Ocean breezes. Music from the party downstairs. Dancing. Whispering in her ear. Flirting. Laughing. A slow dance. Rum and Coke on his breath. His sandy brown hair, blue eyes the color of his shirt. Tan pants. The teasing. The argument. The anger. Their Scavenger Hunt the next day. Across the island. The fun. The bonfire on the beach. The laughter.

The look in his eyes before his kiss that started so tender before turning so deep, so strong, his embrace so -- no no-- no no--

"No. No. I keep telling you. Virgil Caine was a real person, douchebag."

"I don't think so, fool. Levon made it up."

"All I can say is thank you, Levon Helm, for singing the best damn song to rile up the South. Yessirree. 'The Day They Drove Old Dixie Down.' As if we needed encouragement."

"Hell, yeah. The South shall rise again, boys, and we'll be blasting Levon's song to those Yankee sonsabitches."

"Look, all I'm saying is give Virgil Caine, a war hero, some respect, dammit."

"I'm telling you he wasn't real, just a name to represent the South's view of--"

Feeling irritable after napping for a nanosecond, she wanted to shout. Do you boys know what is happening? Can you stop your one-up-man-ship? Do you see how testosterone-fueled arguments that escalate to rage are the beginning of all battles? Like the battle between unarmed students and armed government troops in Ohio hours ago?

But how could they know what happened at Kent State? The nightly news would not be on until six o'clock. And they would miss it anyway. They would be partying before the Monday night curfew.

Of course, she could tell them. But she hated announcing news, hated the "I know something you don't know" spotlight when she wasn't being a tour guide. Better to be an observer. Keep your eyes open. Don't participate. That's what true historians do. Observe patterns. Connect details. Write it down for posterity.

Besides. These boys could not care less about news from Kent, Ohio because none of them cared a whit about what happened in a Northern state. Bet they have no idea where the state of Ohio even is.

"Isn't Levon Helm from Ohio?" Tally stood and stretched, her mini-dress climbing up her thighs, almost reaching her panties. There were lots of ways to get boys to stop arguing.

"OH—HI--OH, OH, OH. Looking good, Tally. Looking good, except it looks like you spilled something on your dress."

"You have to be kidding, Tally? You think Levon Helm is from Ohio?"

"Where the hell is Ohio?"

"Levon Helm? A Yankee? Tally, the heat's messing with your brain. But I do like that dress you got on. Hot damn. Those psychedelic brown spots are messing with my brain too. Do we agree, my Rebel friends?"

They chorused, "Woooo-ha."

At least everybody was smiling now.

"Levon Helm's from Turkey Scratch, Arkansas." Jimbo Carson clarified as some of the boys nodded. "Saw him at the filling station once, with my grandpa. He drinks Nehi Orange."

"Touché. Fellows. Touché." Research accomplished. They knew nothing about Ohio, even though William Tecumseh Sherman, the man they most despised for all of time, was born and raised in Ohio. She waved to the boys and said she would be right back. She strolled along the boardwalk flanked by the grove of flowering mimosa trees that buffered the brisk Atlantic breezes coming in from the beach.

She could hear voices singing the lead-in to The Band's hit song. *"Look Away, Look Away, Look Away, Dixieland."* The strains of "Dixie," the South's anthem, plaintive as could be, coaxed Southerners to listen again and again to "The Night They Drove Old Dixie Down," a title as inexplicable as the song lyrics were heartbreaking.

Seagulls roosting in the tiers of mimosa branches squawked. As Tally meandered along the walk, wondering if her friends had found Dr. Logan, she also wondered when The War Between the States would ever end.

The War of Yankee Aggression, the term for the war by many in the South, happened only eighty years before this generation was born. The Centennial commemorating the end of The War Between the States was only five years ago, stirring up Southern passions about heritage and causes once again.

The Georgia state flag, towering atop a flagpole, snapped with a sharp bang as if a firecracker lit by wind instead of fire. She despised the Confederate X at the center of the flag. The Confederate symbol riled up folks on both sides of the Mason-Dixon and both sides of the Confederate legacy for Southerners. It was another reminder that continued to divide.

Her daddy always said, "The past still haunts the present, Shug, and, sad to say, not in an illuminating way. I see it every day in court."

Tally had already proposed her history project for senior year to Professor Dodge. She wanted to explore how people defeated in war continue to grieve, how losers in a war further dismissed by the victors will rebel in their own way, in their own time.

She wanted to discover how defeated and dismissed people experience loss by regaling stories of their defeat for generations, by being sucked into "the depression of defeat," by not being recognized for their suffering, which they endured, no matter the moral merit or lack of merit of their position.

She worried about what happens to these groups of people when they are dismissed. Do they succumb to bully behavior, hold a grudge? Do they seek revenge by becoming vocal, aggressive, dangerous, even criminal?

One thing all Southerners could agree upon, other than "The South shall rise again," was their galvanizing Creed: "Dismissed and defeated people *will* rebel."

Now she wondered if she should write her Oxford essay on this topic and cite the Kent State murders as a present-day example?

Tally waved when she saw her sorority sisters rounding the bend. "Did you find him?"

"Emergency faculty meeting. Because of some protest at a college up north I never heard of. Good grief." Khaki's voice shrilled. "How come students in the South don't protest? Why is it always people in California or New York or wherever? The west, the north, the east, they're all troublemakers. But *we* get blamed for being rebels and stupid and backwards."

When Khaki got angry, she twisted strands of her hair around her ears like earmuffs. The way she was shaking her head, one was already unraveling as she continued.

"Dadgum. We go to school and football games and graduate and join the military and don't cause trouble. What the hell! Not very fair."

"Khaki, when you feel you're right, you sure know how to say it." Virginia tucked a strand of Khaki's hair back in her circular earmuff mess and patted her back.

"Thanks, Gin. So, listen up. Good news. We only have to do one experiment on the field trip now because Dr. Logan's late. That's the rule and I'm going to remind him of it."

"I hope it's that one where we get to see the leaves curl up." Virginia braided her long black hair in a romantic Renaissance style, bobby-pinning it to stay in a unique hair-do all her own.

Tally noticed tears in Becca's eyes. She also noticed Becca wearing the mint eyelet mini-dress Tally had planned to wear to the birthday tea for Tess Hamper at the Country Club tomorrow. The ends of Becca's hair looked jagged and frayed as if she had scorched them while forgetting her hair was wrapped around the curling iron.

"You okay, Becks?"

"Not really."

"Sweetie, I hardly got to talk to you earlier at the cabin. Besides, Becks, you seemed fine. Was the Home Ec. Final hard?"

"No. I showed them my game of how to put a kitchen in order by color-coding cabinets and showed them how an engineer would design a kitchen and had them play the game for extra points. Miss Davis said she had never had so much fun during a Final Presentation."

"Becca, you are brilliant. Congratulations."

"You too, Tal. You so deserve your history honor. I just, I don't know, going to the Gala tonight without Shawl but with all the military men makes me--I swear if Shawl doesn't hurry up and write and get home, I may--" Becca's voice wandered off.

"Hey Khaki, Virginia. We're right behind you." Tally shouted.

Virginia turned and blew a kiss.

Khaki called back, "Just as well. *We* found out the information about why Dr. Logan is late so *I'll* tell the fellas." There had never been a time when Khaki did not want to be the town crier. If Khaki Carson had lived in Boston during April 1775, history books would not even know the name "Paul Revere."

"Tally, I swear I'm going crazy. Khaki and Gin checked on Logan. I zipped to the sorority house. I couldn't wear my ROTC uniform anymore. Too suffocating."

"It's hot outside so that makes sense. The cotton in those uniforms is woven so tight, it doesn't breathe like it's supposed to." Tally hesitated to explore this any deeper. "And that dress looks gorgeous on you. You'll have to wear it when Shawl comes home."

"Oh, Tally. Can I?"

"Only if you cheer up and imagine how excited he'll be to see you, you nut."

"Tally, don't you dream of that day too? When you'll hug your brother and I'll hug my sweetheart? Feel my hands. I'm shaking just thinking about it."

Becca had known Shawl since Tally grabbed Becca's hand and told her to sit by Shawl at her birthday party. Tally had told Becca she needed her to keep her chair warm while she opened presents at the table stacked with gifts. Tally and Becca were three. Shawl was seven.

Yet as many times as the three of them had been together, on McCall family vacations to Paris, climbing trees in their backyards, cheering Shawl when he became President of the Student Body at Hamper High and Becca when she was named the youngest varsity cheerleader, Becca and Shawl did not begin dating until a year ago.

Now that they were engaged, Tally could not imagine the two of them with anyone else.

"Becca, I've dreamed of that day ever since he left." Tally cleared her throat. She started coughing and motioned to the water fountain.

Becca smiled and patted Tally's new hairdo when a breeze gusted it upward.

"Hurry. I'll keep your place in line on the boardwalk, Tal."

Tally sipped water and nodded.

"If we're standing next to each other, Loafin' Logan will have to put us on the same team." Becca blew her a kiss.

Thank heaven. Becca's back.

But will Shawl ever be?

A breeze whooshed Tally's hair over her eyes as she leaned against the fountain and waved to Becca.

The topic of breezes was the last thing she had talked about with Shawl on the veranda during his final visit home before departing for Vietnam. They agreed to write each week. They promised to play tennis when he came home. They promised to take good care of themselves while he pointed to her skirt.

"Hey, Miss Sorority Girl-College Junior. Listen to me. When it's breezy, you better not wear those miniskirts of yours. I don't want to be reading headlines in 'Nam about a girl from Hamper, Georgia who is stirring up all kinds of trouble on her college campus. And find out that girl is my sister."

Tally grinned and punched his shoulder. "Hey, Shawl, Mr. Army man. Seriously. I mean it. Be serious. You know what I find curious about breezes?"

She knew she was making small talk to avoid the farewell that was about to happen when their parents came downstairs to personally drive Shawl to Fort Hamper.

"No, Squirt, but I know you're going to tell me. Just make it quick, a word that, of course, is not in your vocabulary. 'Cause *seriously*," he mimicked her, "I got to get to the base on time."

"Or," her voice cracked, "you could just let Mother and Daddy leave without you."

"Focus, Tally." Shawl's voice deepened. "Everything's going to be okay. Now, what's your new, wacky discovery about breezes?"

"Shawl, you're going to miss me. And my discoveries. Okay, think about this on the ride to the Fort. Have you ever wondered how a breeze may be the only thing in the world you cannot see until it moves something?"

"Okay. Physics is not your forte. Besides, you're babbling, Squirt."

Shawl tossed his army hat on her head.

Thank goodness it plopped down to her nose.

If he kept calling her "Squirt," the nickname she'd begged him to ditch yet now she knew she'd miss hearing, her eyes wouldn't be so blurry.

He lifted the hat from her head and twirled it around his finger.

"Hey, Tally. No tears now. I'm coming home, remember?"

He changed to his TV anchor voice imitating Walter Cronkite announcing the news.

"Viewers, just because I signed up for this gig, just because I enlisted, making Delphi Aviary McCall proud that his son would uphold the McCall family tradition of military service, allowing Babette Bouviette McCall to tell everyone her son is visiting the South Pacific, and offering Tally Gigi McCall the opportunity to write her long, rambling, fascinating letters in her elegant handwriting to someone who will actually read them--"

Tally did not know if she wanted to laugh or cry.

She tried to sear the image of this moment into her brain with him standing beside her so she would never forget. Trickles streamed down her cheeks. Oh. No. Now he was twitching a fake cigar as if he were Groucho Marx and shifting his voice to that uber-confident schtick.

"--and because, ladies and gentlemen, I was destined to visit the South Pacific anyway given that I was born a handsome young lad on September fourteenth, nineteen hundred and forty-six, winning the prize, yessiree, the prize I tell you, as the first birth date chosen in the draft lottery. So, let's play *You Bet Your Life* and the secret word, ladies and gentlemen, is--"

Tally laughed when he mentioned his favorite TV show and shrugged her shoulders.

"The secret word today–is--'Fair.' That's right. Fair. Can I let those other lucky birthday boys go without me to the South Pacific even though my daddy could pull some strings and keep me stateside? No. Can I finish my Doctorate in Philosophy when I get back? Yessiree. I can. And that's our secret word, ladies and gentlemen. *Fair.* Now what'd'ya think of them marbles, chickadee?"

"Shawl, stop. I can't breathe. You've got to do your impressions with your army buddies. They'll love it. Promise? Promise you will?"

"Promise, Squirt. But just remember, you nut. I'm coming home. Got to keep my promise to be best man at your wedding, that is, if anyone on the planet is ever crazy enough to marry you."

Tally punched his shoulder and grinned.

"As I was saying, Private McCall, about breezes." She mock-saluted him. "Before *you* started babbling."

"Touche'."

She heard a door slam upstairs and footsteps.

"Shawl. Promise you'll remember."

"Remember what, Squirt?" He sounded serious.

"When you see a flag fluttering or leaves dancing or curtains sailing from an open window of a kitchen over there, when you feel cooler or wonder why your hat tumbled off your head, you'll remember there's a breeze near you, wanting to make things cooler or happier or prouder, wanting to make things move to remind you we are all thinking of you, promise?"

"Promise." His voice was hoarse.

"Good. 'Cause that's the curious thing about breezes. A breeze can only truly be seen by its actions, what it stirs up and touches. Now, isn't that the greatest discovery that's right in front of us?"

Shawl cleared his throat.

Tally kissed his cheek and whispered, "Hurry Home!"

Shawl kissed the top of her head as he hugged her, whispered, "Love you, Squirt," squeezed her tight, and left before she could say another word.

"Jimbo Carson! Don't throw paper in the mimosa trees." Tally wanted to laugh at his rebellion yet after seeing Jimbo eat chalk during Vacation Bible School, she knew he would do anything to get attention.

"Lighten up, Tally. It's just stupid botany notes. They'll blow away. Besides, we're done with these notes. Shit. Here comes Logan. Got to hurry." He wadded up papers and zinged the paper balls into the branches.

"Jimbo, what if prospective students touring the campus see this mess you're making? The law school is touring today."

"Hot dog. Forgot. Saw the sign for the barbecue."

He threw another wad of paper at a seagull at the top of the tree.

"Jimbo, do you know Levon Helm hates litter?"

"He does?" Jimbo stopped tossing to look at her.

"James. Tally. Please stop talking."

Dr. Logan had arrived during their banter. He apologized for being tardy. He said there were events happening up north that were causing havoc with Finals Week on campuses everywhere.

"Who cares about the North?" Jimbo hollered.

"James. Your opinion about a news event has no merit in our Botany class."

Without further explanation, Dr. Logan proceeded to remind the students of the phenomenon of thigmonasty and its relevance to mimosa trees.

"Thigmonasty," he paced the boardwalk, "is a botanical phenomenon. A plant's response to touch, vibration or warmth. The most noted example? The Venus Flytrap. An insect landing on the open curves of a Venus Flytrap triggers an immediate closing of the curves. The Venus Flytrap ingests the insect as food."

He noted that this information should be in the notes he would be grading during the final science project for each of the teams of students he was about to announce.

Jimbo mumbled, "Shit."

Laughter could be heard as if skipping atop the breezes.

"James, as you may recall, thigmonasty has a different purpose for mimosa leaflets. A mimosa leaf with its splayed ferns, as if a hand with its fingers stretched out, will trigger an immediate retraction when touched or injured, making the fingers skinnier until they finally droop, as if lifeless. Technically, one reason this phenomenon happens is because the leaflets store calcium ions as a response to loss of water in dry weather or as a mechanism of curling up to protect themselves from the grazing of herbivores."

Male voices groaned.

Jimbo smacked a wad of paper at the "No Littering" sign.

Dr. Logan said, "Quiet, students. Now before I ask you to demonstrate how this happens, put yourself inside the perspective of a mimosa leaf."

Jimbo pulled his baseball cap over his face.

"Imagine you are a mimosa leaf. If the sun gets too hot, if you need to store water overnight, don't you appreciate the ability to take care of yourself? Most importantly, if someone touches you roughly or if you need to protect yourself, don't you value an immediate, unexpected response to anything or anyone threatening your safety? Students! That is an example of empathy, when you imagine being a tree or a mimosa leaf. Technically, it's called an empathetic response."

Someone in the crowd started humming "Dixie."

Jimbo launched into his usual tirade in an aside to fraternity brothers close by.

"Yeah. Like empathy those sons-a-bitches Yankees need to have toward us. And our land they destroyed. Fuck you, Sherman." Jimbo ripped another sheet of notebook paper from his spiral binder, wadded it into a ball and with his pitcher's arm, zinged it at a mimosa blossom that shattered, petals exploding into the breeze.

"James! It's not time for the empathetic experiment yet and why do I keep hearing the tune, 'Dixie' being sung?" Dr. Logan shouted.

"Logan, shut your flytrap." Jimbo covered his mouth and whispered loudly. His fraternity brothers laughed.

Dr. Logan looked like he wished he had a gun.

Dr. Logan assigned three students to each mimosa tree for the experiment that would encompass their final grade. With Dr. Logan's back turned, Tally scurried to retrieve her guitar case, racing to stand with Jimbo and Becca at the tree where most of Jimbo's papers were still stuck in a cluster of blossoms, deep in branches near the trunk.

Church and campus bells chimed five o'clock. Seagulls nesting in the mimosas shrieked. Dr. Logan approached Tally's group who, per their agreement, blocked the lower branches of the tree from his view. He asked each student to explain the role he or she had chosen to conduct the experiment.

Becca said she would read the instructions then record observations in the logbook. Jimbo said he would light the match and protect the tree as safety monitor. Tally said she would explain thigmonasty as the experiment proceeded.

"Dr. Logan, we need to ask you a question." Khaki yelled from a distant mimosa-team.

"Be right there." Dr. Logan shouted back. "Tally and James, switch."

"What?" Jimbo looked shocked. "No way. I'm great with matches and I'm the only guy here to protect the tree."

"Your final grade depends on this experiment, James, and my observations. You may also be aware that holding a flame to a tree is not a gender-dependent assignment."

"Say what?"

Dr. Logan's voice floated away at the swirl of a breeze.

"And I trust Tally will prove competent. Conduct the experiment several times. See what you observe each time and record this in your notes, Becca. And, James, here's a stopwatch to record the seconds it takes for the leaves to react to the heat. I'll return shortly."

He jogged toward Khaki's team.

"Now that's what I'm talking about." Jimbo tossed the stopwatch high in the air and caught it as if catching a fly ball. Announcing "time to go," he disappeared behind the tree. With the sound of a thundering stream so close by, Becca pointed her finger to her head as if to shoot herself.

Tally closed her eyes at the image.

At the whiff of urine in the breeze, confirmation that Jimbo was relieving himself without a care for others present, and with Khaki's whining and attention-seeking, she understood why Mr. and Mrs. Carson seemed so timid, so exhausted, so 'at wit's end' whenever they leaned behind a pillar at church as if hiding from the world.

The vibration of shoes clomping on the boardwalk sounded as if horses galloping toward them. Tally had just struck the match, watched it puff out immediately, and was searching in her bag for her sterling silver lighter engraved with an outline of the Eiffel Tower when she heard Becca squeal.

"Rye!"

"Becca Brown." Rye's voice sounded surprised and delighted. "What luck. Damn, you look stunning." He hugged Becca.

Tally looked into his eyes as if in a daze. Sandy planks of hair. Tanned skin. Those eyes. That grin that made her dizzy. Blue shirt, white pants, navy coat. Handsome as all get out.

"And, wow, Tally McCall. You look, how shall I phrase it? Inexplicable."

"Rye Somerset." Good grief. With all the mini-dresses in her closet, she's wearing this?

A group of young men, wearing business suits, walked past.

"Rye." One man pointed. "Headed to the picnic tables. See you there?"

Rye nodded. "Sure thing."

"Aren't you going to show me some Southern hospitality, Georgia? Nice haircut, by the way." Rye grinned.

Tally blushed. "Thank you for noticing, Mr. Somerset, and welcome to Hamper."

She tilted her head to her shoulder and extended her hand, which he held in both of his. The sudden touch and warmth of his skin triggered waves of tingles to gush down her body.

"It's a pleasure to welcome a Yankee to Georgia."

"Who said Yankee?" Jimbo emerged from behind the tree.

"Rye Somerset. Jimbo Carson, Khaki's twin."

"Jimbo. Met your sister on the cruise in April." Rye, seemingly assessing Jimbo's absence, put his hands in his pockets and nodded toward him.

"Wait. You're the one. Khaki said you and Tally were hugging on deck the first night. Hot and heavy. Teammates on the Scavenger Hunt. She said everybody was talking 'cause y'all didn't show up for hours. Way to go, buddy. Reckon if Tally's sweet on you, you're okay."

Tally was sure her face was as red as a fireball.

Fire!

"Rye, I'm so sorry. We're supposed to be conducting an experiment for Botany class. We have to hurry. But can I speak with you for just a second?"

Jimbo was fiddling with the stopwatch. "No time, Tally. Aw, hell, go on. Hurry."

Rye put his arm around Tally's shoulder.

Becca waved. "Take your time. I'll read the instructions. Jimbo can light the match. We'll give the logbook to Logan. Then scoot back to the Chaucer House to get ready. Rye, did you know? Tally's the Gala Queen at Fort Hamper tonight."

"Becca!" Tally shook her head and gave her a look. "Rye has a barbecue to go to." She stood on her toes to whisper in his ear. "I read your letter. Thank you so much for writing."

He whispered back in her ear, his breath so soft on her skin she wanted to kiss him that minute. "Hey, you. Great to see you, Georgia."

Aloud he said to her, "Congratulations, Tally. Barbecue's just a picnic. Becca, since your sweetheart is overseas, may I escort you, as Shawl's proxy, to the Gala?"

"Rye! You remembered? About Shawl?" Becca glowed. "Thank you."

"It would be my honor. What time and where do I meet you?"

"Seven is perfect. At the Chaucer Sorority House on Poet's Row."

"Team One?" Dr. Logan's words surfed in their direction. "Turn in your observations to me in the next five minutes. Breezes are picking up."

"Rye." Tally sucked her bottom lip and lowered her voice. "That's the sweetest gift to Becca. Can I thank you properly during another dance tonight? Like the one we shared on your birthday in the moonlight?"

He grinned. "Best birthday gift ever. In fact, after touring today and now seeing you, Georgia, my decision is clear. I'm coming to Hamper Law School in the fall."

"You are? Really?"

"Hey. Can you two quit playing lovers' reunion and start this stupid experiment?"

"Jimbo, sorry. Rye, we're going to be in deep tapioca if we don't hurry."

"Need some help?" Rye grinned.

"Hot damn. We accept." Jimbo looked over his shoulder. "Logan's still with Khaki."

Becca asked Rye to read the instructions, fast, while she took notes. Jimbo set the stopwatch. Tally noticed the breezes had died. Rye's instructions were a blur.

"Thank God for fast-talking Yankees." Jimbo shouted. "Tally, go."

Tally flicked the lighter under the tip of a mimosa fern, careful not to get too close. Jimbo counted the seconds out loud. Becca scribbled. Rye stood behind Tally. His presence, his closeness, dizzied Tally's concentration.

The delicate ferns looked like wrists touching, hands jutting forward, palms up, fingers stretched apart to make a fan. They began to curl from their tips toward the center.

Becca whispered, "Look."

Tally's hand began to shake as Rye whispered in her ear, "Looking hot, Georgia."

It only took that moment.

Dry leaves, crisp from days without rain, curled in a domino collapse toward the wadded papers. The ferns were ablaze.

"Tally! Fire." Rye squeezed her bare arms, picking her off the ground, her feet stepping lopsided on the guitar case where she landed. He pulled his coat off.

Jimbo hollered, "Smother it, Yankee. I'll time you."

Becca yelled, "Hurry," just as a gust of wind swirled. The flames jumped, skipping toward the papers, devouring the paper balls.

Rye lifted his coat over the flame.

"Rye! Please. Move the branches above me."

Tally clutched the tomahawk.

"What the hell?" Rye dropped his coat and pushed the branches high above her, opening a space for her to get closer. "Careful, Georgia."

Raising the tomahawk, while leaning into the circle of flaming paper, she chopped at the fiery branch, hacking it next to the trunk, dodging flames. Oozing the sticky sap for which mimosas are known, the branch tumbled onto the sand.

"Good girl." Rye grabbed the blackened branch, stomped the wads of fire under his loafer, and disappeared between the trees.

"Becca, head Dr. Logan off at the pass." Tally squeezed the wooden handle of the tomahawk.

"Becks, I'll tell him I was smoking a cigarette and my notebook caught fire if he asks about the smell." Jimbo put his arm around Becca as they huddled and walked toward Dr. Logan, Jimbo pointing to the stopwatch as Becca's hand jerked across the logbook, scribbling fictional notes.

Tally stared at the gash in the tree trunk. She killed the tree. No. Saved the tree. The ragged wound, yellow and raw, might never heal.

She felt a tug on the tomahawk.

"Georgia, come here." Rye's voice coaxed her from her stupor. He motioned to her to come closer, arms outstretched. She wanted to be scooped up in them, embraced in them, to feel safe in them, to smell his shirt, sniff his English Leather cologne, feel his warmth, feel his strength. But she couldn't move.

"Georgia, it's my fault. I distracted you. What you did was incredibly brave." He raised an eyebrow. "And I don't say that just because you used a tomahawk."

She shook her head and dropped the tomahawk on the sand.

He frowned. "What's wrong?"

"I don't know. I don't know if I saved it or killed it."

She looked up at Rye. Pink cupcakes surrounded his head. The concerned look on his face reminded her of the night they met and the worried, regretful expression he wore after he proved his point about what to do when in peril.

She pursed her lips and curled her finger. He bent down.

She whispered in his ear, her cheek touching his. "When in danger, make sure you know how to protect yourself. Remember?"

She could feel a muscle in his cheek move upward. She knew he was grinning. His mustache tickled her skin. She heard his voice, husky and firm, whisper, "That's my girl."

Without hesitation, she kissed his smoky cheek, her lips lavishing little pecks from his ear to his mouth until his lips smothered hers with a kiss so tender, so searching, so deep, a fresh wave of abandon coursed through her body rendering her oblivious to anything but the rush of anticipation for that ultimate surrender, her most personal historic event, that first-time event she couldn't fight much longer.

Fourteen

The smell of grass, freshly mowed in time for the Gala, infused the air with summer. Along the brick promenade leading to the most historic site at Fort Hamper, candlelight danced in lanterns that swung from iron posts. Streaks of sunset, hot pink tinged with gold, reflected on the ballroom windows of Hamper Hall.

A soldier in full dress uniform stood at attention on the portico between the American flag and the state flag of Georgia. An occasional breeze pouched the flags as if sails on ships before the weight of stifling air drooped them again.

The weather report for May 4th, 1970 predicted an oppressive night.

Hamper Hall, an edifice of pink Georgia marble, was named for Lord Horatio Hamper, the quick-thinking leader of the Georgia colonists who repelled Spanish invaders in 1733 in what history books cited as "The Legend of Hamper Marsh."

According to the tale told to children in Georgia through the years, Horatio attended Oxford University with classmate and founder of the Georgia colony, James Oglethorpe, who appointed his friend, "HH," to be Provost of the "Georgia-Yamacraw School," nicknamed the "Georgia-Craw," in the fledgling settlement north of Savannah.

Horatio was charged with instructing Yamacraw Indian children and the colonists' children the rudiments of language, history, writing, and arithmetic.

One afternoon Horatio spotted a Spanish galleon in the Atlantic. The threat of invaders, their diseases, murderous behaviors, pillaging and kidnapping was a constant fear. Horatio gathered tribal Yamacraw and Georgia colony leaders to a powwow about strategy. Knowing words in the Spanish language, Horatio also offered to make a sign.

Yamacraw leaders beat drums to alert the tribe of danger. Colony leaders played bagpipes to rally settlers to the beach. Yamacraw women gathered children and huddled with them in a shelter deep in the forest. Female colonists scurried across the beach with baskets and blankets before vanishing into the thicket. Yamacraw men gathered live oak branches and built a bonfire on the sand according to Horatio's directions.

Logs crackled. Sparks spewed into the sky. Flames illuminated the men lifting and lowering blankets soaked in saltwater over a mound of driftwood, mimosa ferns and sea grass. Gray smoke-puffs signaled a greeting to the ship.

At dusk, Spanish scouts brandishing swords landed on the beach. The natives and colonists were nowhere to be seen. Sand dunes, live oaks and weeping willows prevented the intruders from seeing those hiding. In the glow of the roaring fire, the Spaniards pointed to the sign that had been hurriedly painted by Horatio on a giant board he used in class.

The first line stated in broken-Spanish:

Paz. Regalo es para ti de la Medica.

It meant: "Peace. Gifts for you from the Doctors."

The second line issued a dire warning.

Upon reading the words, a Spaniard grabbed a basket of watermelons, kumquats, lemons, oranges and bricks of indigo wrapped in magnolia leaves. Another stuck his sword into a watermelon, sucked the sweet juice, and fell to his knees in prayer. The Spaniards hurried to their skiffs with the bounty and paddled back to the ship. The next day ocean waters were calm.

The galleon was never seen again.

The Yamacraw Tribe and colonists met on the beach to roast sweet potatoes, dip peach slices in goat's milk, and celebrate. They peppered Horatio with questions. How did Horatio know the Spaniards would sail away once they saw his sign?

"A knowledge of history," he said, "is the key to survival."

Horatio noted that "The Great Plague of Seville," the bubonic plague called 'The Black Death,' devastated Seville, Spain only fifty years before. He said he would refrain from describing the horror with ladies and children present, however, he said the disease made one's skin turn black before the victim died. He reminded them that the source of power is to know what others fear most, especially one's enemy.

"To know history is also to know strategy," Horatio tapped a finger to his temple before touching his lips, "and to speak a man's language is to honor a love most dear to a man's heart."

He told them the second line on the sign read: *Cuarentena: Negro Muerte Colonia.*

"Can one of my students translate?" he asked.

A girl of eleven years raised her hand. "Quarantine: Colony of Black Death?"

"Well spoken, Constance."

She raised her hand again. "But, sir, will we be quarantined here forever?"

"No, Constance. We are not quarantined now. There is no Black Death in Georgia. I beg forgiveness for a regrettable yet justifiable lie. My intent was pure."

She raised her hand again.

"But we gave them watermelons. What if they give us Black Death from Spain?" She began to whimper. "And those people who already turned black? The ones painted in your book of history? You said they live in Carolina, near us. What if they come to visit? Will Black people bring Black Death to Georgia?"

He shook his head. "Black people do not have Black Death. They are born with black skin. Now remember the history General Oglethorpe made here?"

She nodded and wiped her eyes with the hem of her pinafore.

"Slavery is outlawed in Georgia." He patted her head. "General Oglethorpe pledged this to King George II. It is the most important Trustee Rule in the Royal Charter of Georgia. The King's namesake colony is the only colony in the new land to be a utopia. There will be no Black Death here. There will be no slavery. And if there is no slavery, there can never be any Black people in danger here in the Georgia land."

Horatio lived seventeen more years, succumbing one silvery-moon night to old age. A year after he died, on January 1, 1751, the law was overturned and slavery was allowed in Georgia. One hundred and twelve years later, on January 1, 1863, the Emancipation Proclamation freeing slaves became law in the war-torn States.

A statue of Lord Horatio Hamper holding his legendary sign next to a bronzed Yamacraw man and a young girl with her hand raised stood amidst blue hydrangeas in the courtyard of Hamper Hall at the spot where HH established the Georgia-Craw School.

Beside the statue was a historical marker and the cast-iron cannon never fired that fateful day. The cannon, too heavy and fragile to move, was unfortunately pointed toward Hamper Hall's elegant ballroom now serving as the location for military galas, officer commencement ceremonies, and receptions for visiting generals.

The ballroom was also where the Queen of the Annual Military Gala would have her picture taken on the first Monday of May each year for *The Hamper Herald* and *The Fort Hamper Army Gazette* at the moment the surprise celebrity guest presented her with a scepter and the Fort Hamper Medal of Service. It was the moment her year of community service representing the Fort would officially begin.

At half past seven, a black sedan carrying the Gala Queen of 1970, Miss Tally Gigi McCall, arrived at the promenade. A soldier opened her door. A wave of heat threatened to force Tally back into the air-conditioned sedan. Instead, she placed her hand in the Sergeant's gloved palm, her cheeks blushing when a breeze swirled the yellow chiffon scallops of her tea-length gown above her knees.

She wished she had worn her black-sequined sheath. No breeze could fluff that form-fitting dress. But her sorority sisters had convinced her she should not wear black. Even if she was determined to pay homage to the students killed hours ago at Kent State, it was unheard of to wear black to a gala, especially by the Queen. She finally agreed. But only after Becca reminded Tally that yellow was her brother Shawl's favorite color.

"Miss McCall, are you ready to do something you have never done before?" The Sergeant's voice boomed as he swept his hand toward the VIP side of the walkway, partitioned by a red velvet rope dividing the promenade.

"Yes, Sergeant. I've always wondered what it would feel like the very first time."

The way the Sergeant cocked his head and smiled made her wonder. Did she say that too loud? Is it unladylike to admit that you have always wanted to know what it feels like to be a VIP? Why is his smile triggering his dimples to show?

She glanced over her shoulder to see her sorority sisters, Becca, Khaki, Phoebe and Virginia, talking with friends. Rye, however, was standing next to the rope with his hands in his pockets. Wearing a black suit, a white shirt and aqua tie, he looked like an oasis in a sea of uniforms. Curiously, one eyebrow was arched upward. Now he was motioning to her.

"Sergeant, one sec, please." Tally leaned over the rope as Rye pulled back strands of her hair. The brush of his mustache and touch of his lips tickled her earlobe. Her shoulder instinctively lifted toward her ear.

"Careful, *Virgin* Queen," he whispered. "Do you want your kingdom to know? Or just fellows like me who try and fail to--"

"Rye!" She stood on tiptoes, cupped her hand and whispered "Shhh," purposely blowing warmth into the cave of his ear. Her hand began to jitter. He pulled it down and placed both of his hands over hers.

"You'll do great. Be confident. Say what you most want to say. Just think first."

Without thinking for a moment, she kissed him smack on the lips. He grinned and mumbled, "Or not," as he gave her a laid-back salute.

She had never entered the ballroom on this side of the rope line before. In previous years, in her capacity as Honorary Lt. Colonel of the Hamper High ROTC, she had attended the Gala as a guest, lining up on the right-hand side of the rope. She always felt certain she would like the feeling of being a VIP.

Yet the more she passed by ladies with their pearl necklaces stuck to their necks, their lace fans like windshield wipers on high speed, their mascara smudging at the corners of their eyes, she realized it was not fair for some folks to breeze by while others wilted like peonies in the Georgia heat.

Not fair. Good grief. The theme of her life today. Khaki splashing her white mini-dress with hot cocoa. On purpose. Her presentation in Georgia History class about "The Trail of Tears" and Georgia's injustices to the Cherokees. Winston's request to help Franklin improve his grades so he would not get drafted. The ultimate injustice? Kent State students being shot by the National Guard.

"We can go slower, Miss McCall." The Sergeant stopped in the shade of a magnolia tree bordering the promenade. Tally adjusted her yellow satin choker with the black cabochon fob. Nobody could stop her from wearing black jewelry in her private homage to the Kent State students who did not deserve to die so young.

"Thanks, Sergeant, I'm fine. And please call me Tally. I just wish the folks waiting in line were allowed to move to the covered portico."

Tally felt hairs on her neck getting moist. Thank goodness the Mimosa Oil had soothed her ankles.

"Aren't you broiling in that uniform, Sergeant?"

"You get used to it. Part of the duty. Besides, it's Georgia weather. Same latitude as 'Nam. That's why we built a Vietnam Village on the base." The Sergeant pointed to some distant place where an outline of huts could be imagined. "Red clay, hot and humid, an ocean nearby, mosquitoes, vines, snakes. Best place for boot camp and training before heading overseas."

"That's what my brother said when he enlisted."

"Hold the fort. Your brother is Shawl McCall?"

"Do you know him? He was stationed here for boot camp."

"Sure do. Great fellow. Good soldier. Amazing rifle skills. Funny as all heck. Heard him telling stories one night at the mess hall. Everybody was in stitches." The Sergeant shook his head. "He sure could make us laugh."

Tally's sheer sleeves puffed in a sudden breeze. They might as well have been her lungs swelling with pride. She wanted to listen to the Sergeant talk about Shawl all night.

"After we told him there was a rumor that he had volunteered to serve even with the clout to get out, he finally, sheepishly, told us he could've gotten drafted, what with his birthday, September fourteenth, being the first one picked in the lottery, but he volunteered instead. That's my kind of soldier. Proud to meet his little sister."

"Thank you, Sergeant Cook."

"Larry." The Sergeant tipped his hat. "Is he still in Da Nang?"

"I don't know. We haven't heard from him since his first days in Vietnam. He used to write me and Becca, his fiancée, every week during boot camp."

"Not to worry. Ever hear of Operation Graphic Hand?"

They started walking again. She shook her head.

"Didn't think so. It's kind of hush-hush down here. Jeez. I'll tell you flat out. The Army can drive tanks, train the best soldiers in the world, pinpoint the weakest spots in an opponent's defense, and defend a nation like no other. However, we sure as hell can't deliver mail. I know. I was there."

She heard someone call her name. She turned to look behind her. What was that girl's name? She's pointing to, what? Good grief. Is she expecting? But she just bought her wedding dress at Mother's boutique a couple of months ago. She's not even married yet. Tally waved. It must be the heat. She could not remember what she and Larry were talking about.

The soldiers in uniform and their guests inched forward while lightning bugs clicked about the crowd as if tiny yellow flashbulbs taking pictures of celebrities.

"Sergeant, I mean, Larry, have you heard who the celebrity guest is this year?"

"Affirmative. But orders state the Gala Queen is not supposed to know the identity until after she gives her speech. Then it's announced. Something about a winning photo?"

Tally flipped her hair, hoping to give it some bounce, at the reminder of a photo being taken.

"I hate surprises." They reached the steps leading to the portico. "And the photo? I intern at *The Hamper Herald* so I know. It's a big deal. Every year the photo wins a newspaper subscriber's award. Tess Hamper, the editor, says people like seeing a girl with wonder and awe and excitement on her face after all the pictures of injured soldiers from Vietnam on stretchers or in body bags. Oh, goodness, Larry, I apologize."

"She's right. I prefer a picture like that too."

Tally glanced at another woman waiting in line, leaning her head on her husband's Army stripes. She looked radiant. No. Sunburned. No. Flushed.

Tally felt a hand pounding her back as if she were choking. She turned around.

"Hello, Commander Hemming. Mrs. Hemming."

The Commanding Officer of Fort Hamper returned the salute from the Sergeant. Mrs. Hemming, wearing a striking cream couture gown, nodded and congratulated Tally on being the Queen of the Gala.

"Thank you, Mrs. Hemming. You look divine." Tally turned to the Commander and wished his glasses weren't so thick. It was hard to see his eyes. No wonder he was forced from the battlefield into an office job. At least, she hoped he could not see how nervous she was.

"Commander Hemming, since tonight's a special night, I wonder if you might grant me a favor?"

"Unless it's against protocol, the young lady who represents Fort Hamper at charity events for a year earns a favor."

"Thank you, sir." Tally pulled an accordion fan picturing Versailles in pastel pink images from her clutch and offered it to Mrs. Hemming who eagerly accepted. "It's the heat, sir. Could we invite the guests to stand on the portico where it's cooler?"

"Yes. Well, that is not--" The Commander paused when his wife excused herself, placed the fan over his ear, and began whispering. "Yes. Mrs. Hemming reminded me that VIP guests are still arriving and we need to keep the rope separating guests."

"And the burgundy rope is tradition, of course." Mrs. Hemming's dress was beginning to form wet smiles under her arms.

"Besides, rank has privileges."

The Captain and Mrs. Hemming smiled.

"Yes, sir. I appreciate that. However, one day when I asked my father, you remember my daddy, don't you?" She knew he did. She wondered if he knew that you cannot be a lawyer's daughter if you do not know how to cross-examine. And you cannot be a Southern woman if you do not know how to circle an issue before revealing its center.

"Delphi Aviary McCall is a fine lawyer, well, except for now he's a judge for the high court."

"Thank you, sir. Now that I think about it, he says the same thing about you being such a fine commanding officer. He's going to be here tonight." Rubbing the onyx fob that dangled from her choker, a gift from her father, her fingers froze. A news bulletin flashed through her thoughts. One of the Kent State students had been shot in the throat.

"Look forward to having a cigar on the porch with him."

"I'm sure he'd enjoy that, sir. He's probably got half a dozen H. Upmann cigars in his coat pocket right now."

Commander Hemming smiled and wiped his brow with his handkerchief. "He sure knows how to persuade. Now what were you saying, Tally?"

"Yes, sir, Commander. It's about a favor. You see, one day I asked Daddy when he used to be a judge at the County level, I said, 'Daddy, how come do you refer to prisoners in your courtroom as 'Sir' or 'Mister' when they are charged with awful crimes?'"

"I'd like to hear the answer to that." Mrs. Hemming leaned closer.

The cool from her fanning was a relief.

"Daddy said, 'Shug,' short for Sugar, of course, in my courtroom you see democracy in action. Everyone is equal under the law. When my bailiff asks those defendants to rise as I enter the room and instructs them to call me, 'Your Honor,' I'm going to reciprocate by calling them 'Sir' or 'Mister.' Daddy said that's the least he can do to acknowledge that a man is presumed innocent before the jury declares his fate."

"Fine man, your father."

Mrs. Hemming tugged at her husband's sleeve. "Let's move this chit-chat to the portico, Henry. It's too warm for my up-do here."

Tally and the Sergeant followed, per protocol, behind the Hemming's.

"Mrs. Hemming, I love that pearl choker wrapped around your bun."

"It's the latest, dear. They call it 'a French handcuff' at the beauty parlor because it's fashionable and," Mrs. Hemming patted the protrusion, "it won't let go of its purpose." Her underarm stain now looked like a mouth saying, "O!"

"Fine suggestion, Harriett." The Commander puffed up his chest as if he could not be prouder of his wife. "Much cooler here thanks to the shade and cross breezes."

"Commander Hemming, that's the favor I'd like to ask. Not only would your guests be cooler up here, but it would also be a treat for VIPs to have the entire promenade, without lines and ropes, to themselves so everyone is waiting at the end of the promenade for the VIPs to arrive. And," Tally's voice strengthened, "wouldn't it be the highest tribute to the democracy for which our soldiers fight if the soldiers and their guests could be treated with the equality and respect they deserve?"

"Now that's what I like to hear. Finally. A college student advocating *for* soldiers. Especially after what happened today in Ohio." The Commander's voice sounded stern. He marched to the soldiers guarding the flags.

"Ladies and Gentlemen." His voice boomed. Soldiers stood at attention. So did the guests. "I've opened the portico for your use. It's cooler and closer to the Receiving Line. Lieutenant Hayes, direct the guests to enter quickly. There are still VIPs arriving including our special guest. I expect an orderly re-formation."

Fifteen

Tangerine and hot pink Gerber daisies blossomed from crystal vases in the center of each table in the ballroom. Prisms dazzled from chandeliers. Swags of daisies formed a daisy chain that draped over the yellow and white bunting in the front of the dais.

Tally smiled. Within the word, *daisy*, is the word, *dais*. She couldn't wait to tell Tess Hamper, the famed author of the *Within the Word* books, of her "aha," even though Tally's favorite book of Tess's would always be the one titled *Within the Word "Sacred" is the Word "Scared."*

"Larry. It's so cheerful. I wish Chaucer could see this now."

"Chaucer? *The Canterbury Tales* guy?"

"Yes. The English Daisy was his favorite flower." Tally noticed the Sergeant's perplexed look. "I should have mentioned before. I'm in the Chaucer sorority at Hamper University. The daisy is our sorority flower."

"All I know is they choose a decoration each year that connects to the Gala Queen. Bet that's why they've stuck daisies in everything they could find."

Tally chewed peach gloss from her bottom lip. She remembered Walter Cronkite's voice on the CBS Evening News an hour ago. He had reported the story of a girl sticking a daisy in the barrel of a gun held by a National Guardsman at Kent State. Walter Cronkite stated the girl told the soldier, *"Flowers are better than bullets."* He also stated that she was believed to be one of the students killed today.

"Tally, my escort duties are complete. It was a true pleasure to meet you."

"Larry, thank you. It's so great to meet a friend of Shawl's." Tally shook his hand before squeezing it tight. "Goodness, I almost forgot. Two things. One. You aren't from Georgia, are you?"

"New Jersey." He made Jersey sound as if he had marbles in his mouth.

"Lovely, Larry. It's just that folks in Georgia don't ever say, 'Hold the fort.'"

"And guys in New Jersey don't ever say, 'how come,' but how come?"

Tally smiled. "We don't say 'Hold the fort' because it's a phrase first used by William Tecumseh Sherman. And, trust me, no one from Georgia *ever* quotes Sherman. So, I thought you might want to know. Second. What is Operation Graphic Hand?"

He grinned.

"First, good reconnaissance on Sherman. Didn't study The Civil War much in Jersey."

"Really?" Tally had heard that from Rye too. Why do Yankees not study a war where 620,000 men died, the costs were astronomical, and the South was left in ruins?

"Second. Operation Graphic Hand? Remember the National Postal Workers' strike? Back in March? Unprecedented. Got to give it to those mailmen. They stood their ground for more cash. President Nixon had to call in National Guard and Army troops to deliver the mail." The Sergeant leaned closer. "Overwhelmed. That's what we were. Mail is still being found and delivered. Checks, letters, bills. It's a mess."

What was he talking about?

March 1970.

Could that have been a busier month?

Becca's engagement tea hosted by Chaucerettes at the Country Club. Hot pants and bikini shopping for the Spring Break cruise to the Caribbean. Sorority initiation and the delivery of too much white gauze for the ceremony. Oh, my gosh. Maybe the manufacturer never got the letter canceling the original order. The pressure from Mike Parish to go all the way. Breaking up with him because she was not ready to do *that*. Wishing she could explain to him how she would only do *that* with someone she truly loved as her sweetheart but she would never want to hurt Mike's feelings.

"But, Larry, we've been getting mail. Was it only happening in the North?"

"That's where it was the worst. But letters from overseas are still being sorted."

"You mean it is possible Shawl has written and his letters are—"

"In New York. Where it all started."

Tally wanted to squeal.

She hugged Larry.

"Could this night get any better?"

By the time the band played "The Caissons Keep Rolling Along," followed by "The Star-Spangled Banner," and a recitation of the Pledge of Allegiance, Tally was ready to bite her fingernails or bum a cigarette from Khaki.

Commander Hemming instructed everyone to continue standing. He ordered those in uniform to repeat the Soldier's Creed.

Chaplain Cane offered the invocation. The word, *amen*, had barely been uttered when an army of waiters, all Black men wearing white uniforms and gloves, attacked their duties with precision. Tally waved to Winston and Franklin as they rushed past the dais. Winston winked. Franklin nodded.

In succession, the waiters offered wine, shrimp cocktail appetizers, Waldorf salads, rib roast, fried chicken, sweet potato soufflé, butter beans with herb-butter melting on top, fried okra, black-eyed peas with bacon, and pitchers of sweet tea for each table.

Tally looked around the room. Where was Daddy? She felt a pain in her side. He would only be late if, wait, did something happen to Mother during her trip to Paris?

Too worried to eat, she made table talk with the Commander. He told her he had just gotten word that President Nixon had cancelled his trip to join Governor Lester Maddox at the Stone Mountain ceremonies in Atlanta.

"Why would he--?" Tally saw Rye escort Becca to the place where a photographer took her picture with Sergeant Cook who must surely be proud to pose next to Shawl's fiancée.

"Kent State. The President needs to stay in Washington. He's sending Agnew instead. National Guard troops are ready if Blacks boycott the festivities."

Tally sipped sweet tea. The United Daughters of the Confederacy might boycott Agnew since the UDC had paid for the giant carvings of General Lee, Stonewall Jackson and Confederate President Jefferson Davis on the monument and expected President Nixon to be there. There had been pictures in the paper for a week showing UDC ladies getting ready for "Tea and Teacakes" with the President.

By the time desserts arrived, she was starving. Presented a choice between lemon meringue pie and Georgia Thirteen-Layer caramel cake, a delicacy of the thinnest layers beloved by Georgians in homage to their state being the last of the Thirteen Original Colonies, she chose both. Soon it would be time for her to speak. She tasted the caramel frosting melt in her mouth, one sugar crystal after another. Oh, my lord. Please let this cake be on a buffet line in Heaven.

She searched for the table where her friends were sitting. Thank goodness for Rye's suit. Abruptly, she asked Commander Hemming to excuse her. He stood and pulled out her chair. Gliding between tables, she acknowledged congratulations. Finally, she paused at the table where the diners, her friends, began to clap.

"Thank you, kind subjects." She laughed. "Enjoying dinner?"

Everyone, most with mouths full, nodded, smiled, or said, "Delicious." Becca squeezed her hand. Tally rubbed Becca's shoulders.

"Just think, Becca. Mother will be home from Paris next week with winter wedding dresses for the boutique. You'll choose the fanciest one and be ready to marry that brother of mine when he's home for good in December."

Becca laughed. "Won't he be surprised? Wait. Tally. Someone said the surprise guest might be—No, no. You have to guess. A native Georgian, a former Marine who walked with Dr. King, his fellow Georgian, in Selma."

Tally's eyelashes, lush with violet mascara, fluttered like hummingbird wings. "Becca? No! I'm going to scream. Are you serious? Could it be? Truly him?"

"That's the rumor. Pernell Roberts. Would you die if you got your picture taken with Adam Cartwright himself? You, the biggest *Bonanza* fan on the planet."

"Becca." Tally felt her pulse throb against her choker. "Don't tease. I could faint."

Tally took a sip of Becca's lemon water, picked up a Gala Program, and fanned herself. She leaned over the table, twirling her hair around her index finger.

"Excuse me, Rye. May I speak with you please? In private?"

Woo-hoos erupted from the table. Tally's cheeks turned as pink as the Gerber daisies. She grinned and pleaded, "Shush, fellas."

Rye scooped her hand in his. They walked out the side door into the cool night air. The smell of cigarette smoke lingered from stubs glowing in a bucket of sand.

"Everything okay?"

"Rye, you, just being here, makes it okay. Good grief. Daddy's not here yet. Mother's in Paris. Shawl's in Vietnam." Tally sniffed, accepting the handkerchief Rye pulled from his pocket. "Thank you for being here, Rye. You know, I remember what you said on the beach that night we were alone. You said there's one sure way to know if a person is feeling confident. You said, 'Give a person a compliment and see if 'thank you' is his or her first response.' Remember?"

"Merci beaucoup, Georgia." His lips kissed her hand. "And how could I forget? That night. The beach. Your yellow dress slit up the side."

She laughed. "Thank you for remembering that detail, Mr. Somerset. Seriously, Rye, you compliment me just by being here. Your presence comforts me in ways I can't express. I want you to know, Rye. I feel more confident when you are near me."

In the darkness, in the quiet, she heard his low, husky voice whispering her name. She felt his arms tug her close in a swirl of sensations before she tasted a hint of caramel on his lips, triggering a blush of tickles across hers. She could not wait for the Gala to be over so they could be alone. Only the sound of the band playing "Ruffles and Flourishes," the signal for the speeches to begin, could force her lips from the force of his.

Sixteen

"Distinguished guests," Commander Hemming began his opening remarks. "I welcome you to the annual Fort Hamper Military Gala. Tonight, we say thank you to Betty "BeeBee" Persons, our 1969 Gala Queen who will remind us of her 'Queen's Quote' that guided her through this year. Will everyone please applaud Miss Betty Persons, daughter of Mayor Buddy Rod Persons?"

Betty "BeeBee" Persons, a blonde beauty, former "Miss Georgia" runner-up and cousin of Truman Capote, waved from her place on the dais next to Mrs. Hemming as the band played bars from "Sweet Georgia Brown." Lifting the microphone from its stand, Betty looked as if she were about to sing. Instead, she thanked the Commander, Mrs. Hemming, the soldiers, her parents and her fiancé.

"My 'Queen's Quote' was a favorite lyric from one of the songs I sang in the talent portion of my first 'Miss Georgia' pageant. 'I Say a Little Prayer for You' is still my pledge to all soldiers everywhere."

Betty blew kisses and hugged Tally.

Commander Hemming replaced the microphone. His voice boomed. "Thank you, Betty, for your service and your prayers. Now I'd like to introduce our 1970 Gala Queen who is the first young lady to serve while one of her family is currently serving. Her older brother, PFC Shaw Philippe McCall, who completed his basic training at Fort Hamper, is presently serving the United States of America as a member of Delta Force in South Vietnam."

The crowd cheered.

"Ladies and Gentlemen, please welcome a young lady who served admirably as Honorary Lt. Colonel in the ROTC Program at Hamper High School. A young lady majoring in Georgia History at Hamper University. A young lady who won the 1968 Miss Georgia Peach Majorette Award. A young lady with a sterling reputation. A young lady with impressive recommendations. A young lady we can be proud to welcome to our military family of service. It is my pleasure to introduce the Queen of the 1970 Fort Hamper Gala, Miss Tally Gigi McCall, who will offer a few comments and her Queen's Quote before our special guest arrives and the dancing begins."

The crowd applauded. A few whistles shrilled the air.

Tally stood and turned to thank Commander Hemming. His eyes, however, looked past her. He popped up from his seat and bellowed into the microphone.

"Excuse me, Miss McCall. Two important people should also be mentioned. Tally and Shawl's parents. Georgia Federal Court Judge and retired Army Lieutenant who not only landed on the beach at Arromanches during D-Day but also brought home to Georgia his most beautiful conquest, his lovely wife. Ladies and Gentlemen, please welcome Delphi and Babette McCall."

The crowd stood, clapping enthusiastically. The band played "Over There."

Tally twirled. She squeezed Rye's monogrammed handkerchief, turned and saw her mother walking toward her with a bouquet of white gardenias, the flowers she always offered a bride to sniff when nervous.

"*Maman?* Oh, my gosh, how can you—oh, you're here."

"*Cherie*, I wouldn't miss this for the world."

"*Maman*, the best surprise. I-I can't believe."

Their words overlapped the way their arms did when they hugged. Her father gave her a kiss on the forehead.

"Sorry we're late, Shug. Plane was delayed. Trust you know I'm mighty proud of my girl."

Tally stepped to the microphone after her parents and the crowd were seated. She felt even more giddy and more at peace than she had felt all day. The pungent-sweet aroma of gardenias propped atop the podium energized her.

"Commander Hemming, thank you so much."

The commander interrupted once again.

"Ladies and Gentlemen, I have also just received a note from Jax Boudreaux, the Managing Editor of *The Hamper Herald*, that Miss McCall, an intern at the paper, was nominated today to be the first recipient of the prestigious Oglethorpe-Oxford History Honor. Looks like our Queen is beautiful like her mother and smart like her daddy."

Laughter and applause erupted.

Tally blushed. Mr. Boudreaux brought that to Commander Hemming's attention? Today my life changes, for sure. She grinned at her parents who blew kisses to her. She searched the room and saw a man with an Afro placing a plate of hushpuppies, watermelon and cake in front of the girl who pointed to her pregnancy earlier.

"Thank you, everyone. Thank you, Commander Hemming, and thank you so much, Mr. Boudreaux, sir."

Should she say it? Yes.

"And Ladies and Gentlemen, would you please applaud also for Mr. Winston Churchill Crockett who is here with us tonight. He and I were both nominated today for the Oglethorpe-Oxford History Honor to earn a graduate degree in history at Oxford. Winston, would you please join me?"

The crowd pivoted in their seats. Winston's Afro glistened under the prismatic light. He sauntered to the dais. The audience clapped politely and murmured.

Mr. Moretti stood up so abruptly at *The Hamper Herald* guest table, his chair toppled over. He positioned himself in front of the podium, clicked pictures of Tally and Winston, her shoulder next to the middle of Winston's arm.

Becca, Virginia, Khaki, Phoebe, Rayleigh, Rye, Jimbo, and Travis stood and cheered. Louie stayed seated. Winston nodded, shook Commander Hemming's hand, waved to the audience, and said, "Thank you" into the microphone.

Turning, he whispered in Tally's ear, "*This* is your first act as Queen, girl? Good golly, Molly." He squeezed her hand and strode toward the kitchen.

Tally sipped water and began her speech.

"It is a privilege to be named your Gala Queen and an honor to represent Fort Hamper at charity and social events this year. I follow in BeeBee's, I mean, Betty Persons' footsteps and appreciate her sweet encouragement."

Betty blew Tally a kiss.

"Thank you also for your kind introduction and bright surprise of acknowledgement, Commander Hemming. Thank you, Mother and Daddy, for all you did to be here tonight."

She looked at Commander Hemming. "Not only do I agree with you, sir, that my mother is beautiful and my daddy is smart. However, I also cheer my mother for being a brilliant businesswoman and my daddy for being mighty handsome too."

The crowd laughed. Mrs. Hemming, fluttering the fan Tally gave her, folded it and tapped her husband's shoulder.

Commander Hemming lifted his glass. "I wholeheartedly agree, Miss McCall."

"Thank you, sir." Tally smiled. "Thank you also to my brother Shawl and each of you who serve our country through military service. I especially want to thank Travis Brinkley who is here with us tonight. Let's please raise a glass to him as a welcome for his safe return home."

Travis waved. The crowd cheered.

"Thank you also to one of my two special guests joining us tonight, Private Second-Class Gus Garner who served as one of the peacekeeping forces in Tokyo after the surrender. Today he serves as an important member of *The Hamper Herald* staff." The audience clapped as she signaled for Gus to stand. He did with his hand over his heart.

"And thank you," her voice sounded reverent, "to each family member and sweetheart waiting for a letter or a postcard from a distant land. John Milton once wrote a sonnet titled *On His Blindness* that ended with these words, *'They also serve who only stand and wait,'* and tonight, I especially want to honor Mr. Lastings Livingston Bentley who is here with us. Mr. Bentley, our treasured friend and colleague at *The Hamper Herald*, is the most devoted soldier of the "stand and wait" brigade. And, Mr. Bentley, Commander Hemming has a surprise for you. Would you please stand, sir?"

Commander Hemming lifted his glass.

"Mr. Bentley, for conducting yourself through the years as one of the most honorable citizens in Hamper, for supporting our troops with your taxes, for your volunteer work, for your Red Cross tapes sent to soldiers in Vietnam, we thank you for your service. Furthermore, to grant the first official request of our new Gala Queen and with the appreciation of Fort Hamper officers, I am honored to present you with our first Medal of Valor for Citizen-Soldiers."

Applause erupted. Mr. Bentley, dressed in a yellow linen suit, stood and saluted the Commander who signaled to soldiers to escort Mr. Bentley to the stage. Tess blew a kiss to Tally. Boudreaux pointed to Tally and nodded. Tally felt tears puddle in her eyes as Mr. Bentley accepted the silver medallion boasting red, white and blue ribbons. His smile beamed bright. The crinkled lines on his cheeks looked like pink rivers as he blushed. He thanked the Commander, Tally and the crowd.

The band struck up the chorus of "For He's a Jolly Good Fellow." Commander Hemming welcomed Tally back to the podium.

Tally touched her onyx fob. Soon she would be called on to give her speech. Should she say what she really wanted to say? Should she be more cautious? Quotes raced through her mind. She saw Franklin pouring coffee into a cup at a nearby table and made her decision.

"Distinguished guests, I was asked to offer a quote to be inscribed on the Queen's Plaque, a quote dear to me that may inspire you too. There were lots I liked. Yet I kept coming back to one that is a favorite of my brother Shawl, who was a philosophy major, I mean, who *is* a philosophy graduate student earning his Doctorate in Philosophy when he comes home."

She glanced at her parents. Her mother's head was resting on her father's shoulder. Her father nodded.

She sniffed the gardenias.

"The quote is by Shawl's favorite Greek philosopher, Heraclitus, who observed that *'You can never step into the same river twice.'* Of course, anybody who has stepped into the Hamper River knows your feet are always going to sink into soft warm mud, no matter how many times you step into it." She flipped the ends of her hair and paused as people smiled and nodded. "Yet, my brother explained to me that each time you step into any river you will also be older and the river will be too. A river cannot stay the same. Neither can we."

She glanced at *The Hamper Herald* table and saw Mr. Boudreaux twirling his finger to speed it up.

Stuttering, she said, "Just-just-the-the other day, I was talking with my friend Franklin who asked if I knew the story of *The Peach Blossom Spring* and I wonder if anyone here knows that story?"

Tally grinned as she saw Franklin raise his hand. She wanted to recognize him yet worried he would be embarrassed in front of the crowd if she did. He smiled a big smile, as if hearing his name was the greatest surprise. His handsome grin reminded her of his exuberance when he took bow after bow at the end of the play, *The Wrong Brothers.*

"Happily, Franklin Roosevelt Crockett is here with us." She clapped as others looked around and applauded as if in slow motion. Franklin waved.

"Franklin, would you be kind enough to join me?"

Franklin took long strides to the podium. Commander Hemming looked apoplectic. Mrs. Hemming batted the fan about her face and cleared her throat loudly.

When Franklin reached Tally, he poured her a cup of coffee and turned to leave.

"Thank you, Franklin. Ladies and gentlemen, Franklin Crockett. Franklin and his twin brother Winston just happen to be my favorite storytellers. So, Franklin, would you be kind enough to tell us the story of *The Peach Blossom Spring?*"

Franklin dutifully changed places with Tally. Instead of speaking, he bowed to the Commander and to the crowd. He approached the microphone and bent down to its height.

"My brother says taking a bow is not just about folks clapping for you. He says it's about thanking folks in a real respectful way."

Franklin raised the microphone and stood straighter. He began speaking without hesitation, as if he were just taking direction as an actor again, only this time from Tally instead of Winston.

"A long time ago, there was this fisherman rowing down a river looking for the best fishing hole. He kept rowing and rowing and, before too long, the river started changing. Smelling better. Looking brighter. He could see all the way to the bottom. The fisherman saw bass and trout swimming ahead of him as if they were leading the way. The fisherman felt so happy. His arms weren't even sore. All of a sudden, there was this bend in the river and peach blossoms everywhere. Trees so pink, so summer-sweet smelling, he thought he was surely in Georgia during a peach festival."

Commander Hemming chuckled. Others smiled and nodded.

"Well, the people by the peach trees were all kinds of folks. Short, tall. Young, old. Men, ladies, children. Different colors of skin. Different homelands. And every single one of them was really happy. Smiles on their faces bright as sunshine."

Franklin pointed to Tally. "That's what I call Tally. Sunshine. Even when she isn't wearing a yellow dress."

Tally blushed and whispered, "Thank you, Frankie."

"The fisherman stepped onto the sand. He felt welcomed like a long-lost cousin at a family reunion. He asked where he was and learned he was in a utopia, a place where folks are kind, where folks look after each other and laugh a lot, a place where, the folks told him, outside problems do not float down the river to their homes and do not weigh down the air they breathe. Most of all, there is no war in a utopia. Only peace and peaches which Tally always says is the only fruit that has all the letters of the word *peace* in it."

Coughs were heard in the ballroom.

Franklin continued in a quieter voice, "The fisherman left to get back to his house and family. He told everyone about this place that reminded him of the best day he ever lived. Ever since, for years and years, fishermen would put their boats in that river and row until their arms tuckered out, trying to find that *Peach Blossom Spring* place, the place that seemed like heaven. But no one could find it. But every fisherman knows. Fishing is really about patience. So, we just reckon one day one of us will find it, 'cause it's out there. It's out there."

Franklin's voice trailed off. He seemed mesmerized by the twinkling facets of the chandelier. The ballroom hushed. Tally clapped as Franklin lowered the microphone.

"Thank you, Franklin." She shook his hand before giving him a hug.

She could hear Mrs. Hemming say, "Well, I never. Talking about peace during wartime. Unheard of. And how many more colored people are coming up on this stage?"

Tally remembered what her daddy always said. *The best way to get out of a tight jam is to use a crowbar of appreciation.*

"Commander and Mrs. Hemming, and distinguished guests, thank you for being so generous to me tonight. Thank you for welcoming Winston and celebrating his achievement. Thank you for welcoming Franklin as you so kindly did and listening to his story. Even though fishermen through the years stepped into the same river, it was not the same river as it was on that idyllic day in the story. The fishermen who tried to find the *Peach Blossom Spring* could not find the utopia. Yet they did not stop trying. They did not stop being restless. Oh, one other thing."

Tally's eyes searched for Rye. He lifted his glass. She wished she could throw her baton in the air about a dozen times just to release the energy streaking through her body.

"Franklin learned this story that originated in China from a Vietnam veteran, Private Gainty, a native of Hamper, who heard it while he was in Saigon. Private Gainty told Franklin that peach blossoms are treasured in Vietnam. He told Franklin how seeing peach trees on a distant hill comforted him when he was in the jungle. He told Franklin that the weather was just as hot, the mosquitoes were just as big, the rivers were just as muddy in Vietnam as they are in Georgia and that made him feel like Vietnam and Georgia have a whole lot in common, including, peach blossoms blooming every Spring and, as every Georgia school student knows, Georgia was originally intended to be a utopia too."

"Thank you, Commander Hemming, for the honor of being your 1970 Gala Queen. I hope to represent all of you as best I can. In conclusion, I give honor to four people whom I will never meet yet will always remember: William, Sandy, Allison and Jeffrey." She had heard Walter Cronkite confirm the names of the four students killed at Kent State moments before she departed for the event.

The crowd hesitated as if trying to figure out who the four people were. A murmur swept across the dais with dignitaries and soldiers saying their names.

Tess Hamper stood and applauded.

Mr. Boudreaux followed suit.

Rye stood, grinned and applauded.

The crowd began to cheer.

Tally looked at her parents who were beaming.

Her mother was blowing kisses.

Standing beside Commander Hemming, Tally awaited the arrival of General Carlyle and the Gala's special guest after the two of them finished their private dinner in the Brigadier's Club.

The rumor in the ballroom made her spellbound with hope. If only the guest could be her favorite TV star who played Adam Cartwright, Ben Cartwright's eldest son on *Bonanza*, and who was Georgia's favorite son, Pernell Roberts, from Waycross, Georgia. If she could meet him, shake his hand, hear his voice which reminded her of Rye's voice, she could die happy and go to heaven right now.

The crowd hushed. She heard footsteps. The profiles of her parents and others on the dais blocked her view. She heard someone gasp. She glimpsed shiny black shoes before they disappeared behind the black curtain. The curtain billowed at her back.

Commander Hemming stuck his head through an opening of the curtain. Mr. Moretti gave the signal. Commander Hemming's baritone voice boomed across the ballroom as he asked Tally to turn and greet the Military Gala's special guest, the Honorable Governor of the State of Georgia, Lester Garfield Maddox.

The moment the flashbulb popped she knew. She knew she would regret this moment the rest of her life. She couldn't speak. The Queen's scepter Governor Maddox held in his hand looked like the pickaxe handle with which he threatened to beat Negroes when they tried to dine at his restaurant years ago.

In that split second, surrounded by military officers and a governor, she had no choice to say 'Stop.' She had no voice to protest. She had no words that would matter or change the way things were.

Mr. Moretti shot her again and again.

Early the next morning, after fitful dreams of slow dancing and deep kisses with Rye interrupted by gunfire like staccato sounds of typewriters, and waking up in a panic about the O-O Honor essay she needed to write, Tally tugged on her peignoir and scooped the newspaper from the driveway of the Chaucer House before anyone else was awake.

She popped the rubber band off *The Hamper Herald* and opened the paper.

On the front page, in an unprecedented sight, there were three pictures of her: a picture of her smiling with a group of men behind her in the *Meet the Staff* photo and a picture of her smiling with a group of girls dressed in ROTC uniforms surrounding her at the Georgia Glen Cabin.

In the center of the page was also a picture of a lifeless-looking girl, clutching gardenias, a scepter and a medal as the new Fort Hamper Gala Queen. Next to that picture was a girl with shock on her face and outstretched arms over the body of a dead student in a parking lot at Kent State.

She felt distraught as she looked at the boy face down on the pavement. It was Jeffrey Miller, according to the caption, the first student killed. A dark stream of blood trailed from his throat. The image, raw, shocking, heartbreaking, staggered her.

She ripped the page into tiny pieces. How dare this young man's lifeless body be viewed by strangers! Her palms turned black from newsprint. Confetti scattered in the breeze.

Still, the agony on the face of the girl at Kent State haunted her. The face of the other girl at the Gala, her own face, looked stunned. The only connection she could see in their expressions was that they both looked helpless without power to change the past, the present or the future.

Seventeen

Tally closed the door to the Initiation Room and glanced at the clock. 11:08 a.m. on Monday, June 1st, 1970. She placed her baton on the chiffarobe. Meandering through panels of shimmery gauze hanging from ropes high above her, she skimmed her fingers over the soft fabric. Flickers of déjà vu sparked memories.

Gliding through sheets hanging on laundry cords in her grandmother's backyard in Arromanches, France was one of her happiest childhood moments. The smell of sunshine on cotton. The feeling of no one being able to see her as she hid between the sheets. The popping crack when breezes flapped the fabric. The bumpy feel of wrinkles before the sheets were ironed. The memory of the pillowcase that puffed when its tethers snapped and blew away one morning like a pink cotton balloon.

Sitting on the shag rug amidst the gauze, she remembered her grandmother laughing that the pillowcase was *"emporté par le vent"* or "gone with the wind."

That phrase was reminiscent of Margaret Mitchell's childhood too. Her travels in a buggy with her aunt to see the ruins of plantations in Georgia revealed an era that was 'gone with the wind.' Tally marveled that Margaret Mitchell was born on November 8th, or "11-08," in 1900 on her parents' eighth wedding anniversary and forty-nine years later, Miss Mitchell was struck by a car on Peachtree Street in Atlanta, on August 11th, "08-11," in 1949.

Tally had studied all she could about the Georgia author of *Gone with the Wind* in the *Encyclopedia Britannica* as well as from newspaper clippings at the library. She was struck by the fact that Miss Mitchell and her husband, John Marsh, were on their way to see the movie, *A Canterbury Tale*, when a car swerved, skidded, and hit Miss Mitchell. She was taken to Grady Memorial Hospital where she died five days later on August 16th, 1949.

Tally had read that Grady Hospital would be celebrating its birthday today with a cake and balloons in the lobby. The Hospital had opened its doors on June 1st, 1892, seventy-eight years ago, with one hundred beds, fifty reserved for Black patients and fifty reserved for White patients. Grady Hospital is also where the Black medical students, for whom Miss Mitchell "anonymously" afforded scholarships, went to school.

Tally's scholarship to Oxford, if she won the O-O Honor, would afford her the opportunity to visit Canterbury and Kent where Chaucer was once Justice of the Peace. Kent and Peace. Kent State and Peace. Four weeks ago, on a long-ago Monday, the students were rallying for peace. She promised never to forget them.

She had also promised Miss Perry, who was visiting her sister's horse ranch in Kentucky before the sisters traveled to Royal Ascot festivities for six weeks, that she would stop by the Chaucer Sorority House to check on Miss Perry's gardenia bushes and open the windows in the suites upstairs, especially the turret, at least weekly.

Officially, the sorority house was closed until the first of August each year. The only exception was for the reunion of Chaucerette alums and resident Chaucerettes staying in the house during the week of celebrations around the fourth of July.

Lula had the summer off with pay "just like the professors at the college," she would tell her friends and family. Phoebe was taking a poetry class in France. Their absence left Tally as the designated senior sorority officer in Hamper.

Trying to write her essay for the Oglethorpe-Oxford History Honor, Tally found there was no better place than sitting in the Initiation Room in her favorite velvet chair.

Under the glow of a Tiffany-lamp she could study uninterrupted. The soft whirr of a ceiling fan floated the gauze panels in the air as if they were ghosts. Finally, Tally could settle and read her autographed copy of *Hamper*, the Pulitzer Prize-winning non-fiction book by Tess Hamper written when Tess was just twenty-two years old.

Tess had first earned national notoriety when she wrote in *Hamper*:

"Southern women did not faint because Clark Gable as Rhett Butler said to Vivien Leigh as Scarlett, 'Frankly, my dear, I don't give a damn' during the premiere of *Gone with the Wind* at Loew's Grand Theater in Atlanta, as it was reported in newspapers all across the country. What assumptions, stereotypes and lazy journalism. The truth? It was hot as hell in that theater with all the women wearing furs in December and every seat filled and the heat turned up high for four hours. Good God Almighty. No Southern woman is offended by hearing the word, 'damn.' We've been calling Northerners 'damn Yankees' for years. What was really offensive was not the word, "damn," but the fact that newspapers were so condescending to the intelligence and fortitude of women in the South after all they have survived and endured."

The quote, in its entirety, was featured on the back jacket of the book and discussed in every interview Tess would allow. It surely helped Tess's book become a bestseller.

Tally laughed reading the passage again. Ahhh. Tessie. She sure knew how to stand up for what she believed even as a young woman.

"Still does." Tally stretched and riffed a quick twirl of her baton through her fingers. With all the writing and typing ahead of her, she needed to keep her fingers nimble.

Of course, all her friends were enjoying summer, getting suntans, shopping summer sales in Atlanta, flying to Paris to take cooking classes, driving to Pawley's Island for a girls' weekend, vacationing in Venice, purchasing an array of pastel leather gloves to give as Big Sister-Little Sister gifts, and attending bridal teas at the Club.

Yet, here she was, still trying to understand history.

Rifling through record albums she stored in the Initiation Room including ones from Diana Ross and the Supremes, Jerry Butler, Creedence Clearwater Revival, Glen Campbell, and The Temptations, she chose her favorite, dropped the needle on the vinyl and sunk into the velvet chair as if in a dreamy cocoon with gauze all around.

The piano intro led to the voice of Elvis singing her favorite song about wise men and fools. She had listened to his *Blue Hawaii* album and the song, "Can't Help Falling in Love," so many times already, she began to wonder if she should write her essay on the flowing river

Elvis sang about, like the one in the legend of *The Peach Blossom Spring* or about Heraclitus.

Should she say something profound about how the colony of Georgia didn't rush in to join the other colonies when they declared independence from England?

Should she state that Georgia was the only one of the original thirteen colonies to refuse to declare independence from England in 1777, yet when all the other colonies "seceded" from England, Georgia did not call them "treasonous?"

Or should she focus on how wise men in Georgia were pioneers in allowing eighteen-year-olds to vote in 1943, long before other states agreed to do so?

Amidst studying how Scottish settlers had influenced the culture of Georgia in ways that were different than the influences of the Dutch and the Germans in the North, while also looking up information about her own Scottish ancestors, the McCall Clan, all she truly wanted to do was rush into Rye's arms and stay there for one whole night, just the two of them.

She felt too restless to study. Climbing the grand staircase, Tally could smell wisps of perfumes, Shalimar, L'Air du Temps, Chanel No. 5, even Jean Naté lemon shampoo, still lingering in the suites.

Lula had warned the girls year after year that spritzing perfumes too close to the curtains or while sitting on the plush window seats would defeat the purpose of fresh air coming into the rooms through plantation shutters.

"Spritz those perfumes close to your skin, rub your wrists together or spray the perfume on your bra and panties when you get out of the shower. Just don't splatter those oils on cotton fabric or I'll never get 'em out."

Now the scents just reminded Tally of her sorority sisters and how much she missed them. Stroking her fingers on one of the pale blue French desks, she felt soothed to be surrounded by the yellow striped wallpaper, gold-leaf mirror frames, photos from softball games played in the quad, and of bonfires on the beach.

The closer she got to the turret, the more Tally smelled paints and pottery clay, a whiff of art glue, and an Arts & Crafts room that needed airing out. She unlatched windows, lifted a pink Hula Hoop over her head and started swaying her hips in a circle.

One of her favorite majorette exercise routines was swirling a Hula Hoop around her waist. Not only did the movements keep her waist toned for the tight costumes she needed to wear but she also believed her hips could somehow appreciate, as they undulated in pronounced Figure Eights, what it might feel like to be gyrating as if a baton.

Ahhh. Thigmonasty.

Professor Logan would be so proud.

Even when some ladies at her church said it was disconcerting to see majorettes dressed scandalously in their tight, skimpy outfits and boots when cheerleaders were much more wholesome in their darling knee-length skirts, letter sweaters and Rah-Rah shoes, Tally had found the courage at age sixteen to intervene.

She reminded them that cheerleaders did not whip flaming sticks around their bodies and have to worry about bulky clothes catching fire.

The ladies had sniffed and pursed their lips. They countered that a cheerleader's biggest fear was not fire but a boy cheerleader looking up her skirt while holding her high in the air.

Tally had grinned and agreed. That *would* be worse.

As Tally reached for the latch to close the turret window, she heard seagulls squawking furiously. Grabbing binoculars from a shelf, she saw a male figure sitting on a sandbar. He threw what looked like an envelope in the ocean.

"Oh, my lord!" She dropped the binoculars and rushed to the mansion's tunnel.

Rolling her Capri pants to her knees, Tally swished through warm water trickling through the trough that splashed at her ankle bracelet as she approached the sandbar.

"Hey, Frankie! Didn't want to scare you." Tally fanned her straw hat at a gull. "Do you mind if I join you and the gulls or do you want to be by yourself?"

She really wanted to ask, "How on earth did you get to the sandbar?" considering the lack of access except from the private Chaucer Beach.

However, she waited for Frankie to nod toward the sand before she sat with her legs to the side.

"Just needing a place to think."

Tally inhaled briny air and closed her eyes. Respecting Franklin's need for quiet allowed her time to respect her own. The warmth, the steady sound of waves, the occasional squawk of a seagull soothed her to her core. She did not realize how focused she had been on her essay and how anxious she was about seeing Rye again until she was forced to sit in the sunshine and relax.

"Wondering how I got here?" Frankie's voice seemed far away as she nestled her head on her hat.

"You don't have to tell me, Frankie." Tally yawned. "Lay down, just take a little nap."

"Tally. Tally!" He shook her arm. "Wake up. Can't sleep on a sandbar, Sunshine. Remember those two girls in the news last week? Swam out to a sandbar. Fell asleep. Only one body was ever found."

Tally blinked and lifted her head. She remembered. You could not live in Hamper during the summer without hearing on the evening news about teens, especially tourists, sunbathing on sandbars, falling asleep and drowning or tempting fate by leaving the 'bar too late and being sucked into the undertow. She imagined that is what happened to the couple, now called the "Sunset Sandbar Sweethearts," for they had never been found.

She wished she had a vanilla fountain Coke with lots of crushed ice.

"Frankie, let's talk about something happy. How's Lydette?"

"Broke up last night."

"Oh, gosh, Frankie. I'm so sorry." She could not stop a yawn. "There's another lucky girl out there, Frankie. Promise."

He bent his head, shaking it slowly from side to side.

What could cheer him?

"Hey, Handsome. Want to meet me at the library so we can study together for your Summer School classes? I can help you with history and other things too. And we can get a grape snow cone afterwards."

"Wish I could, Sunshine." Franklin scooped wet sand, squeezed it in a ball and hurled it in a high arc, as if a gritty rainbow, into the ocean. "Look. You know how you like it when I'm frank?"

Tally nodded, worried what she might hear next.

"Got my grades. Three F's and one D. Can't show 'em to Mama. She'll never see 'em now. Shoot. She'll never see me again if I don't figure out what—"

"Frankie. Hold on. What's your average? You didn't flunk out, did you?"

"It means I don't even qualify for the first month of Summer School. I have to take a test to try to get into the second month. Going to lose my deferment if I'm not in school or get married which won't happen now or get the grades that keep me--shoot, it's not even worth talking about."

Franklin moved closer to Tally as water crept to his feet.

"Franklin. You're scaring me." She touched his arm.

"Promise not to tell Mama?"

"Promise."

"Got a call-up letter too. Telling me to get ready." His voice seemed choked with sadness.

"Oh, Frankie. That breaks my heart. What did Winston say?"

"He said something I can't repeat to you, Sunshine."

"Frankie, how did you get on the sandbar?"

"Just saw the gulls on the 'bar from Papa's shrimp boat. That's when I told Papa I needed some thinking time. He said he'd get as close as he could so I could swim to the 'bar and sit with the gulls for a while." Tally noticed how quiet the gulls were when Franklin spoke. "Papa said he'd wait but I told him, 'nah, I'll climb the dune, grab that Historical Marker up there, pull myself up and help Mama at the shrimp stand." Franklin tugged at his shirt. "Already dry."

"Frankie, we better go. Sandbar's shrinking. Gulls are flying to the mimosas. And you're not grabbing that Marker, Mister Crockett. You're my guest and you can walk across our beach to get to the Park."

Franklin grinned for the first time, his hand tapping his shoulder.

"Hop on my back. Give you a ride. No need you getting your pants wet too."

Eighteen

After stroking Canter Berry's neck as Chaucerettes always did for good luck, Tally exited through the wrought iron gate and opened the door of her yellow MGB convertible parked on the cul-de-sac of Poet's Row. With the sorority house closed for the summer and no parking attendant on duty, it was safer to park on the street rather than navigate the meandering driveway in the bright sun to the private parking lot bordering Hamper Park.

Placing her shoulder bag, books and baton on the passenger seat, she had no time to dash gloss on her lips.

That night she would be back at the Chaucer House to join the girls arriving from their trips to attend their "Daring Daisies" secret meeting on the beach. She had to hurry if she was going to find Winston and get back to the sorority house with fixings for campfire s'mores.

Pressing the clutch with her left foot, she pushed the accelerator with her right, steered around pink azaleas in the circle median, admired their bright color and feathery blooms, and skidded as she almost hit a car entering the roundabout.

"Careful!" The male driver with long, dark hair to his shoulders, shouted.

Tally, already unnerved by her conversation with Franklin, tried to shift gears while pushing the clutch and the accelerator yet the car seemed stuck. Good grief.

"Need help?" The male driver approached her car.

She turned the key to the "off" position.

"Thank you so much." How embarrassing. No Lip Gloss. "I'm fine. I think I flooded the engine."

"Looks like you did. Smells like it too." The young man patted his palm against his leg. "Why don't you get out for a minute, Miss, uh, I don't know your name."

Should she get out? Tell him her name? They're alone. He's a stranger, Rye would caution her.

He opened her door and held his hand for her.

"Thank you for your offer." She placed her hand on the door, shutting it behind her. "So sorry about the stall. Are you able to back up so you can get out or were you trying to park at the Park?"

He smiled. "You have a way with words."

Tally blushed.

"I'm not going to the Park. Just taking a drive around campus and decided to stop at the Chaucer House to see if anyone's there. Just got back from Key West last night to start summer school, you know, got to keep my deferment, and I'm not sure which houses are open for the summer."

His voice. Key West.

"Wait—is your name Ted?" Her voice sounded incredulous.

"Holy sh—Your voice. Is your name Gigi?"

"Oh, my gosh. Ted Alton Beckett! I can't believe it."

"Tally Gigi McCall, nice to meet you." He leaned over and gave her a hug.

What a surprise. Meeting Ted and hugging a man you have only known for one minute.

"Ted, it's so nice to meet you too. Ever since I hung up on you, I mean, we hung up after the interview, I've wanted to thank you for your help with my sidebar, article, column--I mean--" She was feeling nervous just looking into his brown eyes. "My assignment that day."

"I read it the next morning. Saw your byline. Impressive, Gigi. I don't know how you juggled those quotes. Especially since you were still absorbing the news yourself."

"Ted, thank you. No one's ever said that, about me absorbing the news too, I mean. I still can't believe it happened. And Sandy Scheuer, one of the girls who was shot and killed while walking to her dorm, was in a sorority. I think about her all the time."

"Innocent. All of them. Jeffrey, William, Allison, Sandy. Did you read the *Newsweek* article? May 18th? I keep a copy in my car. What slays me is the quote from, wait, I'll show it to you." Ted reached into his glove compartment. "Okay. Look at this: *A 22-year-old drama student named James Minard charged that he saw an officer give the command to fire. 'This lieutenant had his arm raised and carried a baton,' Minard said. 'When the baton came down, they fired. I was apparently the only one who saw it; nobody believed me.'* And you know who the Brigadier General was in charge of the Guard troops that day?"

"Brigadier General Robert Canterbury." Tally shook her head, dabbing moisture from the corners of her eyes.

"It's heartbreaking, right, Gigi?" Ted pulled a napkin from his front seat, placed the magazine in the glove compartment, and offered the napkin to Tally who accepted with a "Thank you so much, Ted."

"And eleven days later the murders at Jackson State in Mississippi by police?" He shook his head. "You were right when you wrote '*College students are in danger.*' Now the North and the South have killings of innocent students on campuses in common."

"Wow, Ted. I never thought about it that way." And the South already had the Orangeburg killings too.

Ted crossed his arms and leaned against her car. "Look. You gave context to the tragedy from a Southern view that is rare because most of the country doesn't seem to care what a Southerner thinks. There's an assumption that Southerners are dumb, sorority girls are dumb, and your acknowledgement in your piece of being a member of a sorority and writing a provocative piece surely made some readers stop and think."

"Ted, I, I don't know what to say except thank you. And thank you for stopping to help me and sparkling my day."

"You're welcome, Gigi. And my theory? How a person hears news or learns history shapes how that news or history is processed." He looked serious. "And, Gigi, I'll always remember I heard the news from you."

"Ted, I, I'm so touched. And I'll always remember I heard about *the chirping of grasshoppers* from you. I'm so happy Mr. Boudreaux agreed to keep your quote, well, Emerson's quote, in the column." Tally put her hand to her heart. "I cannot believe I'm talking with you again. Oh, I almost forgot. What did you want at the Chaucer House?"

"You. I wanted to meet you." He cocked his head and smiled, his mustache like a horizontal black piano key above ivory teeth.

"Gigi, let's move to my car and sit for a minute unless you need my help starting your car. You in a hurry?"

"I have a few minutes but, Ted, this may sound silly and I should have asked earlier but I was so shocked to meet you…."

"I know the feeling. What's up?"

"Well, I've always been afraid that cars will blow up."

"If they're flooded?"

"Or if someone hits them in a fender bender or if the car overheats and you have to lift the hood." Her voice trailed off.

"Sounds like there's a lot you're scared of, Gigi. So, even though none of those things will ever happen, to give you peace of mind, let's get these things out of your car and safe into mine." Ted reached into her car, pulled out her books, bag and baton. His burgundy bellbottom pants and paisley shirt on his slim body were the perfect combination of attitude and style.

"My brother always tells me not to worry yet I do."

Ted balanced the middle of the baton on the tip of his finger, spinning it the way basketball players swirl a basketball on the tip of theirs.

"Ted, that's amazing."

"Thanks. I do this with drumsticks at every gig."

"I forgot. You're a drummer with a band."

"Yep. *Oh, Canada-Bound!*"

Ted turned toward his car with her belongings.

"Ted, please forgive me. I wish I could sit and talk. It's just I need to hurry home, change clothes and meet my sorority sisters here in an hour." Tally looked at her watch. "Could we get together some other time and talk? I would love to do that."

"It's a date. How about Thursday? June 4th? Dinner at the restaurant of your choice."

"Ted, that would be one month since we first spoke on the phone. One month since Kent State."

"You know, I was thinking about the fact that today is a Monday and it was four weeks ago today. That's what got me thinking about you. So, don't you think it's about time we made a new memory Thursday night, Gigi?" Ted placed her items back in her car except for the baton, tossing it to Tally.

"Actually--" Tally dropped her baton as Ted pitched it to her. She needed a moment to think. She wanted to get to know Ted better, of course, however, she would never want him to consider their next meeting a *date*. That would not be fair to Rye.

"How about lunch on Thursday at Patchett's Fish Camp? That would work better for me."

"That little hangout? Best fried hushpuppies, fish and homemade tartar sauce in town."

After a quick hug goodbye, Ted stood near the azaleas.

Tally pumped the clutch, pressed the gas, waited for the engine to turn over, and let her car idle for a moment before waving goodbye. Her watch showed 6:01 p.m. It never fails. Seeing 6:01 on 6/01. A golden moment. Today's date and time aligned.

If only she had time to call Winston.

Maybe tomorrow.

Nineteen

The girls tucked in close by the bonfire. Tally strummed her guitar as their voices harmonized the lyrics of "Michael, Row the Boat Ashore," the Negro spiritual that became a hit song by The Highwaymen. The salt air, aroma of burning wood, whiffs of cigarette smoke, and bouquet of perfumes in the breeze could not have soothed her more.

Being with Becca, Rayleigh, Virginia and Khaki on the beach as they used to do when Miss Perry was asleep and they would sneak out to sit under the weeping willow to talk and laugh was a tonic she needed after seeing Franklin so worried.

"They say it caused her to miscarry her baby." Khaki opened another bottle of wine.

"Well, I will never use those kinds of pans, ever." Virginia mumbled through a mouthful of popcorn.

"Aluminum has a more even cooking surface anyway." Becca lifted her crystal wine glass as if about to make a toast. "But if a tiny piece of that new, what's it called, Khaki?"

"Something called Teflon."

"If she swallowed a tiny piece of Teflon and it made her miscarry, well, it should be taken off the market right now!"

"She wasn't on the pill?"

"She said it made her sick."

"That's so sad. The only thing she can do, I reckon, is grieve for her lost baby and then get married without having to let out her dress." Rayleigh blew a bubblegum bubble.

Tally wanted to say, *"She didn't lose a baby. She lost a fetus. A baby can only be a baby, by definition, if it is born. And if we, as young women, keep talking about babies in our stomachs instead of fetuses in our uteruses that may or may not be carried to term to become babies only at the moment of BIRTH, a prerequisite for the word 'baby,' we are perpetuating language that is not precise, conflates a stomach with a uterus as a euphemism to deny the fact that conception occurred as a result of a choice to engage in sexual activity, except in cases of artificial insemination or incest or rape, and confuses the real issue of the opportunity to give birth and the right to give birth that is--"*

"Speaking of dresses, Khaki, have you found one?" Becca asked.

Tally placed her guitar in its case, and sipped her favorite cucumber water from a thermos, glad she let the moment pass. Another discussion for another time. But, wow. She should read Tessie's quote more often. A surge of energy warmed every cell in her body like sunshine on daisy seeds. Be passionate, bold, direct, not an ingénue. Winston was right. She would have to speak to him soon.

"Yes, Khaki. We're your bridesmaids. You can tell us." Virginia pleaded while drinking from a can of Tab. "We know we're wearing those khaki-colored satin dresses with ice-blue piping that Vera's making for us but we don't know what you're wearing!"

Tally smiled. She had seen Khaki's dress in a vault at her mother's salon and it was a white satin, architectural masterpiece, absolutely stunning, however, she had promised Vera she would not tell a soul. She had also promised Vera she would not mention to anyone that Khaki was gaining weight and Vera was worried about the satin seams.

"Vera is adding more columns of tiny pearls and a shimmer of--, wait, I shouldn't be saying anything." She pointed to her wine. "Good lord, this stuff is truth serum! I can just say my dress is gorgeous, truly one of a kind, and a big surprise."

"And, after the wedding, you and your dress will be featured on the Society Page of *The Herald*." Tally scooped a handful of peanuts.

"In color. I'm sitting for my portrait next week. Amidst the magnolias in the garden at the Country Club and also at the Garden Club gazebo at the Museum since my grandmother, Miss Myrtle Indigo Carson, was Founding President of the Garden Club."

"That was where you had your debutante photo, right?"

Tally had stood next to a Historical Marker for hers.

"Wait. You know Mrs. Benson, don't you, Becca?" Virginia exhaled a steady stream of smoke from a Virginia Slim which she teased was named after her except for the "slim" part.

"Reverend Benson's wife? Of course! The Reverend is going to marry me and Shawl." Becca took a quick drag from Virginia's cigarette.

"Well, she looks gorgeous in all her photos at the Missionary Luncheons because, think about it, even when she is sitting in church, she keeps a smile on her face."

"Virginia, what on earth does that have to do with my portrait?"

"Well, if you keep smiling, Khaki, no teeth showing, just keep your lips curling up all the time, like Mrs. Benson does, your face will get used to smiling like that and you'll look even more beautiful in your portrait."

"Rayleigh, honey, you okay?" Tally observed her staring into the distance.

"Just wondering what my wedding pictures will look like with Travis on crutches and one leg."

"Your pictures will be perfect, Leigh." Tally squeezed her hand. "You will look prettier than any of your beauty pageant pictures and Travis will look dashing in his tux. And if you wrap his crutches with black velvet, you know, ask Vera to help you, no one will even notice."

"Besides, who cares, Rayleigh?" Khaki's voice sounded tender. "You love him and he loves you."

"It's just different now." Rayleigh's words seemed swallowed by the breeze. "I'm so grateful he made it back. I just wanted him to be the same Travis he was when he left. But it's, it's really hard." She wiped tears from her cheeks.

The girls were quiet, their gestures alternating between squeezing her hand, rubbing her back, blowing her kisses and dabbing napkins about their eyes.

"We love you and Travis, Leigh." Tally hugged her sorority sister while looking at Becca whose expression mirrored Rayleigh's—numb, distracted, heartbroken.

Just Becca's mention of Shawl moments ago had brought back Tally's worry that something would blow up soon.

"I'm not supposed to say anything but if you promise, as Chaucerette sisters, with our special pledge, not to tell--" Rayleigh hiccupped. "I can't keep it inside much longer."

"What, Leigh?"

"Chaucerette-swear not to tell? Becca, you and Tally should have hope. Even if Shawl, heaven forbid, got injured like Travis."

Tally squeezed Becca's hand as Becca downed the rest of her wine. Tally took a drag from Virginia's cigarette.

"Everything may be okay."

"How come, Rayleigh?"

"Well, I don't know all the specifics. Travis won't tell me. But it seems when the mine blew up, he blacked out and when he woke up, he was on a ship with a doctor tending to him."

"Was he found near a river or something?"

"I don't know, Gin. I think he was by the ocean. I didn't ask too many questions."

"But why is that a secret?"

"Because the ship had some kind of symbol, like a red cross or something official like that, that protected it from being attacked."

"How wonderful for Travis." Khaki rolled up a beach towel, stretched out on her tummy and propped herself on the towel with her elbows. "But I still don't get why that's a secret."

"Because," Rayleigh lowered her voice, "the ship took Travis all the way through the Panama Canal. He said he heard the clanging of the locks and voices giving the okay to sail through. Finally, he got to an island where he stayed for weeks and where he said there were lots of other soldiers, some injured, some not. He heard one of them say 'missing action' or 'missing in action.' When the doctor said Travis was ready to come home, a yacht brought him home at nighttime, without any fanfare which he never wanted in the first place, y'all know Travis, and he walked on crutches right up to his parents' door and surprised them."

"Oh, my gosh." Becca squealed. "That had to be the greatest surprise ever."

Tally turned away, her eyes brimming with tears.

"They didn't even care about his leg being gone. They didn't even care that he couldn't tell them what had happened. They just praised the Lord for him being in their arms again."

"Rayleigh, I haven't had anything to drink yet I feel like I'm drunk." Tally felt dizzy. "But what about the Army? Was this island some kind of Army hideaway for injured soldiers? And the ship? And the—"

"I don't know, Tally. Travis says there was a doctor who came for a visit to his parents' house and they talked for a long time in the den behind closed doors. Travis just said there is a secret benefactor and had Travis sign some papers and that Travis still has medical benefits and, you know what? A sweetheart doesn't have to know everything. Right?"

"Right!" The girls agreed.

Becca lit a cigarette and grinned. "Oh, Ray. You've given me hope. And you told the truth about sweethearts and secrets, 'cause isn't it important to have mysteries in our lives? Things we've done, like what we're doing now, that no one knows about, other than "us," as sorority sisters?"

"Absolutely, Becks." Tally massaged Becca's shoulders.

"And, Tally," Rayleigh sat on her knees. "I really like the idea of covering those ugly crutches with black velvet for the photos. I can't wait to surprise Travis!"

The girls laughed and shared hugs. After throwing sand on the fire, Virginia, Khaki and Becca gathered picnic items, confirmed with Tally that the door to the tunnel was unlocked, and said their goodbyes.

Tally and Rayleigh strolled to the water's edge to rinse their hands and bid their Big Sister-Little Sister Farewell to the stars.

"Oh, Tally. I just remembered. The name of that island? *A' Becket Cay.*"

A sudden light rippled across the willow fronds. The girls hushed and moved into the shadow of the mansion.

In the moonlight, Tally saw Mike Parish leaning against the Historical Marker, looking out to sea.

Twenty

Tally hung up the phone after talking with Winston. He could not talk long, he said. He was working the early shift. He also said he was working on a plan to get Frankie free from the damn draft. The stress of constantly worrying about the mail or someone showing up at their front door to take Frankie to Fort Hamper, as absurd as that might sound, was killing his family.

No one was sleeping anymore. His mother cried all the time. They all felt trapped with nowhere to go for relief. He said he kept dreaming of stealing a small airplane and flying Frankie to the Bahamas if only he knew how to fly.

Tally arrived at Patchett's Fish Camp early. She waved to Mrs. Patchett and told her how she was looking forward to celebrating her 20th birthday there in two weeks. Tally asked if Winston Crockett was available. Mrs. Patchett said she would check and walked around the reception desk to the kitchen.

After Winston placed a platter of fried catfish, hushpuppies, tartar sauce and dill pickles on a nearby table, he sauntered over to Tally. He looked exhausted.

"Welcome to Patchett's, Amelia. Where's your date? Reckon it's time for me to meet this guy you're so sweet on. We got a table set up for you two by the window."

"Winston, you're the best. I'm so glad to see you. But I'm not meeting Rye. Now, don't start grinning. Nothing scandalous here, Mr. Incorrigible. I'm meeting Ted Beckett, you know, the fraternity member I interviewed for the sidebar? He's in town for Summer School, we bumped into each other and we're just having lunch."

"The guy with the Emerson quote about 'The Trail of Tears?' Impressive. You two should have a lot to talk about. And one day I'll meet Rye, right?"

"Sooner than later, I hope!"

"Sooner or later. Around my house, we don't even use those words."

"Look, Win. I want to talk with you about Frankie. We'll figure this out, okay? We're history majors, for heaven's sake! We know the past has all the answers."

Tally smiled.

Winston let out a low whistle, as if exhaling, and nodded.

"And, in the meantime, here's a little something for you."

Tally gave Winston a gift-wrapped box from V.V. Vaughn Jewelers.

"What in the--?" He shook his head and pointed to a corner where a life-size anchor provided décor and a measure of privacy. Opening the box, he whispered, "Wow," and held up a thick gold chain with a gold dog tag dangling from it.

"See? It's engraved '*Sapere Vedere*' and your name." She frowned at the sudden realization that a dog tag, the jeweler's newest design, was the worst thing she could give him today.

"Girl, you never cease to amaze me. It's what Professor Dodge always says. Da Vinci's quote: *To know how to see.* Going around my neck right now." She helped him clasp the chain around his neck. "I don't know what this is for but it couldn't come at a better time, girl."

"It's for your nomination for the O-O Honor, you nut. I ordered it a few days after we learned the news—about the nomination--but Mr. Gallops, the engraver, was on vacation so I just picked it up this morning. Congratulations, Mr. Crockett."

"Winston!" Mrs. Patchett called out.

"Be right there, Miss P."

"Girl, I gotta go. I'd give you a hug but you know the name of that tune. Anyway, you really know how to surprise a guy, Tally." He started to walk away but turned back. "Oh, and thanks a lot for giving me a reminder of my competition every day. Good strategy, you."

Tally laughed.

By the time Ted bit into one of Patchett's famous homemade biscuits, he said he might have to move to Hamper permanently.

"I swear I'm eating a cloud. An absolute cloud."

"I know. Aren't they the lightest biscuits you've ever eaten?"

"Indescribable. Now before I got this little glimpse of heaven," Ted held up half a biscuit, "you were giving me an idea for the project in my business class. The assignment is to create a solution that I can market for truckers falling asleep at the wheel. And you were saying?"

"I was just saying the Business School students, the MBAs especially, have a history of going to all the Hamper U football games and sitting as a group with their professors. Did you ever see them?"

Ted shook his head.

"No? They all have short hair. All wear business suits and ties. To a football game, of all things! Well, the professors are forever giving assignments based on football stats, management decisions during a football draft, those kinds of things."

"How do you know all this, Gigi?" Ted buttered another biscuit.

"I just listen to my brother's friends and observe folks."

"Like historians are supposed to do?"

"Exactly!" Tally tilted her head and grinned.

"So, I was saying that if I were given that assignment myself, I would get some football shoulder pads, you know, that go across both shoulders and I would put some Shalimar-perfume-powder in a pouch on each one so that whenever a trucker tilts his head on either shoulder as he's starting to fall asleep, his head would hit the shoulder pad, the perfume scent would escape, the powder would tickle his nose, and the scent and tickle would wake him up!"

"I swear I could listen to you all day, Gigi."

Tally blushed. "Thank you, Ted, you sweet talker, you."

"And with your permission, I just may use your idea and buy some Shalimar perfume soon."

"No, wait! Even better! White Shoulders by Evyan. Smells like gardenias and it's the perfect name!" Tally laughed. "Now. Equal time. What were you saying about *A Canterbury Tale*? You know, when I mentioned that was the movie Margaret Mitchell was going to see the night she was hit by the car."

"Right. When we were referencing how you almost hit me with your car." Ted pointed his finger at her. "Have you ever seen Kubrick's movie *2001: A Space Odyssey*? No? Well, there's a scene at the beginning of the movie, *A Canterbury Tale*, where Chaucer's fictional pilgrims are on horses in the countryside of Kent on their way to the Cathedral to pay homage to Saint Thomas A' Becket at Canterbury. A hawk, you know, the bird, flies into the air above them and in the same sky-scene, when the image of the bird descends it becomes a plane diving over men in tanks at the same spot in World War II."

"How odd."

"It's unforgettable. And one of Stanley Kubrick's favorite movies. So, in the beginning of *2001: A Space Odyssey*, as an homage to *A Canterbury Tale*, it seems, Kubrick has a man-ape throw a bone into the air that twirls and transforms into a satellite to show the march of time. Just another way of showing respect for what has come before."

Winston approached the table. "Sorry to interrupt the party. Do y'all want Lemon Meringue Pie for dessert?"

"Sounds good, Winston. Tally tells me you are up for the Oxford award too. Congratulations."

"Thanks, man. Tally and I want it to be a tie."

"I also understand your brother and I have something in common. Birth certificates."

"Sorry to hear that, man."

'My draft-number? 03." Ted pulled cash from his wallet. "And to think I used to celebrate the numbers 'oh-three' with my birthday on December 'three-oh.' Like a cruel joke, right?"

"The cruelest."

A flurry of events cartwheeled through Tally's thoughts. December 30th. Asa Candler of Coca-Cola fame, Emory University benefactor, Atlanta's former mayor, and owner of Candler Field that he gave to Atlanta to build the Atlanta Airport, was born on that date. Cousin Kathy's birthdate too. But December 29th. Why did that date jump to the forefront of her mind when—what is Ted saying?

"Hey, I'm here in Summer School to keep my deferment too. Played too many gigs, missed too many classes this year. I shouldn't have been in trouble. But my continued bad luck? I had a professor with a crew cut who said he was, 'disgusted by guys,' well, he said, 'young gentlemen,' with long hair. And he graded accordingly. Unfortunately, I've got him for Summer School too. Shoot," Ted shrugged his shoulders, "I've been thinking of ditching school altogether, especially if my business project doesn't work out," he winked at Tally, "and heading to the place I named my band after."

"Where's that? I mean, what's your band's name?" Winston, pouring sweet tea in Tally's glass, splashed the table with a rush of tea and ice cubes. "Sorry, girl."

"Nothing to worry about, Winston." Tally wiped the table.

"Oh, Canada-Bound."

"Know how to get there, man?"

"Winston," Ted's voice lowered, "we should go out for a beer. You, your brother, me. Tonight good?"

Something in Ted's voice seemed like code, deliberate, odd.

"Sure thing—I'll check with Frankie. Look I'll bring you some pie, two forks and you can split it. No charge."

"Thank you, Win." Tally winked.

Winston left. Ted excused himself and caught up with Winston. Tally looked at the anchor and wondered when she would hear from Rye again.

By the time Ted got back to the table, he was carrying a piece of pie on a plate.

"Did Winston Crockett charm you into working for him?" Tally looked around and saw Winston leave out the back door.

"Something like that."

Twenty-one

In the early morning hours of June 15th, 1970, Tally pulled her Birthday Journal from the top shelf of the chiffarobe in her bedroom at home. She closed her eyes and inhaled the zest of lemon sachets and lemon drawer liners. Fresh, clean, crisp, energizing.

Could there be a better way to begin her birthday, her new year, her new decade?

She glanced at the ivory garment bags where her majorette costumes were stored, the batons in their wicker baton rack, her history books atop shelves. She opened a drawer where bathing suits nestled. She scooped her favorite, a one-piece black and white polka dot suit with a flirty white ruffle across the top, to wear to the pool party at the Country Club. It was the one that caused Rye to whistle, the one he said made him a fan of ruffles forever, especially when breezes were blowing.

Every birthday morning since she turned thirteen-years-old, Tally wrote her hopes and plans for the year ahead in her Birthday Journal for future historical perspective. Sitting at her desk, she wrote her new entry:

Happy New Year ~ June 15, 1970

*I will do my best to write a winning essay for the Oglethorpe-Oxford History Honor and be prepared to celebrate Winston if he wins instead.

*I will work hard as Fort Hamper Gala Queen, visit the Veterans' Hospital once a week, and send "Hurry Home" cards to as many soldiers as I can.

*I will be Maid of Honor at Shawl and Becca's wedding!!!

*I will tell Mother and Daddy about my decision not to marry. (Time to be honest with them. Time to be true to myself. Encourage Mother to focus on Shawl's wedding more than ever. Help Daddy get used to the idea.)

*I will graduate from Hamper University with a B.A. in History in May 1971.

*I will share SPECIAL, private moments (!) with Rye Somerset.

Rye had called the week before. He had told her that, regrettably, his plans had changed. He had intended to drive to Hamper to help her celebrate her birthday and meet a law professor at Hamper U, however, he had subsequently been asked to prepare a paper on Criminal Intent for his summer job as a clerk for a lawyer in Niagara Falls.

Tally told him she understood but she sure wished he could come.

She asked him if she could ask him a question. He chuckled and said sure. First, though, he wanted to compliment her on the way she charmed men with her circuitous chatter. Secondly, he wanted to assure her she would confound any prosecutor on the planet with her charm. She said thank you so much, however, there are women prosecutors too. He laughed. Her words sounded like a wink, he said. She said she would be happy to be a witness for the defense and confound any prosecutor if Rye would promise to be the defense attorney. He made that growling noise she loved and said he just might take her up on that one day.

In a serious tone she shared with him that she had been thinking the National Guard could be charged with criminal intent for what they did at Kent State. Did he think they would be? He acknowledged that the National Guard probably would not be charged in criminal court since they were ordered to be at Kent State by the Governor.

It seemed to her, however, that the fact the Guard had ammunition in their guns proved they had intent to kill or injure those unarmed students. So why would that not make the shooters who fired shots filled with intent to commit the crime of murder or, at least, manslaughter? Rye said it might merit an indictment, albeit with circuitous logic, yet it would probably never see the light of day in a court of criminal law.

She told him that she and her daddy were going to Ohio at the end of June for their annual summer "Daddy-Daughter Trip" at the time each year when her mother was busy with June weddings. She wanted to see the Kent State campus. Her daddy wanted to visit an old friend on the judicial circuit in Akron who was about to retire. She wondered if maybe Rye could meet them there, since they would be closer to New York the further north they traveled.

Rye said her father might object. Tally said her daddy would like to see Rye again. After all, their meeting at the Gala was so brief. That reminded Rye of the brief he had to prepare. Before they hung up, he told Tally he would call her on her birthday.

Tally looked at the clock in her bedroom suite. 9:14 a.m. Shawl's birthdate on her birth date. It was as if her eyes kept looking for that date. How else to explain why she saw that time, those numbers everywhere? On a clock. In a *Photoplay* magazine biography of dancer Joey Heatherton whose birthday was September 14th, 1944. In history books: Francis Scott Key wrote "The Star-Spangled Banner" on September 14th, 1814. The first lighthouse was lit in America on September 14th, 1716. Ironically, Congress passed the first peacetime conscription bill called the "draft law" on September 14th, 1940.

A letter from Shawl to Becca had finally arrived weeks ago. It was in a big postal envelope. The Postal Service included a letter of apology and indicated the missing mail had been lost in the logjam during the postal workers' strike. It was just as Sergeant Larry Cook suspected.

Shawl told Becca that he was fine, missed her, found it hard to write and would not be writing for a while because he was assigned a scouting assignment in the jungle. He said he loved her and would see her soon and not to worry. He told her he was writing a note to Tally too.

Tally never got an envelope from Shawl.

Tally opened the French doors leading to her private balcony that wrapped around the corner of the second floor from one set of French doors to another. She preened to see the mailbox. Aqua balloons danced in the breeze. Her daddy always tied birthday balloons to the mailbox each year. Unfortunately, it was too early for mail delivery. Too early for a phone call from Rye too.

Except for a distant seagull squawking, all was quiet.

She plopped on the hammock in the alcove of her bedroom. She swayed on the Pawley's Island rope, still so firm and strong, having never been in inclement weather. Its black wrought iron stand was crafted in Savannah. She hugged her Birthday Journal, and looked up at the gray storm clouds painted on the ceiling.

She had been given the indoor hammock by Tess Hamper, as a "Goddaughter's Housewarming Gift" to help Tally, who was four years old at the time, settle into her new house and new bedroom. Tally had whispered to 'Tessie' that a hammock was what she wanted with storm clouds on the ceiling too. When Tess and her parents asked why, Tally crossed her arms and said, "'Cause y'all never let me stay in the hammock when gray clouds show up in the sky. And that's not fair."

According to stories her parents told during their family car trips to Atlanta when Tally and Shawl were little, Tally had exhibited a streak of determination all her life.

As Tally swayed in the hammock, memories of car trips floated like untethered balloons in her thoughts. For years, the McCall family had made a pilgrimage in their light blue Cadillac each month from Hamper to Atlanta to visit elderly family members. Her father drove the historic route, the same one, albeit in reverse, that Sherman followed on his March from Atlanta to the Sea.

Her daddy would tell the story of how Hamper survived Sherman's wrath, a story Tally and Shawl asked him to repeat each year.

Delphi, in the same monotone voice and using the same words, would tell them of the citizen of Hamper, a Mister James Walter Fitzgerald, a traveling barber heading down the back roads toward

Atlanta to see an elderly client, as the person who first warned the citizens of Hamper about Sherman's devastation.

It seems Mister Fitzgerald, her daddy would say, smelled smoky air all about him and heard from his friend, Mister Phinizy Beauregard, that Yankees were getting closer and killing folks along the way and he, Mister Beauregard, needed a shave and a haircut so he would look presentable when he arrived at the Pearly Gates.

Mister Fitzgerald galloped back to Hamper to tell town leaders about the scorched earth in Sherman's wake and the Yankee General's imminent arrival in Hamper. The quick-thinkers of the town vowed to take a stand.

That cold December night in 1864 the townspeople, including all the women, gathered at a bonfire on the beach that was hidden from sight by a grove of mimosa trees. Aware that their homes would be ransacked, their silver stolen, their houses burned, their mimosa trees torched, their women potential victims of the evils of the Yankee males, their men forced to watch the terror before being killed themselves, and the town destroyed, the frantic citizens concocted a desperate plan.

Throughout the night, carpenters hammered, women painted, and children sorted nails by the light of the bonfire. The next day as General William Tecumseh Sherman rode into town followed by fourscore of males in blue uniforms so caked with dust from the red dirt-roads they looked bloody, the General abruptly reared his horse, spit tobacco on the ground and smiled.

Everywhere he looked were signs. Sherman's General Store. Sherman's Apothecary. G. D. Sherman's Saloon. F. Ulysses Sherman's Horse and Buggy Shop. Tombstones, crudely chiseled to mark the graves of the Sherman Family of Hamper, Georgia, were scattered throughout the cemetery. A sign that looked like a precursor to a Historical Marker stated the influence of the founding fathers of Hamper, Georgia, the illustrious Dickie Sherman Family from Hamper, England.

General William Tecumseh Sherman ordered his men to douse their flaming torches in the horse troughs. He shook hands with Hamper's Mayor. He listened to a contingent of women and children who welcomed him. Hamper's Mayor presented Sherman with a key to the city, citing him as a descendent of the Sherman founding fathers and a distinguished member of the Sherman family.

The only smoke in the air that day puffed from a daguerreotype camera. General Sherman told the citizens shivering in the cold that Hamper would be the only town he would spare from Atlanta to the sea. He owed that to his heritage, to his newly-discovered Sherman ancestors, and also to the fact that Hamper had abided by the original rules regarding "No Slavery" set forth by King George II when Georgia, the King's namesake colony, was founded as the last of the original Thirteen Colonies.

"Lucky thirteen," Sherman was quoted as saying. "Lucky Hamper. It is known to me that you have no slavery, no plantations, no cotton here. There is no need, therefore, to burn your buildings and your homes. The bold citizens who built this town will not see it destroyed. If only Georgia had stayed true to its original intentions, as you did, other towns would be spared too. History will judge your deeds accordingly."

After eating collards, grits, sweet potato soufflé, fried shrimp, and ham spiked with rum, the Yankees departed Hamper. General Sherman captured Savannah a day later yet also spared it from burning because of its extraordinary beauty, an act Hamper citizens celebrated.

Tally and Shawl, as they grew older, would invariably wonder out loud why history did not judge Sherman accordingly. Shawl stated that Sherman's policy of "total war," of "scorched earth revenge," of "psychological devastation" and of "terror" with his intent to "*make Georgia HOWL*" would not adhere to the principles of the Geneva Convention standards in today's world.

Shawl argued that even though Georgia, from "Atlanta to the sea," could rebuild their buildings and homes, the morale of the citizenry was still affected a century later.

He pointed out that every child he knew went to bed ending their bedtime prayers with "Amen" and "The South Shall Rise Again."

He said his friend Corky always talked about his great-grandfather telling him stories about how all the brothers in the family, except for him, were killed at Shiloh and how he had to take care of all the women and children in the family when he returned to Atlanta and they had no food.

Their Daddy would say, "History is told by the winners, Shawl. Plain and simple. *To the victors go the spoils.* And legends of triumph and tales of glory. Son, when the descendants of slave-owners acknowledge the immoral past of their ancestors, albeit based on economics that united the states as intensely as any Declaration of Independence, and when Northerners acknowledge how complicit they were in the slave-trade by also owning slaves and by gladly consuming the cotton products made as a result of slavery, only then will life in the South get better for everybody, especially our Negro brothers and sisters."

Tally had said, "Daddy, what were the stories the little Negro children would hear from their grandpas?"

"Sugar, nothing could ever be as devastating as losing your freedom, your children, the sanctity of your body, your boundaries, your hope as a human spirit on this earth than being forced to be a slave to another person just because of the color of your skin." Delphi had pulled the car to the side of the road, put the car in park, turned around and said to Shawl and Tally, "One day those of us with white skin may know what that is like here in America to be the minority and it makes me think of *The Golden Rule*."

"Do unto others as you would have them do unto you."

Tally said it faster than Shawl and giggled as he grabbed her in a bear hug.

During each trip, her parents would also keep the children entertained by singing songs, playing games and oohing and ahhing at signs.

Delphi would point out filling station and speed limit signs, marveling at how gas had gone up to thirty cents a gallon and how one could accelerate up to forty-five miles an hour now.

Babette would point to giant billboards that enchanted her. She had never seen signs that big when she was a little girl in France.

Shawl would get excited to see Brylcreem signs, reading each of the progressive phrases on the half-dozen signs aloud.

Tally, however, would be so in awe whenever she spotted a Historical Marker, she could not even speak a complete sentence. Instead, when she was just two, she would stand behind her daddy, her feet on Shawl's knees in the backseat, tug on her daddy's collar, and whisper "coo-coo" in his ear until he pulled off the road, and held her in his arms so she could rub her fingers on the words, while he read the sign to her. Eventually she would read them aloud too.

Her parents also entertained their children by telling stories. Delphi would tell a story about the doves his father raised on the family farm in Griffin, Georgia and the times he would ride with his father to events where his father would release doves from baskets at funerals, weddings, baptisms or revivals. Her Daddy-Delphi's job was to softly sing "coo-coo" to the doves to keep them settled while in the baskets before being released.

Her daddy would also tell the story about how he was named after the Oracle at Delphi so that he would have a leg up on being smart. His middle name was a tribute to the species of creatures his father cherished with the hope that he would remember to be a peaceful man. Her daddy would say the only thing worse than being named Delphi Aviary McCall would to have been named Delphi Dove McCall.

That was when Tally's mother would scoot closer to him, put her head on his arm and remind him that at least dove rhymes with love. This would trigger groans from Shawl and giggles from Tally. Her mother called her father "Dove" yet only family members knew why.

One story her parents inevitably told during the car trips was of the Sunday morning they realized they would be forced to buy a new baby doll for the church nursery because they could not pry the baby doll Tally held in her arms away from her. Tally had insisted to her parents that Baby Bay was *her* baby. She had pointed to the toy box where she had found the baby doll and said, "MY Baby Bay." She had sat in the little red rocking chair cuddling the ragged baby doll until her parents agreed with "Miss Luna," formally, Mrs. Luna Mary Melanie Grier, the Nursery Leader, that the two should not be parted. Miss Luna told them she had never seen a little girl so devoted to something she loved. Tally was twenty months old.

Today, at noon, she would officially turn twenty years old.

Twenty-two

Tally brushed her teeth, tossed on hot pink hot pants and matching eyelet blouse and tucked her journal back on the shelf in the chiffarobe. Before mounting her bike to zip down the long curving driveway to the mailbox, she straightened the sign on the wall by her door.

Her fingers brushed against the sign's slick surface, one index finger tracing the ridge of the round protrusion. She shook her head. Talk about memories. It was the sign she had decoupaged at camp ages ago, a sign she also read every day while she was home. The words on the sign were *Huckleberry Friend*, from "Moon River," the first song she learned to play on her guitar.

Her camp counselor had encouraged campers to cut out words and pictures from the stack of magazines on the table to compose a special phrase on their wooden boards. She promised to help them with the decoupage process.

It was during a summer afternoon Arts and Crafts class in July 1966. Tally had turned sixteen weeks before.

While others scoured *Photoplay* and *TV Guide* magazines to spell "I Love Paul" or "I Love Ringo" or "Stop! In the Name of Love," Tally searched the titles of *Reader's Digest* to find letters big enough for her phrase. She also cut out a full moon and angled it so that its path of bright white light streamed onto the words.

One day an announcement blared over the loudspeaker instructing teen campers to gather on the tennis courts at two o'clock that afternoon. The youngest campers were instructed to take a tumbling class in the barn.

At the tennis courts, the leader of the camp had talked to the teen girls about personal safety and boundaries. She told the girls about a tragic event in the national news.

Tally glanced at her black wrought-iron bed. She had long ago found a way to crawl under the bed skirt and hide behind tiers of black polished cotton just as the one surviving nurse had done when she hid under a bed during the horror of a stranger murdering her eight roommates in their apartment in Chicago.

The camp leader's words still echoed in Tally's thoughts.

"My request is that you, who are our oldest campers and hoping to be Junior Counselors next summer, will take this opportunity to be strong and brave and not frighten the little ones with your conversations. I also expect each of you to set an example of how to take good care of yourself and think of creative ways to protect yourself throughout your lives."

Tally kept the sign in her bedroom through the years to encourage three personal reminders:

1. to always be on the lookout for danger,

2. to know what to do in a threatening situation, and

3. to remember that when something happens in a distant place, a person can feel haunted by the news and feel heartache for those nurses in Chicago or soldiers in Vietnam or, now, for students in Ohio even when you are far, far away.

Bicycle pedals pressed grooves in the soft skin of her bare feet. She stood on the rubber slats gathering speed to coast down the meandering driveway. She closed her eyes. Warm breezes brushed her hair upward. She inhaled the sweet scent of hyacinths bordering the drive. At the first whiff of mimosa blossoms, however, she opened her eyes, braked and skidded to a stop at the mailbox.

Aqua balloons were anchored with white ribbons to the black iron mailbox. She took pictures with her Kodak camera in the shade of a towering pine, the flashcube popping with each one, before unlatching the mailbox door, and loading a beaucoup of pastel envelopes into the basket on her bike.

Racing back to the house, she waved to Mrs. Dodge, Virginia's mother and Professor Dodge's wife, who shouted "Happy Birthday, Tally."

In the kitchen, Tally kissed the dark brown forehead of Alida, the lady who had started as a maid to the McCall family when Shawl was born and was now considered the manager of the household and a member of the family. Alida shooed Tally away from counters decorated with lilacs in Waterford crystal vases. A cut glass pitcher of ice water, cucumber slices and ice cubes in the shape of fleur-de-lis glittered in the rays of sunshine next to a sterling tray laden with napkins that were fresh from the dryer and in need of ironing and folding.

"Scoot. Back to your room. I'm fixing to make your bed since it's your birthday. But I've got to ice your cake first."

Alida acted so flustered and giddy, Tally did not want to disturb her. Yet she wondered why Alida had not given her a birthday hug.

"A-lye-da, lye-da, lee! The cake smells delicious. However, I've already made my bed and written in my Birthday Journal. You know what I wrote?"

"That you want our boy Shawl to get himself home and you want that Yankee fellow to get himself to Georgia." Alida hummed as she beat the icing, taking moments to lift the spoon in the air and squint at the stream of caramel dripping into the bowl.

Tally stuck her index finger into the stream and sucked the sugar from her skin.

"Divine, Lida-Lee."

"Almost thick enough, honey. Almost done."

"Alida, you always call me 'Birthday Bunny' on my birthday."

Alida stopped. She did not look at Tally as she touched a dishtowel to her eyes.

"I just can't believe my baby is twenty."

Odd. Either Alida is forgetful today or preoccupied. She always made such a big to-do about calling her, "Birthday Bunny," again and again, on that one day each year.

"Alida, I have to meet Maman and Vera at the Boutique to make rice bundles, you know, so guests can throw rice at Tricia Lynne McLean's wedding. I better scoot to read these cards, get dressed and dash. Thank you for my cake. Can't wait to taste it."

Tally dipped her finger back into the bowl as Alida turned to pull wax paper from one of the made-from-scratch layers. "And, yes. I do want Shawl home. I do want that Yankee fellow named Rye here soon. However, my birthday wish right now? For you, Alida, to lay in my hammock today and take a nap. You must make it come true."

Tally hugged Alida as a puff of flour from Alida's apron tickled her nose.

Tally sneezed. "Gracious. Excuse me. Now, if you'll excuse me again, I have some reading to do." Tally held up cards in both hands, kissed Alida's cheek and called out as she jogged up the staircase, "I love you, Lida Lee."

"Love you too, my Birthday Bunny."

Tally tossed the cards on her aqua bedspread. She placed Baby Bay next to a needlepoint pillow that Tessie had made for her when Tally was nominated for the Oglethorpe-Oxford History Honor weeks ago. In black letters on an aqua background, it stated:

"Isn't it time for Herstory?"

She propped a pillow beneath her tummy to study the handwriting on the cards. Sorority sisters, majorette friends, camp buddies, Sunday school teachers, and neighbors had all sent birthday cards.

However, the one she most wanted to see was the first card she opened.

The envelope was white. The ink was royal blue. On the front of the dark gray card was a moon shimmering a glittery path atop ocean waters. She caught her breath. It looked like the moon over the ocean the night they met. Inside Rye had written:

> Tally,
>
> Let history show that you, Birthday Girl, are an original. Your passion for life? Contagious. Your joie de vivre? Intoxicating.

Your freckles? Adorable. Your passion for history? Admirable. My passion for recent history focuses on a certain Southern belle who was kind enough to dance with me on my birthday. I wish I could dance with you on yours and whisper "Happy Birthday, Georgia," into your ticklish ear. Wishing you a year filled with "all" your dreams coming true.

Rye (aka "Guy")

"Guy." Tally laughed. The melody of "Moon River" trilled in her thoughts as she moved to the hammock, the card with Rye's keepsake sentiments in her grasp. The swaying reminded her of the rocking of the ship. She immersed herself in the memory, in the body of the girl she was just two months before. The night she kept reliving. The night she would never forget.

That night she could not wait to see the moon. On the top deck of the cruise ship, she had leaned against the railing. She remembered the ruffled hem of her gold mini-dress along with her shimmer wrap fluttering in the cool night air. Her hair danced past her shoulders, down her back.

She extended her hand as if to touch the moon. Her wedding-ring finger sported her solitary pearl ring, nearly the same size of the distant orb in the sky, nestled in a swirl of pave diamonds. The sparkle around the pearl looked like twinkling stars.

"*Boys, take a good look at the moon.*" Her shout boomeranged in the breeze as she toasted the moon with her glass of lemonade.

"Cheers to James Lovell." A male voice had interrupted.

She swiveled. Her hand hit the railing. Her glass sailed into the churning water below.

"Lovell? You know his quote too?" She pulled the silk sparkle wrap across her breasts, her fingers grasping a tiny spritzer hidden in a pouch on her gold polished cotton bra strap, a patented invention her mother had created. Not only was it the perfect spot to conceal perfume if she ever wanted a fresh spritz, but it was also easy to reach if she needed to spray perfume into the eyes of a potential attacker.

"Nice ring."

"My birthstone."

"Stoned? Oh, yeah. You bet guys are getting stoned. What a day." He placed his glass on a nearby tray. "Sorry to startle. Just saw you standing there." He grinned and hitchhiked his thumb toward stairs descending to the disco ballroom where a band was playing The Beatles' hit, "I Saw Her Standing There." "Taking a break to salute that big beach ball in the sky tonight. Sorry. Forgot to introduce myself. Rye. Rye Somerset."

He stuck his hand out.

"Nice to meet you, Guy." She smiled and gave a firm handshake. A shiver rushed through her as he placed his other hand over hers. His skin warmed her hand. It felt as hot as the heat above her knees, between her thighs, the place she nested her hands when in bed on a cold night, the place where her body was the hottest. She slipped her hand from his grasp and gestured to the stairs. "Folks having fun?"

"*Cokes*? Yeah. Beer, shrimp, enough to feed an army," his words skipped like pebbles on the wind, "lined up, ready for the Limbo. Going down?"

Why did he say drown?

She shook her head and pointed to her ears.

"Sorry. Hard to hear."

He gestured to a row of lounge chairs in an alcove where paper lanterns dangled from bright blue ropes. The color reminded her of the color of his eyes. She hesitated, wondering where the waiters were, if the light was too dim, if she would be safe. He touched his hand to her back, asking her preference as they passed a deserted bar.

"Ginger ale, please. With a lime."

There was not a girl in her sorority who had not heard about squirting lime juice up a fellow's nose if he got too frisky and would not listen to the word, "no."

He offered her a glass with a tiny pink umbrella and guided her to chairs under a lantern casting a soft glow.

"Didn't mean to scare you. Man, that was loud." He grabbed yellow beach towels from a rack and spread them across the chairs. "Hope you don't mind if we get away from that noise. Besides, we can have our own mixer up here. Now, what's your name?"

What could it hurt? He seemed safe enough. Besides it was time to celebrate.

"Tally. Tally Gigi McCall."

"Tally. Nice. Unforgettable. Tally is a family name?"

"No, but thank you for liking it." A sip of liquid soothed her suddenly parched throat. Whenever her adrenaline kicked into overdrive, her throat would feel dry as chalk.

"My mother's from France. It never dawned on her that I'd hear 'tally-ho' the rest of my life. I was supposed to be Cecile, a sweet Southern name. But, *Mon Dieu*, the day I was born, mother changed it." She shrugged her shoulders and took another sip. "Out of appreciation to the stranger who saved my life and hers."

"A stranger? Wait. What do you mean? A stranger delivered you?"

"Well, he's not a stranger now. He comes to my birthday parties every June fifteenth." She laughed at his puzzled look. "Guy, this ginger ale tastes different from any other ginger ale I've ever had."

"Glad you like it. Now what were you saying about a stranger delivering you?"

"I'll give you the quick-quick version. I wasn't due until the end of June in Hamper, Georgia. My mother didn't speak English too well. Alida Lee, the maid who helped Mother care for my four-year-old brother, was at the grocery store buying cucumbers for my mother. She craved them so much she says that's why I love cucumbers. Anyway, a strange man knocked on the door. My mother invited him into the house for croissants."

"What?" He waved off a waiter strolling by and raised an eyebrow. "A stranger is in the house and she's serving him food? Man, I've heard of Southern hospitality but—"

"It's her favorite thing. She serves warm croissants to the ladies at her shop, Babette's Bridal Boutique." No need to say the original name, Babette's Bridal Brassieres Boutique. How could she ever say the word, "brassiere," to a fellow she just met?

"Anyway, my mother talks with the man and says goodbye. He walks to his car. Just as my mother was about to close the door, my brother falls from his tricycle onto the brick floor of the screened-in patio, scrapes his knee and starts crying. My mother rushes to comfort him, slips on a row of army men in the hall, hits her head and faints. My brother jumps back on his tricycle, his little knee still bleeding, rides out the front door, down the sidewalk and hollers at the stranger, 'Mister. Mister! Mama fell. Mama fell.'"

Tally took another sip. "So, the stranger rushes back to the house and calls the operator who switches him to the hospital, but I reckon

I just couldn't wait to be born. The man quick-quick gave Mother crushed ice from the icebox freezer, made sure my brother was happy eating a banana popsicle in the kitchen, heard the noon church bells as he delivered me, wrapped me in a blanket that he found in a baby carriage on the patio, and handed me to my mother to hold."

Tally opened her arms as if 'viola.' "So, I owe my life--and my name--to a census taker."

"Wow. *Tally*. What a story." He lifted his glass. "To strangers."

"To strangers who save our lives!"

She clinked her glass with his. Her wrap fell from her shoulders to her hips. The deck was empty. She licked strawberry gloss from her bottom lip, the zest of fresh berries in a summer-sweet-sizzle of flavor.

But what would her sorority sisters think if they knew she was by herself with a stranger?

They had all heard the rumors of that college girl, a freshman at Ole Miss, who was raped by a member of the crew during a recent cruise. Tally's parents made her promise she would stay with her sorority sisters at all times.

"Now it's my turn to apologize. Your name is Guy?"

"Rye. Rye Somerset."

"Rye?" She blushed. "Sorry, I've never heard that as a name before."

"Family tradition. Firstborn named after the place where my parents met. Lucky me. Rye, New York."

She knew Rye, New York. Where Amelia Earhart had lived.

"Oh, Rye, how romantic. So sorry I couldn't hear you earlier."

"I know. I mentioned Jim Lovell and you said something about the boat."

"Haha! No. His quote. Wait. Jim Lovell? You know? *Boys, take a good look at the moon.'* Can you believe he said that right before the oxygen tank exploded in the cabin and doomed the mission? Don't you imagine that broke Captain Lovell's heart? Oh, my gosh. You heard the news too?"

"Best news ever. Hot damn. Cheers to Apollo 13 for landing safely today." He took a swig. "But Jeez. Bet they will always regret choosing the number thirteen. Nothing good has ever come from that number."

Sounds of "Love Potion No. 9" and off-key voices drifted up the stairs.

"This Georgia History major would kindly disagree, sir." Her head moved in time to the music, her shoulders shimmying slow. She took another sip and closed her eyes. She had the strangest urge to take off her dress. "The state where I was born happens to be the thirteenth colony." She twirled the umbrella between her fingers, mesmerized by a blur of pink. A breeze swished it away. She lifted her wrap to her shoulders. "And Georgia is the only colony in America founded as a utopian experiment. Even slavery was outlawed."

She took a taste of the delicious, bittersweet liquid.

"I stand corrected." He leaned closer and patted her knee. "Let's just not get into the ways that well-meaning intent can change to criminal intent."

"You sound like my daddy. He's a lawyer." She tilted her head, "Oh, I just remembered. Guess what else is great about the number thirteen?" Closing her eyes, her voice cooed about kissing a cop on--

"You okay there?"

"Love this song. But, Rye, what was I saying? Oh, yeah. Guess what's even better? The Thirteenth Amendment. Emancipation Proclamation." Wow. So hard to say.

"Damn, Miss Georgia," he lifted his glass, "Cheers to the number thirteen." He downed a gulp. "Hell, I'm just happy that Lovell and crew landed safe and sound on my birthday."

"Rye! Happy Birthday. How many?" She lifted her glass in a toast.

"Twenty-two. Never forget this day. Or this night. Hey, thanks for helping me celebrate. Hell, the whole world's celebrating. Right?"

Their glasses touched.

Tally laughed. "Right!" The ginger ale was strong. It really did taste different.

"Great to meet you, Tally. Away from the crowd." He leaned back on the lounge chair, his hair flying up like fireworks with each whoosh of wind, his khaki pants and powder blue shirt the perfect complement to his tanned skin, blue eyes and caramel-colored mustache.

Away from the crowd. Stay sharp. Don't look at those intoxicating eyes.

"Thank you, Rye. Nice to meet someone from New York."

"Yankee through and through. Pre-law. Rebel of the family so far. Until my two little sisters get to be teenagers. Dad wanted me to follow him into medicine at Syracuse. Soon to be my alma mater."

"Wait. The Syracuse basketball team is on the ship. I met them this morning."

"Gang's all here. Spring break. Then finals. Then our last trip as a group to the Kentucky Derby."

"I'm on Spring Break too. Hamper University. Hamper, Georgia."

"Great law school there. Plan to check it out. Especially after meeting you, Miss Georgia. Now do I call you Peaches, Georgia or Grits?"

"Grits? Love it." She laughed. She had no idea what a New Yorker would be called other than 'Yankee' or 'Damn Yankee.' "So do I call you Derby?"

Sounds of calypso music infused the air.

"Hey, Tally, great idea. An invitation to the Derby. Saturday, May second. My special guest. Want to come?"

She thought of a dozen pastel hats she could wear. "Maybe."

"I make a mean mint julep." He leaned forward and touched his finger to her lips. "How did you get pink umbrella paper on your lips? And how did you hear the news about Lovell?"

The scent of lime lingering on his skin energized her as if it were smelling salts.

"My father knows the captain." It was just a little white lie but it put fellows on notice. "And he, the Captain, Captain--"

"Swenson."

"Yes, of course. I know." Why was he grinning? She would never order ginger ale with lime again. It left a strange taste in her mouth. "Captain Swenson greeted me when I was at the lifeboat drill. I told him I'm besotted with the astronauts. My sorority sisters blurted out that I'm a history major. Wait. Did I tell you that? Did I tell you about the award at Oxford I hope to be nominated for?"

"Oxford? England? Seriously?"

"Oglethorpe-Oxford History Honor named after the Founder of Georgia, James Oxford. I mean Oglethorpe. He went to Oxford. I want to be the first winner. Go to graduate school there."

"Damn. They don't even allow girls to be Rhodes Scholars there. Quite a coup. Good luck, Georgia. Wish I could be one of the judges. You'd win, for sure."

"Rye, thank you so much. That's the sweetest thing. Oh, the astronauts. I was dying to hear the news. Yet worried to death they'd die on re-entry. The captain invited me to listen to the ship-to-shore radio in his private quarters."

"Private quarters? Alone? With the Captain?"

"He sat with me on the bed as we listened. How did you hear the news?"

Rye had a funny look on his face like he was trying to remember something.

"I heard the news at dinner. Captain made the announcement in the ballroom."

"Wow. Can you believe it? From '*Houston, we've had a problem*' to '*Boys, take a good look at the moon*' to splashdown just--" She looked at her watch. "Nine hours ago. Good grief. How can it be ten o'clock already?"

"Here's to Apollo 13."

He lifted his glass. Tally lifted hers. They both took gulps.

"Hey, Rye. This doesn't taste so much like ginger ale."

"It's the ale brand they make on the islands. And when they say 'ale' they mean 'ale.' They add a little—Tally—whoa--you okay?"

The rocking of the ship reminded her of the time Shawl snuck up on her while she was asleep in the hammock in the back yard. He had pushed and pulled the ropes until she fell out. She had thrown a book of Rod McKuen poems at him. Wow. She felt dizzy. She needed a biscuit. Shawl cannot prank her now. Blanket. Warm bed. Does Shawl have warm bed in 'Nam? Maybe Guy or Ryan or whatever his name is, such a handsome man leaning over her, could just hold her for a minute. To stop the ship from tipping over.

She felt Guy prop her feet on the towel, take off her strappy sandals, but how come, and wrap yellowy terrycloth over her legs and feet.

"Tally. You don't drink much, do you?"

"Nope. Promised daddy. Waiting til twenty. Like my mother. Not a teenager. A Young Lady."

She heard him say *Spit*. Doesn't he know? A lady doesn't spit in public.

"How old are you?" His voice sounded like a judge.

"Nineteen. Then twenty. Then twenty-one."

"So, you're twenty in June?"

"If I have a Country Club party, will you come? Please. Slow dance. Champagne. Daddy's toasting me with champagne for waiting to be twenty before drinking alcohol."

Why did he say *spit* again?

"Close your eyes for a second." His fingers were pressing her wrist. "Breathe. I'm going to get you some water. Cool compress. Then you're going to take a little nap."

Sounds of "My Girl" floated by her ears. She hiccupped, whispered, "I'm sorry," and smiled at her faux pas as she fell asleep.

Tally heard a phone ring. She opened her eyes. She rushed to the phone. She felt disoriented after being with Rye again, on the ship that night. She hated being awakened from a daydream.

"Cherie. Did you see the balloons?" Her mother's voice sounded effervescent.

"Oh, yes. I took pictures of them. My bed is filled with cards. The kitchen smells like a bakery. I can't wait to see you at the Boutique."

"Could you arrive a little before noon, cherie? Oui?"

Tally could hear her mother laughing with Vera Sanders, her business partner. She had forgotten how her mother's laugh was contagious to anyone who heard it.

"Cherie, we are putting the paquettes of rice on the sterling tray, they look magnifique, and, s'il vous plait, come at midi, ma cherie. Then go to the splash party at the Club before the birthday dinner?"

Babette is babbling. Something is wrong. Or right? She is mixing French with English. She does that when she is worried, tipsy or excited.

"Maman, I'll be there just before noon. Is Vera there? Is Becca? Everything okay?"

"Oui, darling. All is well. I can't wait to see you, ma cherie, my birthday baby."

Tally hung up the phone in a daze. It was as if she had heard her mother's voice, so happy, so giddy, so excited, for the first time in forever.

Tally walked to her dresser. Pink peonies stretched from the crystal vase, healthy, strong, fragrant. She lifted one of the stems from the water. Touching soft petals to her nose, she strolled to the balcony. She stared at the tennis courts where Shawl would be practicing backhand strokes if he were here.

All of a sudden, she had a new birthday wish.

She wanted to hit a backhand stroke at him. She wished it would hit him in the stomach. She was tired of everyone raving about his guts, his grit, his gumption for enlisting. What about safety? What about brother-sister talks? What about finishing his Ph.D in philosophy? What about her peace of mind?

Down deep she was still mad at him. Just because his birthday was picked first in the lottery, why did he have to enlist two days later? Why didn't he wait? Just because he wanted to meet his obligation, just because he had some rush of patriotism, just because he wanted to do his tour of duty and be done as soon as possible, just because he wanted to make Daddy proud, just because he knew that everyone who shared his birth date would be drafted although Daddy could have pulled some strings. Why did he have to enlist?

The past six months since the lottery had been surreal. Now, it was her first birthday without Shawl. And no word from him. Nothing. Not even a card. She hated everything about the Vietnam mess. She hated Nixon. She hated war.

She leaned against the railing. She felt helpless. Tears flooded her eyes until they streaked down her cheeks. She collapsed on the rocking chair, sobbing. Just hearing her mother's voice. So light, airy, bubbly.

It was the greatest gift she could receive on her birthday. Something in her mother's voice sounded carefree for the first time in months. Crying, finally, just letting some of the worry go, felt refreshing, a release of emotions as quick as pulling rubber bands from braided hair only to feel the braids untwisting, the scalp relaxing, the hair free to tumble down.

Tally closed her eyes and rocked in the rocking chair. The petals on the peony in her grasp felt soothing, soft, the way Alida's skin felt when she stroked Tally's hand before naptime when Tally was a little girl. The quiet of the moment soothed her until a buzz sounded close.

A tickle on her hand. She opened her eyes to see a bee creeping up her finger.

She jumped. Shook her hand.

The bee hovered over the petal until it buzzed near her face. She shook her head, wishing she had some hairspray to spritz the bee. That would stop it from moving.

The bee flew back to the peony. She gripped the railing, tossed the flower and watched it splash in the birdbath below. The feel of the railing, the fall of an item so recently in her hands, now soaked in the water, felt visceral.

She remembered the gold-shimmer wrap she wore that night on the ship and how she lost it in the ocean.

Waking from her nap on the chaise lounge aboard the ship that unforgettable night, she remembered seeing Rye's face still frowning. He asked how she was feeling. Becca came to check on her.

Tally heard Becca chatting with Rye—Rye telling Becca he would escort Tally back to her room at the end of the party—Becca giving Tally a roll of Butter Rum Lifesavers to "perk you up with some sugar." Tally hugged her and said she would be back to the cabin soon.

"Tomorrow. You'll feel better." Rye offered Tally a cup of water. "There's the Road Rally on the island. Scavenger hunt." He seemed to be talking to help her wake up. "Why don't I sign us up for a Jeep with a cooler and no ginger ale?"

Tally laughed. The Lifesavers hit the spot. She felt alive again. She felt as light as the bubbles she loved to blow into breezes.

"Sounds fun. But, Rye. How did my shoes come off?"

"Family tradition. Something my dad always did when my mom, sisters or I felt sick. He would take our shoes off, wrap a blanket around our feet for comfort and warmth. He said it makes a person feel secure."

"That's the sweetest thing."

"Sorry about not asking first, Georgia," Rye raised an eyebrow, "but you didn't seem to know—"

"Oh, Rye, I love being barefoot! Hey, let's dance before your birthday ends."

"Here? On the deck?"

"In the moonlight."

He pulled her up. "You sure? You feel like it?"

She nodded. She heard cheers erupt from the ballroom. The band announced they had been playing a medley to celebrate the astronauts' safe return with CCR's "Bad Moon Rising," and Cat Stevens' "Moon Shadow". Now they were ending with Henry Mancini's "Moon River."

"Perfect, Rye. Your birthday. The astronauts home safe."

He wrapped one arm around her back, the other cupping her right hand. She placed her left hand on his shoulder. He smelled like cocoa butter.

Rye pulled her closer. He nuzzled her neck and whispered in her ear, "Thanks for a great birthday, Georgia."

His mustache tickled the curve of her ear. She stood on tiptoes, whispered back, "You're welcome, *Huckleberry Friend.*" His arms pressed her tighter. They slow danced until the music stopped.

"Let's go downstairs for the final songs." Rye grinned. "Join the group."

"No. I like dancing here." She felt energized. Happy. Safe.

A drum roll announced the next song then a roar from the crowd as "Ain't Too Proud to Beg" began to pound from below.

Tally cheered. "Great song."

Rye sang a few words, wrapping his arm around her waist. Their swaying hips moved them closer to the railing.

Wait. Say something. It can't get too lovey-dovey if one person is talking.

Rye leaned in, kissing her neck.

Is that why men have mustaches? To start an avalanche of tickles?

"Hey, Rye. Have you ever seen the Captain's Quarters?"

"Nope. Never been invited." His palm seemed the same size as her back.

"Oh, you would be impressed. It's huge. With a great view of this deck. Rye, the Captain said I'm welcome there anytime. Wasn't that sweet of him? He said I could use his guest robe, take a nap there, just relax on his bed. It wouldn't bother him a bit."

"What? Wait. What?" Rye stepped back.

Perfect. Works every time. Distract a fellow with chatter, even a little bit of a fib, then they are not so insistent. If only she could twist around. Her back touched the railing, so cold against her warm skin.

"Rye, let's keep dancing. I was just saying that the captain is so nice. He told me to stop by anytime."

"This is your father's friend?"

"Well, they, uh, don't know each other too well." It never fails. Say one thing that is not a hundred percent the truth and keep trying to remember what you said.

"Tally. Promise you'll be careful. Especially with guys on a ship."

"Rye. I'm fine. Trust me." She crooked her finger. He leaned down. She whispered in his ear. "I know how to take care of myself."

"Really?" He raised an eyebrow, nodded and stepped back.

"Absolutely." She waved at a crewmember gathering beach towels from the chairs and shouted, "Thank you."

"How are you so sure of yourself?"

"I'm an observer. That's what historians do. And," she tugged at the silk wrap that kept slipping off her shoulders, "I used to teach Self Protection to campers at summer camp. How old are your sisters?"

"Claire is nine, going on eighteen! Courtney is twelve."

"I bet they're darling. I taught campers who were early teens."

Rye put his hands in his pockets. The band announced they would be playing their last song. Someone yelled into the microphone, "New Orrrrr-leeeeans! 'House of the Rising Sun.'" Whistles shredded the air.

"Georgia. Got a question. Do you feel safe here with me?"

"Yes, of course. Besides. I know what to do if I didn't."

"Really?"

"Absolutely. I used to tell the girls if you feel you're in danger, go along with it until you find your way to escape. I was taught that it's better to be raped than killed." My God. She said the word, "raped," in front of him.

"Seriously? You told the young girls this?"

"No. I was very careful not to offend the junior campers with words that might frighten them." Good grief. How did they even start talking about this? Why is he so interested? Probably wants to tell his sisters one day. "Hey, birthday boy, can we dance?"

"Just wondered what else you know that you didn't share with the girls."

"That the attacker doesn't want anything sexual." She couldn't believe she said that word in front of him either. Good grief. They just met. "I mean, he doesn't want anything romantic. The attacker wants to be stronger. Besides, he's angry."

"So was the captain angry today?"

"What?" This is a great slow dance song even if the words made no sense. "Rye. Let's dance. Okay?"

"Good idea."

He scooped her into his arms. She put her head on his chest. His body seemed stronger than before. She never noticed how his muscles could feel so hard, so tight.

It dawned on her. What if the captain or anyone else could see her now? His suite was above the deck. She remembered looking out his window earlier and seeing a couple argue. What if Rye kissed her? How embarrassing.

"Rye. This has been the best. I'm sorry but I think it's time to call it a night. Thank you so much. What an unforgettable evening."

Rye nodded. "Sure. Let's move away from the captain's glare."

Is he clairvoyant? Had she said something out loud?

They strolled to the opposite side of the ship. So much quieter. Less breezy.

Rye seemed lost in thought as if he were figuring out how to approach a jury.

"Georgia, before we say goodnight, how about a birthday kiss?" Rye put his hands on either side of her on the railing. She felt a bit claustrophobic, a bit excited.

"Well, how about one on the cheek since we just met a few hours ago?"

Did he not know how to be romantic? His voice sounded sarcastic.

"Sure. Why not?"

She leaned up to kiss his cheek.

"Damn. You smell like fresh ferns in a forest, Georgia. Ferns. That's it. The color of your eyes. Intoxicating."

"Why, thank you, Rye. You're a sweetheart to notice. It's MaGriffe, from France."

"The French sure know how to keep a guy's attention. Georgia girls do too."

She felt her cheeks warm up. "Thank you. Are you ready for your birthday kiss?"

He had the most incorrigible grin on his face.

She licked her lips slowly with her tongue, glossing the flavor of butter rum over the tender skin of her lips, and grinned back.

"I can't think of anything I want more." He put a finger up to her lips. "But first, I'm curious. Why did you learn self-defense? Have you ever needed to use it?"

"Well, once. I've never been in a really dangerous situation, thank goodness, but thanks for asking." What a caring man. "I learned how to take care of myself during camp that summer when that despicable male, and I say 'male,' because a 'man' would never kill those nurses. Don't you remember? In Chicago? I used to remind the campers that one nurse escaped by hiding under a bed. So, they should always be on the lookout for a chance to escape."

Rye turned and moved away from the railing as a member of the crew whistled while carrying a tray of drinks and asked if they wanted a last round.

"Thanks, buddy. Want something, Georgia?"

"No. Thank you though."

Rye stuffed a ten-dollar bill in the man's shirt pocket. The man winked at Tally as Rye took a big swig of his rum and Coke. She smiled and waved. The waiter disappeared down a staircase. The smell of rum was exhilarating. If there was anything that could make her feel sexual, it was that smell. Sexual. That word again. If she kissed his cheek, soft and gentle, surely that could lead to another kiss, delicious, deliberate, decadent, deeper. If only she could feel his arms hug her close. If only they could share a tender, blissful kiss. In the moonlight. How romantic. The end to a perfect day.

"Georgia, you sound like *you're* convinced you'll be safe. Think you can convince me?" He raised an eyebrow.

"Rye Somerset. Is that a challenge?"

"You decide."

"Look. Here's the quick version." She winked. "If someone attacks you, you're supposed to act crazier than he is. So, if someone attacked me—"

"Like me?"

"Yes. Let's say you're crazy or crazed, angry, whatever, and you try to attack me. But don't, of course. This is just an example. I'm just going to tell you."

"Sure, Georgia." He nodded. "I challenge you to show me exactly how you would protect yourself."

He put his drink on the arm of a deck chair then put his hands behind his back and stood at attention.

"Well, if I were holding books," she pretended there were books in her arms, "I could push them into the bottom of your nose. Except that you're standing up too tall. But if you bent down a little bit--"

He did.

"Perfect. Or I could bash my fingers into your eyes."

"Really?" His voice sounded taunting. "Have you ever tried that?"

He grabbed her wrist the moment she darted her hand toward his face.

"Well, of course, you could stop me like that, Rye." She shook her hands as if they were wet. "Because I told you exactly what I was about to do. So, there was no element of surprise."

"Is the element of surprise important? If you were teaching my sisters how to protect themselves, would you tell them to surprise their potential attacker?"

"Well, your sisters are too young to have to worry about anyone trying to kiss them, Rye. Gracious! When they are older, I would tell them, 'Yes, Claire. Yes, Courtney. Surprise is important!' I hope you tell them that too."

She wanted the feeling of being back in his arms. She wanted them to share a birthday kiss and have him stroll with her back to her room. She wanted to make plans for the Road Rally tomorrow. She wanted their conversation to be flirty and romantic again. Good grief. She wished she had never started this conversation yet she was frustrated by his disbelief that she would know what to do to stop an attack.

She wished she could bonk him on the head with her baton, if it weren't in her room, and say, "I know what I'm talking about!"

But how could he know that she had flown to Paris alone to see her grandmother when she was sixteen and, one night, while walking by herself from the Rue di Rivoli back to their Ritz Hotel in the Place de Vendome after buying a saucer of cherry crepes from a street vendor, she had encountered a group of boys who surrounded her, flattered her in broken English, laughed with her as they told her they would escort her back to her hotel, offered to hold her crepes even as she refused, and talked with each other in French until she heard one boy urging the others to stand guard as he pulled her beneath the darkened awning of a bespoke cufflink boutique.

Trying not to panic, she had immediately spilled the plate of warm, gooey crepes on the boy's shirt, apologized profusely, slid her perfume dispenser from her bra strap, spritzed it several times in the air, the fragrance seeming to distract the boys for the instant it took her to dash into the glow of a lamplight where a man was lighting a cigarette.

In fluent French, she begged for his help. As he approached the boys who had already begun to scatter, she shouted, "Merci beaucoup, Monsieur," ran across the cobblestones past the historic obelisk in the Vendome square, greeted the bellman at the Ritz who must have seen fury in her eyes as he asked, "Mademoiselle, est ce que vous allez bien?" and entered the revolving door that led to the carpeted safety of the hotel.

Rye also could not know about the time she visited Pompeii, Italy with her mother when she was seventeen and the handsome young man who was their tour guide had flirted with her, called her "Bella," and asked her mother if he could walk with her daughter on the beach near their hotel in Naples that night. Tally had told him, "Oh, you don't have to ask my mother. Thank you for your offer, however, I don't know you well enough to do that. Would you like to walk on the beach with Mother and me tomorrow morning, in the sunlight, instead?" She had smiled as the young man hurriedly directed their attention to Mt. Vesuvius and its hovering proximity. Later, her mother had praised her for not being swayed by his handsome face and abundant charm.

"Georgia? Are you in a trance? You haven't had a sip of ginger ale since your earlier fiasco so I know you're not drunk." He snapped his fingers.

"Sorry, Rye. Why you don't believe me? You think I'm weak and not smart enough to--"

"Georgia, I care about you, you nut, and I don't think you really know what you're talking about. Or at least you haven't proven it. It's one thing to be smart. It's another to be savvy."

Okay. That does it.

"Well, I do know what I'm talking about! I could kick you in the— well, you know!"

"Not very savvy. That's the first place a guy defends."

"Okay. I could surprise you, do something unexpected, make you think I'm crazier than you are, you know, act like a monkey, make weird sounds to throw you off, distract you, make you pause so I could run away. Or I could stick my finger down my throat, throw up—"

She never finished "all over you."

In one swift move, he pushed his body against hers, his hands on the railing. She could not move. His force pressed her against the metal barrier. His weight, his strength, his intensity, his power overwhelmed her. She couldn't breathe. *Dear God! What is he doing?* She struggled, tried to move her arms. His body pressure, his hands gripping the railing, prevented her escape. So hard to breathe. Her voice felt paralyzed. Everything seemed in slow motion. His lips almost touched hers. She could smell rum on his breath. She felt panicky. Too shocked to scream. Dizzy. *You idiot. He could push you overboard. No one would ever know.*

In a motion as quick as the moment he pushed against her, he let go of the railing. Stepped back. Arms behind his back.

He said in a low voice, "Do not scream. Do not run. You know I can stop you."

His voice sounded angry.

Her legs felt paralyzed. Her brain, shocked. Swirling. Furious. Afraid.

She wanted to sob.

He stared at her. She stared at him. A rush of energy. Her fists clenched. If only she could slap him, kick him, spit on him. If only she had her baton.

"Tally. I won't touch you--unless you run or scream. Are you clear about--"

"Why did you do that? Why did you treat me that way?" She could not stop babbling in her embarrassment and shock. "I just met you. I'll call the captain." Her body kept shaking. "Why did you scare me like that?"

"Tally. You have no idea how much I want to hold you right now. I know you won't let me. But I do. I know I caused you panic and I'm sorry for having to--"

"Sorry? Are you kidding me? How dare you. I don't ever want to see you again. And just so you know. That was a horrible thing you just did. You ruined my night, my day, my trip, everything."

"Tally, if you don't listen to me, I'll have to tie you to that railing." He glared at her. "Listen."

She started to inch along the white metal barrier. Her wrap fell from her shoulders. She tried to grab it before it tumbled to the water below.

"Tally. Do you hear me? Look. I need to tell you something. Hear me out."

Tally said, "Swap places. You against the rail. Me on the outside. You've got two seconds before I yell for the captain."

She stood behind the chair, shivering. He stood, ramrod straight, against the railing.

"Tally. I apologize. My actions were outrageous to you, I'm sure. I may have pressed too hard, gone a little overboard."

"I wish *you* had gone overboard. You scared me! Not fair!"

Oh, my gosh! The best birthday gift ever! You're here. I can't—" She never finished, "thank you enough."

With one arm cradling her derriere, Rye tightened his grip around her as their laughter melted into deeper, slower kisses until a feeling of dizziness overwhelmed Tally again with one clear anchoring decision.

Tonight, she would make love for the first time in her life with this man of her dreams. The most memorable birthday gift she could ever give herself. And the deepest thank you she could ever offer him.

"Now when do I get to meet this handsome fellow?"

At the sound of Vera's voice, Tally lowered herself from Rye's embrace to squeeze Vera's hand.

"Vera! It's Rye. I mean, please meet Rye Somerset. He drove all the way from New York to Georgia for my birthday. And, Rye, please meet Vera Sanders, the most talented and beloved seamstress in Georgia."

"Thank you, Tally. Nice to meet you, Rye. You are mighty generous to drive all that way to celebrate our Birthday Girl today."

Tally knew the word "generous" was Vera's way of sounding cordial yet still having reservations about someone.

Vera shook Rye's hand after tucking a thimble into the pocket of her pink sewing apron that complimented the beauty of her ebony skin.

"Wouldn't have missed it, Vera. Tally has told me a lot about you. Your place here is impressive. Congratulations."

Tally hoped Vera would not say anything about the lipstick on Rye's lips or surely the smeared lipstick on hers.

"Thank you, Rye. Did Tally tell you about our Creed? Our history? And you do know, of course, that history is the *true* love of her life?"

"I could prove that to a jury any day of the week."

Rye offered Vera a croissant.

Vera took a bite. "And I'm sure, Rye, from all Tally has told me about you, that jury verdict would be unanimous!" She rolled the tips of her fingers on a cotton napkin before offering it to Tally and motioning to her lips.

Tally dotted the napkin about her lips. Remnants of lip gloss sparkled the soft fabric.

"Our Birthday Girl has a thing for history and creeds, as I'm sure you know. Lord, have mercy! She was just the age of a flower girl when she asked, "What creed do you love, Vera-dear-a? She got that word, 'creed,' from her daddy and she never let go of it."

"So, Rye, our creed here at Babette's Bridal Boutique is based on the premise that every girl in the South needs an exquisite wedding dress at some time in her life, preferably sooner than later." Vera raised her eyebrow at Tally whose cheeks were blushing.

Rye nodded his head as if he were listening to a witness who was saying more during cross-examination than he had asked.

"Of course, I give credit to my grandma for teaching me to sew," Vera rubbed her calloused fingers on the napkin Tally offered her back. "Gracious. I've made thousands of dresses since Babette and I met but we first started our business with--Tally, did you tell him? She still blushes about our origins. You see, Rye, we started with brassieres."

Tally rolled her eyes and shook her head, her cheeks feeling warmer by the second. Rye leaned against the banister, shaking his head and smiling, as Vera started what Tally called "Vera's greatest hits-routine."

Tally had never had a chance to tell Rye that Vera did not believe in the word "decorum," that she refused to sugarcoat an awkward topic or use euphemisms.

"Babette learned to sew in Arromanches, France, her hometown."

"Talk about history." Rye leisurely tickled the soft spot below Tally's ear. Her reflex squeezed her shoulder up to her cheek, almost trapping his finger. He grinned. "That's the famous Mulberry Harbor. D-Day's secret weapon."

"Yes," Vera nodded, "where Babette and Lieutenant Delphi, as he was called then, met. He was in the Navy and helped to secure the coastline north of Omaha Beach on D-Day. And Babette, oh, you should hear her tell the story, Rye. She fell in love with Lieutenant Delphi the night she first met him."

Tally licked her bottom lip.

Rye winked at Tally.

"Babette gets dreamy, speaks in French and even though I've never really understood all of what she says, I can read their love story just by watching her expressions. It's a talent I have."

Rye scooped up a mini-croissant and popped it in his mouth without taking his eyes off Vera.

"She was only nineteen. They married in the garden of her home—Lieutenant Delphi in his uniform, Babette in a dress she had designed and sewn herself. Oh, and it was beautiful. We have it in the vault waiting for Tally." Vera tilted her head and raised her eyebrow at Rye, her shiny black curls studded with pink silk tea roses.

"Veeeerrra!"

Rye laughed.

"Anyway, Babette came to America with a revolutionary idea. She wanted to be a—what does she call it, Tally?"

"A *corsetiere*."

"Yes. She had designed a bridal brassiere, an architectural masterpiece, that was functional, comfortable, supportive and sensual. The only thing is--she didn't want satin. Not affordable or durable enough, she said. That's what she told me when we first met. She invited me to her house, Tally here was sitting in her little yellow rocking chair, rocking her baby doll, sucking her thumb and looking at me like she was listening to every word I said. Anyway, Babette served me champagne and crepes suzettes, and told me she wanted to work with me, the best seamstress in the South, she had heard. I told her I had never had crepes in my life but if she would keep making them from time to time, I would be happy to work with her."

Vera laughed.

"Yessirree, Babette and I started a revolution. See this corset with a built-in brassiere?" She pointed to a dress form displaying an old-fashioned corset decorated with bows and ribbons. "Wires, literally steel wires, in brassieres, through the years, had always been used to support the female anatomy causing all kinds of pain, especially in hot weather in the South, when the weight of the garment and heaviness of the fabric made it so you couldn't breathe or move without hurting. When I was little, I used to see my mother sigh the biggest relief when she took hers off at night after working all day and on weekends for the Carson family."

"Khaki and Jimbo's family." Tally clarified before whispering under her breath, "So sorry about this."

Rye squeezed her hand.

"That Miss Carson, Khaki's grandmother, was an absolute tyrant. She still is if you ask folks in my old neighborhood. My mama said that Miss Carson would holler that she, Mrs. Myrtle Indigo Carson, would not embarrass her friends by having them see her maid, Annie Love, my mother, looking 'floppy' when they came to her house for Prayer Meetings, Dinner on the Ground-planning meetings, Picnic by the Ocean-fun meetings or 'Spit in the Ocean' card-playing tournaments. So, my mother scrubbed floors, fed the Carson children, washed clothes and styled Miss Carson's hair every day while wearing a brassiere with wires that marked up her skin. It was the only one she could afford and she washed it every night. That is, until she brought home a buttercup pastel tablecloth made of polished cotton that Miss Carson was about to toss in the trash and decided to design her own brassiere without wires."

Vera tugged Rye's hand to glide over the fabric on the most elegant blush pink bra in the salon, "It's Georgia's own Sea Island cotton, polished in the mill to shimmer like sunshine on top of water, and no other cotton blend is finer. When mama brought Miss Carson's tablecloth home, my sisters and I couldn't stop touching it. Mama measured herself, made a pattern, and cut strips of the cotton to cradle one's bosoms in a way that made mama smile every day."

"Impressive, Vera." Rye's fingers stroking the bra mesmerized Tally. "Your mother was quite a problem solver."

"Thank you, Rye. I showed my mama's brassiere to Babette and the two of them collaborated on the design and the *Annie Love-Babette Bridal Brassiere* was born. Judge Delphi made sure the patent was in both names and my mama still gets royalties. Best of all, she just bought some property on the street where Miss Carson lives."

"And Mama made Vera her partner right away."

Tally gave Vera a kiss on the cheek.

While Rye asked Vera a question about the patent, Tally's thoughts swirled about serving as Vera's "Bridal Assistant" through the years.

As a kindergartener, Tally held pincushions and tape measures for Vera, whom she idolized, as she dreamed of standing on that pedestal one day in a princess white gown too. The brides would ooh and ahh over Tally's organdy dresses and the bows in her baby-fine butterscotch hair.

As Tally grew older, she fluffed hems of wedding gowns for Vera and buttoned hundreds of satin-covered buttons on wedding dresses.

Tally grinned at the memory. When she was younger, Vera would hug her and whisper in her ear, "Baby girl, look how strong your fingers are." Years later, Vera would take credit for Tally's dexterity to twirl batons through her fingers as a direct result of Tally doing her "finger exercises" while buttoning wedding gowns on Wednesday afternoons after school.

Tally had even twirled her baton when Vera would ask the Bride-to-be to "focus on the twirling and be still now" while Vera tediously marked the hem of the satin, silk, brocade, jersey, polished cotton, tulle, taffeta, organza or lace wedding dress being fitted.

As Vera was sharing with Rye how she and Babette decided to change from Babette's Bridal Brassieres Boutique to a more focused approach to become Babette's Bridal Boutique, the sound of Vera's voice triggered Tally's memories of the way Vera guided brides, who desperately wanted to get a tan before their summer weddings, to focus on what was most important instead.

Vera would say, "Now it's a wonder to me how folks with white skin always want to have dark skin yet folks with black skin are proud to be the color God made 'em."

Vera would chit-chat in her soothing voice to put the bride at ease by telling her how pretty her skin was, how delicate and lovely the freckles on her arms were, how complimentary her porcelain skin would be as a cushion for the pearls or diamonds she would be wearing around her neck, how stunning the bride would look in her favorite sleeveless dress even though the bride kept fretting about how the pink splotches on her arms that appeared when she got nervous would take attention away from the dress itself.

Vera would remind the bride that the wedding would be *her* special day to celebrate love and that her groom would surely love his bride looking like herself whether she had a tan or freckles or birthmarks or scars or splotches on her delicate skin.

"It's not the color of your skin that matters to him, honey. No, sirree. You know what matters to him?" Vera would squeeze the girl's jittery hands. "The way *you* make him see the world *in color instead of just black and white.*"

Tally was amazed to see the shoulders of the brides-to-be slump down, the smiles return to their faces, their laughs fill the room.

"He fell in love with you, honey bunch," Vera would say, "now don't you forget that. He loves your smile, your pretty blue eyes, your laugh, your sweet personality."

"Now everything's going to be just fine." Vera would give the bride a cotton handkerchief to dab her eyes before giving her a hug. "And you can go get yourself a tan on your honeymoon! I'll even buy you the cocoa butter. Just promise me you won't get your skin blistered before the wedding or every spot of your skin this dress touches is going to hurt like the devil! Okay, you Beautiful Bride! Everything's going to be just fine."

Even though Tally heard the most endearing words through the years in the Bridal Salon, she also heard arguments between mothers and daughters about the plunge of the neckline on the wedding dress being too low for church; about the mother's insistence that there would be no secular music like "Love Letters in the Sand" played at the Baptist church during the ceremony reducing the bride to tears and shouts between the two; about the mother's snide remarks that even an empire waist Juliet gown would not hide the fact that the bride was in the 'family way;' or about the groom's hair being too long; or his family not being rich enough.

Every Wednesday night, Tally wrote notes in the Wedding Guest Book her mother had given her to practice her cursive on the lined pages.

Finally, after years of observations trying to figure out why girls would ever marry in the first place since it seemed like such an emotional ordeal and, as a teenager, seeing former brides come back after a divorce for a brand-new wedding dress, Tally made her decision never to marry and never to put up with the expectations and heartaches she had witnessed during those fittings.

After all, she just wanted a sweetheart, not a groom, a word that always reminded her of a person who took care of horses.

Now what was Vera saying?

"*Revolutionary* is the word *The Hamper Herald* called our partnership as a Black woman and a White woman owning a business together when there was a clamor, remember, Tally, that time you won the 'Georgia Girl' award and you were in all the papers and Miss Tess wrote a column to introduce your family and included me too? Did you tell him, honey?"

"No, Vera. He's not interested in—"

"Sure I am. What's the 'Georgia Girl Award'?"

Vera practically stumbled over her words in her rush to tell Rye.

"The owner accused him of stealing a Baby Ruth candy bar even though Larchmont told him he had put the money on the counter. Larchmont even pointed to the money that had somehow ended up on the floor just before being handcuffed by the police but it seems the owner wanted to make an example to his customers."

"Daddy said if only Larchmont were a Georgia citizen, Daddy could have intervened in the process but all he could do as a Georgia Judge for an Alabama citizen is give Larchmont a character reference and talk to the judge in Andersonville, Georgia. And the judge, a University of Georgia alum, refused to hear about the 'Bama Bad Boy,' as he called Larchmont."

"Judge Delphi drives to see that judge whenever his court is out of session to get to know him better and to talk to him on Larchmont's behalf and to visit with Larchmont at the jail and give him hope for another appeal."

"Oh, Vera! Last week Daddy said it's time for the 'Jello strategy' so Daddy, Tessie and Mr. Moretti drove to Andersonville to see Larchmont. They took him a cake, comics and crossword puzzles to celebrate his birthday. Tess interviewed Larch, posed with him beside the cake, and her editorial will be in her *Wednesday Wisdom* column."

"*Jello* strategy?" Rye raised an eyebrow.

"In the South, we always say that the only way to nail Jello to a tree is to *shine a light on it*. That's what the article and photo aim to do. Shine a light on Larchmont and his plight and the injustice he's endured. Yet Daddy says Larchmont's ordeal is an example of the price of fame."

"A double-edged sword." Rye shook his head.

Tally looked at Vera who was wiping a tear from her cheek.

She gave Vera a hug.

"Well, if anyone knows about fame, it's Vera. Not only is she famous for being the best seamstress in Georgia and a pioneer businesswoman."

Vera smiled.

"But she was famous from the moment she was born."

"Really? Congratulations, Vera. Should I get your autograph?"

Vera shook her head.

"I had nothing to do with it. It's just that my birthday is January 1st and my sisters and I were the first New Year's babies born in Georgia in 1929."

"Sisters?

"Can you believe it, Rye?" Tally hugged Vera's arm. "Triplets! Vera Velmarie, Lula Louise and Alida Lee Sanders."

Vera tucked the frame under her arm, shook Rye's hand, blew a kiss to Tally with a shout of "Happy Birthday to the Birthday Girl. See you at Patchett's Fish Camp," and shut the door to her office.

Tally gasped. "Rye, Mother forgot about Vera not being allowed at the Country Club tonight." Tally made a mental note to remind her mother about Vera.

Church bells chimed the noon hour.

Tally took a deep breath. Oh, my gosh. Twenty years old. A new decade. A new romance. A new identity of being a full-fledged woman after tonight. Tingles bubbled inside her. She was closer than ever to making love with Rye in just a few hours.

Rye nuzzled her ear, whispering, "Happy Birthday, Georgia," and pulled her into his arms, lifting her off the ground.

"Rye Somerset. Thank you for being my favorite gift ever."

Rye hugged her tighter as the tip of his tongue traced her earlobe.

Tally closed her eyes. His voice sounded like a growl. Her voice sounded, to her ears, like a purr.

"And isn't it about time to start granting me some birthday wishes?"

Rye's laugh tickled her ear. "Turning twenty hasn't changed you a bit, Tally McCall."

Tally cocked her head against his arm. She crooked her finger. He leaned closer. She could smell chocolate. Their lips touched in a slow, meandering, consuming kiss as Rye's tongue filled her mouth with the flavor of sugar until he pulled away.

"You taste so—" She felt wobbly.

Rye shook his head. "You have no idea what I want to—"

Tally knew. She wanted the same thing. To go upstairs to the guest bedroom, lock the door and make love that very second.

"Well, until your idea happens, Mr. Somerset, will you keep kissing me like that?"

Rye's blue eyes never wavered from her gaze. "Let's skip dinner and I won't stop kissing you like that," he raised an eyebrow, "and more."

The look in his eyes, the serious tone of his voice, the beat of her heart pounding in her ears, the bells sounding like drumbeats. She felt as if she were plunging over the top of the Ferris Wheel, free-falling with flutters like butterflies being released in her core. A wave of abandon gushed into a seriousness of purpose.

What would it hurt if they went upstairs right now to the guest bedroom? Or drove to the weeping willow near the Georgia Glen Cabin and parked under the fronds, hidden from view? Or slipped into a dressing room, locked the door and made love on the chaise lounge? Or, or, or—she could not stop thinking of what it would feel like if she were in Rye's arms and he was stretched out beside her, kissing her and touching her where she had never been touched before.

She could feel her resolve melting as she sensed her expression changing from delight to desire, from ingénue to seductress. Rainbows danced on the wall. Rye's hand fell to her hip. If only she could make time stand still. If only the bells could keep pounding. If only that moment would never end.

Suddenly, Rye lowered his arms and put her feet on the floor again.

"Georgia, what am I going to do with you?" Rye coughed.

"You--you're going to be my gift all day today!" Tally stuttered as she tried to compose herself. She blew him a kiss. "Tonight too!"

Rye grinned. "You know the perfect band name? The Temptations. You know the perfect lyric? *Get ready*—"

He whispered the rest of the lyrics in her ear.

"Well, until you do—" Tally blushed at her boldness, "you handsome man, you can solve a mystery for me. Why did you say the phone call between Coach Bryant and Coach Butts was on September 13th when I know it was on September 14th?"

"How do you know it?"

"Because everybody in the South knows that *The Saturday Evening Post* article starts out with the sentence, *On Friday morning, September 14, 1962, an insurance salesman in Atlanta, Georgia, named George Burnett picked up his telephone and dialed the number of a local public-relations firm.*" Tally wanted to throw her baton to the skylight. "And that is when George Burnett was mistakenly put on a party line with Coach Bryant and Wally Butts and heard their conversation."

"And that first sentence was one of the reasons for the *Post* losing its case. The phone call didn't happen on the 14th. It happened on the 13th. *The Saturday Evening Post* published the wrong date in the first sentence of the article that doomed the story's credibility as a thoroughly researched work. Their rush to publish the story damned their case in court and provided another example of their sloppy journalism in this article and their inaccurate historical facts."

Tally heard his voice yet could not reconcile what he was saying. Accuracy was the hallmark of historical facts and she couldn't believe—now what is he saying—doing?

"You see," Rye traced a finger along the edge of Tally's halter-top as he spoke slowly, quietly, "the author of the article didn't get the date right. And," his finger slipped under the soft fabric, beneath her bra to the top of her nipple, "if you're going to do something as important as upset the whole damn football nation in the South, seems to me," his lips were nuzzling her neck, "you'd better get all the details right. Right?"

She nodded.

His finger touched the tip of her nipple, as solid now as a pearl.

Twenty-four

Tally careened her MGB convertible past weeping willows bordering the promenade to the Hamper Country Club. The Splash Party in her honor would start soon and she wanted to speed up the events of the day. Sunset and moonlight could not come fast enough. A blur of green leaves and sunshine dappled her view as she imagined what tonight would be like when she finally made love for the first time.

Her fingers squeezed the stick shift. Her feet alternated between the clutch, the gas and the brake, each jerky action reminiscent of the way her flirting, French kissing, and verbal brakes of saying "No" to boys through the years had driven her to remain a virgin. Her past decisions, dashing faster in her memories than her convertible as it raced around the curves, and her present plans for making love to Rye seemed clearer than ever.

At the curve near the tennis courts, a young man with blonde hair backhanded a tennis ball. Through the haze of sunbeams and shadows,

Tally saw Shawl, throwing his arms up in the air in victory the way this young man did.

"Shift, Georgia!"

Rye's voice sounded muffled yet stern.

Tally stomped the brake. The car steered back to the pavement. Tires squealed as she rounded the bend. Pressing the clutch while shifting gears, she felt the baton she always kept in her car bounce between her legs to the floor. Rye leaned from the passenger seat, his arm crossing her leg.

He reached for the baton as it slid across the floorboard under the brake. His hand brushed her inner thigh. Tingles sparkled up her leg.

Skidding on gravel, Tally pumped the clutch, shifted to first gear and braked. Rye placed the baton on a blanket nestled between the seats and the folded accordion-convertible top. Tally's black and white striped dress bag secured with yellow ribbons to the back of her headrest, floated like a banner in the wind, landing askew, its black bordered hem touching the ground.

"Oops! Sorry about that, Rye." Tally could feel her cheeks getting redder.

A siren shrieked. In the rearview mirror, a police car, screeching to a halt, looked like a tank about to ram her.

"Tally! Listen to me. Don't admit you were speeding." Rye grabbed her quilted Chanel bag, placed it on her lap and squeezed her leg just above her knee as if in reassurance. "Just show him your driver's license. Be calm. Don't incriminate yourself."

While Rye was talking, Tally had stepped out of the car, slammed the door, and approached the police officer.

"Or not!" Rye shook his head. Mumbling, "Damn," he opened his door.

"Mike Parish, why are you following me?"

Lieutenant Parish pulled out his thick ticket book, with carbon sheets between pages, without saying a word.

"I thought I saw you hiding behind the mimosa trees near the entrance, Mike. Were you waiting for me?" Tally looked up at him. His sunglasses hid his eyes. He kept writing.

"Mike, I will fight this ticket. I'll go to court if I have to. I wasn't going any faster than I normally do. And those other tickets? I went to the courthouse and paid them but this one isn't fair. Besides this is a private promenade and not even a city street, Mike!"

Rye cleared his throat and moved closer. "Hello, Officer. Is there a problem here?"

"Nothing I can't handle." Mike signaled Rye with his hand to move back. "Miss McCall, even though this is a private promenade, as you correctly state, it is still within the police jurisdiction of this county. If someone happens to be killed by your reckless driving as they walk along the promenade to the tennis courts, would that felony just be handled privately by the Hamper Country Club?"

Rye coughed although it sounded a bit like a laugh.

"Mike!" Her voice lowered as Mike's hat tilted above her head. "Are you trying to embarrass me?"

"Officer," Rye cleared his throat. "I think that scenario could be considered—"

"Appropriate." Mike stated, his hand on his holster.

Tally looked at her watch. "Mike, I don't have time to—"

"Miss McCall," Mike interrupted. "Drive slower. You'll live longer. And everyone else will too."

Mike placed a white envelope in Tally's hand.

"Besides," Mike touched her nose with his finger, "isn't that what today is all about? Celebrating life?"

Tally grinned.

"Mike, you remembered!" She opened the birthday card, read Mike's note and rolled her eyes. "Coupons at the Piggly Wiggly for Baby Ruth candy bars? What a hoot!"

Tally placed the card by her bag and reached to hug Mike as he bent down, embracing her. His hands touched her bare back. Stiffening, he suddenly moved upward. In his lurching action, silk threads of Tally's blouse caught on his badge. Trying to untangle her blouse without ripping a hole in it, Tally leaned closer to Mike. Fidgeting with the threads, trying to extricate them from Mike's badge, she fretted as Mike hands neared the center of her breast in his apparent wish to help.

Tally squeezed Mike's hands.

"Mike. Sooo sorry." Tally plied his fingers from the silk. "Mike, hold on. The fabric could tear. Better yet, I think I can get this all by myself."

Mike's radio crackled, belching the sound of a female voice from his car. "Hey, Mike. Want to meet me at Blue's Bar-B-Q for a late lunch?"

Tally knew that voice. "Connie May?"

"Oh, hey, Tally. Mike told me he was fixing to surprise you and wish you a Happy Birthday." Connie May began singing "Happy Birthday to You."

"Tally, if I was still at the diner, I'd bring you an extra scoop of blackberry cobbler with Miss Sharon Marie's homemade vanilla ice cream on top."

"Connie May, you sweetie pie! Thank you. And congratulations on your new job as the dispatcher. But I miss you at the diner."

Mike twisted slightly and hollered back. "Connie May, meet you there in fifteen minutes, give or take."

Tally looked up at Mike. He was blushing. If they were hugging, they could not be more entangled.

"Can I help you two?" Rye arched his eyebrow as he approached.

"Oh, gosh. Rye, please meet Mike. Mike, this is Rye."

Rye held out his hand over Tally's head. Mike shook it.

"Nice to meet you, Mike. Mind if I help?"

Mike had barely nodded by the time Rye unlatched Mike's badge from his blue shirt. In a quick motion with his knuckle brushing Tally's breast, Rye left Tally holding the badge still attached to her halter top.

"Sorry to take that off your shirt, Mike. Seems it's the only way Tally can have some privacy to untangle herself."

"Sure. Yeah. Thanks."

Within moments, Tally had followed lavender threads around the tiny protrusion on Mike's badge and gingerly removed the silk from the silver star. Both of the fellows were staring at her. She handed Mike his badge and gave him another hug, this time without incident.

"Have fun at the party, Tally-ho. Nice to meet you, Ryan." Mike tipped his hat to her before securing his badge on his shirt again. "And slow down," his voice sounded stern again. "With everything. Know what I mean, Jelly Bean?"

Mike saluted Rye who nodded his head. Mike sounded his siren in two short bursts as he peeled onto the Promenade exit.

Tally blew Rye a kiss as they resumed their places in the convertible. "Alright, my knight in shining armor! That's how it's done. And no speeding ticket for the Birthday Girl after all."

"So, that was your last boyfriend? Nice to know my competition."

"Now, Rye Somerset! You know nobody compares to you."

Tally winked and zoomed to the veranda where valets were waiting near her girlfriends who held yellow balloons and squealed her name as she stepped on the brake.

Twenty-five

Like a scene from every beauty pageant, dance recital, Debutante Ball and Majorette Contest, a group of young ladies stood in front of a mirror. In the Ladies' Lounge at the Club, Tally, Virginia, Becca, and Rayleigh applied Pot O' Gloss lip shimmer with their fingers as they compared tan lines from the afternoon's Splash Party.

After washing her hands, Tally blew air kisses to her sorority sisters. In the Bridal Dressing Room, decorated in white and gold for the weddings and receptions held at the Club, she selected L'Air du Temps perfume from a silver tray and spritzed it on her neck and down her arms. The light, sea breeze fragrance calmed her nerves. The moisture felt cool to her tender skin. Gingerly, she pulled a sleeveless aqua mini-dress over her tender-to-the-touch-shoulders that seemed to grow pinker by the minute.

Rushing down the back stairs, she inquired about Winston's whereabouts at the valet check-in. Told he would return soon, she waited until he strolled to the desk carrying a set of keys that he placed on a board next to gold numbers corresponding to parking spaces in the valet parking lot.

"Hey, Winston." Tally greeted Winston with a smile.

"Hey, Girl. I mean, *Birthday* Girl."

Winston apologized for the change of plans. "Tally, I got to work as many gigs as I can to pay for that trip to Oxford for the interviews."

"Winston, I, uh, I think Professor Dodge has a surprise donor who's going to pay our way. But, shhh. You can't say anything. Promise?"

Winston's face lit up. "You're not messing with me? When is he planning to tell us?"

"Soon, I'm sure. Hey, Winston," she pulled out a white lace-wedding fan and started breezing it back and forth, "try to finish early so we can celebrate, okay? Even a quick toast with champagne during the band break? At the gazebo. Please? Besides, I want you to meet Rye and I want Rye to meet you. He's heard so much about you."

"Do my best, girl. Impressed that guy drove down to see you. And your Mama went on and on about Rye's surprise when I called this morning." Winston shook his head. "Haven't heard her voice that excited since, wow, I can't even remember when."

"Not having Shawl here for my birthday, for the first time in my life—" Tally stopped fanning as if in a daze. "Well, Rye being here is a great distraction for Mother."

"Sounds like a great distraction for you too, girl." Winston patted her arm as he grabbed a set of keys. Tally grimaced in pain.

"Sorry, girl. Guess there are benefits from having black skin, after all."

A car honked.

"Better get some cream on your skin, pronto. There's some kind of coconut-smelling lotion by the valet station. And, girl, if I don't see you later, call me. We need to talk strategy. I say let's both win the award. Shoot, Oxford needs a Black guy and a White girl from the South to make history. They gotta believe in the power of two, baby."

The car honked again.

Winston started to jog to the valet stand, turned and pulled a paper airplane from his pocket and sailed it to her. "Catch, Amelia."

Tally grabbed the airplane as it sailed toward her. She grinned seeing a red fox drawn on one wing and the phrase, "Once a fox, always a fox" written on the other.

She stood by the striped yellow and white canvas curtains on each side of the valet check-in, and took a bow.

"Amelia's curtain call just for you, Win!"

She reached for the coconut lotion and smoothed it on her arms.

Winston laughed, waved to the driver, hollered, "Happy Birthday, Girl," and dashed to the black Barracuda driven by Louie Larson. Khaki waited in the passenger seat until Winston opened her door.

Louie tossed the keys over Winston's head and laughed. Winston ran to pick them up as other cars arrived.

Khaki slapped Louie's hand, pointed to the keys and, in the midst of their angry voices, Louie hollered, "Sorry, man. Got a Jackson for you," before placing a twenty under a windshield wiper and receiving a kiss from Khaki.

Tally strolled to the balcony outside the dining room alone. She had not seen Rye since they split up to change clothes after the pool party. Soon it would be dinner. Then dancing. Then darkness. Then, oh my gosh, where would they go to make love? Back to the Bridal

Boutique? Sneak into the guest house in the forest behind her parents' home? In Rye's car? On the beach?

It was almost time for the dinner dance and her birthday dinner to start.

She looked out over the flower gardens, the fountain, the golf course. In the distance she could see the flags and the rooftops of the barracks at Fort Hamper. Tears spilled to her cheeks, like kisses to her tightening skin. She could not reconcile the absurdity of her frivolous life of leisure compared to Shawl's life of rigor.

If she thought about Shawl too much, if she thought about Shawl missing her birthday, she would never make it through the night. She reached for a linen napkin on a table inside the ballroom, dabbing the corners of her eyes. The Club orchestra was tuning instruments. As her eyes cleared, she saw Rye talking with the pianist. She walked over to the two of them.

Rye put his arm around her, his hand on her upper arm, and mentioned how hot she felt. Tally winced, kissed his hand, tugged it from her shoulder, and twirled under his raised arm as if making a dance move.

Rye grinned and asked if the pianist could play the song they had discussed. Rye placed two ten-dollar bills in the silver goblet on the piano.

"After you raged against Andrew Jackson during our dance at the Gala," Rye whispered to Tally, "I've started asking for Hamilton's instead."

Tally laughed and whispered in his ear, "Merci for remembering, Rye."

The pianist signaled the musicians to take a break.

Before exiting, the men in white tux jackets and black tux pants quickly dimmed the lights, lit candelabras adorning tables by the windows and closed the French doors.

Rye led Tally behind sheer panels of blue billowy gauze where private dances were reserved.

The pianist played a tune Tally had heard before. She could not remember the title or the lyrics. She loved the melody, the mesmerizing tempo, the way she felt as if swept away to a distant place as Rye held her tight, slow dancing inside their cloud of blue.

She closed her eyes. Rye's arms held her gently, his hands clasped behind her back, at her waist. Her arms nestled behind his neck. They swayed to the music. Rye kissed her shoulder. The touch of his lips soothed her skin. The final notes echoed. Rye cradled her head against his chest, cupped his hand over her ear as if for privacy and whispered in her ear, "You belong to me."

At dinner, the orchestra played songs requested from the audience until the pianist's fingers flourished the keys from one side of the piano to the other. He asked everyone to join in singing "Happy Birthday" to Tally McCall on the occasion of her twentieth birthday.

Rye, Tally's parents, her sorority sisters, their dates, Tess Hamper, and Mr. Tillery, the census taker who delivered her and who was a special guest each year at her birthday party, raised their glasses and sang. Diners throughout the Club sang along, clapping as the song ended.

Tally's father stood. Guests and diners quieted.

"Thank you, good friends, for your indulgence of time as I say 'Happy Birthday' to my baby girl. Only thing is, she's not a baby anymore."

Delphi winked at Tally.

"I could go on and on about the joy Tally has brought her mother, her brother and me, the joy she has brought us all, however, I know the orchestra wants to play and my esteemed fellow diners want to dance. So, let me just say this to my girl."

Delphi cleared his throat and raised his glass.

"Tally Gigi McCall, my only daughter, who was born on June 15th, 1950, the 735th anniversary of the Magna Carta, that Great Charter of Freedoms that was sealed by King John at Runnymede, you have acquitted yourself well. In school. In baton twirling. In learning about history. And in life. You have championed freedom and fairness and justice your entire life. Most of all, you have acquitted yourself well as a daughter who would make any father proud. I'm blessed and honored to be yours."

Diners clapped.

"However, as your Daddy, I must also say my verdict is 'guilty,' for, Shug, you have been stealing my heart from the moment you were born."

Guests laughed, oohed and ahhed.

"Here's to you, cherie," Babette stood and joined Delphi. "To the next chapter of your life. Your Twenties! Your Roaring Twenties!"

Babette kissed Tally on both cheeks. "Je t'aime plus que tout au monde."

"I love you to the moon and back too, Maman."

Babette whispered in Tally's ear. "And, darling, I talked with Vera. We're celebrating with her at Patchett's later this week. More parties to start your year, cherie."

Tally nodded and sipped champagne from her flute. Bubbles danced in her throat. She waved and thanked the diners. Guests applauded, returning to their chats and laughter.

Delphi handed Tally a letter. Upon seeing Shawl's handwriting, Tally felt faint. Becca wiped a tear as she smiled at Tally. Her father pulled Tally close yet her tender skin could not feel a thing.

"We've been keeping this for you, Shug. Shawl insisted in a letter we received that we were to wait until your birthday to give it to you so he could be part of your special day, like always."

"Cherie, do you want to read it at home or keep it with you now?"

"I, I, oh, Daddy! This is the best birthday gift I could ever receive! Oh, Maman. Shawl wrote me! I don't even care if he just wrote, 'Hi, Squirt.' Knowing he is—" She felt the weight of the world lifted from her shoulders. "Will you please keep it safe and put it on my bed?"

She felt giddy. She started shaking. She wanted to sit outside in the breeze, hold the letter next to her heart, and cry. In the dearest way, Shawl was with her right at that moment, on her birthday, a gift she never expected.

She grinned.

All's right with the world, almost.

"And, Daddy, could you please grant me one of my Birthday wishes?"

"I reckon I'd be honored to, Shug."

"Could you please ask Professor Dodge to inform Winston tonight, while it's still my birthday, about a generous donor--?"

"Talk slower, Shug."

"About a generous donor who is going to pay for all of Winston's expenses to England during the Award Interviews and Ceremony, you know, the ones Oxford doesn't pay, so Winston doesn't have to worry about money and can spend time writing his essay?"

Delphi shook his head.

"And who would this generous benefactor be, Shug?"

"Well, *you*, of course! Pleeeeaaassse, Daddy!"

"As you wish, Shug. My pleasure. Although I'll never understand your logic. You do know he's your competition?"

"Au contraire, Papa. Remember what you always say?" She hugged her father tight and kissed him on the cheek. "I'm only competing against myself."

Franklin Crockett delivered a fresh coconut cake with tall, lit candles from the kitchen, placing it gently on the table. Guests cheered. Tally, excited to see Franklin, hugged him without thinking about the protocol of hugging a server, let alone a Black man, at the Club, an absolute cultural faux pas.

Franklin froze. He looked stricken. The maître d' scowled and motioned to Franklin. Guests stopped talking.

Judge Scarlett, a friend of Tally's father and a keen observer of people and actions, raised his glass of bourbon and said in a loud voice from a nearby table, "What's your wish, Tally-gal?"

"Thank you, Judge Scarlett." She waved to the pianist. "My wish is, uh, for our wonderful pianist, Mr. Patterson, to play "Happy Birthday" one more time. Only this time we will all be celebrating Franklin Crockett."

Mr. Patterson seemed startled but began to play the familiar tune. Delphi, seated next to Judge Scarlett, stood up. Other diners obliged, some by singing along, a few by standing, all by adding "Franklin" to the lyrics.

As voices crooned, Tally whispered, under her breath, "Frankie! Pretend it's your birthday. Act like you're saving your life!"

Franklin held his hand up and nodded to the guests. "Thank you, ladies. Thank you, sirs. Can't believe this is happening."

"Franklin and I will be blowing out the candles together," Tally announced as guests clapped, "after we each make a silent wish."

Bending down, they blew out the dancing flames, looked at each other and smiled at the absurdity of the moment. Tally cut Franklin a piece of cake, served it on a plate and whispered, "Take a bow, Frankie!" Franklin waved to the crowd as he walked toward the kitchen. Abruptly, he leaned down to the microphone on the piano and tapped it with his free hand.

"I'm giving my cake to Mr. Patterson for being such a good piano player."

Mr. Patterson laughed, skated his thumb down the keys in a flourish while accepting the cake with his other hand. "And that birthday wish I just made when I blew out the candles?" Franklin continued, "Well, it was for everybody to have a real good time tonight."

The maître d' smiled and applauded along with others in the room. Everyone at her table, except Rye, knew she had lied to protect Franklin from the wrath of his boss or the Country Club regulars.

"Thank y'all for going along," she raised her glass, "with my little white lie."

Louie tossed his napkin on the table. "You mean your little black lie."

Rye guided Tally to a vacant spot on the dance floor. The orchestra was playing "True Love," Tally's favorite song from the movie *High Society* with Grace Kelly and Bing Crosby.

"That was some quick-thinking about Franklin, Birthday Girl."

"Whew. Thanks, Rye. Don't you love this song? Grace Kelly made this movie right before she married the Prince of Monaco."

Rye asked her why she felt she had to do that.

"Do what?"

"Lie about Franklin's birthday. That's what you said, right?"

"Well, protocol, of course." She told him about protocol at the Club and how she wanted to protect Franklin and not get him in trouble. She explained that the Southern Country Club-crowd tended to feel gracious and generous when they were offering charity to Black people like the meager gift of wishing Franklin a "Happy Birthday."

"Why couldn't you have hugged him, done nothing afterwards and let others deal with their own prejudices?" Rye's voice was tender yet serious. "Why wouldn't it be more important to be true to yourself instead of needing to make others feel more complacent or comfortable? Remember, you did nothing wrong."

Tally retorted, "Isn't that what Jesus said on the cross--'I've done nothing wrong'-- and he still got crucified?"

"Objection. Hearsay." Rye raised an eyebrow, shaking his head. "We can't prove what Jesus may have said on an alleged cross."

Tally stood on tiptoes, blew warmth in his ear and whispered.

"You are incorrigible."

Rye grinned, leaned down and whispered back.

"You are intoxicating."

Tally let out a little squeal.

Rye made a growling sound in her ear. "Be bold when you believe in something. There's no greater rush than that." He pulled her tighter. "Well, there is one greater rush."

Rye waved to the pianist. Mr. Patterson announced that this next song would be a special birthday song for Tally McCall requested by Rye Somerset. The dance floor cleared. The tune they danced to earlier swelled with all the instruments playing. The soloist, a young man with a baritone voice, sang the lyrics to "You Belong to Me."

Tally nuzzled into Rye's chest. Her feelings felt as clear as the soloist's voice.

She was going to be true to herself that night.

She wanted to be bold and feel both "rushes" at once.

Twenty-six

Rye drove Tally in his Mustang to Hamper Park. Parking under a weeping willow near *The Hamper Herald* mansion, the fronds formed a green parasol around them. Gazing through the dangling fronds, Tally pointed to the crescent moon, a smiling light in the sky. Rye pointed out stars, constellations.

Finally, alone, Tally snuggled next to Rye.

"How was your birthday, Georgia? Will it stand out in your own history book?"

Feeling the effects of champagne, nervous and excited about what would come next, happier than she had ever been in her life, she curled her finger enticing him to come closer.

"I will never forget this day."

"I just want to make sure you never forget this night."

Rye kissed her lips. His hands cupped her ears. Tally imagined she would open her eyes and it would be morning. That is how long the kisses lasted. After changing from her aqua mini-dress earlier to her party dress of butter yellow polished cotton with peach piano pleats down the V-neckline, Tally could not wait to finally take her dress off or feel Rye slip it off her body.

Before the undressing began, however, she paused, inhaled salty air and turned to Rye, as she unbuttoned the second button of his shirt.

"Rye, can I please ask you a question?"

"Ahh, Georgia, I'm going to miss you."

"Rye, I'm going to take that as a yes because in the South when folks talk to each other, they respond directly to the comment or when they ask a question, they answer directly to a—"

"Yes. You can ask me a question."

"Thank you." Tally licked her bottom lip slowly and smiled her brightest smile. She knew the answer she wanted to hear. She just wanted to hear him say it again.

"Well, you know, that song you chose for us to dance to? I just want to advise you that you took a big risk having someone sing 'You Belong to Me' in the South after all that happened to cause The War Between the States."

Rye grinned. "Point well made, 'cakes."

She loved how he called her "Baby cakes" or "cakes."

Why did she feel so conflicted by not wanting to belong to anyone yet wanting to belong to Rye, as if he belonged to her and she belonged to him, and the longing within the word belonging and the—

"Georgia, what's on your mind?"

"I, uh, I was just wondering, Rye, why did you request that song we danced to?"

She wanted to hear him say, "Because you belong to me always."

Rye sat up straight, as if the romantic moment had passed, like the sandbar disappearing in distant waters.

"Hemingway. A passage from *The Moveable Feast.*"

His voice lowered, as if in reverence, as he shared how the passage still mesmerized him.

"It was the passage that first encouraged me to think about how powerful one's mind could be, how a moment can change one's world, how the memory of a person can stay with you, and how one has the power to own each moment of time merely by reframing what really happened."

"Rye, I love the way you talk. Do you remember the passage? Can you tell me?"

"You've not heard of it?"

"Sorry to say I don't know much about Hemingway, except that I heard he committed suicide a few years ago."

Tally could tell she was babbling. The energy in her body felt like a firecracker about to explode.

"Look. There are things you know and things I know. And this passage is something I know by heart. So, there's Hemingway. Sitting in a café in Paris, where a girl, a stranger, seems to be waiting for someone to arrive."

Rye's voice softened like velvet as he recited verbatim the story.

"A girl came in the café and sat by herself at a table near the window. She was very pretty with a face fresh as a newly minted coin if they minted coins in smooth flesh with rain-freshened skin, and her hair was black as a crow's wing and cut sharply and diagonally across her cheek.

I looked at her and she disturbed me and made me very excited. I wished I could put her in the story, or anywhere, but she had placed herself so she could watch the street and the entry and I knew she was waiting for someone. So, I went on writing.

The story was writing itself and I was having a hard time keeping up with it. I ordered another rum St. James and I watched the girl whenever I looked up, or when I sharpened the pencil with a pencil sharpener with the shavings curling into the saucer under my drink.

I've seen you, beauty, and you belong to me now, whoever you are waiting for and if I never see you again, I thought. You belong to me and all Paris belongs to me and I belong to this notebook and this pencil."

Tally knew in that moment that this is what it would feel like if time stood still. Mesmerized by his voice, his accent on certain words, his emphasis whenever he said, "the girl," she felt transformed by the sound of his passion.

Say what you most want to say. Don't be the ingénue.

She tugged at his tie. "Do I belong to you?"

Her eyes met his, unblinking, utterly bound to that moment.

"You belong to me for all of time. Every memory we've made belongs to me."

"And to me," she whispered. Melting into his arms, she kissed him, deeply, passionately. Her mouth moved to his ear. She whispered, "Someone, a handsome fellow from the North, told me tonight to 'Be bold.' He also once told me to 'take great care of myself.' So," she licked the top of his ear, "may I be so bold to ask if we can make another memory tonight?"

She felt his hand move up her leg. He kissed her, slipped his hand under her dress, stroked the skin near her panties, and whispered back, "I thought you'd never ask."

"Still, Georgia, I'd rather go someplace more private." His voice sounded raspy. "More special, more—"

Tally kissed his lips as if she were starving for the taste of his breath. She didn't want to wait any longer. "No. Rye. This is perfect. Promise."

Rye started the engine, pressed a button and raised the top of the convertible. It locked into place. Rye turned off the engine, strolled to Tally's door and helped her into the backseat.

Abruptly, a beam flashed, bathing him in light.

Rye instructed Tally to lock the doors and stay in the car. He moved away from the car. She pushed down the locks.

Tally heard muffled voices. Rye's voice. *Mike's* voice? She felt a cool breeze through an open window. The light disappeared. She heard a door slam. Rye pulled up on the lock, slid back into the driver's seat and started the car. Tally hurried back to the front bucket seat.

"Change of plans. Your old beau Mike Parish just happened to be on patrol in the park, saw New York license plates and wondered if the car was mine. He also wanted to make sure you were okay. I assured him you are in good hands."

"You are in good hands, right?" He stroked her inner thigh.

"The best."

Rye asked Tally to direct him to her sorority house as they pulled out of the Park.

A siren blared behind them.

"Shit! What now?" He slowed down.

The patrol car sped past them.

"Time to move on," Tally whispered as if in Mike's ear.

She directed Rye to the Chaucer Sorority House parking lot. It was empty. Rye parked under the weeping willow tree near the Historical Marker on the cliff high above the water.

Tally put her index finger to her lips. She placed the slender strap of her beaded purse on her shoulder, lifted the blanket and pillow Rye kept in his car so he could pull over and sleep on his drive back to Niagara Falls, placed her baton on the backseat for safekeeping, squeezed Rye's hand, and led him back to the Park in the moonlight.

Crossing the footbridge over the creek, they stood in front of the Georgia Glen Cabin. Cool ocean breezes bounced Tally's hair about her face.

Rye turned to Tally with a quizzical look. Tally held his hand as they reached the porch. Scooping the cast iron key from her wallet, Tally opened the door.

The smell of cinnamon permeated the room. Tally lit candles by the fireplace.

"Georgia Glen loved cinnamon candles. Do you love cinnamon?"

Rye wrapped his arms around her.

"Cinnamon--I like. You--I love."

Tally felt Rye's mustache as he nuzzled the back of her neck.

"Will you prove how much?"

Rye grinned. Slowly his face took on a look of seriousness. Tender kisses pressed stronger. Soft growls in her ear echoed sexier. Hands stroking her body soothed her skin as if caressing each nerve ending.

He tossed the pillow and blanket over the rug by the hearth.

"Georgia, are you sure this is safe? Sure this is private?"

"Everything is perfect." Tally pointed to the latches on the logs covering the windows. "No one knows we're here," Tally whispered as she bolted the door.

"Georgia. Come here, 'cakes. Take my hand." Rye's voice, lower and thicker than she had ever heard, tingled her ear as if his breath were blowing her favorite invitation from "Can't Help Falling in Love" deep inside.

She placed her hand in his. He guided her to the hearth where her last thought before he kissed her lips was that within the word hearth is the word heart.

As an incandescent moon shimmered above the cabin, candle flames danced around them. Restlessness and force consumed them.

In the place where young love was finally consummated, the most private, passionate, powerful historical moment Tally had ever experienced illuminated how life can change in an instant—or two.

Twenty-seven

After whispering devotions in Rye's ear, Tally kissed his lips as they sat in his car, idling in her parents' driveway, lights off, while saying their goodbyes before he drove north. The taste of sweet tea they had found in the icebox at the Georgia Glen Cabin lingered on his tongue as it slow-danced inside her mouth until the tang of salt washed a bittersweet longing into their farewell.

Rye whispered, "Come here, Georgia. Why the tears?"

"You'll drive safely?" Tally could not look at him, only the clock next to the car radio.

"Promise."

"Rye, I'll worry about you so much and—oh, look. It's 4:17 a.m. Your birthdate."

Rye shook his head. "You call me incorrigible? I won't be able to drive if I keep thinking about you and--tonight."

"Are you crazy about me?" Tally whispered in her best flirting voice.

Rye tickled her side. "Who you?"

"See? You are incorrigible."

"Georgia, have you ever figured out why you see numbers all the time that somehow have meaning to you?"

Tally cuddled in his arms. She pointed to the moon.

"You know how the moon and tide have an order to them? Low tide, high tide. Full moon, harvest moon, crescent moon."

Rye whispered in Tally's ear. "You can moon me anytime."

"Ooo-la-la!" Tally laughed. "As I was saying, Mister Somerset, I think numbers, especially ones so dear, keep reminding me that there's an 'order' to life, especially these days when there seems to be no order in the world at all."

She snuggled her head on Rye's shoulder, kissing his neck.

Rye hugged her tight, his hands caressing her back, past the curve of her derriere.

"I also know I've never been with a boy, I mean, a man all night long."

She could hear the wonder in her voice as her cheeks grew warmer.

"Just make sure, Miss McCall, you don't do it again—except with me, of course."

Tally smiled. "I'll try to remember that while you're gone."

Rye pinched her cheek where his hand had just been patting.

She muffled a squeal.

"You'd better hurry back though." Tally stroked his chest.

"Trust me. July 4th can't come soon enough. My vacation week on the horizon. Can't wait to drive back down." Rye traced his finger down the bridge of her nose.

"Or fly? You know, to get back faster."

"Either way," Rye kissed the tip of her nose, "I can't come back if I never leave. And you need your sleep. Remember? You have to be up, bright and early, so you can tell your parents how you stayed in the guest house, not wanting to disturb them, and dreamed the whole night through."

Tally nodded. If only this night would never end.

"Georgia. I hate to say goodbye, 'cakes, but it's time. You ready?"

"Never."

After another rush of kisses, Rye opened Tally's door. They hugged and kissed until Rye escorted her to the path. Blowing kisses, she walked on cobblestones in the moonlight to the guesthouse tucked along the edge of the woods behind her parents' home. The glow of the carriage lanterns helped her find her key. She waved Rye's handkerchief in the air, their signal that she was safe. His car eased out of the driveway with headlights off, turning them on after the car drove slowly around the cul-de-sac and away from the house.

Inside, she pulled a cord on an heirloom lamp.

Light splashing on the pine-green leather chairs looked different to her. The lapis blue swirls on the mantle above the fireplace seemed brighter. The bed with its down comforter of pine-green Sea Island cotton looked more handsome. The vases gushing with fresh irises on the nightstand sparkled more.

Stripping her clothes, leaving them in a pile on the pink-striped chaise by the bedroom window, Tally opened a drawer in the dresser and shimmied a soft periwinkle gown over her shoulders to the top of her thighs.

Crawling under a sheet that smelled like a lemon teacake, she pulled up the comforter as soft and light as whipped cream frosting.

In the darkness, with moonlight seeping through shutters, Tally reminisced about the moments she spent with Rye that afternoon, that evening, that night, those moments ago.

She could still smell his cologne on her fingers, feel his tongue thick in her mouth. Images of dancing swirled in her thoughts. Waves she had first felt deep within her body hours before still rippled inside her as if a tide coming in and going out, again and again. Nothing could ever compare to this birthday. Nothing could ever compare to the rush she felt in Rye's arms. Nothing could ever compare to the force of Rye's gaze as he moved his hands down her body to part her—

Insistent tapping jarred her thoughts. What? Knocks on the door? Who?

Tally jumped out of bed, grabbed a shimmer-wrap from the closet and looked through the window. Flinging the door open, she squealed. Rye scooped her in his arms, put his hand over her mouth. An upstairs light in the mansion flicked on.

"Rye!" Her voice muffled as he pulled his hand away. "Hurry. Come inside."

"I thought you'd never ask."

"Oh, I'll always let you in!" Tally winked, smiled and closed the door. "Oh, my gosh! Rye, what are you doing here?"

"Started down the road," Rye grinned, shrugging his shoulders, "and didn't want to leave. Besides you said you were going to sleep in the guesthouse so you wouldn't wake your parents and—" He winked as the upstairs light turned off. "—I figured you might want some company."

"But you have to get back to Niagara Falls. You have to—"

"Shhh. I parked my car down the road for now. Don't worry. No one will see it and think thoughts that are none of their business. If it's okay with your folks, I'll leave my car here, fly home tomorrow, use my dad's extra car for two weeks in the Falls and fly back down here for the fourth of July." Rye traced his finger slowly along her earlobe, "and drive back home, leisurely, during my summer vacation week."

"Rye! You can't imagine how much that tickles." Tally squeezed her shoulder to her ear.

"But, as I recall, Georgia, isn't that your second-most ticklish spot?"

Tally kissed him until she felt dizzy. Still in his embrace, she looked into his eyes.

"Rye, you're my sweetheart, you know." Her voice sounded vibrant. "And you belong to me, right?"

Rye raised an eyebrow, nodded slowly and grinned.

"So, Rye," Tally stood on tiptoes whispering in his ear. "Will you please take *my* hand and sleep with me tonight?"

The next morning Alida knocked on the door, gave Tally a kiss and a sterling tray topped with chocolate croissants, a pot of coffee, a ramekin of mint pillows, and scrambled egg biscuits with strips of bacon on a platter covered in tin foil and a napkin.

Grinning, Alida also pulled an envelope from her apron pocket and said, "It was on the bed you never slept in last night, Birthday Bunny."

Tally blushed and whispered so Rye wouldn't hear her. "Thank you, Lida-Lida-Lee—for everything."

Alida winked, blew her a kiss, and closed the door.

Tally placed the tray on the coffee table. Curling her legs beneath her on the chair, Tally pulled a crocheted daisy Afghan over her lap, and gently opened the thin envelope.

May 17, 1970

Dear Squirt,

Happy 20th Birthday to a girl I'm mighty fond of. Okay. The truth? To a girl who's mighty fond of me. Yes, you goof. It's time to get your tissue ready. I'm about to say a few things that just might bring on the waterworks.

First of all, I miss you. I really do. Secondly, I feel the breezes. I know you're thinking of me. Promise. Thirdly, I hope you're feeling the breezes too. I'm thinking of you, Squirt. And, speaking of breezes, get Vera Velmarie Sanders to put weights in the hems of those miniskirts of yours! Fourthly, I want to meet this Yankee friend of yours. Want to thank him for taking good care of you on the Cruise. Having protected you for twenty years, I know that's not an easy task.

Hey, Squirt, just thought of something. I happened to see Travis Brinkley over here. About a month or so ago. Can you believe it? A fellow from Hamper and tennis team buddies at Hamper U meeting in the jungle in 'Nam? He was jogging past me with his platoon and lobbed me a tennis ball, one he had carried for good luck. Said he didn't need it anymore 'cause he was headed home soon. He stopped for a minute or two, told me he couldn't wait to finish his tour of duty because he was going to propose to Rayleigh. I know you won't say anything. Right? Told him we'd play tennis when I get home. It was great to see him. Gave me a boost.

I'm fine. Wish I could be with you for your birthday, Squirt. Hope you had a fun time. How's this? I'll be there next year and I'll take you to the diner for lunch. And maybe you'll bring Rye to Patchett's for the party that night.

He sounds like he may be your guy.

With love from your biggest fan, always,
Shawl

P.S. One other thing, Tally. With all that's going on, the protests, the murders at Kent State we keep hearing about, please remember this. Every generation thinks they are living through the worst time in history. Every generation thinks no other generation could have possibly experienced such heartache. What we know is that each period of time is difficult for the people living through it. I ache for those families of the students at Kent State. I appreciate the protests for peace there. Just please remember, Tally. There are lots of ways to protest. Sometimes in the light of day. Sometimes in the dark of night. Sometimes by living the most courageous life you can live in spite of all that is happening around you. Know I love and miss you, Squirt.

Tears tumbled down Tally's cheeks. She read the letter again and again before reading it, over croissants and coffee, out loud to Rye.

Twenty-eight

Tally's pen skidded off the page of her journal as her father swerved the Cadillac convertible to the left lane of the highway.

"Daddy! Why did you lower the top just when I'm writing? The date doesn't even look like Monday, June 22, 1970." Tally looked up. "And now you're swerving? How can I take notes for my essay?"

Delphi tilted his head and adjusted the rearview window.

"Just trying not to hit that baby raccoon meandering across the highway, Shug."

Tally twisted her body. The baby raccoon stood frozen near the center yellow line of the highway. A larger raccoon in short grass lay at the edge of the road.

"Daddy, stop! Please!"

"Dadgum. Knew I shouldn't have told you. Especially since we're almost at our exit." Delphi had already slowed the car, merged into the right lane, and pulled onto the side of the road.

Tally urged him to go in reverse. Delphi complied. The sedan came to a stop, its tires crunching gravel at the edge of the road.

Tally jumped out. She grabbed a red blanket from the back seat and her baton with red glitter ribbons on each end. Observing the mother raccoon bleeding on the opposite side of the highway, she tossed the blanket onto the highway behind the baby raccoon as if a barrier the baby should not cross.

Twirling the baton above her head, she moved closer to the baby. The driver of an approaching car honked his horn and swerved into the opposite lane. The baby raccoon scurried toward its mother, stopped on the highway, seemingly frozen in fright, and crouched in a sitting position.

Delphi slammed his door, opened a red golf umbrella and used it to signal another car to change lanes.

"Hey, what the hell?" A passenger in the swerving car lowered his window, yelled and pointed to the back of the Cadillac. "Go back to Georgia, Redneck!"

Delphi waved.

"Shug, hurry up. Getting dangerous."

Tally shouted, "Yankee hospitality."

"No time for name calling." Delphi stood by the blanket.

Tally sprinted to the car, threw her baton on the front seat and snatched packages of peanut butter crackers they always carried on road trips. Breaking the crackers, she crumbled a trail of pieces from the baby raccoon to the edge of the road. The animal grabbed one tidbit, gobbled another and waddled toward the path of crackers. Tally tossed a handful of the crackers near the mother raccoon, wished her "Godspeed," and rushed to pick up the blanket.

Delphi slammed his car door as a truck sped past.

"Young lady, your desire to rescue critters is not always wise or safe." Delphi arched an eyebrow of gray hairs that looked like a weary rainbow.

Tally grinned, reached across the armrest and kissed his cheek.

"But how can I live with myself if I don't try?"

"My fearless girl."

Delphi pointed to the exit sign for Kent, Ohio on the side of the road. "Almost there."

Tally plopped the blanket by her baton, pulled a Polaroid camera from her shoulder bag and turned to her father.

"I love your idea, Daddy. Taking photos on this trip to illustrate my essay for the Oxford Committee. I just hope they like my *'Tale of Two Campuses'* theme and the Ohio-Georgia connections I propose. Now if you could just slow down a bit. I want to take a picture of the sign."

Tally grabbed the white rectangle as it ejected from the camera and shook the film to help it develop.

"Wait—oh, my gosh--Daddy, look! There's a girl by the sign. She's in the picture. She's, good grief, she's coming toward us. She probably thinks you were pointing to her. What if she thinks we're about to pick her up?"

"Tally, we are never going to get to the campus, take the tour I arranged," Delphi looked at his watch, "and meet Judge Fox for lunch back in Akron at this rate."

"I know we're running a little bit late, Daddy. But it's not fair for the girl to think one thing is going to happen and then dash her hopes. It's not justice, either."

Delphi shook his head.

"There's a big difference between justice and fairness, Shug."

The hitchhiker, a tall, thin girl with long strawberry-blonde hair wore bell-bottom jeans and a yellow t-shirt with words painted in blue. As she got closer, Tally read the words, *"Tin soldiers and Nixon coming."* Odd. How could anyone be fond of Nixon here?

The girl slapped the front of the car as Delphi braked to a stop.

"Thanks for the ride, mister."

"I regret there seems to be a mistake, Miss. I do apologize."

"For what? You pointed to me. I need a ride to town and you've got your blinker on for the Kent exit."

"Yes, well, what's your name, young lady?" Delphi squeezed the steering wheel.

"Bright. Bright Capelli."

"Nice to meet you, Miss Capelli. I'm Delphi McCall. This is my daughter Tally. May I ask why you are out here -- hitchhiking—alone?"

"Sure. No big deal. Sold my car to pay tuition. And my stupid boyfriend pissed me off when I told him I needed a ride to town this morning. He's gone fishing so I told him to drop me off by the sign and I'd hitchhike."

Tally looked at her father who was frowning and pursing his lips, and turned back to the girl.

"Bright, I love your name. It's so unique." Tally juggled the camera and semi-wet picture, offering her hand to the girl. "I'm so sorry it seemed like my Daddy pointed at you to offer a ride. And thank you for asking but I'm afraid we're not going into town. We're going--"

"Hey. No sweat. Another car will come along. Just figured you were taking the exit and heading to Kent."

"No, we're going to Kent State." Tally tucked her hand back by her side as Bright crossed her arms, covering the words on her t-shirt.

"Kent State. The new travel destination. You want to take pictures of the parking lot, the hill, the crime scene?" Bright rolled her eyes.

"Look. Sorry if I sound sarcastic. It's been a rough morning. Anyway, hate to disappoint you but you can't get on campus. Judge's orders. Been on lockdown since the shootings."

Tally gestured to her father. "But my daddy is a--"

"Bright." Delphi interrupted. "We'll be happy to take you to town. Get in, young lady."

As Bright opened the car door, Delphi excused himself for the delay and walked to the car that had stopped behind them on the edge of the exit ramp. Tally heard her father thank the driver, explain he did not have a flat tire, and ask, in his booming voice, how to get to the Kent State campus from the town of Kent.

"You an Ohio State fan?" Bright pointed to the red blanket and ribbons on Tally's baton.

"Heavens, no!" Tally laughed at the thought of cheering for a Northern team. Well, maybe Syracuse, Rye's soon-to-be alma mater. "I'm going to be a senior at Hamper University in Georgia. And my baton? That's what I use, you know, to twirl, if I need to stop traffic for some reason."

"You? Twirling a baton to stop traffic? Hell, I bet that works every time."

"Thank you, Bright." Tally smiled. "And the blanket is to appease my mother who always wants a red blanket in any car we've ever had."

"Because?" Bright asked.

"Well, of course, she says having a blanket provides warmth on long car rides."

"Sure."

"But my mother insists on a *red* blanket for the same reason she puts a red washcloth in a gift basket of French perfume and soaps for the brides at her Bridal Boutique when they marry."

Bright got out of the car, shut her door, leaned against the car and lit a cigarette. Tally wished she could ask for one but her father had no idea she had ever smoked.

"Mother says her brides stop by the Boutique and thank her years later for those washcloths."

Bright exhaled and shook her head. "Is red good luck or something?"

"No, it's her family's tradition to give brides a red washcloth in anticipation of the bride having a baby. My mother knows the bride will need a red washcloth one day when her baby has a cut and sees blood. If you have a red washcloth, the baby won't be frightened because a red washcloth never shows blood to upset the baby or the mother. Same for an accident in a car, heaven forbid. A red blanket won't panic anyone."

"Never heard that before." Bright took a long drag on her cigarette. "I'll have to remember that if I get pregnant again."

"Bright. Oh, my gosh. You have a baby?"

"No."

"But you said—"

"I said I was pregnant. I didn't have it."

"Oh."

"Abortion clinic saved my life. The last two months have been shit. Found out the morning of the shootings I was pregnant. Left the clinic to get back to campus for the peace rally at noon." Bright tossed the cigarette to the gravel.

"I'm, I'm so sorry for your loss, Bright."

"Thanks." Bright swiveled the toe of her navy leather clog on the cigarette, grinding the fiery tip into the gray road.

Tally wondered what to say. "Bright, I can't believe you went through so much in one morning."

"Hope to horror."

"Hope?"

"Yeah. I just said. I went to the clinic, found out I was pregnant then went to the rally."

"Wait. You didn't have an abortion?"

"No way. I'm Catholic."

"But you said--"

"Don't you have abortion clinics in Georgia? Or women's health clinics? That's where you go to find out if you're pregnant without paying a doctor. They give you a test for free."

"I didn't know that. But your baby, your fetus, your--?"

"Miscarried. Right after the funerals. Just as well." Bright twirled the fringe on her shoulder bag. "Why bring a kid into this stupid world?"

Tally had never wanted a cigarette more. She stepped out of the car, shook the blanket, hugged it to her chest and finger-twirled her baton.

A driver zipped past, honked his horn and yelled, "Screw Ohio State!"

"Why don't you put that stuff in the trunk since scarlet and gray are the colors of *The* Ohio State?" Bright lit another cigarette and offered Tally a drag. Tally glanced at her father, deep in conversation, with the driver behind them, took the cigarette and inhaled.

"Wow. Menthol. Hits the spot, especially when I'm nervous." Tally took another drag and hoped her breath mints and perfume were easy to find in her shoulder bag. "Thanks, Bright. Daddy doesn't know I smoke at all."

"Got it. My dad smokes morning to night but he doesn't want me to smoke either. Go figure." Bright tapped ashes from the cigarette, took a final inhale and stomped on the stub. "Like I was saying, OSU's a rival to KSU. Woody Frickin' Hayes, Ohio State's football coach, is a suck-up to Nixon. Around here you better get something blue and gold, Kent's colors. Especially after May 4th." Bright reached in her bag and gave Tally a giant blue and gold ribbon flower pin.

"Thanks, Bright. And, I'm so sorry about what you just went through." Tally fastened the pin on her powder blue blouse.

"Thanks, Tally. You're easy to talk to."

"So are you, Bright. Thank you." Tally lifted the trunk and cushioned the baton on the blanket next to the suitcases. "Could I ask you a quick question though?"

"Want me to take your picture?" Bright lifted the camera. "Stand by the sign." Bright clicked the button after Tally rushed to pose beneath the giant Kent, Ohio sign and beside the smaller Kent State exit sign.

"Thanks, Bright. I just wonder," Tally softened her voice as Bright shook the film rectangle like it was a fan, "are you a fan of Nixon after what happened?"

"God, no! I hate the son of a bitch."

"Well, your shirt...."

"You haven't heard the song? "Ohio" by Crosby, Stills, Nash and Young? Holy shit. You will before you leave. Radio stations are playing it non-stop. This is the opening lyric. I just painted it yesterday."

"I'd buy a t-shirt like that, Bright, in a heartbeat."

"Yeah? Hot damn. I'll make you one after I go to the clinic today. I'll borrow my sister's car. We can go to the meeting at Byron's house tonight and I'll give it to you."

"The clinic? Bright, are you okay?"

"Just have to go see the doctor today for my check-up. And to get more birth control pills."

Tally blushed. She needed to get a prescription too. Only one week ago was the night with Rye that changed her life. He had used protection but she needed to protect herself too. This time last week she could not imagine all she now knew.

Tally heard her Daddy laugh. She scooped her bag into the backseat where Bright had settled. Admiring Bright's photo, she placed it in a yellow leather satchel with other keepsake pictures of the trip.

"Bright, did you make it to the rally? Were you there when," Tally's voice grew reverent, "the students were shot?"

Bright nodded. "A car length, if that, behind Sandy. Heard the shots, saw her fall and thought she had tripped. That's how fast it happened."

Tally felt as if she were standing in a freezer.

"Sandy invited me to go through Rush, join a sorority, but I'm not the sorority type. And even though I couldn't afford it, Sandy said that didn't matter. She said there were ways to work it out." Bright had tears in her eyes. "She was just walking to class, for god's sake."

Tally felt tears brimming at the thought of Virginia, Becca, Khaki, Phoebe or Rayleigh being shot while walking innocently to class.

"Bright, I'm heartbroken. For you. For Sandy. She sounds like a wonderful girl. How could she die when she did nothing wrong?"

Tally impulsively hugged Bright. Bright stiffened her back.

"Because of the assholes who considered us target practice, Tally. Some idiot in the local newspaper wrote that none of us should complain when boys our age are being killed in 'Nam.'"

Tally brushed at tears as she whispered. "My brother's there now."

"Damn, Tally. Didn't know." Bright hugged Tally. "So, are you all-*I love the military*?"

"Well, I appreciate the military and Daddy was at Normandy on D-Day and I'm the Military Gala Queen for Fort Hamper."

"Say what?"

"But my brother's a philosophy major who would have been on the Kent State campus protesting for peace too if his birthday wasn't September fourteenth."

"September fourteenth? Talk about bad luck. Ho-lee Shit," Bright shouted and let out a whistle.

Delphi opened his door at that moment and turned to look at Bright.

"Go, Golden Flashes!" The driver who had been talking with Delphi merged onto the highway.

"Golden Flashes!" Delphi shouted back.

Delphi closed his door.

"So, Mister, are you a fan of the Kent State Golden Flashes?"

"I am, young lady. But I'm a bigger fan of decorum."

Twenty-nine

Delphi stopped at the entrance to the Kent State campus. Police stood behind sawhorse barricades, rifles in hand. Delphi spoke to an officer and showed his license. One officer pointed to buildings in the distance while another moved a barricade.

"Shug, the officers said no pictures are to be taken. We have an hour." Delphi opened the convertible top. He buttoned his tan seersucker suit coat over his royal blue tie and patted Tally's hand as he turned onto a winding road.

"Yes, sir. But what about lunch with the Judge?"

"We'll make it. The officers said there's not much to look at."

Tally wished Bright could be their tour guide. However, they had dropped her off at the clinic moments ago.

The buildings on campus were a blur of brick. Tally sucked on a Butter Rum candy. A breeze tussled her hair. The campus was deserted. A police car was parked near the entrance to a parking lot.

Tally shivered as they passed the sign for "Nixson Hall," the Health Sciences building, on Theater Drive. Who could fathom that a name so despised for its association with killings in Vietnam, Cambodia, and Kent State, under his watch, would be the phonetic twin, albeit spelled differently, of a building celebrating health on the Kent State University campus?

Delphi put the car in park. Both father and daughter sat still, as if mesmerized and in reverence, to finally be at this scene of death and heartache just seven weeks after these surroundings became part of history.

Gently tugging her fringed bag over her shoulder, Tally stepped onto the pavement of the parking lot. The Prentice Hall coed dormitory was on her right. Blanket Hill, where members of the National Guard had abruptly turned at the top and fired at dozens of unarmed students, was directly in front of her. If she had been standing at this exact spot, on Monday, May 4th, she might have been shot too.

Each of the four students who were killed had been shot on this pavement, this now-hallowed place, that would forever connect them all. Jeffrey, shot in the mouth, died instantly, his blood streaming a river on the concrete. Allison Krause, shot in the left side of her chest, died in a hospital hours later. William Schroeder, shot in the back, died within the hour. Sandy Scheuer, shot on the left side of her neck, died within a few minutes.

Police markers and dead flower bouquets designated the locations where each fell, a scattershot from each other. Without cars in the parking lot, it seemed to Tally as if these four victims, Jeffrey, Allison, William and Sandy, were the only students still at Kent State right now. Their bodies were not there any longer. Yet the essence of each young, vibrant, hopeful spirit was still there, in the parking lot, in the place where they had last been alive, as innocent students. She had seen pictures of each of the victims and was certain if they appeared right at that moment, she would recognize them and feel as if she could talk to them.

Having grown up with the iconic image of Georgia Glen in her own hometown, Tally knew the power of a legacy left by a person who died too young. She felt restless thinking how the lives and deaths of Allison, Jeffrey, Sandy and William would surely force a profound and long-lasting legacy of "what if" and "if only" and "why did this have to happen" through the years.

She felt her father's arm around her shoulder. She leaned into his chest. He pulled a handkerchief from his front pocket. Tally nodded as she touched it to the tears trickling down her cheeks.

In silence, they walked around Prentice Hall through wild daffodils and daisies, down another hill to The Commons. Where the hill smoothed into a giant field of grass, the Victory Bell held court. The only structure at the foot of the hill, the bell hung inside a blue iron-embrace in the middle of a "window" designed into the brick.

The former Erie Railroad bell had witnessed not only the peaceful rally but also the request by a member of the university administration to stop the gathering before the rally began. The Bell had witnessed the attempt by an officer with a megaphone to calm the crowd and the actions of the National Guard loading their rifles with tear gas canisters before launching them at student protesters who refused to disperse. Ultimately, the Bell witnessed the Guard forcing the students to the top of Blanket Hill with the parking lot far below.

Fortunately, the Victory Bell could not witness the protesting students who were rushed down the other side of Blanket Hill by the uniformed Guard members or the shouting of the protesters at the soldiers.

Its view of the final moments before the shooting began was blocked by Taylor Hall, the architecture and communications building, the place where a bullet was found in a sculpture in front of the building and where the iconic pagoda at the top of the hill, at the place where the National Guard turned suddenly and started shooting, could be seen from the building's windows.

Tally's fingers touched the bell in reverence. Delphi sat on the low brick wall jutting out from the Victory Bell. Tally wondered if her father was thinking what she was thinking.

A copy of the U. S. Constitution was buried at this spot, on Friday, May 1st, "Law Day" in America. It was the same Constitution to which her father had pledged his professional duties and judgments. The same Constitution her father read, in excerpts, before going to bed each night. And it was the same document he would read to his children whenever he wanted them to fall asleep quickly.

At this place of rebel energy, Tally looked at her father who was staring in the direction of the charred ROTC Building that was set on fire the same day as the Kentucky Derby.

She reached into her bag, pulled out her camera and snapped photos of The Commons, the Victory Bell, the daffodils and the daisies, not caring a whit if anyone in authority tried to stop her.

Thirty

Judge Fox and Judge McCall, college roommates at Mercer Law School in Macon, Georgia, laughed about a case Delphi had tried when he was a young lawyer in Macon. The three of them were having lunch at the Akron Country Club. After the Club's famous cherry pie à la mode was served, Tally and Delphi dipped their sterling silver forks into the decadent pie while Judge Fox held his fork in the air and patted his friend on the back.

"Delphi, you asked the jury of twelve men if they had ever picked up the wrong hat from the hat rack when they left a restaurant and after they all nodded, you proceeded to point to your client and said," Judge Fox sipped from his cup of coffee and shook his head, "that your client had just picked up the wrong car when he left the restaurant and, surely, they could understand how that could happen. Tally, honey, the jury acquitted your daddy's client of car theft in five minutes. Now that should be in the history books."

Tally smiled and winked at her daddy. She had heard a version of this story every time her father and Judge Fox got together. She, however, could not laugh at anything right now.

Rye had called their hotel room while Tally was at the Kent State campus and left a message that he could not meet her in Ohio, after all. He was sorry that something had come up with his job and he hated the change of plans, especially since she was so close by. He said he would see her when he flew to Hamper on July 4th for the festivities at the Chaucer Sorority House and he couldn't wait.

Tally knew she would see him in ten days. She knew Rye was careful in what he had said on the phone in case her daddy was the person who picked up the message instead of her. She knew his clerkship was important this summer. But, good grief. She just wanted to see him, talk to him, feel his mustache tickle her lips, feel his hug, and feel him inside her in the most intimate way again.

After the emotion of touring the site of the Kent State shootings and the disappointment of Rye's change of plans, now all she wanted to do was go home. However, she had to write her essay and get ready to—

"Shug, Judge Fox was just asking you about Oxford." Delphi cleared his throat and asked the waiter for another glass of tea.

"Judge Fox, I'm so sorry. Ever since Daddy and I got back from visiting the campus today, I've been thinking about so many things." Her father nodded to her. "And thank you, sir, Judge Fox, so much for your help in arranging our opportunity today and for your willingness to write a recommendation for me too."

"Tally, dear, you're most welcome. I'm mighty proud of you. And Shawl, of course. Makes sense you have a lot on your mind."

He signed the tab on the silver tray with a flourish.

"Seems they're about to open the school any day now." Judge Fox placed the Mont Blanc pen in his coat pocket. "What a mess. The faculty is doing a yeoman's job trying to get in touch with students to finish exams and help them complete the school year."

Judge Fox waved to a woman wearing plaid slacks and a golf shirt.

"Bob White, the President of Kent State, and I are golf buddies and when I explained that you are a history major nominated for the Oxford scholarship and Delphi is a Federal Court Judge and one of my oldest friends, he was most accommodating."

"Well, your kindness means the world to me, Judge Fox. I will never forget seeing where the murders happened."

"Murders? Is that what the newspapers are calling it in Georgia?"

Tally was taken aback by the sarcasm in his voice. She looked at her father. Delphi wiped his mouth with his pale blue napkin and stared at her with one of his "Careful, Shug" expressions.

"Well, Judge Fox, sir, the newspaper, you know, *The Hamper Herald* where I work as an intern, just reports the facts."

"Have you read any interviews with the National Guardsmen who were there?"

"Oh, goodness, sir. I haven't seen any." Tally wanted to say she would rather read interviews with Jeffrey, Allison, William and Sandy and hear *their* voices more than anyone else's, however, she sensed something curious in Judge Fox's demeanor.

"Well, let me just say that as the only daughter of one of the finest Federal Court Judges I know, Delphi Aviary McCall, I trust you want to acquit yourself well as you prepare your presentation to Oxford."

"Yes, sir. Thank you. I do."

"Then it seems to me you need all sides of the story, young lady."

Judge Fox leaned closer and quieted his voice.

"My nephew, remember Sam? Sam Richardson? My sister's son? Well, he was one of the National Guardsmen called by the Governor to protect Kent State that weekend."

"Sir, could I please take notes for my essay?"

"Of course. Just know we talk fast in the North, Tally."

The three of them laughed.

Tally needed to go to the bathroom after drinking so much tea, however, she decided to cross her legs, pinch her thighs and write fast.

Judge Fox explained that Sam had joined the National Guard as a way to serve his country since his birthday number for the Military Draft Lottery was 365 with no chance for him to be called for duty.

Tally's teeth bit down in tiny jumps on her bottom lip as a way to transfer her sudden urgency to rush to the Ladies' Room and her increasing urgency to know more about Sam. Obviously, Sam could have volunteered to go to Vietnam if he really wanted to serve his country yet she saved judgment to appreciate Sam's desire to serve in another capacity. Besides, she did not want to interrupt Judge Fox.

"Sam was at the top of Blanket Hill, Tally. He said the students were disrespectful to the Guard with their hand motions and their rock-throwing; and one student looked like a hippie and was waving a black flag and shouting at the soldiers."

"Did Sam explain why their guns were loaded, sir?"

"Sam said part of the duty of the National Guard is to be prepared for any situation. And they were. The Guard left the truckers' strike here in Akron where there were shots fired at them. Their guns were already loaded when they got notice from the Governor to go to Kent State. You have to see how dire the situation was from the view of the Guard, Tally. Delphi, you probably read the report that the authorities found ice picks, a machete and railroad flares at the ROTC fire. Now, you tell me there aren't agitators in this country going from campus to campus stirring up those who are innocent students. That's what the Guard was up against."

Judge Fox tossed his napkin on the plate. The blue napkin, red cherries and white Lenox plate proved the perfect patriotic reminder.

"Yes, sir. I can imagine Sam was worried and scared that day. Was, uh, Sam shocked at what happened?"

Judge Fox pushed his plate away.

"Tally, he hasn't slept more than two hours a night since May 4th." Judge Fox's voice sounded raspy. "Nobody seems to care what the Guard soldiers are going through, what their families are going through and what these young men saw and experienced. The Guard members are afraid to talk to the press and have actually been ordered not to. Just remember, honey, there are two sides to every story, right, Delphi? Like that innocent car thief of yours."

Thirty-one

Tally kissed her father on the cheek.

"Back in two hours. Bright promised she would not keep me out late since we've got a long trip home tomorrow."

"Shug, I expect you to call me from your room when you get back. 10:00 o'clock. No later. I need a good night's sleep. You do too."

After today's events, Tally did not think she would ever sleep again.

"Sorry about the car. Had to borrow my sister's." Bright leaned across the passenger's seat and opened the door. The white VW Beetle sported a giant iridescent peace sign painted on its top. Tally smiled and imagined Bright's sister was probably named "Kite" or "Sprite" or "Moonlight."

"So, how did it go today?"

"Oh, Bright. We toured the campus. Walked to The Commons. Stood in the parking lot. It broke my heart to think of what you and your classmates went through."

Tally chose not to tell Bright about Judge Fox and his nephew Sam. She did not want to upset Bright who seemed so happy to see her.

"How was your day?"

"Great. Thanks for the ride to the clinic. Your dad's a sweetheart, Tally. Gruff but a sweetheart. Oh, and I got you a present."

"You did?" Tally hoped it was the T-shirt Bright had promised.

At the red light, Bright grabbed a paper bag from under her driver's seat.

"Here. One gift is expected. One is a surprise."

Tally dipped her hand into the bag. Pulling out a blue T-shirt with the inscription in yellow-sparkle letters about soldiers and Nixon, Tally raved.

"Thank you SO much, Bright. I cannot believe you were able to paint this for me so quickly."

"Some folks think I'm a fast girl." Bright laughed.

Tally grinned.

"I think you're wonderful, Bright. And, I think you're a hoot! Please come visit me in Hamper. We would have so much fun."

None of this made any sense to Tally. After all, she, a Southerner, and Bright, a Yankee, had little in common yet Tally liked how Bright did not sugarcoat anything. It was refreshing after all the circles girls in the South had to draw around a conversation before getting to the center. And Bright was sweet as she could be.

Bright offered Tally a cigarette and flicked her lighter as Tally leaned forward.

"Thank you for knowing exactly what I need after such an emotional day, Bright."

"Look inside the bag. There's another surprise."

Tally pulled out a cylinder of pills, birth control pills.

"What? What on earth? I don't know what to say!"

"Remember when your dad got out of the car to fill the tank with gas? Remember you asked about how to get the pill?" Bright shifted gears, turned left and parked at Byron's house.

Tally was thrilled she was not under a lamplight anymore. She couldn't hide her blushing cheeks.

"Well, I figured you're new at this from what you said and I told the doctor I was going out of town for a few months and needed extra pills. And when I run out, I'll just tell her I dropped a whole container of them, by mistake, in the river one day when I was fishing. Just little white lies to get what you want, right?"

"Bright, please let me pay you for—"

"Nope. At the clinic, the pills are free. That's the good news about being poor."

Tally accepted another cigarette as they stood on Byron's porch.

"Bright, I didn't mean to imply—"

"No sweat, Tally." Bright pulled open the screen door. "Besides, it's important that some folks have status and know what to do with it."

"What do you mean, Bright?"

"I mean you've got status. I know you're rich, eating at Country Clubs and all that. And you've got gumption and it seems to me that only folks with status can actually change the status quo and, man, do we need you to do that right now, my friend."

Tally stared at Bright as if she were Eleanor Roosevelt. As Tally entered Byron's incense-fogged house, she could not wait to get home and talk to Winston.

Thirty-two

Gazing at the full moon from her bedroom balcony where she had been pacing, Tally grabbed the phone on the second ring. Please, please let it be Rye. It was Friday, June 26th, and Rye would be flying to Hamper in a few days. She could not wait. She had gotten three letters since he left Hamper ten days ago. She knew each sentence by heart. Now she just wanted to hear his voice again.

Holding the phone close to her ear, her heart aflutter in anticipation, she heard a voice she never expected.

"Tally, baby. It's Lula. Can you meet me at the Chaucer House?"

"Lula. Is something wrong? You okay? Your boys?"

"Just need to talk with you. How 'bout eight? In the kitchen?"

"Lula, I'll be there."

Tally knew there was nothing in the refrigerator or pantry at the Chaucer House. Soon she would join Lula, Khaki, Virginia, Rayleigh and Becca to open the House up for the annual "Fourth of July

Reunion Weekend." They would be getting rooms, sleeping porches and the kitchen ready for alums to stay in the House before the legendary July 4th festivities.

Tally layered napkins, plates, apples, chicken salad, Alida's lemon teacakes and a jug of sweet tea in a picnic basket, grabbed her baton and hopped in her car.

The portico light flickered on at the Chaucer House. The spotlight on Canter Berry was bright. Lights were also on in the kitchen where Tally placed the wicker basket on the counter.

"Tally, baby. I thought I saw you come in." Lula was dressed in a purple muumuu. "And look at all you brought. My goodness. You sure know how to fix a pretty picnic. You sure do now, you sure do."

Lula was babbling. What's wrong? Tally hugged her.

"Lula, I learned everything from you and Alida. Now have some tea, let's settle down on the comfy, cozy chairs by the patio, and talk."

Lula wiped her eyes and snuggled into a chair. Tally placed a napkin and a plate of teacakes on Lula's lap and pulled her own chair closer.

"You tell me when you're ready to talk, okay?"

Lula nodded.

"I have to talk fast, baby. They'll be here any minute."

"Who will be here? Lula, are you in trouble?"

"No, baby. My dearest friend is in trouble and I have to help."

By the time Lula told her everything, Tally could have knitted a baby blanket. She still felt as if time were standing still when she heard the knock on the door.

Within moments, Mrs. Crockett, Winston, Franklin and Ted were being told by Lula to please take their shoes off in the foyer and slip on the footies for gentlemen with the skids on the bottom, the ones wrapped in tissue paper, in the "Welcome Closet" where umbrellas, footies, shawls, pastel dusters, and an army of coats were stored in linen covers.

Winston was carrying a bucket of fried chicken. Franklin was toting a bowl of shrimp salad. Ted was lugging two pitchers of lemonade. Mrs. Crockett was carrying a chocolate cake.

Lula hugged each of them, even Ted.

Tally hugged each of them too. She had not seen Ted in ages.

At first, everyone was chattering about the food and how beautiful the sorority house was and offering thanks to Tally for letting them meet there on such short notice.

"You're welcome. I, uh, just can't believe you're all here."

Mrs. Crockett wiped her eyes with a yellow-striped napkin.

"Tally. A long time ago, Lula may have told you, she and I went to kindergarten together. We loved playing with our baby dolls at Double Churches Elementary, you know the one that has breezeways connecting the Hallelujah Baptist Colored Church and the United Methodist Negro Risen Church. We went to Vacation Bible School every summer. Bridesmaids in each other's weddings. Mothers to the cutest baby boys you've ever seen. She's as close to me as a sister, if I weren't an only child. So, I sure do appreciate how Lula and you are helping me get through this."

Franklin nodded and, for the first time, Tally noticed a smile on his face.

"Sunshine, you make the best teacakes. Almost as good as Aunt Lula's." Franklin hugged Lula and she leaned up to kiss his cheek.

"Thank you, Frankie. All the credit goes to Alida." Tally could hear Alida telling her she should have taken some paper doilies to display the teacakes on the plate appropriately.

"By the way, how's everything going, you know, with, well, everything?" Tally whispered to Franklin.

"Aunt Lula didn't tell you?"

"She did, Frankie, in her own overwhelmed way. I just wonder how you are taking things."

"What can you do? Final call-up letter from the draft board yesterday." Franklin pointed his teacake at Ted who was chatting with Mrs. Crockett. "He didn't pass the midpoint of his summer school class either. "

"Oh, my gosh, Frankie. Poor Ted. He's brilliant."

"Well, Ted says—hold on--Win, what does Ted say about people being smart?"

"That grades are not an accurate measure of one's intelligence." Winston draped his arm around his twin's shoulder. "But we've known that for a long time, right, Frankie?"

"Thanks, Win. You know what Mama says, 'When you're right, you're—' "

"Right!" The brothers chorused.

"It's not right that Ted got the same professor who flunked him last time."

Winston patted Franklin on the back. "That's what happens when power finds itself in the least capable or most impotent hands. The guy has tenure. Bulletproof. Gave Ted an 'A' for his perfume project for which, by the way, girl, Ted credits a certain gal named 'Gigi,' and then the damn professor gave Ted two 'F's'."

"Winston, I was happy to help Ted but that's awful."

"Yeah. One F for failing to turn in a paper on time even though Ted said the ass--, I mean, the, uh, teacher locked his door before the deadline and Ted couldn't get in even though the guy was sitting there and Ted was knocking on the door." Winston took a piece of paper from the stack on the counter that Chaucerettes would use to write each other notes and folded a paper airplane. "The other F was for Ted not cutting his hair for the mandatory Marketing Class Picture in the paper. The teacher told Ted to do it or get an F for insubordination and Ted refused. Reckon that guy just has it in for Ted."

"Winston, I can't believe how cruel! That's heartbreaking for Ted. And for you too, Frankie, about the letter." It was all Tally could do to hold back the tears in her eyes.

"Shrimp boats are full, Sunshine. You'll see." He reached his arm around Tally's shoulders and gave her a squeeze. "Now these teacakes—think I'll have another."

"Please do, Frankie." Tally had no idea why Frankie and Ted were not apoplectic right now. "Alida sure knows how to--"

The sound of horses galloping overhead thundered the air.

"What on earth is that?" Ted froze, the shrimp in his hand dripping tartar sauce on the counter.

"Oh, our housemother, Miss Perry, loves horses so much, she made a tape of them galloping and—excuse me, please, I need to see who's at the door."

Tally peeked through the beveled windows and, hurriedly, opened the door.

"Tessie! Miss Penny Grace!" Tally hugged them twice. "I can't believe you're here, even before the House is ready for the festivities."

"Tally, honey, neither can we." Tess Hamper shook her head and smiled. "Sounds like Amanda Perry is at it again with her horses."

"She was in our Initiation Class, Tally, and, I promise you, she's never changed." Mrs. Penny Grace Hamper Clark laughed. "Just saw her in London before I flew to Hamper and we had so much fun shopping for hats to wear to Royal Ascot. Now she's decided to spend July touring France too. Oh, Tally, it's so wonderful to see you again, darling."

"You too, Miss Penny Grace. Welcome home. How's LeeLee doing at camp?"

"She's the Counselor for all things drama-related and happy as a chickadee."

"Tess, Penny Grace, so happy to see you." Lula hugged them both. "Thank you for being here. I know you just got home, Penny Grace. We've got lots of food for you."

Tally moved closer to the "Welcome Closet." Lula called the women by their first names. She had never heard Lula call any White woman anything but "Miss" or "Mrs." The three women chittered like seagulls and started all over with hugs and laughs as Mrs. Crockett joined the group.

"Camille Crockett, I have one question for you." Miss Penny Grace sounded stern. "Do you have your whistle?"

Mrs. Crockett placed her fingers down her décolleté, into the bridge of her brassiere, and fished out her whistle just as Miss Penny Grace pulled an orange whistle from her Chanel pocketbook.

Tess held hers in the air. Lula pulled one from her pocket.

"Well, now we know—"

"The gang's all here!" The four women said in unison and laughed, wiping moisture from their eyes, except for Tess, as Tally stood dumbfounded.

After sharing with the group how the four of them had known each other since they were asked to speak at a Georgia Garden Club meeting years ago, Tess and Miss Penny Grace raved about the hydrangeas and the special plant food Lula and Camille had brought that day to show the ladies.

"Prettiest, healthiest, bluest hydrangeas I've ever seen in Georgia." Tess sipped lemonade.

"That's because we don't feed the plant. Remember, Tess?"

"We don't feed the plant," the women chorused. "We feed the worms!"

"Worms love a little bit of shrimp as they dig around in the dirt making air pockets for the 'drangeas," Mrs. Crockett told the group, "And, my goodness, do we have shrimp."

"Penny and I were asked to talk about, what was it, Penny?" Tess placed a teacake on her plate.

Miss Penny Grace shook her head.

Camille answered. "The English Daisy, remember?"

"That's right. We gave a presentation on Chaucer and his favorite flower."

"The picture of the four of us was in the Society Section of *The Herald*, thanks to Tess, and before we knew it, we got to talking about flowers and Hamper and how we wanted to work together to plant a new floral display around the fountain in the park, and, here we are, friends for life." Miss Penny Grace squeezed Camille's hand.

"Yes. And now? Here we are," Tess announced, "about to make plans to keep these boys safe."

As the group began to discuss specific details, including the legality of some of the plans, Tally excused herself. She knew all about the plausibility of denial and the consequences of perjury. After all, her daddy was a Federal Court Judge. Her sweetheart would be a lawyer one day soon. She was nominated for the prestigious Oglethorpe-Oxford History Honor with its Creed about integrity. She needed to breathe. Her dilemma was that she wanted to participate, do something, help in some way even though she knew she shouldn't.

Twirling her baton slowly through her fingers, she found herself in the Knight's Hallway, new electric hurricane lanterns along the walls flickering, paint strokes on the oil portraits shiny in the dim light. Placing her baton in the hand of a suit of armor, she sat on a swing hanging from the roof in one of the alcoves and began pumping her legs.

The swings in each alcove were not supposed to be playthings. They were historically meant to stop any amorous behavior when Chaucerettes would say their chaste farewells to their beaus at night. Instead of benches, cushioned chairs or settees, the girls would sit with their dates on the swings where nothing more serious than a goodnight kiss could take place, even if both individuals wanted more.

The thought of wanting more, knowing Rye would be in Hamper soon, made her anxious to be with him, and slowly take off her hot pants and white lace top with ruffles and feel the look in his eyes, the look that was already turning her cheeks pink.

She closed her eyes and dreamed she was outside, the smell of pines and hyacinths fresh in her memory.

"Hey, you."

Tally, startled, squeezed the ropes and opened her eyes.

"Winston, we need to talk."

Winston put his arm around Geoffrey, crooning lyrics to "What Becomes of the Brokenhearted" to the suit of armor.

"Oh, Win. I adore that song."

Tally jumped off in mid-swing. Jitterbugging with Winston down the hallway, Tally sang with her friend an acapella rendition of her favorite Jimmy Ruffin song, the two of them seemingly without a care in the world until they stopped, sat on the Grand Staircase and proceeded to talk about what to do next.

Thirty-three

Tally juggled a platter of biscuits, a jar of preserves and a thermos of tea as she searched for an open space on Khaki's door to knock. Good grief. Typical Khaki. Forever changing how she decorated her door.

At the beginning of their junior year, instead of stenciling a favorite word or quote in pink paint on a white door as many did in the Chaucer Sorority House, Khaki had painted the door to her private suite with black and white stripes and a large pink "C" in the center.

Khaki had assured Miss Perry that the "C" was her personal tribute to "Chaucer." Khaki's sorority sisters knew, however, that the "C" was actually Khaki's homage to her idol, "Coco Chanel."

The door at the end of the third-floor hallway once looked like the entrance to a boutique in Paris. In January, however, Khaki began to attach clear sheet protectors to the door using stick-on pink bows to secure them. Each week she would insert pages from *Women's Wear Daily* or *Town and Country* magazines into the sheet protectors as if creating a storyboard like the ones students crafted at the Hamper University Design School where Khaki was majoring in Fashion Design.

When Miss Perry asked what those pages had to do with Chaucer, it was rumored that Khaki said, "Why Miss Perry! You don't want your girls looking as unattractive as the Wife of Bath in *The Canterbury Tales*, now do you?"

According to witnesses, Miss Perry had laughed, tucked a tendril of Khaki's copper-colored, shoulder-length hair behind Khaki's ear and told Khaki she was the brightest, dearest girl.

Privately, Khaki announced to sorority sisters how she was sick and tired of seeing the same old tweed skirts, white blouses with Peter Pan collars, cable-knit-boring sweaters, and Pappagallo ballet flats that made everyone look as matchy-matchy-gross as their mothers. Never mind that most of the girls wore miniskirts, flouncy tops and platform sandals with Pappagallo pocketbooks. When Khaki had a rant in mind, facts did not matter at all.

At the private sorority sister meeting in January 1970, while dressed in a chartreuse mini-skirt and purple blouse that oddly seemed to intensify the blue of her eyes, Khaki stated she was making it her New Year's "Chaucer Resolution" to educate her sorority sisters on the latest fashion trends.

By May, however, the door was a mess.

It was cluttered with pictures of Khaki and Louie on the Spring Break Cruise, photos of them at a market in the Bahamas trying on straw hats, dancing the Shag at his fraternity dance, stomping a sandcastle on the beach, and drinking Margaritas with their arms intertwined. In one enlarged black and white photo, Khaki was sunbathing on a rock in her bikini with Louie's hand covering her navel.

Tally had no choice. She banged on the photo of Khaki smiling, her peach lipstick smudged around her mouth, her heart-shaped face aglow in the rays of a sunset, showing her three-carat marquis diamond engagement ring to the photographer.

The more Tally thought about it, the more she wondered if Khaki had barricaded her door with photos so she there would be no place to knock and she would not be disturbed.

Khaki shouted, "Who is it?"

"Delivery of biscuits and blackberry preserves."

Khaki flung open the door, dressed in sweatpants and a Chaucer Sorority jersey.

"McCall! What are you doing here? I told Lula to fix me some biscuits and bring them up here as soon as she could."

"I know, Khaki. I was in the kitchen talking with Lula when you called."

"So why didn't Lula deliver the food like I asked?"

"I volunteered to bring it to you instead. Besides I need to ask you a favor."

Khaki grabbed a biscuit from underneath the tin foil and without waiting for preserves or butter, plunged it into her mouth.

She signaled for Tally to come in as she plopped onto her black leather Breuer chair.

Tally closed the door behind her and set the thermos of sweet tea on Khaki's glass coffee table.

"Oh, Lord! Are these fabulous? And still warm." Khaki reached for another biscuit and scooped preserves in the center. "Thank God for Lula and for letting us have this week at the Chaucer House so Lula can cook for us. So, spill the beans. What favor do you need this time? Holy cow, where did you get that bracelet?"

"Isn't it the most beautiful bracelet you've ever seen?"

Khaki grabbed Tally's hand and touched the delicate gold bracelet. A dazzling center heart studded with pave´ diamonds, Rye's birthstone, embraced a smaller heart of tiny cultured pearls, Tally's birthstone.

"Rye gave it to me to celebrate my birthday."

Actually, Rye had surprised her by having the bracelet delivered with a bouquet of peach roses and a card that stated cryptically, "Please wear this, Georgia, to remember your guy and our cabin."

Tally blushed thinking of that night.

"About the favor, Khaki. You see, I received too much gauze a few months ago for Initiation and—"

"Tally, how many times have I told you to measure on the bias? Good grief. It's Fashion 101."

Tally wanted to inform Khaki that the receipt of too much gauze was not because of any measuring hiccups but because of the mail snafu in March that caused the manufacturer not to receive Tally's cancellation notice of the extra gauze she thought she needed.

Instead, Tally picked up Khaki's favorite bottle of perfume.

"No! Stop!" Khaki shouted, biscuit crumbs spilling from her mouth. "Don't spray it! I don't want the whole room reeking of gardenias."

Confirmed. Khaki was definitely pregnant. Her room always smelled of gardenias.

"Look, Khaki, on July 4th at our sorority Independence Day picnic and pageant, I need you and Louie to portray *Troilus and Criseyde* for the marriage ceremony behind the gauze, you know, in silhouette, with tea candles." Tally sucked in her breath and tried to sound casual. "Rayleigh and Travis were going to do it but Travis is having trouble with his leg again, and, anyway, Daddy is planning to officiate the wedding and since he's a judge, he can perform a real wedding too."

Khaki stopped eating. She squinted at Tally. The room was so quiet Tally could hear someone playing "Chapel of Love" by The Dixie Cups on a record player next door.

"Go on."

"Well, I was just thinking that Daddy could actually marry you and Louie, you know, if you want him to. You would have a fabulous story to tell everybody years from now about your secret wedding and then you and Louie could have your beautiful ceremony at the church. You could wear your bespoke dress that Vera is making for your wedding and you and Louie could still get married as you are planning on Wednesday, August 19th, Coco Chanel's birthday."

Tally wished her words were not tumbling all over each other. She poured herself some tea. She had heard Vera cursing the other day while letting out seams on Khaki's satin empire-waist wedding dress and that is when she decided to hatch her plan.

If she and Winston were going to create deterrence while they helped Franklin and Ted escape from the sight of military officers who would attend the July 4th picnic and pageant as they did every year at the Chaucer Sorority's invitation, it might as well benefit Khaki too. Yet no one else could know the escape plan. Not even Khaki.

"Wait. That would be a couple of days from now?" Khaki placed her hand on her stomach. "Okay. Alright. Gosh. That could solve every, I mean, I could do that for you as a favor this one time."

"Thanks, Khaki." Both girls exhaled at the same time. "The crazy thing? Daddy will marry you as *Troilus and Criseyde* according to the play about Chaucer's star-crossed lovers."

"Well, that won't make it legal for me and—"

"But Daddy can also call you and Louie by your real names behind the gauze if you want him to do that, you know, while the harp is playing and, in the most romantic way, make it a special, secret, legal ceremony between the three of you."

For the first time, Khaki smiled.

"You know my favorite memory of your Daddy, Tally?" Khaki dabbed a napkin around both eyes.

"No, what?"

"When I worked at the Dairy Queen that summer to qualify to compete in the *Miss Georgia Dairy Queen Pageant* which, of course, I won," Khaki pointed to a crown, sash and bronzed ice cream cone on her glass shelf. "I remember your Daddy encouraging me. I remember Judge McCall would drive through the drive-through, stop at the window, order a banana milkshake, two burgers with pickles and a chocolate dipped ice cream cone for your mother." Khaki sniffed.

"Your sweet mother would always lean across your daddy's lap and say to me, 'You look so lovely, Khaki' and your Daddy would say, 'Khaki Katie Carson, you make the best curl on a Dairy Queen cone I have ever seen.' I couldn't believe he admired me."

Tally cleared her throat imagining how something so small and insignificant could mean so much.

"He meant it, Khaki." Tally squeezed Khaki's hand. "Now isn't he the perfect person to marry you and Louie?"

Khaki squeezed Tally's hand tight and reached for another biscuit.

Thirty-four

Chaucerette alumni and current sorority sisters gathered on the lawn of the Chaucer Sorority House for the annual July 4th Garden Party and Pageant. Fathers, mothers, brothers, sisters, husbands, fiancées, boyfriends, sweethearts and children played lawn tennis, badminton, volleyball, horseshoes, softball and tag in the Georgia sunshine from noon until sunset each year. Prizes were won. Pictures were taken.

Chaucerettes served pound cake slices near the famous Dogwood Tunnel on the cliff. Hamburger and hot dog stands were located near picnic tables. Barbecue and steaks were grilled on the path that led to the cliff. Canter Berry presided over it all.

Tess Hamper and Penny Grace Hamper Clark, cousins twice-removed, were Alumni Co-Chairs of the event. They welcomed everyone to the festivities, with a special introduction of military officials from Fort Hamper, using a microphone on the stage originally used for the "Third of May-Chaucer Day" event just two months and one day before. To the attendees, their voices may have sounded enthusiastic, gracious, celebratory and appreciative of sorority sisters and their guests for joining in the fun.

To Tally, however, their voices seemed higher-pitched, more shrill, more strained. She could not believe what she and Winston had planned. She also could not believe it would happen before she saw Rye again. Would he approve? Would he understand? Would he be proud of her quest for justice?

Tessie announced that the wedding of *Troilus and Criseyde* would commence soon, a wedding to which all were invited.

Tally glanced at the American flags bordering the walkway leading to the Chaucer House in a flutter of red, white and blue. Soon it would be sunset. The garden party would be over. The flags would need to be removed, out of respect, according to the *Flag Code*, before the sun went down.

Earlier, Tally had performed a flaming baton routine to wild applause. Rayleigh had sung "Edelweiss," dedicating it to her beloved Travis who sat in a wheelchair and waved to the guests. Becca had worn capris and wowed the crowd as she walked on her hands from one weeping willow to another before cartwheeling into a perfect split.

Tally observed Winston, Franklin and Ted carrying silver trays aloft, one tray with throwaway cups of sweet tea, one with fresh chocolate-chip cookies and one with cups of watermelon as dessert offerings for guests preparing to enter the Chaucer Sorority House for the wedding ceremony.

The trio looked as if Independence Day was their favorite holiday. They talked animatedly to guests, laughing and bowing to the children, pointing to their patriotic uniforms with red and white striped-seersucker pants and pale blue shirts. The only time they seemed reticent was when serving the military recruiters, especially when Franklin dropped peach biscuits on a Sergeant's polished shoes.

She wondered exactly when Rye would arrive. His flight had been delayed. He called her at the Chaucer House just before the party began to wish her a fun afternoon and to say he would get a ride from the airport to his car and meet her at the Chaucer House. He also encouraged her not to worry, he would see her soon, and yes, he could not wait to kiss the sweetest lips in Georgia again.

Louie Larson and Jimbo Carson, soon-to-be brothers-in-law, began taking down the flags as Miss Penny Grace waved to Tally to come over and join the Farewell Chorus of Chaucerette Sisters harmonizing "Georgia on My Mind" with Ted soft-brushing on drums and Winston on harmonica.

As Chaucerettes sang, Tally wished she could have Georgia on her mind. However, she had the families of the Kent State victims on her mind. How could these families celebrate the fourth day of any month ever again knowing each date was a numerical reminder that another month had passed since the last time their children were alive on the fourth of May, 1970?

"Tally, darling. Can we speak with you for a moment?"

Tally turned to see Tess and Miss Penny Grace gesturing to her. She was the last person on the stage and had not even realized it.

"Sorry! What a great job y'all did with the party this year!" Tally hugged both of the women and pointed to the sunset. They oohed and ahhed over the pinks, yellows and scarlet streaks in the sky above the Hamper U campus.

"The sunsets in Hamper remind me of the ones at Crinoline Cay." Miss Penny Grace wrapped her arm through Tess's. "Don't you agree, Tessie?"

Tess smiled and said, "Penny, you'll be seeing those sunsets come tomorrow. And I love you for taking the risk."

Tally blew kisses their way and excused herself to go change her outfit for the wedding ceremony. She wanted to slip on her new silk sheath, pistachio green with a dash of periwinkle accent, and her new periwinkle panties. She also wanted to shimmer more lip gloss on her lips. Rye could be arriving in an hour or so. She could not wait to see him and be in his arms again.

"Tally, baby, don't go just yet. Penny and I need to talk with you."

Tess and Penny Grace led Tally under a weeping willow tree.

"Dearest, we are only going to give you the silver lining around the moon, not the moon itself; the forest, not the trees; the silhouette, not the fashion details; the--" Miss Penny Grace hand shook as she held Tally's. "You see, today is Independence Day and we intend to free our boys."

"Ma'am? Miss Penny Grace? I'm not sure what you mean."

"Tally, darling, what Penny is babbling about, in her own British poetic way, is this: We are not going to let Nixon take Franklin and Ted and send them to 'Nam. We are women who are finally going to take a stand about something in which we believe."

Tess ran her hand through her hair, her emerald ring gliding through waves of silver.

"Pumpkin, I shared with Penny your essay on the military draft being modern-day slavery months ago. You wrote that a military draft is the antithesis of our Constitutional freedoms, an outrageous affront to the equality of males and females. You cited Chaucer's story of

Chanticleer in *The Canterbury Tales* as the perfect example of our government flattering our young boys with tales of glory, service, patriotism, God and country, while making them our slaves to do as they are told and follow orders." Tess seemed out of breath. "Well, by God, we are not going to allow slavery in Georgia ever again."

Tally knew Tessie was talking. However, she was struggling to comprehend her words yet she knew she had just been paid a compliment.

"Th-thank you, Tessie. I don't know what to—"

"Don't say anything, sugar. Just listen. We have to hurry. We are going to put the boys on Penny's ship tonight, the one anchored in open waters near our Chaucer Sorority Beach and, by God, Penny and I are going to sail with them to Crinoline Cay, you know, Penny's private island off the coast of Georgia."

"It's named that because the waves scallop the sand like crinolines scallop—"

"Edit, Penny-pie, edit. We need to ask Tally a question, remember?"

Tally could not speak. Her throat felt as if breezes had sucked her voice from her. She and Winston were planning to secure Franklin and Ted on the Crockett's shrimp boat during the wedding ceremony and Mr. Crockett was going to take them to his uncle's cabin near St. Simon's Island. It was the only place they could think to hide them until the next phase of the escape when—wait, what did Miss Penny Grace just say?

"We are going to be as outrageous as the Wife of Bath in *The Canterbury Tales*." Penny laughed a nervous laugh.

"She had five husbands, Penny Grace! So much for the sanctity of marriage." Tessie sounded more effervescent than Tally had ever heard.

Tally grabbed Tess's hand. A surge of passion, born of force and restlessness, soared from her toes to her thoughts as if a baton sailing from her fingers to the moon.

"Tessie, I love you and I promise I want to hear more and please know I'm thrilled for the boys. It's just that I have to help Khaki get ready for her wedding, I mean, as *Criseyde*, of course, and I need to talk to Winston."

Tess kissed Tally's cheek. "My goodness. You feel like you got a sunburn today, baby."

That will be my defense in court. Sun poisoning, heat stroke! Tally fingers felt numb. She needed to hurry. Wait. Did Winston know about Tessie's plan? Did Mrs. Crockett? Did Mr. Crockett talk to his wife about it? And what about Franklin and Ted? Good grief. She felt so confused.

"And we're not going to get caught. And, if we do, we'll make sure the boys are not discovered." Tess winked at Miss Penny Grace.

"How come?" Tally's eyes were opened so wide, she didn't dare to blink.

Miss Penny Grace looked around as if someone might hear even though there was no one in sight. "Tally, honey, do you remember my birthdate?"

"I-wow-let me think. It's December because you always wear blue topaz, your birthstone. It's after Christmas because you always tell the story of when you were a little girl, you told your mother and daddy that you, all by yourself, made sure you were not going to let the stork bring you to their house on Christmas Day because you wanted another day, a birthday all your own, for more presents."

"Oh, I can see Penny now, stomping her feet as everybody laughed." Tess wiped her eyes.

"And you wanted to be a Chaucerette because, oh, my gosh! Your birthday is December 29th. The day Archbishop Thomas a'Becket was murdered at Canterbury Cathedral which was the purpose of the pilgrims riding their horses to Canterbury Cathedral in *The Canterbury Tales* to pay homage to the dead Archbishop."

"Brilliant, Tally, brilliant. And this year, I'm throwing a big party in London on my 70th birthday for it is also the 800th anniversary of the day the Archbishop of Canterbury became a martyr. I'm having a dance in the ballroom and a church service earlier in the day."

"You're not going to have it at Crinoline?" Tess waved to someone in the distance.

"Not this year, Tessie." Miss Penny Grace tugged Tally closer. "And, Tally, we call it Crinoline Cay to outsiders. However, my closest Chaucerette sisters in my Initiation Class know my little island is officially named A'Becket Cay, my personal homage to the Archbishop of Canterbury."

"She even built a chapel there." Tess sounded impressed.

Tally looked at lights blinking on across the lawn and in the Chaucer Sorority House with one bright spotlight on Canter Berry. She felt energized and numb at the same time. The island where the soldiers were taken? Miss Penny Grace's island? What on earth? She needed to find Winston. She needed to hurry.

"However, and this is just between Chaucerettes, dear one. While my little Cay is a beautiful place to visit, by invitation, of course, it is, well, let's just say it's my *creed* to offer a private refuge for soldiers who yearn to be free."

"Lula, we'll be right there." Tess shouted. "Come on, girls. We've got lots to do."

Tally grabbed Becca in the Knight's Hallway.

"Becks, you have to help me. I'm losing my mind."

"Sure, Tally. What's up? Great baton twirling, by the way."

"Thanks, Becca! And Shawl would love how you walked on your hands! You know he's wild about that talent of yours, sweetie pie." Tally heard a phone ring. "Becks, can you please help Khaki get her dress on? Virginia is in charge of lighting the candles for the ceremony. Oh, and could you remind Daddy of the arrangement he made with Khaki and Louie—don't worry, he'll know—and could you please—"

"Tally, call for you." Nora Faye waved to her.

"Thanks, Nora Faye!" Tally blew a kiss to Becca who waved while dashing down the Hallway. Grabbing a fan from a silver tray, Tally cradled the phone on her shoulder, fluttering the fan near her face.

"Georgia. Hey, 'cakes. Just landed. Headed over. You okay? You're breathing hot and heavy. I trust that's because you're hearing my voice." Rye laughed.

"Rye, I can't wait for you to hold me again. And for me to hold you too."

"Oh, trust me, Georgia, there's going to be a whole lot more than holding going on tonight."

Tally found Winston in the kitchen.

"Winston! What in the world is going on?"

"Girl, you have no idea."

"Oh, yes, I do. Tess and Miss Penny Grace told me they are rescuing the boys."

"Did you tell them our plan?"

"No, Win, I wanted to talk to you first."

"Look," Win took her hands that were gesturing wildly and held them steady. "One way or another, Frankie and Ted are going to be safe tonight. They have to be."

He kissed the top of her hand, grinned and scooped her in a hug.

As sounds of "He Don't Love You Like I Love You," the hit song by The Iceman Jerry Butler that Khaki and Louie insisted on playing during their ceremony, Lula, Tess and Penny huddled with Tally in the Knight's Hallway. Tally rolled her eyes when Tess asked what song that was and why it was appropriate. Tally responded that it was a modern-day retelling of what happened to *Troilus and Criseyde* without sharing that it was Louie's favorite song to sing to Khaki after she broke up with Hugh Prentice.

Camille Crockett and her husband, Woodrow, stayed with Franklin and Winston in the kitchen. Camille's sobs could be heard through the door. Ted was talking on the Chaucer House phone to his parents, stroking his fingers through his shoulder-length hair. Tess grabbed Tally's hand.

"Tally, you must know the truth. Penny, Lula, Camille and I were not going to ask you to be involved. We wanted you to have plausible deniability. However, we need the boys to escape through the tunnel to the beach and you are the only one who has the key. To the Initiation Room."

"Thank you, Tessie." Tally squeezed her godmother's hand and whispered. "The problem? No one is allowed in the Initiation Room other than Chaucerettes. I'm sorry, Tessie. I just need a moment to think how we could—sure, yes. Please go talk with Ted's parents. I'll figure it out."

How else could they get the boys to the beach except through the Initiation Room? And why did Winston ditch the plan they crafted to walk with Frankie and Ted to the dock where his daddy's shrimp boat would be ready while Tally provided cover at the party?

Tally plopped on a swing in the alcove. She swayed slowly, trying to make sense of it all.

Mike Parish came to mind. The night they met near the weeping willow tree. Could Franklin, Winston and Ted somehow get to the beach that way, the way tourists used to ignore signs to follow a path to the private beach?

According to Mayor Buddy Rod Persons, interviewed by Jax Boudreaux for his recent *Wake Up!* column in *The Hamper Herald*, they could not. After the girls died on the sandbar down the coast, the Mayor and Police Chief Parish had seen enough.

They erected Hamper's famous driftwood-gray, plantation shutter-fences all along the dunes with no access to any private beaches anymore. High enough to deter jumpers, quaint enough to please Hamper's old moneyed residents, functional enough to allow scenic views to be undeterred, the happiest beneficiaries seemed to be the seagulls roosting atop the fences, night and day.

Another thought about Mike Parish dashed through Tally's thoughts. What if he is on patrol tonight? Good grief. What type of danger merits being an acceptable risk?

Thoughts raced through Tally's mind. Tess was on the phone. Rye was on his way from the airport after picking up his car. How could she justify her actions, even now, or if she needed to in the future?

She wanted to change clothes. Her majorette costume felt dated, like something she used to wear when she was younger yet not what she wanted to wear now. Most of all, she wanted to throw her baton in the air, ask Shawl for his wisdom on what she should do, and feel Rye's arms around her in the warm glow of candlelight in the Cabin.

The memory of the Historical Marker high on the dune, glinting copper in the moonlight, just two months and one day ago, jumped into her thoughts as she sat on a swing, staring into space.

The Marker that enlightened folks about the original Trustee rule of Georgia. *No slavery permitted in the Georgia-land.* Just as Tessie said. They would be following the original rules of the colony of Georgia.

She, Tally McCall, could help to free men forced against their will to be military slaves of the government, slaves forced to see images that would haunt them the rest of their lives, slaves forced to kill people.

She pumped her legs higher.

Why doesn't the military tell all the convicted murderers in prisons that they are going on a "field trip," give them rifles and swap the convicted murderers for the American farm boys from Georgia and Ohio who are killing and being killed?

Good grief. Why not employ people who like to kill as our killers during a war? Aren't there enough murderers on Death Row to take on a field trip where they can do what they are good at?

Why not allow people who like to kill, on either side of a war's battlefield, the opportunity to do their government's bidding, unless we can get the old men, in the United States and Vietnam too, the ones who start the wars, to fight the battles themselves?

Why do men who have come back from war decades before, often shell-shocked and maimed, think younger generations need that same experience to "serve" their country when, in fact, she knew her generation of young men forced into military service by the draft would never be the same?

Wouldn't the best way to serve one's country be to protest wars?

Wouldn't the best way to serve be voting for leaders who keep us out of war?

Wouldn't the best way to serve one's country be a gathering of artists with creative minds who could use their imaginations to propose creative ideas to wage war like dropping swarms of mosquitoes or gallons of molasses or tons of Milk Duds on the warriors just to get them to pause and stop fighting, if only for a moment; or gathering artists to predict events that might seem fictional now yet could prove to be dangerous in the future; or a coalition of youth with exuberant dreams and fresh ideas who could offer their unfettered views and original thoughts without fear of recrimination if the ideas seemed revolutionary; or a gathering of mothers whose views are often dismissed instead of revered for the perspectives they have earned and the children they want to protect more than their own lives; or a convention of historians and philosophers who could offer their abilities to "know how to see?"

She was shaking.

The phone rang.

"Gigi, it's for you." Ted called out.

She jumped off the swing.

"Georgia. Damn airline lost my luggage. I've got to file a report and buy a toothbrush before I get to the Chaucer House."

"Rye." Tally whispered. "You don't really need clothes, do you?"

"Now that's my girl." He laughed. "Can't wait to see you, 'cakes, and I can't wait," he lowered his voice, "to kiss you and *dance* with you again." The word, *dance*, was their secret word for making love.

"Oh, Rye! I can't wait to *dance* with you too." Tally whispered.

Soothed by Rye's voice, encouraged by the history of this night in which she would be a participant, not an observer, devoted to the cause of justice with hopes that one day the laws of the land would catch up to the justice the laws should honor, Tally made peace anew with her decision to protest the war, the military draft and the absurdity of one's birthdate potentially leading to one's death date by helping Franklin and Ted escape.

Her only dilemma? Logistics.

With the rocky cliff too dangerous to descend at night, with fences barricading the beaches and patrols by police everywhere, with the "Invited Visitors' Entrance" down a stairway on the side of the mansion to the Chaucer Private Beach under construction for the summer, the only way the young men could escape with Tess and Miss Penny Grace was through the private Initiation Room and Tunnel under the sorority house. Tally had the only key. Phoebe and Miss Perry were still out of the country so Tally would be the only—wait a minute.

Horatio Hamper. His famous quotes: *A knowledge of history is the key to survival.* And *To know history is also to know strategy.* She remembered her own history. She knew the past had all the answers.

The "Third of May-Chaucer Day Celebration" popped into her thoughts.

Tally waved to Tess. "I'm checking on something. Quick-quick. Back in a moment."

Tess blew her a kiss and looked at her watch. "Ten minutes?"

Tally nodded and blew a kiss back.

She heard her Chaucerette sister, Cecile, playing the harp. The wedding ceremony and the telling of the story of *Troilus and Criseyde* had begun and Khaki and Louie would soon be married. *Troilus* and *Criseyde* too.

Walking past a series of portraits featuring horses with young women sitting sidesaddle in antebellum dresses and ruffled pantaloons and progressing to a young woman in jodhpurs, all alone in a forest, straddling a horse that was jumping over a fallen tree limb, Tally neared the Giant Staircase. She unlocked the door to the Initiation Room, swished the remaining panels of gauze to hide the secret Initiation artifacts, and eased into the blue velvet chair.

Closing her eyes, she summoned memories of the event on that Sunday afternoon, May 3rd, just two months before.

Thirty-five

Her champagne pearl, perched atop diamonds, had shimmered on Tally's finger as she shook hands with guests arriving for the Sunday, May 3rd, 1970, afternoon ceremony. Escorting ladies in tea-length dresses and gentlemen in linen suits to the entrance of Hamper, Georgia's famous Dogwood Tunnel on the grounds of the Chaucer Sorority House, she observed them stroll through soft pink light, many pointing to the canopy of intertwined dogwood branches, lush with pink blooms, above them.

"Don't worry, sweet." Becca swooped her arms around Tally. "They're all here to celebrate him."

"Can you believe this day has finally arrived?" Tally hugged Becca. "After all those handwritten invitations, engraved programs and costume meetings? And on the other side of that tunnel—"

"—is the one tale Chaucer forgot!" Becca interrupted with a "ta-ta-ta-ta" trumpet sound.

"*The Ingénue's Tale.*" Tally laughed and tugged a pleated fan from the pocket of her taffeta skirt, swanned it into a half-moon and fluttered it about Becca's face.

Offering homage to Chaucer by modernizing *The Canterbury Tales*, updating the group of travelers from peasants, knights, millers and The Wife of Bath to sorority sisters on their way to Chaucer's crypt in Westminster Abbey, sharing anecdotes of the Chaucerettes' trip last summer to tour Versailles, buy leather gloves in Venice to gift the underprivileged girls they sponsored in Hamper for Christmas each year and as Big Sister-Little Sister gifts, visiting Normandy to pay their respects to soldiers their daddies' age who did not come home, and honoring Chaucer with a group prayer at his gravesite in the Abbey energized the group.

"If only our stories could make our guests think of Chaucer as being relevant in a bright new way. That would be my dearest dream, well, *one* of my dearest dreams come true."

The dearest reason Tally wanted to win the Oxford Honor was to immerse herself in understanding Chaucer's rebel influence on literature, delight in his humor and earn the honor of being named a "Chaucer Scholar."

She had squeezed Becca's hand and swung her best friend's diamond engagement ring into the sunshine.

"Becks, speaking of a bright new way, look how your ring's sparkling in a bright new way, Miss Bride-to-be!"

"Dazzling, Becca. Just like you, darling." Miss Perry, their Chaucer Sorority Housemother, marched up to the girls leading her beloved chestnut filly named "Legacy" on a rope.

"Speaking of rings, that is what you should be wearing, Tally McCall."

The horse whinnied as if in agreement. Tally shoved her fan back in her pocket.

"Diamonds, darling. Not pearls. Lord, have mercy! My mother forced me to wear my pearl necklace to bed every night." Miss Perry tied Legacy to the newest Georgia Historical Marker beside the tunnel. "She thought I would stop going to the stables if I got used to wearing pearls. Ha! I took my debutante photo for the society page dressed in a white satin ball gown sitting on my stallion, Thunder. My diamond engagement ring was as big as Thunder's eye. And then, wouldn't you know it, the very next day my sweetheart, my Freddie, was killed at Pearl Harbor and—"

"Oh, Miss Perry. That's the saddest thing!" The girls said in unison.

"Still hurts my heart. Nearly thirty years. Life sure is a journey. Right, Legacy? Just goes to show, you can keep folks beside you the whole way even if they are only beside you in your mind." Miss Perry petted Legacy. "Anyway, mother was a hoot."

Miss Perry freshened the buttercup bows on Legacy's mane.

"Never liked pearls though. Good lord. Such irritants. Literally. Ask an oyster. Figuratively? Ask a fraternity boy. You need a diamond solitaire on that finger, Tally McCall. Like the stunners I saw at the Derby yesterday."

Miss Perry, who had just arrived back in Hamper from the Kentucky Derby, was wearing a purple straw hat that dripped red silk roses to her shoulders.

"I bet those rings were decadent, Miss Perry. You know what? You would have been a hoot yourself, telling your stories, if you had been one of the pilgrims on the way to Canterbury."

Tally brushed sand from the letters of the Historical Marker.

"And, Miss Perry," Tally fidgeted with her ring, "this pearl is my birthstone, remember?"

"Most unfortunate, dear." Miss Perry sneezed into a lace handkerchief.

The distant sound of a sorority sister strumming a mandolin signaled the musical prelude to the ceremony.

Becca dotted the tip of her ring finger about her eyes. "I hate to hear about your fiancé, Miss P., and I'm so sorry, ma'am, but I have to hurry you along."

"I will remember you and your fiancé, Miss P., whenever I study Pearl Harbor." Tally began to untie Legacy's rope. "The ceremony's about to start, ma'am. Do you want me to take Legacy back to her stall?"

"What for? Tally McCall, you are in charge of this ceremony as Chaucer Sorority Historian. Therefore, in honor of Chaucer and his *Canterbury Tales*, you are taking Legacy with you."

"What? Ma'am? Miss Perry, I can't—"

"Now, don't you say you *can't*. Always say you *can*. The word *can* comes before *can't* in the word 'Canterbury,' remember?" Red roses bounced about Miss Perry's head in a dizzying display. "And Legacy here will remind folks of the horses that carried those dear Pilgrims to Canterbury."

Cecile, the Chaucerette sister who played 'Love Me Tender' on the harp as her talent in the 1969 Miss Georgia Pageant, began plucking the tune, "Georgia on My Mind," the signal for the sorority sisters to begin the processional.

Tally knew there would be no arguing with Miss Perry once she made up her mind. Besides, as Sorority Housemother, she was the authority and, Lord knows, in Georgia, you learn at a primal age never to buck authority.

"Yes, ma'am. Thank you, Miss Perry, for wanting Legacy to be part of the ceremony." Tally gestured for Miss Perry to enter the tunnel. "I'll be sure to celebrate the horses in my presentation and, after I introduce Legacy, I'll introduce you so you *can* take Legacy back to your seat by the stage."

"Lovely, Tally. Lovely."

Miss Perry blew Legacy a kiss as she turned and sashayed with Becca through the tunnel toward the garden party on the lawn high above the sea.

Virginia Dodge's mandolin strumming was accompanied by Rayleigh Scattering singing "Today While the Blossoms Still Cling to the Vine." The tune was intended to evoke campfire songs the Chaucerette sorority sisters sang at summer camp. The girls wanted it to be their personal tribute to the Canterbury pilgrims who told some of their stories while sitting around a campfire too.

Although Chaucer had died 570 years ago, the girls felt this song would be a lyrical bridge to the past, both their past and Chaucer's, and a bridge to the reminiscent tales of his beloved fictional characters.

Tally wished she could focus on Chaucer instead of trying to keep Legacy from lifting her hoofs ever higher in the air.

"Good girl, Legacy, sweet girl. We'll see Miss Perry soon, honey." Tally made clicking noises.

Legacy pulled at the rope, refusing to move.

"Legacy, come on now. No time to protest, sugar." If only Tally had sugar cubes in her pocket. Good grief. She only had a vial of her favorite MaGriffe perfume, the French fragrance that introduced a scent of just-mowed grass into the air before delighting with a second layer of intrigue, forest ferns and clover.

She squirted a spritz into the tunnel.

Legacy whinnied and moved backwards.

The solo was almost over.

There were no other songs on the ceremony program to be sung.

Tally remembered how Miss Perry would coo to Legacy, telling her stories.

"Legacy, did you know Chaucer mentioned the dogwood tree in *The Canterbury Tales*?" Tally's voice softened. "He sure did. In *The Knight's Tale*, he talks about the whipple-tree, another name for the dogwood that was actually—"

Legacy lifted her head and showed her teeth.

"Everything will be just fine, honey." Tally tied the rope around a dogwood trunk.

Promising Legacy she would be right back, she had hitched her skirt to her knees and ran to the other end of the tunnel. Spotting Winston and Franklin, she waved to get their attention.

She whispered to the Crockett twins before racing back to the pony.

Legacy pawed the grass.

Straining to see if anyone was entering the tunnel by the Georgia Historical Marker, the light in front of her darkened as if a shadow putting its arms around her.

Thank goodness. The plan was working.

Tally pulled a sleeve of her peasant blouse over her elbow and down her arm. She tugged the other sleeve off until her blouse puddled at her waist. Cooing to Legacy, she reached behind, unhooked her yellow push-up strapless bra and pulled it from its restraint, freeing her breasts to bounce in the warm breeze.

Closing her eyes, she inhaled. Rayleigh was leading the audience in singing, "Michael, Row the Boat Ashore."

Wriggling the blouse up her arms, the puckered material circled her shoulders. The polished cotton brushed her nipples, puckering them as well.

Untying Legacy's rope, Tally placed her bra across the filly's eyes, hoping the inspirational scene in *Gone with the Wind,* when Rhett Butler used his coat to cover the eyes of the terrified horse during Sherman's burning of Atlanta, was accurate.

Legacy reared up. The bra fell to the grass. Tally let go of the rope. What now? Legacy was free yet seemed so baffled about what to do. The filly shook her head. A buttercup ribbon plopped to the ground. Something--the tunnel, the trees, the sounds of unfamiliar music echoing in the dogwoods seemed to scare Legacy, make her skittish, make her—

"Hey, girl. You okay?" Winston's voice echoed.

Tally swirled. Oh, dear lord. Winston could not see her now! Without her bra on, he would be able to see her nipples through the cotton if he walked into the tunnel to find her. Hurry! Think!

"Fine, Winston." She shouted. "Thank you so much. Great job with the tablecloth. Appreciate you covering the opening and—"

"Get a move on, girl. I got studying tonight. Besides, seagulls keep eyeing the cucumber sandwiches."

"Just keep Rayleigh singing! Please! Be there quick-quick."

Legacy looked tired. Her eyes, so droopy, blinked as she put her head down and chewed on the bark of a dogwood.

Harp, mandolin and guitar formed a string trio as Chaucerettes sang the lyrics to "Tammy." Legacy's ears fluttered. Her eyes looked as soft as cocoa velvet. Tally stroked Legacy's face and kissed the stiff, coarse hair on her cheek.

Singing the song, as if a lullaby, close to Legacy's ear, Tally cradled the rope in her right hand, kicked the bra in the air, caught it with her left hand and softly placed it over Legacy's eyes.

Leading the filly through the tunnel, all Tally wanted to do was cry.

Tally swept open the side of the tablecloth, motioned to Becca and handed her friend the rope.

Lifting the bra from Legacy's eyes, Tally thanked the dark silhouettes of Franklin and Winston through the white cloth, dashed back into the tunnel, stripped her blouse to her sash and, with her breasts free again, inhaled fragrant air.

Her moment to celebrate Chaucer, a man who enchanted the world with his words, with his humor, with his timeless stories had arrived. Hopefully, she could make the past come alive as if it were the present.

She latched her bra back into place feeling the thick cotton cradle her breasts in a cool cushion of comfort and blessed support.

Hallelujah. She had helped Legacy through the tunnel, covered the filly's eyes and calmed her fears, just by using her ingenuity, a word that curiously shared echoes with the word "ingenue."

Now it was time to try that strategy again.

Thirty-six

Tally gathered the group outside the door to the Initiation Room.

"Winston, Franklin, Ted, I apologize for what I must ask you to do. Only Chaucerettes are allowed to see this room or the tunnel. I hope you understand. Mrs. Crockett, Mr. Crockett, I know you want to say goodbyes again to Franklin. And Ted too, of course."

Tears welled in the eyes of all witnessing the exchange of love and hope and good wishes and promises to be together soon.

"Camille." Penny Grace called to her in a cracked voice. "And Woodrow Wilson Crockett. You know I'll get you and Winston to Crinoline as soon as possible. And, Ted, I'll be in touch with your parents as well, for a vacation visit. We'll take good care of these young men."

"And folks will be thrilled when you show up in Hamper one day, hopefully soon, when the draft ends, after fears that you must have been lost to the ages after falling asleep on a sandbar." Tess patted Ted's back.

Expressions of gratitude filled the promenade around the Grand Staircase. Hugs were exchanged. Laughter skipped up the stairs as if it were ether gas floating.

Tally gave Lula and Mrs. Crockett yellow satin "Chaucerette Initiation Blindfolds" to place over Franklin's eyes and Ted's.

Tess also placed a blindfold on Winston who had volunteered to skipper the party boat that was tied to the pier and charter it across the waves to take Tess, Miss Penny Grace, Franklin and Ted to Miss Penny Grace's ship that would be waiting for them.

Tally turned the key and unlocked the Initiation Room.

"Hey there, Tally-ho! Where you going? And what are those fellows doing with those blindfolds on?"

Mike Parish's voice.

Oh, my gosh.

Think.

Quick.

Mrs. Crockett gasped.

"Mike, are you lost?" Tally twirled around and put her arm on Mike's back. "The buffet is in the Dining Room, here let me show you, and the Wedding Ceremony is—"

"Hold on. Where does that door lead?" Mike turned toward the Initiation Room door, tipped his hat to Tess and Miss Penny Grace. "Miss Hamper. Miss Clark." He nodded to Mr. and Mrs. Crockett. "And why are the Crockett boys and the other fella blindfolded?"

Hurry. Think. Laugh. Do something. Ted, Winston and Franklin began taking their blindfolds off, staring at each other.

"Oh, Mike, that's my friend Ted. We're showing them a, uh, special historical keepsake but they can't see the Initiation Room because it's private and they have to—"

"What Tally-girl is saying, Mike? You just saved us from one of her history tours when all we really want is a beer. Know what I mean, Lieutenant?"

If Mike had observed every face, he would have seen mouths wide open, eyes not blinking, faces in shock.

Franklin was walking toward Mike, imitating Winston who was staring in disbelief at his twin.

"Hey, Winston." Mike shook hands with *Franklin*, Winston's voice-doppelganger. "Can't have a beer myself. Still on duty. Good to meet you, Ted."

"Sure, yeah, you too."

"Franklin," Mike looked at *Winston* who was beginning to smile. "Heard you got your call-up letter. Some of the military brass were looking for you earlier. Think they're still here. Will that tour take long?"

Winston shook his head.

Franklin turned to his father. "Pops. It's mosey-on-down-time to the shrimper. We'll be taking the *Rendezvous*, right?"

His father stared at him.

Franklin winked at Tally.

"No can-do for the tour, girly-girl. And, Frankie, my man. Shrimp boats are full, brother."

Franklin waved to Winston, kissed his mother, and whispered something in her ear.

Feeling dizzy, Tally began to cough. Mike thumped her back as Miss Penny Grace lifted a goblet of water from a silver tray nearby and offered it to Tally.

Tess Hamper stepped forward. Touching Winston on the shoulder, she said, "*Franklin.* Ted. Secure your blindfolds, boys, and follow us. We'll show them the keepsake, Tally. You take care of *you.*"

Tess opened the door to the Initiation Room.

Franklin, posing as Winston, and Mr. Crockett strolled down the Knight's Hallway, ever closer to the front door and freedom.

"Winston," Tally called out to *Franklin,* "I'm still going to take you on that tour and show you the keepsake even though you escaped this time." Tally tried to keep her emotions in check even as her voice cracked.

"You better get to studying, girl, or I'll be taking you on a tour of Oxford when you come to visit me there. See you around, Mike."

Franklin, in his best imitation of Winston, saluted Tally, pointed to Mike, put his arm around his father and sauntered out the front door.

"Mike, thank you so much for being my escort once again." Tally pointed to the lighted portico. "Just need a gulp of fresh air."

"Happy to be your knight in shining armor, Tally-ho."

Mike bent his elbow, tucked her hand inside it, and saluted Geoffrey at the end of the Hallway.

Tally's majorette costume adorned with stars of red, white and blue sequins sparkled in the light of the full moon as she leaned against the Historical Marker. Red lights from Mike's patrol car exited the parking lot. He had just confided to her that after his patrol, he was taking Connie May to see *Love Story* at the drive-in, and asking her to be his girlfriend.

The beam of the lighthouse splashed Tally with radiance. She waved to the ragtag sailors, blindfolds in hand, on the beach making their way to the party boat. Winston saluted her. Tess blew her a kiss. Soon they would rendezvous with Franklin and their escape plan to Miss Penny Grace Hamper Clark's private island would proceed.

Tally twirled her baton, adorned at each end with red glitter ribbons, in spins above her head. The next time the lighthouse beam circled, she hoped Frankie, who had saved his own life with his brilliant, talented, courageous, savvy, amazing, quick-thinking actions, would see her.

Mr. Crockett's shrimper, its trawlers vertical, skimmed through the water. Its herald light flickered twice, as if in code, before it joined the flotilla of boats in the moonlight, some shooting flares from their decks toward the stars.

Car headlights rippled across fronds of the weeping willow.

Finally! Oh, my gosh. Rye is here.

A rush of restlessness to kiss him, whisper in his ear, and *dance* with him in the most intimate way bubbled inside her.

She scooped a mint pillow from the velvet pouch in the strap of her bra, sucked its sweet, fresh taste, and grinned at the thought of cinnamon candles burning hot in the Georgia Glen Cabin tonight.

Georgia Glen. A Southern girl who made history. A Southern girl who will always be remembered for her spirit of hope, her exuberance of youth and her dream of loving her sweetheart for all of time.

Tally finger-twirled her baton. Breezes tousled her hair and puffed the fringe of her white boots, tickling the skin below her knees. Ahhh. If only she could be a breeze. Moving things forward. Swirling support around others. Floating energy through leaves to remind others that they are being remembered with love.

She inhaled salt air. Vera. Camille. Lula. Alida. Tess. Babette. Miss Penny Grace. Miss Perry. Good grief. Southern women who do not have to be in history books to make history.

Each person, no matter one's heritage or proximity to the Mason-Dixon line, can create a distinguished, dazzling Historical Marker with words that are a testament to one's life story, one's relevance, one's celebration of personal dreams.

Tossing her baton toward the stars with a force of energy she never imagined she had within her, she wondered if this is how it felt to release a dove to the sky.

She heard a car door slam.

She grinned, twirled twice, her eyes focused on the spinning object, her ears hearing his whistle and his voice exclaiming, "Hot damn, Georgia!" just as her fingers scooped the baton, like plucking a daisy, before its sparkle could hit the ground.

THANK YOU NOTES

As I bid a fond farewell to the cast of characters romping through these pages, I will miss them so much. Happily, I can visit them at any time for this novel will never be far from my reach. Thank you, most of all, to Tally for your irrepressible spirit. You mean the world to me.

I also wish to celebrate the most beautiful "Miss Georgia" (1960) I have ever seen whose name inspired the name of my protagonist. Thank you, Sandra (Sandy) Tally, for being my forever-favorite "Miss Georgia," for inspiring me, and for sparkling my personal image of "Tally Gigi McCall."

My appreciation to another "Sandra," my mentor and dear friend, Sandra J. Scofield, is immeasurable. Sandra has truly seen me through "the best of times and the worst of times" as I have navigated through this story. Thank you, Sandra, for your encouragement and guidance through the years. You were my first creative writing teacher at the Iowa Summer Writing Festival and my last teacher at the Solstice MFA

Program. I treasure our friendship, Sandra, and celebrate the storyteller you are.

If anyone has been on this "writing road trip" with me, it is my friend, Barbara Byer. Thank you, BB, for ten years of road trips to Iowa City for the Summer Writing Festival. Thank you for being my cheerleader, workshop pal, Writing Partner and beloved friend of thirty years. Congratulations also, Barbara, on the 2023 publication of *Shatterproof*, your memoir of love and loss. It's magnificent. So are you.

My forever-gratitude is also offered to my teachers through the years who chaperoned Tally to her debut: Leslee Becker, Sandra J. Scofield, Jaime Manrique, Randall Kenan, Robert Lopez, Dennis Lehane, Ron Hansen, Bret Anthony Johnston, Joshua Kendall, Gordon Mennenga, Sterling Watson, Steven Huff, Laure-Anne Bosselaar, Dzvinia Orlowsky, Anne-Marie Oomen, Kathy Aguero, David Yoo, Terrance Hayes, Helen Elaine Lee, Tom Barbash, David Michael Kaplan, Venise Berry, Marc Nieson, Shannon Olsen, Ashley Warlick, Eric Goodman, Marilyn Kallet, the indomitable Gussie Goss, Mrs. Carmen Perry, Mrs. Evelyn Turnipseed, Mrs. Collier, Mrs. Abel, and my sweet kindergarten teacher, Mrs. Storey.

Thank you to Sterling Watson, my esteemed teacher, brilliant novelist, raconteur and "Watson Cousin," for teaching me about "enveloping action."

Thank you to Steve Huff for your encouragement to "walk the tightrope of writing a novel all the way across Niagara Falls and not turn back."

Thank you to my Critical Thesis mentor, Jaime Manrique, for being a kindred spirit and beloved friend. Most of all, Jaime, thank you for your touching introduction of me before my Residency Reading at Solstice, dearest one.

Thank you to Robert Lopez for the eloquence of your introduction at my Solstice MFA Graduation Ceremony and your encouragement through the years.

Thank you to Randall Kenan who will forever live in my memories as the most brilliant man and innovative teacher. His joy as a storyteller still makes me smile even as his passing breaks my heart.

Thank you, forever, to Bret Anthony Johnston, for your belief in me as a writer, for encouraging me to earn my MFA, for being one of the most important mentors in my life.

Thank you, Josh Kendall, for your support, encouragement and guidance. I have learned so much about craft and editing from you, so much about telling a story in the most compelling way no matter how long it takes to compose.

Thank you to Gordon Mennenga for your unforgettable workshop classes in Iowa City. Your focus on craft and character motivation invigorated my understanding of the layers of a story and the power of subtext. Thank you especially for loving my protagonist.

Thank you to Eric Goodman whose 2019 Iowa Class was pure serendipity for my story. Your writing exercises moved my story forward. Thank you for celebrating the story I most wanted to tell.

Thank you, most dearly, to Ron Hansen, whose novel, *Mariette in Ecstasy*, took my breath away. When I learned my manuscript had been chosen for a Master Class at the Tucson Festival of Books and Ron would be my Instructor, I told my husband the same thing I said after meeting the actress I have loved since childhood, Hayley Mills. I told John that if something happened to me after meeting Ron (and Hayley), no worries. All my dreams had come true. You are a vital contributor to my novel, Ron, and a brilliant, insightful, favorite mentor, author, and friend.

This novel is my tribute to my "Six Southern Storytelling Sisters," the Southern female writers whose storytelling inspired me to be true to my Southern heritage. Thank you to Nelle Harper Lee (my sorority and chapter sister at the University of Alabama, a few decades apart), Carson McCullers (my hometown muse who graduated from the same high school where I also graduated albeit many years later), Eudora Welty, Flannery O'Connor, Margaret Mitchell, and Ellen Gilchrist (a sorority sister at Vanderbilt whose sweet postcard and email of support for my novel are treasures to me).

Thank you especially to Meg Kearney, Director of the Solstice MFA in Creative Writing Program, (now at Lasell University, Newton, MA) who I treasure as a poet, leader, confidante, and admired friend. Thank you, Meg, for believing in my abilities as a writer and cheering my quest for learning. Thank you for encouraging me "to fall in love with another writer's work" while at Solstice. I listened to you, Meg, and fell in love with the works of so many writers during residencies.

A million thanks to the Solstice MFA "Fiction Four" of which I'm honored to be included. Rick Carr, Melissa Ford Lucken and Laura Jones-Pettit, thank you for being my treasured friends and "fiction pioneer-pals" at Solstice. Hugs, cheers, love and appreciation to you.

Much admiration, gratitude and love are offered to my Solstice MFA Fiction Workshop Colleagues including: Ann McArdle, Buffy Hastings, James Anderson, Peggy Sue Dunigan, Mike Miner, Joe Gannon, Mike Farrell, Susan Lemere, and Estela Gonzalez.

Thank you to treasured friends and workshop colleagues who have supported and cheered me as I wrote this novel. I wish I could name you all. Please know how important you will always be to me. With a wish to thank each individually, please see your names on my website: www.carolowenscampbell.com.

Thank you, most dearly, to my fellow Solstice MFA colleagues, for being "Family" I admire and adore.

Thank you to friends who cheered me as I wrote: Joanne Black, Krista Santora, Cherie Millsom, Kathy Monti, Nancy Cone, Michele Stevens, Lesley Morffew, Dianne Poppl, Mary Pat King, Sheila Glazov, Lesley Hightower, Patricia Grace King, Judy Moticka, Paulette Livers, Glenn Vanstrum, Claire Honan, Robin Coe, Ivy Wallace, Debbie Revelle, Betty Michel, Beth Harris, Phyllis Lutz, Celeste Kelly, Jackie Jones, Luna Hollett, Danielle Mathews, Jeff Mathews, Diana Seaman, Pam Van Nostrand, Mary Jane Steward, Diane Maycan, Candy Kyle, Kimberly Kreines, Joanne Carota, Faye Snider, Bill Curtice, Tommy David, Byron Richardson, Don Gallops, Frank Martin, David Kulbersh, Jane Kulbersh, Belita Walker, Andy Robinson, Hal Maloof, Mike Bryan, Kathy Finnerty Thomas, Linda Meak, John Patterson, Ruthanne Martin, Lisa Casper, Camille Ogiba, Jayne Bennett, Dawn Fleischman, Rene Lokay, Jodi Patnoe, Deborah Maske, Colleen Weiglein, Megan Viviano, Ron Smith, Carmen Coraci.

Cheers to BookBaby, the company that published and distributed my novel. I appreciate your Teams' many professional courtesies.

Thank you especially to those whose presence in my life are foundational to me and to the essence of this story including:

*My Daddy, J. Walter Owens, Jr., for your love of history, your love of Georgia, for taking our family to every battlefield of the War Between the States during your summer vacations from the law firm which led to my passion for peace;

*My Mother, Alice Pearl Watson Owens, for your belief in me as a writer, and for driving me every week for two years to the *Columbus Ledger-Enquirer* in Columbus, Georgia so I could drop off my columns as the Richards Junior High correspondent before the deadline, and for your congratulations when you first saw the cover of this novel;

*My extended family for your love and support.

*Thank you to my Chi Omega sorority sisters for this novel is a tribute to the many happy times we shared. Thank you to Cathy Johnson Randall (and her wonderful husband Pettus), Betsy Bethea (and her honorable husband Larry Carmichael), Tade Harrison, Liz Cunningham Pearce (and her fun-loving husband Rick), Jan McKenzie Wells, Ellen Monroe, and all my darling "sisters."

Thank you, Ron Hansen, Jaime Manrique, and Sandra Scofield for your generous comments about my novel.

Thank you to the Judges of the William Faulkner Literary Competition for your celebration of my work and for your Southern hospitality at the Awards Luncheon in New Albany, Mississippi, William Faulkner's birthplace.

There are individuals from Ohio to whom I also offer thanks:

*Daniel Decatur Emmett, an Ohio native, who is credited with writing the music and lyrics to "Dixie." His "look away" refrain was a contemporary expression, in the mid-1800's, of tender longing for home in the tradition of one of my favorite songs, "Shenandoah."

*Alan Canfora who I met at the 40th Anniversary Commemorative Events at Kent State University on May 4th, 2010 (including a candlelight vigil on May 3rd). Alan was one of the nine injured students shot by the National Guard on May 4th, 1970 and is the person waving a black flag in front of kneeling soldiers pointing guns at him in iconic photos. I told Alan I was writing a novel from a Southern sorority girl's perspective about the Kent State murders. He was very encouraging. Our conversation near the Victory Bell at The Commons is indelible in my memories. I feel so honored to have met Alan.

My forever thanks and love to our darling pets who have given me so much comfort and joy through the years while writing this novel: Bambi, Chief, Nicky, Scout, Boo and Wrigley. I love each of you for all of time.

Finally, thank you to Griffin for being the person you are. I am so proud to be your mom. Thank you for being the baby of my dreams and the young man I so admire. Thank you for being my co-author of *Views from a Pier*. Thank you for sharing David Bowie's video with me about artists pleasing their own esthetic and not a "committee's." Thank you for helping me with all-things-computer-related. Thank you for creating the cover for this book with your appreciation for art, esthetics and visual precision. Thank you for your curiosity, Griff, for challenging me to rethink my positions and my knowledge of history, for keeping me laughing, for educating me as only you, one of the most impressive teachers I will ever know, could do. Please know, honey, how much your encouragement and support are reflected in these pages. I love you, Griffin, always have, always will.

Happily, John, I thank you for being my sweetheart for 45 years and my husband for 43 amazing years. Thank you for being my rock, my tether to reality, my muse, my slow dance partner, my cheerleader for this novel. You were my inspiration in so many ways for you are the most fascinating, handsome man of charm, integrity, eclectic interests, curiosity, and brilliance with the ability to make me marvel and laugh like no other. You are my inspiration in life and I cannot love you more or thank you enough for your patience and celebration of my dearest dreams. (And thank you for all the takeout food, golf games, road trips, Cubs' games, and late-night movies to coax me from my "fictional dream" for a bit). Now, a new chapter begins. Time to party! I love you, John. ~ Carolee